SERVANTS' HALL

by Margaret Addison

A Rose Simpson Mystery

Rose Simpson Mysteries (in order)

Murder at Ashgrove House
Murder at Dareswick Hall
Murder at Sedgwick Court
Murder at Renard's
Murder in the Servants' Hall

Chapter One

'Where is it?' demanded Millicent Grayson-Smith, staring in disbelief at her jewel box, the lid of which had been thrown back to reveal its glittering contents.

For a moment, before the rising wave of panic completely overcame her, Millicent admired the various necklaces and trinkets, the gold and silver shining brightly in the sunlight, pouring in at the windows. She stared at the precious stones which caught the light and gleamed and twinkled at her in a most appealing fashion. If she had been alone and at leisure she would have picked them up, giggled and let them trickle through her fingers very much as she had done with sand on the beach as a child. But she was neither idle nor by herself, and the wonderful feeling of peace and abandonment that she had felt as an infant had forsaken her. The harsh reality of the situation bore down on her. For, unless her eyes were deceiving her, which of course was a very real possibility for she always slept so badly in this house and consequently awoke tired and fatigued, *it* was not there.

Millicent sat at her dressing table and with trembling hands began to pull out the contents on to the glass surface with clumsy movements. Two or three necklaces came out together, their chains becoming caught and tangled and the respective gems which descended from them clattered together. She thought she heard a sharp intake of breath abruptly halted. An indication of her lady's maid's disapproval at her mistress' careless actions. However, when Millicent looked up and caught her maid's reflection in the mirror, Cooper's face was its usual expressionless self. There was nothing in the handsome features which gave away her thoughts. And yet Millicent was left with the odd and unsettling impression that, had she looked up only a second or two earlier, she might have just caught the girl releasing her bottom lip as if she had been biting it fleetingly, to contain her annoyance, with those fine teeth of hers. If that were indeed so, Cooper had regained her composure remarkably quickly and Millicent envied her this, particularly when she glanced down at her own shaking hands, which betrayed her own emotions so vividly.

'Where is it?' repeated Millicent. There was a touch of anger and impatience in her voice this time, though she knew it would be most unwise to lose her temper.

'Ma'am?'

'The diamond necklace, of course.' Really, the girl was being very unhelpful. Surely she wasn't really that dense? 'The one I was wearing last night. Where is it?'

'I'm sure I don't know, ma'am. I thought –'

'What did you think?' cut in Millicent. 'I left it on the top of my jewel box last night, as well you know. You must have seen it there when you came in this morning with my tea and toast.'

'I did of course, ma'am. It was staring up at me ever so bold.'

'Well, where is it then?'

'I don't know, really I don't. I'll say this though, ma'am. I didn't see it after I came back from running your bath.'

'What nonsense. It must have been there. And you didn't say anything at the time to the contrary. Why did you take the box down to Mason for safekeeping if you knew the necklace was missing?' Even to Millicent's own ears her voice had become unpleasantly shrill.

'I didn't know how it was missing, ma'am. I just thought you had put the necklace back in the jewel box.'

Velda Cooper might just as well have added 'where it should have been in the first place' or equally something to the effect that any responsible person would have put the necklace away in the box last night, instead of leaving it out to catch dust and tempt even the most honest servant to be light-fingered. At least that was the impression the girl managed to convey to Millicent. Whether this was because of the girl's manner, which had become sullen, or the now impertinent look in her eye, or perhaps a combination of the two, Millicent was not sure. All she knew was that she could read the girl's thoughts as clearly as if she had spoken them aloud. It was patently clear her lady's maid was of the view that if only her mistress had seen fit to shut the necklace away as soon as she had unclasped it from her neck and given her the key, well, then there would be none of this present fuss and nonsense. If madam would discard her necklace in such a cavalier fashion, what did she expect?

'You didn't think to check?' Millicent asked rather weakly. She dropped her head on her hand in such a manner as to screen her eyes from her servant.

'No, ma'am. It didn't occur to me that the necklace had gone missing.'

Cooper now stood there in front of Millicent in an upright manner, her hands clasped behind her back, her face sombre. It was very hard to detect anything behind those large, almost black eyes, framed with rich, thick lashes which required no artificial aid to darken them. Millicent wondered if her earlier impressions of the girl had been mistaken. If only there was a hint of sympathy or empathy in the face thought Millicent. It was obvious that Velda Cooper did not care about her plight. Millicent shivered. Perhaps the girl even got a horrid satisfaction from it. For it was yet another illustration of Millicent's inadequacy to fulfil the role of wife to an esteemed man like Edwin Grayson-Smith.

How dreadful it was to be so unsure of yourself and the role you were expected to play, Millicent thought. Worse still to have a confident and adept lady's maid who did not even try to conceal the fact that she neither liked nor respected you. That was the awful position Millicent felt herself to be in. To make matters worse, the girl was possessed of looks that she, Millicent, could only dream of. Millicent, who had always been rather intimidated by the presence of beauty in others, felt dowdy and lacking, and yes, despite the differences in their stations, distinctly inferior.

A thorough search of Millicent's bedroom, undertaken by the housemaids under the strict supervision of Mrs Field, the housekeeper, did not reveal the necklace. It had not fallen behind the tallboy as Millicent had rather desperately hoped it had, or dropped on to the floor to become hidden in the rich, ornate pattern of the Persian carpet. Nothing was left to chance. Every piece of furniture was taken apart and examined. Drawers were pulled out and their contents emptied on to the floor. Chairs were upturned and their upholstery examined. At one point it looked as if the room had been rifled by a professional burglar, so comprehensive was the exploration.

There was now no escaping the fact. The necklace was definitely missing. Though Millicent could hardly bring herself to consider the possibility, it appeared that the only logical explanation for the necklace's disappearance was that it had been stolen. And to make matters worse, in all likelihood the thief was one of Edwin's own servants. It did not seem at all inconceivable that the impertinent Cooper might be the culprit. Perhaps even now the necklace was wrapped up in an old cloth and hidden under the mattress in her cold and draughty attic room. Trembling slightly at the thought, Millicent insisted that Mrs Field herself undertake a discreet but thorough search of the female servants' bedrooms. Mason, the butler, carried out a similar investigation of the male servants' quarters. It was, however, to no avail. For there was neither sight nor sound of the elusive necklace.

Left alone in her room, Millicent gave up all attempts at maintaining what her husband described as the good old British stiff upper lip, and gave way to her emotions as freely as if she had been a child. Her elbows balanced on the glass top of her dressing table, she buried her head in her hands and sobbed bitterly. She felt a justified anger at the theft. However, the truth was she reserved her harshest wrath towards her own conduct. Why, oh why, had she decided to wear that particular necklace last night? If one didn't count the servants, there had only been the old vicar and his wife to see it clasped around her neck. Of course, she knew very well why. Old Mrs Kitchen was a dreadful gossip. Everyone knew that. Rather an undesirable attribute for a vicar's wife to possess, she had always felt. But it had served her own purposes very well. In a few hours' time everyone in the village of Crossing would know that Edwin Grayson-Smith had bestowed upon his second wife the necklace that he had given to his first wife on her wedding day and which Sophia, the first Mrs Grayson-Smith, had then proceeded to wear at every available opportunity from attending the opera to going to the hunt ball. If one were to listen to what Mrs Kitchen had to say on the matter, Sophia also sometimes wore it to go shopping, though why anyone would wear a heavy and ornate diamond necklace when they were engaged in such a pursuit, Millicent really did not know. The village gossip went further, claiming that she had been wearing the necklace when she had fallen from her horse, the accident which had resulted in her untimely death. Millicent preferred not to think about that, it was too horrid …

She uttered a sound somewhere between a sniff and a sigh. Really, what had she been thinking? Had she really thought that by wearing the necklace she was in some way providing undeniable proof, if indeed such proof were needed, that Edwin Grayson-Smith loved his shy, insignificant and insipid looking second wife as much as he had loved his beautiful, wealthy and accomplished first?

Whatever else, Millicent knew that she couldn't bring herself to tell Edwin that the necklace was missing. He could never forgive her carelessness. She was sure of it. They would not have words. He was too much a gentleman to lose his temper and shout at her. Instead he would gaze at her reproachfully with those sad eyes of his, shake his head, and go down to the drawing room. There he would no doubt stare up at the great portrait of Sophia, which still hung above the mantelpiece. With such a commanding position, it dominated the whole room, the effect of which made Millicent feel as if she were some unwelcome charlatan trespassing on hallowed ground. The loss of the necklace would be one more reason for him to bitterly regret his hasty second marriage. Perhaps he would ask for Sophia's forgiveness, as he stood before her likeness, for marrying again when her body was barely cold in her grave.

Millicent shuddered. I'm all to pieces, she thought, I'm no good. She sighed. She must get a hold of herself. It didn't do to dwell on things one couldn't change. She had made her bed and she must lie on it, as her mother would have said. With an effort, she lifted her head and gazed at her reflection in the mirror. The sight that greeted her did little to improve her despondent mood. Her eyes were swollen and puffy, and her nose was red and shiny, so much so, that no amount of powder was likely to disguise the fact. If it had not been for the servants she might have been inclined to keep to her room while she tried to decide what to do. But she had no intention of giving Cooper and the others any more material to speculate over. It was bad enough that they were probably at this very moment huddled together in the servants' hall discussing the necklace and her carelessness in losing it.

Whatever else, she would go downstairs to the morning room. Perhaps she should summon Mason and lay it on the line, so to speak. She could tell him to inform the staff that, unless the necklace was returned within the next hour or two, she would call in the police. She could stress that she did not require to know the culprit's identity, for she was sure that the butler would administer the appropriate punishment. She desired only the safe return of her possession. It was the most sensible approach to take given the circumstances but … Her resolve fizzled out as completely as if someone had poured cold water on it. What if no one owned up to the deed? She would then be obliged to carry out her threat and call in the police to investigate the crime. And then Edwin would have to know. What would he say? What would he think? The majority of the servants had been in the employ of the Grayson-Smith family for years. He trusted them explicitly. What would he say if his new wife were to accuse one of them of theft? He would instinctively take their side, she felt sure. Perhaps not in public, but certainly in private, and that would drive a wedge between them, something else to weaken their already fragile marriage. Even if he considered her accusation justified given the circumstances, what could he think but that his servants despised her. She put a hand to her burning cheek. She could not suffer such humiliation. Far better that the necklace be lost for eternity than that.

A part of Millicent wished that she had not discovered that the necklace was missing. If she had not decided on an impulse to ask Cooper to retrieve her jewel box, she would now be in blissful ignorance of the necklace's fate. The simple single string of pearls that she had inherited from a grand aunt was more than sufficient to wear in the country, and she and Edwin rarely entertained in the evenings when more formal and elaborate jewellery was required. It might therefore have been months before she had discovered that the diamonds were missing. She bit her lip. But what to do now? That was the question. There was a bit of her that wondered if she might do nothing. If the necklace had not been so very valuable, or held so much sentimental value for her husband, then she might well have been inclined to pretend that it had been found. She could always say to Cooper that she had discovered it in the pocket of her negligée or some such garment and nobody would be any the wiser. It would be very weak of her to do such a thing, of course, but then she was very weak. She had never pretended to be otherwise. She had always hated unpleasantness …

But of course that was not a real option open to her. The desperateness of her situation stretched out before her, long and unyielding, and above all else, hopeless. With such dreary thoughts foremost in her mind, she was just about to give herself up to a further bout of sobbing, when her eyes chanced to alight on her dome top walnut bureau. It was a fine specimen of furniture, mounted on cabriole legs with carved acanthus leaves. The top of the bureau chanced to be open, a piece of correspondence laid out prominently on the embossed leather desk top, a reminder that it still required attending to. A wedding invitation. She bit her lip. It was a miserable reminder of the meagreness of her own wedding, which in contrast had been quiet and secluded. No invitations had been despatched, no one invited to attend the joyous occasion. Instead it had been rushed and hurried for no other purpose than that her husband's first wife had not lain long in the ground. Edwin had considered it would not be seemly to have a lavish affair and she had been happy to accommodate his wishes. It was only now that she regretted that they had not had a longer engagement and that no announcement had been made.

As she contemplated this, her train of thought seemed to accelerate of its own accord. It brought to mind something else that she had forgotten, something that she had recently read in *The Times* newspaper and at the time had thought sounded very grand. If she concentrated, she was sure that she could recall the very words written on the page. *A marriage has been arranged, and will shortly take place, between the Earl of Belvedere, only son of the late fifteenth Earl of Belvedere, and Rose Jane, only daughter of the late Mr Ernest Simpson ...* Her own wedding invitation alluded to a much less grand union, the wedding of Edwin's niece, Miriam Sycamore, to a country solicitor. But the Sedgwick family was not unfamiliar to her. She had met Lady Lavinia Sedgwick briefly at a tea party hosted by a relative of Edwin's, which she had attended rather reluctantly. She had been minded to dismiss Lady Lavinia as being shallow and frivolous, but in point of fact she had delighted the room with stories concerning her brother's fiancée, the woman shortly to become the next Countess of Belvedere. Now what was it she had said exactly? Yes, that was it. Miss Simpson had something of a reputation for being an amateur sleuth.

Millicent sat up with a start. An observer would have seen a glint come into her eyes, as if she were looking at something in the distance far beyond the confines of her richly furnished bedroom. She muttered to herself. It was quite ridiculous of course, for she had hardly said more than a few words to Lady Lavinia other than to exchange the usual pleasantries when they had been introduced. It was very probable that the late earl's daughter would not even remember having met her, for Millicent had a tendency to remain on the very edges of conversations, a spectator rather than a contributor. She blushed at the thought that she might have made no impression at all on her ladyship, as if she might as well have been invisible. However, the potential humiliation that awaited her was not enough to stay her hand. It was very possible that she would be snubbed and dealt with coldly but she could see no other way out of her dilemma. With unusual determination, she made her way to Edwin's study, closed the door firmly behind her, and with a trembling hand lifted the telephone receiver.

Chapter Two

'I do hope you are not having second thoughts,' said Cedric, Earl of Belvedere, looking anxiously at his companion. A frown appeared on his forehead, which had the temporary effect of prematurely aging him, so that for a moment he looked considerably older than a man in his early twenties. The chiselled features, which had a tendency to make his face look almost more beautiful than handsome, became vaguely distorted. 'I don't think I could bear it if you were.'

The young woman to whom he was addressing these remarks stared up at him somewhat taken aback. If he had not been looking so very serious, she might have laughed. Instead she stretched herself up on to her tiptoes and placed her hands firmly on his shoulders. She then proceeded to kiss him in so passionate a manner as to dispel any lingering doubts that he might be harbouring concerning the sincerity of her feelings for him. Only then did she permit herself to take a step back to regard his face. She smiled.

'Darling, of course I'm not having second thoughts,' said Rose Simpson. 'How could you possibly think such a thing?' She giggled and stroked his cheek playfully. 'If anything, surely I should be asking you that.'

Lord Belvedere grinned, showing himself to be suitably reassured of her affection. In that moment, however, the truth inherent in her own words, uttered so carelessly and in jest, struck Rose and caused her to pause and take stock. It was not only the handsome looks of the man before her on which her thoughts dwelt, though admittedly he cut quite a figure with his tall and slender frame and his blonde hair slicked back from a side parting as was the current fashion. Nor were her reflections concentrated on the supposed inadequacies of her own looks in comparison, even though she did not consider these to be slight. In her own humble opinion her face, though not plain, could best be described as pleasant rather than pretty, and her figure, certainly not thin, was no more than pleasing.

Her thoughts that moment, however, were not focused on her own appearance. Instead the strange, almost unbelievable position in which she found herself now occupied her mind. Until recently she had been employed as a shop girl at Renard's, a dress shop in a London backstreet which, though respectable, had not been a particularly fashionable or sought after boutique. Now, however, she stood on the threshold of another world. Her social position in society was on the verge of being greatly elevated. For she was about to join the highest ranks of the British aristocracy by marrying a peer. And it had been to this that Cedric had alluded. The journey on which she was about to embark would change her life forever, and he feared she might have reservations about taking so drastic a step.

If she did indeed have any misgivings, it was on Cedric's account rather than on her own. As might have been expected, the announcement of their engagement had generated much gossip and speculation in the society pages. That Lord Belvedere, one of the most eligible young men in England, had decided to marry outside his class, and to a shop girl at that, was too good a story to ignore. The press was simply having a field day. To some it was reminiscent of the instances in history where peers and rich men had chosen to marry chorus girls and actresses. Much had been made of how Rose and Cedric had first become acquainted. Cedric's sister, Lavinia, had taken up a bet with her brother that she could not earn her own living for six months. The place of employment in which she had chosen to work had been Renard's dress shop. An unexpected friendship had developed between the two girls, despite their very different stations in society, and Rose had chanced to meet Cedric during a visit to Lavinia's aunt.

If only the newspaper comment had stopped there. Rose sighed and grimaced at the recollection of some of the articles she had read. It really was too awful. It was hardly her fault if murders had occurred at country houses at the very time that she herself happened to be there as a guest, or that the dress shop in which she had worked had been the scene of a murder only a couple of months' ago while she was on the premises.

'Darling, in just two weeks you'll be my wife,' Cedric was saying. 'How will you feel about being referred to in future as the Countess of Belvedere?'

'Lady Belvedere,' said Rose, savouring the words. 'Her ladyship this, her ladyship that. I must say it will take a bit of getting used to. Rather different to being referred to as just common or garden Miss Simpson.'

'I rather like Rose Simpson,' Cedric said, linking his arm through hers as they continued their stroll around the formal gardens. 'It has a certain ring to it and, you know, she's the girl I fell in love with. Though 'my wife' sounds even better, don't you think? Tell me, do you think you'll like living here, Rose? You won't find the country too dull, will you? After London, I mean. Of course, we'll have house parties. And we can go up to town as often as we wish. We have the house in the mews.'

They hesitated for a while in their walk. Both took a moment to look out over the Sedgwick Court estate. It encompassed everything that the eye could see from the imposing neo-Palladian mansion to the immense landscaped parkland with its numerous lakes, which looked for all the world like one single body of water, the sunken ha-ha fences and the follies dotted here and there around the wider landscape. The follies were built in the style of castle relics, Greek temples or bridges, and served no useful purpose other than to delight the eye and enhance the view.

As one, their eyes were drawn to what appeared in the distance to be nothing more spectacular than acres of box hedge, but which was in actual fact a maze based on the one at Hampton Court Palace, though on a much lesser scale.

'I find it hard to look at that,' said Cedric, his manner wistful, 'and not think about what happened there, don't you –'

'The murder? Yes, I know,' Rose said quickly, taking his hand and giving it a squeeze. 'It was awful, but –'

'It doesn't put you off the idea of living here, does it? I wouldn't blame you a bit if it did.'

'No, darling, of course not.'

They were silent for a while, each lost in their own thoughts. Memories of the death that had occurred the previous December returned to them appearing almost as vivid as the actual event itself. The happiness that they had experienced until only a few moments ago threatened to dissolve, to be replaced instead by melancholy.

'Please,' said Rose, clutching at Cedric's arm. 'Don't go over it. It doesn't do any good dwelling on it.'

Her companion nodded slightly but otherwise gave no other outward sign that her words had made any impression upon him. Desperately she tried to lighten the mood, clinging at anything that came to mind.

'If you believe what the newspapers say, I attract murder wherever I go. If a murder hadn't already happened here at Sedgwick, it certainly would have after I'd taken up residence.'

Cedric made as if to protest.

'We're lucky in a way that it's already happened,' continued Rose hurriedly. 'We have nothing to fear.' She smiled up at him. 'You think I'm being terribly flippant, darling, and I daresay I am. Of course I mind. I mind terribly about what happened here last December. But I am not going to let it spoil everything. I won't give up on the maze, so there! In the summer months, it's beautiful. It's quite enchanting. And you and Lavinia had such fun playing in it as children. You told me so yourself, do you remember? I want our children to enjoy it too. It will be their heritage.'

'You really are a most remarkable woman, Rose,' said Cedric rallying. 'I know for a fact that not one of Lavinia's girlfriends ever intends to set foot in that maze again. According to Manning, even some of the servants have shown reservations about going anywhere near it. Apparently there has been no end of trouble persuading the gardeners to keep the hedges trimmed. If it was up to most of them, they would give it a very wide berth.'

'Oh, there you are, Rose,' said Lady Lavinia Sedgewick. She was staring with an air of desolation at the image of herself as reflected in the carved wood and water overmantle mirror, which was situated above the fireplace in her boudoir. She frowned with annoyance at her companion's reflection in the glass. 'You've taken simply ages to come. I wondered whether the footman had been unable to find you. I suppose you and that brother of mine were in the gardens mooning over each other like love's young dream.'

'How very beautifully you do put things, Lavinia,' said Rose, not sounding a bit put out by her reception.

She perched herself on the edge of one of the sofas in the exquisitely and expensively decorated room with its rich gold brocade curtains, velvet covered chairs and regency wallpaper. She smiled in spite of herself.

'Well, what is it? The footman seemed to think it was important and I suppose it must be for you to summon me like this?' She cast Lavinia something of a critical look. 'I say, must you always gaze at yourself in the mirror. Haven't you anything better to do? I sometimes wonder whether it is your chief occupation.'

'Don't be beastly,' retorted Lavinia, throwing a screwed up piece of paper vaguely in Rose's direction. Nevertheless, she tore her eyes away from regarding her own image in the glass. 'You know how frightfully miserable I've been about all these scars on my face. Why did I have to go down with that awful chickenpox? It really is too dreadful. I would have thought that they would have faded by now, wouldn't you? My looks are absolutely ruined.'

'Lavinia, don't you think that you may be exaggerating a little?' said Rose, getting up from her seat to go and put an arm around the girl's shoulders. 'They don't notice one bit. I think it's all in your mind, you know. I hate to say anything that will make you become even more vain than you are already, but you're just as beautiful as you were before.'

She spoke the truth. Lavinia's cool, aristocratic beauty was of a startling nature that made her appear aloof and fragile at the same time. Her platinum-dyed hair and delicate, even features offset her tall and willowy figure to perfection. What few chickenpox scars there had been had now faded and were to all intents and purposes invisible to the naked eye.

'Am I really?' asked Lavinia, brightening considerably. She gave a toss of her delightful head. 'Oh, I say, that's frightfully nice of you. I suppose the scars aren't really too noticeable are they?'

'They're not,' agreed Rose, 'unless of course someone were to decide to survey your face under a magnifying glass.'

'How awful. Actually, when I powder my face and put on a bit of rouge, I can hardly see them myself, the scars, I mean,' said Lavinia, dabbing her face with her fingers. 'Eliza is always telling me that I worry about them far too much. She says that they are sure to disappear with time anyway. But she would say that, wouldn't she?'

Eliza Denning was Lavinia's lady's maid, and Rose did not envy the woman her position one little bit.

'Well, what did you want to see me about? Surely you didn't ask me here to reassure you about your looks?' said Rose, her thoughts drifting back to Cedric, who was at that moment pacing the formal gardens without her. She wondered if every now and then he was consulting his watch impatiently, eager for her return. 'Robert implied that you wished to see me urgently. He was almost running when he came upon us and then he wouldn't stop hopping from one leg to the other. I couldn't help thinking it was a good thing that Torridge wasn't around to give him one of those reproving frowns of his, you know, one of those looks that can turn milk sour.'

Torridge was the Sedgwicks' former head-butler, who had at last given in to his old age and inevitable retirement. As a consequence, he was now living out his days in a cottage on the estate on a generous pension. He had been succeeded in his post by the under-butler, Manning, whom Torridge himself had trained. This was something of a relief to Rose; the younger man, in her opinion, was more approachable and less formidable than his predecessor.

'Well, of course I didn't summon you here to comment on my looks,' said Lavinia, perching herself on the edge of an armchair. She leant forward and clasped her hands tightly together as if to try and contain an inner elation. 'No, I wanted to see you about something far more exciting.'

'Oh?' Rose said cautiously.

She wondered how much encouragement to give. What Lavinia considered exciting, and what she did herself, was likely to be very different.

'I received the most mysterious telephone call from a woman whose acquaintance I made briefly the other day at a tea party. To be honest, the poor woman made very little impression on me at the time because she hardly opened her mouth other than to swallow a bit of cake. I do think that's rather rude, don't you?' Lavinia did not wait for Rose to reply, but sailed on with her narrative. 'If one accepts an invitation to a tea party, one really should make the effort to talk and say something amusing, otherwise why go? I probably wouldn't have remembered her at all except for the fact that she left the party early. The poor thing looked terrified. She went as soon as it was polite to do so. However, it did give Miriam Sycamore the perfect opportunity to tell us all about her. She had been absolutely dying to talk about it all, one could just tell.'

'I must say, I feel rather sorry for this poor woman. I expect she was just shy. What was her name?'

'Millicent Grayson-Smith. You've heard of Edwin Grayson-Smith, haven't you? He's a business tycoon or something like that, frightfully wealthy. Well, that poor woman, as you call her, happens to be his new wife.'

'Good for her,' said Rose with feeling. 'She can't be quite as dull or wretched as you make her out to be.'

'Well, that's where you're wrong, because she was, dreadfully, and rather plain too. But I digress,' said Lavinia holding up her hand to prevent further interruption. 'Miriam Sycamore happens to be Edwin Grayson-Smith's sister-in-law. She's married to his brother, Raymond. I need to tell you a bit about Edwin. His first wife, Sophia, died about six months ago. From a fall from a horse, would you believe? She had been something of a beauty and socialite and by all accounts poor old Edwin was absolutely devastated by her death. Absolutely distraught, Miriam says he was. His brother was so worried about him that he persuaded Edwin to put his business interests to one side for a while and go to a little place in Cornwall to recuperate. A fishing village on a quiet bit of coastline. Well, Miriam and her husband heard neither sight nor sound of Edwin for well over a month. They took that to be a good sign that he was overcoming his grief –'

'But he wasn't?'

'Well, in a manner of speaking he was, because, without warning, he suddenly returned home with a new wife in tow. He's got a great pile of a place, you know. It's called Crossing Manor. It's only a few miles from here on the outskirts of the village of Crossing.'

'I still don't see –'

'No one knows the least little thing about her, this new wife, Millicent, I mean. Apparently she has no family to speak of. And Miriam says that she has no idea of how to manage the staff or run a household. If it wasn't for the butler being something of a stickler for things being done properly and particularly strict with the servants under him, Crossing Manor would be at sixes and sevens.' Lavinia lowered her voice. 'Miriam thinks she may have been a governess.'

'Good lord!' said Rose. 'Whatever next? Perhaps she worked in a dress shop.'

Lavinia made a face.

'I'm only telling you all this to explain that we were all a little curious about her, that's all. And then yesterday morning I received a telephone call from the woman herself, requesting that I meet her for tea in one of the tearooms at Crossing.'

'I wonder why she didn't invite you to have tea with her at Crossing Manor.'

'Well, that's exactly what I wondered myself. I will admit I was intrigued. We'd only exchanged a few words at the tea party. I wondered why she should wish to meet with me.'

'Well, did you have tea with her in Crossing?' asked Rose, interested in spite of herself.

'Yes I did. I met her at half past four yesterday afternoon. We went to some rather quaint little tearooms which served some excellent scones with lashings of clotted cream and jam. Poor Millicent was so nervous that she hardly ate a morsel. Those delicious scones were completely wasted on her.'

'But what did she want to talk to you about?'

'You. She wanted to talk about you, Rose.'

Chapter Three

'Well, Mr Mason, this is a right to-do and no mistake,' said Mrs Field, settling herself comfortably into an old armchair, which had seen better days.

They were sitting in what was called the housekeeper's sitting room, though in truth the room was not reserved for Mrs Field's exclusive use. In practice, it was frequented by all the upper staff at Crossing Manor at various times throughout the day and evening. Nevertheless, because of its name, Mrs Field considered it to be her personal domain and was very much of the opinion that any visitor to the room was there on sufferance. This, of course, did not apply to the butler. As far as the housekeeper was concerned, he was always a most welcome guest. The butler, in quiet acknowledgement of this fact, leaned back in his own armchair. Alone as they were, he permitted himself a moment or two of relaxation before he sat upright, picked up his cup and saucer and contemplated his response to Mrs Field's observation. He did not hurry himself as he took a sip of tea. Luncheon had been served and cleared away and he had half an hour or so of leisure before he would be required to return to his duties, the most pressing of which was the polishing of silver too valuable to be delegated to the footman to clean.

'It is that, Mrs Field,' Mr Mason said after a while. 'What's to be done about it, I'm sure I don't know.'

'What'll the master make of it? That's what I want to know,' said the housekeeper.

She leaned forward in her seat in a conspiratorial fashion, further accentuated by a rather furtive glance at the door. As always, the butler was torn between his duty to put a stop to what was surely to follow, idle gossip and speculation on Mrs Field's part, and a desire to know what the servants were talking about behind his back. To her credit, he knew Mrs Field to be discreet and above reproach in the servants' hall. It was only here in the housekeeper's sitting room with just the two of them present that she would open up and speak what was on her mind. He sighed inwardly. He would undoubtedly do what he usually did and adopt a position between the two. It was a tricky balance and one he always negotiated carefully. He would show himself to be not absolutely uninterested in what Mrs Field had to tell him, yet make it clear that he would not hesitate to rein her in if she threatened to overstep the mark and descend to tittle-tattle.

'Has madam said anything to you? About calling in the police, I mean?' Mrs Field began tentatively, perceiving that she had been given some encouragement to continue. 'She's gone that quiet on the subject. After all that tearing apart of the house yesterday, looking in all the nooks and crannies, it doesn't seem right. I could have told her at the time she'd find nothing. Martha and Agnes are good girls. When they clean a room, they do it proper. They don't go about banging into the furniture and knocking things on to the floor or hiding things under the carpet.'

'Madam has not breathed a word about the matter to me since yesterday,' admitted the butler guardedly. He might have added that this caused him disquiet, but thought better of it. One had to be very careful not to be seen to give Mrs Field any morsel which might be used to fuel the flames.

'Perhaps she's found it and is that embarrassed to say so after all that fuss she caused,' said the housekeeper, getting into her stride. 'Fancy making us search the servants' bedrooms and have us question them like we were the police.'

'That was all very proper, Mrs Field, and just as it should be,' said the butler, quickly applying the rein.

'That's as may be, but the girls were that upset. One or two of them might not be that bright, but they did not miss the insinuation that they were thieves.' Mrs Field leaned forward and spoke hurriedly before the butler could stop her. 'If you want to know what I think, Mr Mason, I've half a mind that madam took the necklace herself, perhaps with a view to pawning it or accidently losing it. And I can't say I blame her either. Fancy the master giving his new wife the necklace that he gave to Miss Sophia on her wedding day. It don't seem right.'

'It is not up to the likes of us to question what the master does or does not do,' the butler said, eyeing her coldly. 'And to suggest that madam would behave in such a fashion ... well really, Mrs Field, I'm surprised at you. Words fail me, they really do.'

'All I'm saying, Mr Mason, is that we don't know anything about madam,' Mrs Field said quietly, her eyes averted, well aware that she had overstepped the line, but stubbornly still wanting to make her point nevertheless. 'We don't know where she comes from or what she was before she came here as Mrs Grayson-Smith.'

'And we are not likely to either, Mrs Field. It is not any of our business. She is the master's wife and she is our mistress, that's all we have to remember.'

'For all we know, she might have been a parlour maid –'

'Mrs Field!'

'All I'm saying is that it doesn't seem right not knowing anything about her. She's never had servants before, that I can tell you.' She glanced at the butler who now looked fit to explode. 'And if she didn't take the necklace that means one of the staff must have done. And if it was one of the servants, well you know as well as I do which one it was.'

The butler made an involuntary start. It was almost enough to still the housekeeper's tongue, but not quite.

'And it's no use you trying to protect him, Mr Mason. I'm sure you thought you were doing right by him last time, but bad will out, that's what I say.' She drew herself up in the chair as best she could. 'And if you don't mind my saying, he's a wrong 'un, that one, through and through. You might not want to hear it, but it's the truth. And the master will have to know about it this time. Otherwise there'll be uproar in the servants' hall. They don't like it, being under suspicion, no more than you or I do.'

The butler had visibly paled. If Mrs Field had happened to observe him closely, she would have noticed that the hand which held his cup also trembled slightly, as if he suddenly found its contents were too heavy for him to hold. However, Mrs Field was oblivious to all this. Having had her say and been slightly more forthright in her opinions than she had intended, she had considered it advisable to return to the servants' hall. She therefore left the butler to sit on alone and in silence while he finished his tea.

'What you are saying is that Mrs Grayson-Smith would like me to question her servants about the theft of her diamond necklace?' Rose stared at Lavinia, aware that her mouth was slightly open coupled with a puzzled frown upon her face.

'Yes, she would,' said Lavinia, smoothing her hair with her fingers, though it was difficult to suppose, after all the mirror gazing, that the girl could possibly imagine a curl to be out of place. 'It's not really that surprising, is it? You have gained something of a reputation for being an amateur detective, solving all those murders and whatnot.'

'I just happen to have been in a position to help the police with one or two of their investigations, that's all.'

'Nonsense,' retorted Lavinia, 'and you know it. Why, if it hadn't been for you, the cases wouldn't have been cracked at all, or at least it would have taken the police simply ages. I don't know why you always insist on being so modest about it. If I were in your shoes, I'd simply be telling everyone.'

'That I don't doubt for a minute,' Rose said. 'But I still don't understand how Millicent Grayson-Smith would know about what you call my sleuthing. She might well have read in the press about my unfortunately being present in two or three houses where murders occurred. But how would she know that I had helped the police with their enquiries? As far as I am aware, no mention of my detecting skills, or whatever you may wish to call them, has been made in the newspapers, for which I am extremely grateful. Can you imagine it? The 'countess detective' or something equally frightful. It would be awful.'

'Well,' said Lavinia, suddenly finding that the pattern on the carpet required immediate and greater scrutiny. 'That may have been my fault. It's just possible that I may have been talking about your sleuthing at the tea party, the one that I was telling you about. I really can't remember if I was, but it wouldn't surprise me in the least if I had been waxing lyrical about your various achievements.'

'Oh, Lavinia, you didn't!'

'It's no good looking at me like that, Rose,' Lavinia said, a defiant look on her face. 'Having an amateur detective for a future sister-in-law is quite the most exciting thing. All my friends think so, they're frightfully jealous. You should see some of the hideous and boring women their brothers have married.'

'And it goes a little towards making up for the fact that, until recently, I was nothing more than a common or garden shop girl?'

'Well, there is that as well, of course,' admitted Lavinia. 'You may call me a snob, and I don't doubt for a minute that you are right, but if you had been obliged to suffer what I've had to this past month when your engagement was announced, then you too would have gone out of your way to stress that the future Countess of Belvedere had something a little more about her than working in a dress shop. Really, women can be so catty about that sort of thing.'

'I see,' said Rose, laughing in spite of herself. 'I suppose I ought to feel offended.'

Lavinia had the grace to blush. Rose herself was fully aware that, initially at least, Lavinia had harboured some reservations about her relationship with Cedric, being firmly of the view that her brother should marry someone within his own class and station in life. With that in mind, and knowing her friend's character as well as she did, on reflection it did not surprise her one jot that Lavinia had exaggerated to her peers what had become something of an interesting occupation for Rose of late.

'But, Mrs Grayson-Smith can't really be serious, can she?' said Rose, returning to their original topic of conversation before they had digressed. 'There would be no obligation on the part of her servants to answer my questions and really, why should she think I would have any more luck with them than she has had? I take it that she has questioned them herself?'

'In a manner of speaking,' said Lavinia. 'She delegated the task to her butler and her housekeeper. I understand she did personally demand an explanation from Cooper, her lady's maid, whom she considers in all likelihood to be the culprit. But the girl is quick-witted and devious, according to Millicent, so she did not get anything out of her, certainly nothing in the manner of a confession.'

'If she is certain the necklace has been stolen, and has not just been mislaid, then she ought to call in the police to investigate the theft,' Rose said firmly.

'I agree with you. But she doesn't want to do that. You see, she wants to handle the matter as quietly as possible. If you ask me, she's rather scared of her servants and she's simply terrified of Edwin finding out that the necklace is missing. It was a gift to his first wife and he gave it to Millicent, would you believe?' Lavinia sniffed. 'If I had been her, I think I might have deliberately lost the necklace, but unfortunately she doesn't feel the same way about it as I do.'

'I see. When did all this take place?'

'The theft? Yesterday morning. I'll say this for Millicent, she didn't waste any time in telephoning me. She's hopeful of recovering the necklace. The thief is unlikely to have had an opportunity to dispose of it yet.'

'What is she proposing exactly? That I arrive unannounced and commence an interrogation of her staff, or am I to pretend that I am an old friend come down to stay for a few days?'

'Oh, the latter of course,' said Lavinia. 'And she suggested that I come as well to make a bit of a house party of it.'

Rose grimaced and said somewhat wearily: 'I feel I have been to rather too many house parties and gatherings of late. I've had enough of people regarding me inquisitively, wondering what it is about me that has induced a man in Cedric's position to choose me for his bride. To be honest, I was rather hoping for a few days of quiet before the wedding.'

'You'll be bored to tears.' Lavinia said. 'It can't be much fun having all those letters of congratulation come dropping in and having to acknowledge them promptly. Though, I daresay you and your mother are writing a few replies every day.'

'Yes,' said Rose, fully aware that despite this diligent approach, a mountain of correspondence still required answering. How many times she had written the words: '*Thank you so very much for your kind letter about my engagement. I am indeed very happy ...*' she did not know. Certainly the words had a tendency to appear to her even in her sleep as if they were ingrained on her brain.

'If it were me,' Lavinia was saying, 'I'm sure that I would let them accumulate into a frightening pile. I have always tended to wilt, as a rule, at the thought of putting pen to paper. But I suppose it must be done. The wedding presents will be beginning to arrive soon, and really nothing annoys people more than to have their gift unacknowledged for so long that an apology has to accompany the letter of thanks.'

The recollection of her unanswered correspondence should certainly have had the effect of reminding Rose of her duty to stay and pen her replies. Conversely, it had the opposite effect. If anything, a visit to Crossing Manor, which had only a few minutes ago held little attraction, now seemed distinctly appealing. However, the issue still remained that the visit was unlikely to produce any tangible results with regard to securing the return of the necklace. Rose reiterated this point to Lavinia. To her surprise she discovered that her friend was in agreement.

'Oh, absolutely. It wouldn't work at all. I doubt whether you'd get a word out of any one of the servants. Of course, they'd be perfectly polite and deferential and there would be nothing that you could actually put your finger on, but you'd still know they were withholding information. They wouldn't want to be perceived as telling tales, you see.'

'I suppose poor Mrs Grayson-Smith must have been rather upset when you told her that it wouldn't be any good, us coming to stay, I mean?'

'I expect she would have been dreadfully upset,' Lavinia said brightly, 'if I had told her that. But you see, I said nothing of the sort. I promised I would be coming to Crossing Manor tomorrow. I informed her that, due to a prior engagement, you were unable to join me immediately. I was however quite certain you would follow in a day or two.'

'Why ever did you tell her that?'

Rose felt at once a sense of apprehension. Lavinia was smiling like anything, her eyes bright, her cheeks flushed. It was quite clear, even to the most casual observer, that the girl was up to something.

'Well, you see, the most brilliant idea occurred to me while I was having tea with Millicent,' Lavinia said, clapping her hands together. 'It just floated into my mind as I was taking a mouthful of scone.'

'Oh, did it indeed?'

Rose could feel the girl's excitement as if it was a tangible thing. She could also hear it in Lavinia's voice. It occurred to her that, with all her preamble, Lavinia had been leading up to this very moment.

'Servants gossip like anything,' Lavinia was saying. 'You should hear Eliza on the subject. I expect that's why servants are always among the first to be interviewed by the police when anything occurs, don't you? Nothing can happen in a house without the servants knowing about it. Do you see what I'm getting at, Rose? Millicent's servants must have some idea as to the identity of the thief, particularly if it's one of them. Of course, while they wouldn't dream of mentioning a word about it upstairs, I expect it's all the talk in the servants' hall. I doubt they gossip about anything else.'

'I don't see –'

'Don't you? It seems to me so very obvious.' Lavinia's voice lowered and became conspiratorial, though it was an unnecessary precaution given that they were alone in the room, no footman in sight. 'You must come to Crossing Manor with me, but not as yourself. You must come in disguise.'

'Disguise?'

'Yes, you must come to Crossing Manor as a servant. My lady's maid to be precise.'

Chapter Four

'Oh.'

An inadequate little word, but one that expressed everything Rose felt in those first few moments, foremost of which was surprise. Whatever proposal she had been expecting Lavinia to put forward, it had not been that she arrive at Crossing Manor disguised as a servant. It was such a ludicrous idea any further words escaped her and Rose could do nothing more than laugh and then gape at Lavinia in what she knew to be a ridiculous fashion. The girl in question, meanwhile, stood before her, beaming like the Cheshire cat. It occurred to Rose that Lavinia would, in all probability, have been a most mischievous child. She had given forth her suggestion very much in the manner of a child discussing a game that it knew might not be well received by the grown-ups.

Rose stared at Lavinia's beaming face, at the shining eyes that swam with merriment, at the hands clasped together in barely contained excitement. There was something about the boundless enthusiasm that was contagious and, in spite of herself, she began to sway. Of course, if she were to be entirely sensible, it was easy to dismiss the idea out of hand and yet, much to her annoyance, there was a certain logic to it which Rose found she could not deny. Furthermore, the idea was beginning to appeal to her. There were, however, certain practicalities to overcome and which could not be swept aside. In the end it was to these that she gave voice.

'Lavinia, whatever you may think to the contrary, I have never been in service.' Rose frowned. 'Regardless of the merits of your scheme, I should never be able to convince anyone, least of all the other servants, that I was a lady's maid.'

'Well, I have already given that some thought,' Lavinia said quickly, clapping her hands together.

Rose groaned inwardly, wondering what was to follow.

'I daresay you wouldn't make a very good lady's maid,' Lavinia conceded. 'Not your fault, but there it is. But I have come up with a marvellous idea though I say so myself. We can pretend that Eliza is ill with a head cold or some such thing, and that you are a cousin of hers whom she has suggested attend to me until she is well.'

'Wouldn't you be more likely, under those circumstances, to contact an agency and engage a proper lady's maid?'

'We could say that you're only looking after me for a few days at most. That would explain why I hadn't contacted an agency to obtain the services of a fully trained maid. If it was only to be for a few days, and Eliza had a willing cousin to hand, there would be no need, you see.'

'I suppose so,' said Rose, not fully convinced.

'I daresay you're feeling rather apprehensive at the ghastly prospect of being with all the other servants in the servants' hall. I know I would be, though I would have thought you'd find it rather fun. I've discussed it with Eliza, and she says you are not to worry. You see, you'll be an upper servant. You won't have to wait on the other servants, they'll probably wait on you. They'll serve you dinner and bring you a cup of tea in the morning, that sort of thing. You'll probably take your coffee in the housekeeper's sitting room or butler's pantry with the other upper servants.' Lavinia gave a high little laugh. 'I must say, it sounds rather fun, doesn't it?'

'I don't know –'

'In the evening you'll sit about doing some sewing and mending. It will be an opportunity for you to question the servants informally. I expect you can always pretend to sew if you don't really want to do it. Clutch a bit of material and jab at it with a needle, I mean. Eliza can give you some embroidery that she's made which you can produce if anyone looks inquisitive. And of course, you'll spend a lot of time with me helping me dress and doing my hair.' Lavinia held up her hand in anticipation of a protest. 'Don't worry, I won't require you to do anything complicated with my hair. And the frocks I'll take with me won't need much pressing. Really, you'll hardly have to do a thing at all in the way of work.'

'Good. That's to say, good if I decide to go along with this ludicrous idea of yours,' said Rose rather grudgingly.

'There's nothing ludicrous about it,' retorted Lavinia. 'Why, I can see that you are rather taken with the idea.'

'I'm no such thing. Does Mrs Grayson-Smith have a view on this proposal of yours?'

'Oh, of course not! I haven't told her about it. She'd never be able to keep it to herself. She's the sort of woman who is quite transparent in her emotions. She'd give you away in no time. The poor thing would probably fuss over you, make sure that you were comfortable in your room, that sort of thing … No, I wouldn't breathe a word about it to her. As I told you, I informed her you would be joining me in a day or so. I thought that would put her mind at rest. What she won't know is that you will, in actual fact, be arriving with me, but as my maid, not as Rose Simpson.'

Cedric had quite doubled up with laughter when Rose told him Lavinia's idea. She had returned to him in the formal gardens, where he had been awaiting her arrival impatiently. He had put his arms around her and they had stayed like that for a while until, with some reluctance, Rose had pulled away from him to deliver her news, wondering how it would be received by the young man.

'That sounds just like my sister,' Cedric said, chuckling. 'Everything is a bit of a game to her.'

'Tell me it's quite out of the question,' said Rose. 'Please do. I'm almost tempted.'

She held his hands in hers and squeezed them, imploring him to do as she asked. There was a seriousness about her eyes and her face looked flushed with anything but amusement. Her demeanour unnerved the young earl for a moment or two and he remained quiet as he contemplated his response.

'You know what your sister is like. She can be quite convincing when she sets her mind to it,' Rose said quickly, to fill the silence. 'I was almost persuaded. She made it sound quite plausible, you see, fun even. In her boudoir, it didn't sound so very strange. But out here in the garden where everything appears so real, it seems quite the most ludicrous suggestion.'

'Well, it does sound rather a daft idea. But, saying that, I don't say it wouldn't work,' Cedric said, recovering his composure somewhat and adopting a more solemn tone. 'It would seem a sensible way to go about recovering the necklace, or identifying the thief at the very least. Servants do gossip and I daresay one or two of them have their suspicions. From what you have said, it must have been one of them that took the necklace and they won't be very happy knowing that they're all under suspicion.'

'Yes. Nobody else was in the house besides Mrs Grayson-Smith and the servants. So you see, it couldn't be anyone else. There were no guests staying or some convenient visitor who happened to drop by.' Rose looked resigned. 'When one puts it like that, it makes the most dreadful sense to fall in with your sister's plan, doesn't it?'

'I say, Lavinia hasn't gone about dressing you up as a lady's maid, has she? It's just the sort of thing she would do.'

'Of course she has. It was one of the first things she did.' Rose sighed. 'You should have seen me, darling. She put me in the most frightful old, black rag that had been darned umpteen times. Eliza would never wear such a thing. I looked as if I was in widow's weeds. Your sister was worried that I might be recognised from the society pages, so she went about changing my hair style too. She gave me a middle parting and scraped my hair back into the most awful bun, which aged me terribly.'

'I'm sure I would still have recognised you, whatever you wore. And of course I should still have been madly in love with you,' said Cedric gallantly.

'I'm not so sure on both counts. Not after Lavinia had made me wear some wire spectacles with little round lenses,' said Rose shuddering. 'Apparently she went through a phase where she wanted to appear studious and intellectual and had the spectacles made up with plain glass. I will say this for her, they were very effective in changing my appearance. I hardly recognised myself in the mirror.'

'Well, I do hope you will give me a demonstration,' Cedric said, putting an arm around her and pulling her closer towards him.

'Probably. You see, darling, I think I am going to do it after all. I half hoped you would talk me out of it, say it was all nonsense and all that. But you didn't. Because there is some method in the madness, isn't there? And, I know it sounds ridiculous, but poor Mrs Grayson-Smith is quite wretched with the worry of it all. I feel frightfully sorry for her and … well … if I am to be honest, Lavinia said something that made me stop and think.'

'Oh? What did my sister say?' asked Cedric curiously.

'She said that when I am the Countess of Belvedere I won't be able to do such things. That it was my last opportunity to do something exciting.'

'Oh, I say, I wouldn't have quite put it like that myself,' said Cedric. He had turned away from her and looked distinctly put out.

'She only meant in terms of dressing up and going about in disguise,' said Rose quickly. 'Being the Countess of Belvedere will be exciting, but in a different way. But don't you see? This may be my last chance to go about sleuthing. Well, unless murders keep happening about me, that is. You do see that, don't you, darling?'

'I suppose so. I say, Rose, I wish I was coming with you. But I daresay that you don't want me to, do you?'

'It wouldn't work if you did. I would find your presence too distracting.' She stroked his cheek and laughed. 'In a wonderful way of course, but I would be put off from doing what I was there to do. And I'll only be gone a couple of days, three or four at most.'

'Well, I shall keep you to that,' Cedric said, rallying. 'Whatever you do, promise me you will be back for the wedding!' He tried to put a brave face on it. 'I daresay it will give me an opportunity to finish off some of the estate work before the ceremony. Things that I've been putting off. My estate manager will be pleased. But I should certainly like to see you done up in your disguise before you go. I might even wave you off. Now, darling,' he paused a moment to put an arm around her shoulders, 'are you really quite sure that you want to go to Crossing Manor as Lavinia's maid? She'll run you ragged, you know, you mark my words if she doesn't!'

Rose returned to South Lodge somewhat preoccupied. The house in question was located in the grounds of Sedgwick Court, beside one of the many gates to the park. During its long existence the premises had been occupied by a succession of gatekeepers and more recently by the head gardeners. Like Sedgwick Court itself, the house was Georgian in origin and surprisingly spacious for a lodge house. In addition to its original generous proportions, it had benefited from a couple of small extensions that had been made by previous occupiers to increase its dimensions. This had been done to accommodate the large families of one or two of the former residents. To add to its various merits, the house also boasted a particularly lovely and well-stocked garden, the legacy of having been occupied for years by professional gardeners.

Rose did not stop to knock on the front door. Instead, without a pause, she lifted the latch and walked straight inside.

As she had expected, she found Mrs Simpson on her knees in the sitting room, looking up at a dressmaker's dummy which loomed above her. Her mother was so engrossed in her task that at first she did not spy her daughter and, when she did, her mouth was so full of pins that it was a moment or two before she could speak.

'Oh, there you are, dear,' said Mrs Simpson, removing the pins from her mouth and stabbing them into a pincushion. 'I've made quite a bit of progress today, as you can see.'

She got to her feet and stood back to admire her handiwork. Rose joined her in this occupation and together the two women stared at the full-length dress that clothed the dummy. The gown was of a pale gold satin, cut on the bias. It draped beautifully. So fluid were the lines, the overall effect was of a liquid metal. The gown had a cowl neck and full, puffed sleeves which tapered in at the elbow. Each cuff was fastened with ten tiny satin covered buttons.

'It's beautiful,' said Rose.

'It isn't finished yet of course,' said her mother. 'There are some little details I should like to add. I intend to embellish the neckline with some glass beads, which should catch the light beautifully.'

'That sounds a bit fiddly to do.'

'Oh, yes, it will be. But I think it will be worth the effort. I may even add some diamanté if it doesn't look too much.' Mrs Simpson sighed. 'Oh, Rose. Am I being quite ridiculous? I may be a seamstress, but really I wonder whether I should have insisted on making your wedding dress? It's always been a dream of mine, of course. But on reflection perhaps you should have gone to one of the great fashion houses. It would be different if it wasn't going to be a great society affair. I thought the pattern and colour would suit your figure and complexion perfectly. But now I am wondering whether the gown doesn't look a little too simple and plain.'

'I think it looks beautiful. It's elegant. I don't want anything too fancy. Chantilly lace wouldn't have done me at all.' Rose hugged the older woman. 'I mean it, Mother. It's quite perfect. Cedric will love it and I will feel like a princess in it on my wedding day.'

'If you really are certain,' replied Mrs Simpson looking relieved. 'I think it will look well in the photographs that will no doubt appear in the illustrated papers.'

'Mother, Lavinia has asked me whether I would like to accompany her on a visit to a friend of hers. A Mrs Grayson-Smith. She lives a few miles away in Crossing. We would only be gone a couple of days or so. But of course if you need me to stay here for another fitting, or if you don't want to be left alone –'

'Nonsense,' said Mrs Simpson. 'That sounds to me like a very good idea. You are just twiddling your thumbs here waiting for the wedding to take place. It will give you something to do. The beading on the gown will take me a day or so to complete. And I need to get used to living here in this house alone. After all, it is what I'll be doing after you are married.'

Rose had thought it wise not to mention that she would be visiting Crossing Manor in the guise of a servant. For one thing, she did not want her mother to worry. It had been a constant anxiety to Mrs Simpson that her daughter frequently became embroiled in murder cases and, to make matters worse, insisted on taking an active role in solving them. For another thing, Rose was of the view that her mother was unlikely to approve of this particular venture, especially if she were informed that it had been Lavinia's idea. Rose sighed. The sad truth was that Mrs Simpson did not much like her daughter's friend. She adored Cedric, but she found his sister wanting. Perhaps understandably, on such a brief acquaintance, she considered Lavinia to be shallow, spoilt and self-centred, attributes which did nothing to make her feel favourably towards the girl.

'Have you given any more thought to what Cedric said?' asked Rose tentatively.

'Really, Rose, I don't need hordes of servants. You and I have managed quite well enough by ourselves with only a daily woman coming in to help. I really don't need a butler in a house this size, though I daresay it would have been different if I had taken up residence in the Dower House as Cedric suggested.'

Mrs Simpson had been quite adamant that the Dower House, located on the very edge of the village of Sedgwick, was far too large for her modest requirements. Rose had been in complete agreement. The Dower House, a splendid Georgian mansion in its own right, may well have been fitting for a dowager countess, used to living in a stately pile, but really it was far too grand for someone used to living in a mean little house in a poor part of town. The South Lodge was much more suitable to her mother's needs. It reminded Mrs Simpson more of the sort of house that she had lived in with her husband, before her reduced circumstances following his death had necessitated the sale of the family home.

'Perhaps you could have one or two more servants, like we used to have. Do you remember Doris and Mrs Dobson? I wonder what became of them.'

Before they had fallen on hard times, Mrs Dobson had been the Simpsons' cook and Doris their daily help. As Rose recollected, Mrs Dobson had been most reluctant to leave them.

'Well, I did think about having a housemaid as well as a cook,' conceded Mrs Simpson,' now that there has been a change in my circumstances, so to speak. As you know, I've kept in touch with Mrs Dobson over the years, Christmas cards and birthday cards and the like, and the odd letter when I've had any particular news to impart.'

'Such as my engagement to the Earl of Belvedere?' teased Rose.

'Well, of course. It goes without saying that Mrs Dobson was delighted by that news. I thought she might have reservations about your marrying outside your class. However, she wrote me a very nice letter in which she said that she had seen you grow up from a babe to become a very fine young woman and it was no surprise to her at all that a member of the aristocracy should decide to choose you for his wife.'

'Dear Mrs Dobson.'

'She wrote that Doris is married now. Apparently she has done quite well for herself.'

'I'm glad. And Mrs Dobson?'

'Working as cook for a family she doesn't much like.'

'If that's the case, why don't you –'

'I already have, my dear.' Mrs Simpson beamed. 'She is coming the day after tomorrow. I was intending that it be a surprise. So you see, Rose, you have nothing to worry about. I shan't be by myself after all. It will be just like old times.'

Chapter Five

The next day loomed clear and bright. Had it been an ordinary morning, Rose, in all probability, would have awoken eager and refreshed, keen to start the day. But there was nothing usual about this particular day. To compound matters, she had slept badly the night before, tossing and turning in her bed so that she awoke feeling tired and a little irritable. That she had certain misgivings about the venture that lay before her, there was little doubt. In the early hours of the morning, when sleep had evaded her and a headache had threatened, she had been overcome with apprehension. In those unsettling hours of three or four o'clock in the morning when all worries are heightened and appear insurmountable, she had been fully resolved to inform Lavinia that she had changed her mind, that the whole idea that she impersonate a lady's maid was preposterous. With no experience of life in service, she would not be able to pass herself off as a servant. It was an occupation that was foreign to her. Even if she were to be successful, there was no reason to suppose that her detecting skills, such that they were, and which had been used exclusively to investigate murders, would prove fruitful in securing the safe return of the necklace.

The morning light, however, while doing little to lift her spirits, restored her determination to see the matter through. She still had doubts and reservations, but they no longer ate away at her confidence as they had during the hours of darkness.

Later that day, as she stood in Lavinia's bedroom in what she still thought of as her black widow's weeds, but which her friend had assured her was appropriate dress for a lady's maid, she could not help but think how much more appropriate her sombre wardrobe would be to inclement weather. The sunlight that streamed through the window seemed too bright in comparison with the drabness of her gown. It did nothing but accentuate the shabbiness of her dress, making it appear dusty and faded, highlighting the odd darn that had been made to the material during its long life. She tried to rise above her attire and focus her mind instead to watching what the industrious Eliza Denning did, heeding her words with regard to her mistress' clothes and how to arrange Lavinia's hair. Eliza appeared to manage the latter with quick, swift movements. Rose, when she tried to copy her example, was all fingers and thumbs, even managing to jab Lavinia in the head with a hair pin, much to the girl's annoyance.

It was therefore with some trepidation that Rose embarked with Lavinia on the journey to Crossing Manor. The Sedgwicks' chauffeur drove them and she wondered what he made of it all, Rose dressed as she was in servants' garb. But if her appearance surprised him, the man was careful not to show it on his face. Rose, meanwhile, sat clutching on her lap a bag that had seen better days, and which held her few servant's possessions. She knew herself to be quiet and withdrawn. Lavinia, apparently oblivious to her friend's anxieties, spent the entire journey chattering happily and requiring little, if any, encouragement from Rose to keep her end of the conversation flowing.

Rose's first impression of Crossing Manor, as they turned a corner of the drive and came upon it suddenly, was that it was a rambling old house that had undergone so many renovations and been extended so often that its original structure was hard to determine. Certainly the house managed to combine both Tudor and Queen Anne architecture in a curious fashion, with half-timbered parts coupled with others that comprised classic proportions of red brick and white paint. The porch with its Ancient Greek influenced pillars looked distinctly Georgian. Certainly an impressive looking dwelling, imposing even, but not particularly attractive; some might have called it rather ugly.

A rather thin and delicate looking woman, who had what could best be described as a washed out sort of beauty and whom Rose took to be Mrs Grayson-Smith, hovered in front of the house. She, together with the butler and the footman, greeted them on their arrival or, more accurately, they greeted Lady Lavinia Sedgwick. Rose's own arrival appeared to go unnoticed. The footman proceeded to take Lavinia's luggage, stopping for a moment to direct Rose to the servants' or tradesmen's entrance.

Rose took one last look at Lavinia, who appeared engrossed in conversation with her hostess, and made her way to the back of the house, clutching her bag to her as she went, as if for moral support. Each step she took, she felt more and more exposed, as if she were in very obvious fancy dress and would any moment be found out. It was, however, encouraging that her appearance had occasioned not even a second glance from the butler or the footman who seemed to have taken her for what she purported to be.

The servants' entrance was down some stone steps, which opened out into what could best be described as a small courtyard, hidden from view from the gardens by a high wall topped with wrought iron railings. Rose clung to the ice cold hand rail with one hand, bag in the other, as she negotiated the stairs which were steep and would, she imagined, be particularly treacherous in bad weather. The courtyard was empty, though the noise from the hustle and bustle of the servants' quarters came readily enough to her ears, for across the courtyard a door to the basement of the house was open. She made her way towards the doorway and, peering into the gloom, discovered that it opened into a narrow passage, which had a dark and dingy feel to it due to the lack of natural light.

Rose hurried along the passage, glancing as she went at the rooms she passed, some of which were occupied with servants busy about their tasks: a washroom, a housemaid's closet, a brushing room, a boot room … She knew that the more important rooms must lie beyond: the kitchen, the scullery, the stillroom, the butler's pantry, the housekeeper's sitting room … But it was not towards these that Rose made her way. Instead she followed the passage around until it opened out, as she had hoped it would, into the servants' hall. This she knew was the staff's great communal area with its huge scrubbed wooden table and the bell board, which hung in a commanding position upon the wall, driving the servants' lives.

The room was large but not airy due to the windows being positioned high up on the wall and seemingly insufficient in both size and number to light such a vast room. The sage painted walls and heavy dark wooden chairs that littered the room or were drawn up to the table did little to relieve the gloomy atmosphere. A number of servants were present, engaged in various tasks which ranged from darning socks to polishing silver. They were either too engrossed in their occupations, or in their conversations, the gentle hum from which filled the room, to notice Rose's entrance immediately. This afforded her a moment or two to take stock of the situation and summon the necessary courage to see her deception through. All at once, the conversations stopped abruptly. A few of the servants pushed back their chairs and rose from their seats, others paused or looked up from their various occupations. A small, middle-aged woman in a black dress, not dissimilar to Rose's own, seemed to appear as if from nowhere and bustle forward. A bunch of keys hung from her belt and moved with each step she took. Despite her small stature, the woman had a commanding presence and the other servants appeared to defer to her.

'You must be Lady Lavinia's lady's maid? I'm glad to see you. We didn't know whether her ladyship would be bringing her own maid with her or not. We're a bit short-staffed as you can probably tell, so we would have been hard pushed to assign one of the housemaids to her ladyship. Truth be told, we didn't know her ladyship would be staying until a day or two ago. Mrs Mellor, that's our cook, has been working night and day to prepare the dishes, so she has.'

The woman had been talking very fast, hardly pausing for breath. She did so now as she appraised the young woman before her. Rose felt herself blush, the obsolete spectacles digging into her nose, her scalp aching from her hair having been drawn back into a severe bun.

'I'm Mrs Field,' said the woman. 'I'm the housekeeper here.'

'Denning. Daisy Denning,' Rose said quickly. The name sounded ridiculous even to her own ears, but Lavinia had been insistent. 'If I can't call you Rose,' she had said, 'I'll have to call you the name of another flower or else I'll forget.'

'Well Miss Denning, I daresay you could do with a cup of tea after your journey? As I've said, we didn't know whether her ladyship would be bringing her own maid with her or not, so Martha here will need to make up your bed.' She turned away to address one of the maids sitting at the table. The maid in question had her back to Rose, and she alone had not looked up at Rose's arrival. 'Chop, chop my girl.' The housekeeper inclined her head towards another girl. 'Agnes, you can help her and you can take Miss Denning's bag up with you while you're at it.'

'Now, Miss Denning, you can sup your tea while they're getting your room ready. Mr Mason will want to see you. I'll have your tea brought into the butler's pantry for you. Happen Mr Mason could do with a cup himself.'

Relieved of her bag, Rose found herself ushered out of the room into another passage. She passed the kitchen, the scullery and the stillroom before she came to the butler's pantry. The door was open. A tall and very thin man, she assumed to be Mr Mason, was standing behind a large wooden table. On spying her, he indicated a chair drawn up in front of the desk. As Rose sat down, she quickly and surreptitiously glanced around the room. Her eye spotted what she had been seeking, a mahogany case of Chippendale style with a polished top. This was the Bramah jewellery safe cabinet. If the rather innocuous looking door were to be opened, it would reveal an iron safe complete with handle and lock plate. This was where Mrs Grayson-Smith's jewel case had been kept and in all probability currently resided. It had been returned to this resting place on the morning of the theft, and retrieved from it a little while later at the behest of the mistress who, on opening the case, had discovered her diamond necklace to be missing.

'Begging your pardon, but this is Miss Denning, Mr Mason. She's Lady Lavinia's lady's maid,' said Mrs Field. 'Miss Denning, this is Mr Mason. He is the butler here.'

The housekeeper had remained at the door as if she intended to stop for only a moment before returning to her duties. It transpired however that she intended to stay, ostensibly to oversee the provision of the refreshments.

'Miss Denning.' The butler inclined his head in acknowledgement and gave Rose something of a stern look. Certainly he seemed to draw himself up, almost to puff out his pigeon chest. 'I am glad to make your acquaintance. Welcome to Crossing Manor. You are lady's maid to a member of the British aristocracy. I am sure, therefore, that I do not need to tell you what will be expected of you while you are here. We take very seriously the smooth running of the house, which can only be satisfactorily achieved if each member of staff knows his or her own role and responsibilities in proceedings and undertakes them efficiently and effectively.'

'Indeed, Mr Mason,' Rose said, trying not to fidget in her seat. 'You are quite right.'

She felt herself to be under intense scrutiny and wondered if she was found wanting. Her hair, her clothes, even her spectacles. She reminded herself that the dress she wore was one of Eliza Denning's and as such quite suitable for the role in hand. She stared back politely at the butler. He himself wore a plain dark waistcoat and tailcoat and she thought that the three of them in their sombre black clothes looked as if they had a funereal air about them, quite fitting with the dark green, cold grey and drab brown colours of their surroundings. The room felt small and claustrophobic, likewise the passages beyond. It was as if they were small animals scurrying around in their own little tunnels.

'Good. Well, I think that is all for now.' The butler returned his gaze to some papers on his desk.

Rose got up from her seat. She felt as a child might, dismissed by its school-mistress and sent on its way. The exchange of words had been so brief that there had not even been time for her to have her cup of tea. As she made for the door the tea was being brought in and she almost collided with the tray.

'Miss Denning will have her tea in the servants' hall,' Mrs Field said quickly to the stillroom maid. 'Mr Mason and I will have our tea in here. Nellie, are Martha and Agnes down yet? Miss Denning will want to see her room.'

In the servants' hall Rose gulped down the cup of tea, which was scalding, and then followed the girl she knew to be Agnes up what appeared to be endless flights of stairs. The stairs themselves, used exclusively by the servants, were uncarpeted and steep, a poor relation to the undoubtedly richly carpeted stairs used by the Grayson-Smiths' and their guests. Memories of the grand staircases that Rose herself had climbed and descended while a house guest at various country houses came flooding back. And it was with a sense of distaste that she negotiated the mean little staircases that were now her lot. Agnes, she noticed, was doing her best to tread quietly on the stairs. Rose did not feel the same compulsion to be quiet. However, she considered it best to follow the girl's example.

Breathing rather heavily, they at last reached the end of the flights of stairs. A quick look about her revealed to Rose that they were at the very top of the house. This then was where the servants' bedrooms were located, in the attics themselves. From what Mrs Field had said, the servants had not known that she would be coming. She wondered whether she would be required to share a room. If so, she would need to keep up the deception regarding her identity even in her sleep. The prospect was not an appealing one.

It was therefore with some relief that she discovered that she was to be the only occupant in the room assigned to her. The room itself was very sparsely furnished, having no more in it than a bed, a chest-of-drawers and a chair. The floor consisted of bare floorboards and there was nothing on the walls to relieve the tedious sage green colour. The doors of some of the other bedrooms had been open as they walked passed and she had noticed that some of the occupants had taken steps to make their rooms appear more homely. Some had put pictures on the walls, a rug or two on the floor or small bunches of flowers in vases on the chests.

'We haven't had a chance to air it proper,' said Agnes. 'I'd leave the window open if I were you. It don't look as if it'll rain. Martha unpacked your clothes and put them in the drawers. You haven't brought much, if you don't mind my saying.'

'I don't think we are staying for very long, a few days at most,' said Rose carefully.

'Oh? Well, that will explain it. I'd better go, or Mrs Field will get into one of her moods and then there'll be no pleasing her.'

'Are there only the two of you? Housemaids, I mean. You and Martha, was it?'

That's right. There's only me and Martha now,' said Agnes, putting her hands on her ample hips, which were accentuated by her large, white bib apron. 'Kitty went off and got married last month and weren't replaced. There used to be more of us before the war, so Mrs Field says, when wages were low. Five or six. Housemaids-cum-parlour maids is what they call Martha and me now.' She looked down at her uniform and started. 'Lor', I'm still in my blue cotton twill! I should have changed into my black alpaca dress ages ago. Mrs Field will have my guts for garters.'

With that, Agnes turned tail and fled to the bedroom she shared with Martha, presumably to get changed. Rose hovered in the corridor. She was very tempted to go into her own room and shut the door behind her, pretending to herself it was in order to gather her thoughts. It would, however, only be postponing the inevitable. She must return to the servants' hall at some point; it might as well be now. For further encouragement, she reminded herself why she was there at Crossing Manor. It was no use hiding herself away. She had information to unearth and a diamond necklace to recover. It was with these thoughts in mind that she rather reluctantly retraced her steps and descended the staircases, enclosed and shut off from the rest of the house by the green baize doors on every landing.

'Oh, there you are.' Mrs Field hurried over to Rose as soon as she reappeared in the servants' hall. 'You took your time, I must say. Her ladyship, she's been asking for you these past five minutes. You'd best hurry.'

Rose went back down the passage and retraced her steps up the enclosed, pokey little stairs. Thankfully she would not be required to go up so many flights this time for the guest and family bedrooms were located on the first floor. She followed the brief directions provided her by Mrs Field. Lavinia had been assigned a room, referred to rather grandly as the Sovereign Room.

She pulled open the green baize door and emerged on to a landing which for all the world could have belonged to another house, so sharply did it contrast with the grim and austere surroundings of the servants' quarters. There was a richly patterned carpet upon the floor and the walls were painted a soft green and decorated here and there with portraits and pictures of still life. In an alcove, a marble-topped console table in rosewood balanced a generous and elaborate flower arrangement. She felt for a moment as if she had moved from winter to summer, from dark into light.

The Sovereign Room was located halfway down the corridor, opposite Mrs Grayson-Smith's bedroom. Rose opened the door to find Lavinia, as always, at the dressing-table, gazing at her reflection. The girl was concentrating on dabbing at her face with some rouge, which provided Rose with an opportunity to look about the bedroom. It was a well-proportioned room and beautifully decorated. The hangings of the four poster bed and the window curtains were of chintz and comprised an old French design of rosebuds on a pale gold background. The walls and woodwork had been colour-washed and varnished and tinted yellow, which complemented the pale yellow carpet on the floor. Both a Queen Anne chair and the dressing-table had been covered in a burnished gold damask. Sunlight flooded through the windows lighting up the shades of gold and yellow in the most delightful fashion. The overall effect was of a tasteful opulence. Rose thought disparagingly of her own bare little room high up in the eaves.

'I rang for you ages ago,' complained Lavinia, swinging around on the stool.

'You really must remember that I am not actually your servant,' Rose said firmly, sitting on the bed and removing her spectacles. 'I say, I wish I hadn't let you persuade me to wear these, they're pinching my nose like anything.'

'All part of the disguise,' replied Lavinia. 'Now look here, I didn't want this tea to get cold. I requested a pot so that you could have a cup too.'

'You didn't ask for two cups, did you?' asked Rose in alarm. 'I'm sure it's not the done thing for a lady's maid to take tea with her employer.'

'Well, of course I didn't. What do you take me for?'

Rose thought it prudent not to reply.

'As it happens, I've been frightfully clever,' continued Lavinia. 'Look, I've brought this cup from Sedgwick.' She produced a fine bone china cup and saucer. 'No one will ever know you're having tea with me.' She frowned. 'I would have said take the weight off your feet too, but I see you've done that already.'

'Yes,' said Rose, pouring out the tea. 'I say, where's your luggage? No doubt you expect me to unpack for you and hang up your gowns?'

'The maid has already done that.' Lavinia sniffed. 'She was a strange little creature, I must say. She probably would have been frightfully pretty but her nose was all red and her eyes were swollen and puffy.' She leaned forward conspiratorially. 'Do you know, I think she'd been crying; she looked awfully sad.'

'That must have been Martha. There are only two housemaids and Agnes was busy showing me to my room.'

'Oh? What is it like, your room? I've never been in a servant's room.'

'Not a patch on yours. You wouldn't like it one little bit. It's up flights and flights of stairs right up in the attic. And it's tiny, about a quarter of the size of this room. There's very little furniture and no carpet on the floor and –'

'It sounds absolutely dreadful,' said Lavinia quickly, making a face. 'Now tell me, what have you discovered?'

Chapter Six

'Lavinia, we have been here less than an hour,' protested Rose. 'That's very little time for me to have discovered anything.'

'But you must have met the servants. Didn't one of them look guilty?'

'I've only really met three of the staff, and very briefly at that.' Rose counted on her fingers as she reeled off the names. 'Mason, the butler, Mrs Field, the housekeeper and Agnes, one of the housemaids. I really only have first impressions of them.'

'I always make up my mind about people within five minutes of meeting them,' said Lavinia.

'Good for you!' said Rose. 'Now, listen. We need to find out first who had an opportunity to steal the necklace. You told me that Mrs Grayson-Smith suspects her lady's maid, Cooper. I haven't met her yet, but I think she is definitely a suspect. She and Mrs Grayson-Smith were the last two people to see the necklace.'

'Yes,' said Lavinia, a frown appearing on her face as she tried to recall her conversation in the tearooms. 'According to Millicent, the necklace was there first thing in the morning; both she and her lady's maid remember seeing it on top of her jewel box. It was still there when Millicent went to have her bath but, according to Cooper, it had gone when she came back from running the bath. She assumed her mistress had put it back in the jewel box.'

'In which case, Cooper could not have not returned straight to the room after running the bath,' Rose said, more to herself than to her companion. 'If she had, Mrs Grayson-Smith would still have been in the bedroom.'

'That's right. Now I come to think about it, Millicent said the maid knocked on her door and said something like: "Your bath is ready for you, ma'am." She didn't come in. I suppose she must then have gone off to the servants' quarters to do some chore or other.'

'Or darted into an unoccupied bedroom to wait for her mistress to leave her room so that she could slip back and take the necklace,' said Rose, looking about her. 'If she did do that, this would have been the perfect room to hide in. It's directly opposite Mrs Grayson-Smith's. It would have been easy enough for Cooper to wait in here until the coast was clear. If she kept the door slightly ajar, she could easily have heard when her mistress went down the corridor to the bathroom.'

'Oh, I say, do you think that's what happened?' exclaimed Lavinia, clapping her hands excitedly.

'It is certainly possible. But it is just as likely that she was telling the truth and didn't take the necklace. In which case she didn't return to the room until after the theft had taken place. There would have been a short period of time between Mrs Grayson-Smith leaving the room to go for her bath and her lady's maid returning, when the room would have been unoccupied.'

'In which case anyone could have slipped in and taken the necklace while the room was empty,' said Lavinia looking disappointed.

'Not anyone, no,' Rose said. 'Think about it, Lavinia. The theft may very well not have been planned, but whoever stole the necklace must have known that it had not been locked away, as was the usual custom. If anyone had seen Mrs Grayson-Smith wearing it the night before, they would quite reasonably have assumed that she had returned it to her jewel box with her other jewellery and locked the box. It was rather careless of her not to have done so, to leave the necklace lying out there in full view, as she did.'

'Then the thief must be the lady's maid.'

'Not necessarily. It seems to me that it is just as likely that this was a crime of opportunity. Don't you see, Lavinia? Someone could have come into the room not intending to steal a thing, then seen the necklace lying there and decided to take it on the spur of the moment.'

'I see. At least, I think I do.'

'Good,' said Rose, getting to her feet and putting on the hated spectacles. 'We will also need to find out who holds the key to Mrs Grayson-Smith's jewel box. That's to say, does she, or is it her lady's maid? The same needs to be found out about the jewellery safe. As it's in the butler's pantry, presumably Mason holds the key, but we'd best make certain that is the case.'

'The jewellery safe?'

'Yes. It's just possible that the necklace wasn't stolen until the jewel box was taken down to be put back in the safe. Of course, that would mean that either Mrs Grayson-Smith or Cooper or indeed someone else did put the necklace back in the jewel box before it was removed to the safe. It would also mean that the thief required an accomplice as one person was unlikely to have a key to both the jewel box and the jewellery safe.' Rose paused a moment and put a hand to her forehead. 'Of course, it's just possible that the lady's maid forgot to lock the jewel box before it was sent down to the safe … but, no … it is all getting far too complicated …'

'Well, I think you should concentrate on interviewing the lady's maid,' said Lavinia. 'Whatever you say, she seems to me to be a frightfully suspicious character.' She made a face. 'Millicent doesn't like her one little bit.'

Rose made her way up the flights of mean wooden stairs again, clutching a pair of Lavinia's satin shoes and a brown flecked tweed skirt. The ironing room was located rather inconveniently right at the top of the house in one of the attic rooms. On reaching it, she found the walls to be littered with lockers for guests' luggage. She realised only on entering that she had expected to find the room unoccupied. It was therefore something of a surprise to discover a maid already standing over the ironing board, on which was placed an ironing blanket.

'You must be Miss Denning,' the maid announced, making it sound more like a statement than a question. 'I'm Miss Cooper, Mrs Grayson-Smith's lady's maid.' She looked Rose up and down in so impertinent a manner as to leave the girl blushing. 'I must say, you're not at all what I expected.'

Not for a moment did Rose doubt that she had been found wanting. Her hair, her dress, her spectacles, all of it she felt to be wrong. The woman before her was similarly dressed in black, but her own gown seemed to shine in the sunlight and possess a rich, glossy sheen, rather than looking old and dusty like Rose's own dress. Rose inwardly cursed Lavinia for insisting that she wear such a rag. If she could have thrown off her spectacles and loosened her hair without observation or arousing comment, then she would have done so. To make matters worse, even the simple cut of the lady's maid's dress and the severity of her hairstyle could not disguise the fact that Miss Cooper had an enviable figure and was striking in appearance, attributes Rose considered lacking in herself.

'Has the cat got your tongue?' enquired Miss Cooper, her lips curving into a smile that looked anything but friendly. 'My, you are a timid little thing.'

Inwardly Rose had managed to regain her composure by reminding herself that she was not really a lady's maid. In a few days' time, all this tomfoolery would be in the past to be laughed at and then forgotten. It did not matter therefore if this woman standing before her considered her to be inadequate for the position of lady's maid. Outwardly, however, Rose's manner had not changed. She still appeared unsure and hesitant, for it had occurred to her that Miss Cooper would be more forthcoming with any information if she did not consider Rose to be a professional rival. That she had obtained a position that the other women envied, she did not doubt. The job of lady's maid to the daughter of an earl was no small accomplishment; indeed, to many it was a position to be aspired to. It was usually obtained by skill and training. It was therefore hardly surprising if Miss Cooper was somewhat taken aback at Lavinia's choice of lady's maid, particularly as she appeared to have chosen a woman who seemingly had little interest in her own dress and appearance.

'This is not my usual occupation,' said Rose truthfully. 'My cousin Eliza is Lady Lavinia's lady's maid. She is unwell at present and I am looking after Lady Lavinia in her absence.' She bent forward in a conspiratorial fashion. 'Poor Eliza is dreadfully afraid of losing her position. She is so very sickly, you see, always has been, even as a child.'

'I see.' This time the smile reached the woman's eyes as she perceived a potential career opportunity. 'Well, I'd better not keep you, Miss Denning. Though I'll say one thing before I go. If you're intent on ironing that tweed skirt you're holding, you'd do well to place a linen cloth over it first to protect it from the heat. A damp cloth works best.'

'Thank you, I –'

'These gold satin slippers look very grand,' said Miss Cooper suddenly, swooping unexpectedly and snatching the shoes from Rose's grasp. 'Dust these with a soft brush or wipe with a cloth.' She paused to study them closely. The workmanship was exquisite. 'I say, is Lady Lavinia really intending to wear these shoes this evening?'

'Yes, she is,' said Rose, retrieving the slippers.

'Does she know that they will be dining alone tonight, she and the mistress? Madam is not in the way of inviting guests, unless you count the vicar and his wife of course. A very dull old couple if you ask me.' She regarded Rose curiously. 'I cannot tell you how surprised we all were when we heard that Lady Lavinia Sedgwick was coming to stay.'

'My mistress likes to wear fine clothes whatever the occasion,' said Rose, again truthfully.

'Does she indeed?' There was a gleam of interest in Miss Cooper's eye. 'And does she like to wear fine jewels as well?'

'Yes.'

'Where did they meet, your mistress and mine?'

'At a tea party, I believe –'

'And they struck up an immediate friendship? How very pleasant.' Miss Cooper sniffed, her nose wrinkling in a delicate fashion. She bent forward and lowered her voice to little more than a whisper. 'Between you and me, I am somewhat surprised that Millicent Grayson-Smith made an impression on anyone.'

Rose felt that she had strayed on to dangerous ground. While it was interesting to note that her companion did not hold her employer in very high regard, Rose did not wish to give the lady's maid any encouragement, or indeed opportunity, to pry into the reasons behind Lavinia's visit to Crossing Manor. An invitation to stay was unlikely to have arisen following a chance meeting at a tea party. If nothing else, it was painfully clear that, during the usual course of events, Millicent Grayson-Smith and Lady Lavinia Sedgwick would be unlikely to become friends.

She needed to alter the direction the conversation was going. Even at this very minute, Miss Cooper was staring at her inquisitively. A moment or two more and she would be asking Rose why Lavinia was here. It was even possible that the lady's maid might swoop on her spectacles as she had done the slippers and how would Rose explain the plain glass? She found herself clutching at straws, but also in her desperation she saw an opening and spoke quickly before she could change her mind.

'Lady Lavinia has not brought her jewels with her on this occasion. Mrs Grayson-Smith informed her that there had been a theft, that …'

Rose allowed her words to falter in mid-sentence. She had not said as much, but the implication was clear. Mrs Grayson-Smith had suggested to her guest that in all probability the thief was a member of her own staff and she could therefore not vouch for the safety of anything of value brought into the house. Her words and the insinuation were not lost on the lady's maid. The colour had gone from her cheeks and her eyes blazed. No longer did she appear confident and aloof. Instead she clenched and unclenched her hands as if she were attempting to contain an inner turmoil.

'What did she say? Tell me. Did she say that I was the thief?'

Rose considered it prudent to say nothing. Truth be told, she was now rather regretting her own impulsiveness. She would say no more. Her words had produced a reaction; it was enough. Let the woman believe what she wanted to believe. Perhaps to the good, for on closer inspection she saw that the lady's maid was in a very agitated state indeed. She required no words of encouragement to speak. She could not remain silent for long.

'I knew it! She thinks it was me who stole from her. Me! The cheek of it all and she no better than I am. Well, there's things that I could tell if I wanted to and things I will tell if she's bold enough to accuse me to my face or thinks to dismiss me.'

'Oh,' said Rose. 'What things?'

'Never you mind,' retorted the lady's maid, drawing herself up to her full height with righteous indignation. 'I'm not one to gossip.' She made as if to go to the door.

'Look here,' said Rose quickly. 'If you know something about the theft, why don't you tell me? It needn't be seen as telling tales. I can tell Lady Lavinia and she can mention it to your mistress in passing. No one need know that the information came from you.'

Velda Cooper stopped on the threshold. Her back was to Rose and it was a moment or two before she turned around. When she did, there was a look of indecision on her face and something else that Rose could not put a finger on at first.

'I wouldn't be telling you anything that the other servants don't know,' the lady's maid said finally. 'Afraid of Mr Mason, they are, worried about upsetting him. It's not right, it's not. The master should have been told and it was Mr Mason who should have told him.'

'What should Mr Mason have told him?'

'About the last theft, that's what. It wasn't right keeping it hidden. Anyone else and Mr Mason would have had him dismissed. And it's all very well replacing the snuff box and pretending like it never happened. It was still stolen. That's the point. Mr Mason, he just wants to brush it under the carpet, he does.'

All the while she had been speaking, the lady's maid's voice had risen and with it, her former refined tones and way of speaking had slipped, so that listening to her speech it would have been easy to have mistaken her for one of the lower servants. This was not the proud and haughty woman who had first presented herself to Rose. There was a great deal more behind Velda Cooper's façade than that. For one thing there was a malicious streak that had first appeared with the curling of her lips into that unpleasant smile.

'I'm afraid I don't understand,' began Rose. 'Are you saying Mrs Grayson-Smith's necklace was not the only theft to have occurred in this house? A snuff box … and you say it was replaced?'

'Yes, but the necklace hasn't been returned, has it? At least not to my knowledge.'

'But the culprit,' said Rose, 'the person who stole the snuff box. Are you saying he's known to you?'

'To everyone, at least to all the servants. It's a disgrace, that's what it is. Madam is threatening to call in the police and there he is, going about his business as bold as brass. It isn't right.'

The colour had returned to the woman's cheeks and with it a sense of propriety. She had caught herself discussing the family's business and with a stranger at that. She glared at Rose. True, the girl both looked and appeared to be a little stupid, but you could never tell …

'Look here, I shouldn't be standing here gossiping to you,' she said rather gruffly. 'I've work to do.'

Rose watched her dark retreating figure as she made her way down the corridor to the wooden staircase. She had been tempted to press the woman further, but she felt certain it would have been to no avail. Velda Cooper was undoubtedly of the opinion that she had been manipulated into saying too much already. The purposeful strides, as she tried to put as much distance between the two of them as possible, said as much. Perhaps even now she was bitterly regretting her outburst. And it wouldn't do for Rose to appear too inquisitive.

What was very clear was that there had been a previous theft from the house of which Millicent Grayson-Smith was presumably unaware. What was more, if what the lady's maid had said was to be believed, and Rose had little reason to doubt her words, the identity of the culprit in that case was known to the servants and yet the person was still employed in the house.

Rose pondered this matter while she ironed the tweed skirt. By the time she had finished polishing the satin slippers with a soft cloth, she had quite made up her mind to speak to Agnes. She returned to the servants' hall, determined to put her decision into practice, quite unaware that a surprise awaited her there.

Chapter Seven

On Rose's recommendation, Lavinia had suggested to Millicent Grayson-Smith that they take their afternoon tea in the gardens where their conversation was unlikely to be overheard by the servants.

It was approaching the end of September when the temperature could be so variable. That day, however, the cold winds of October seemed to belong to another season. The weather was fine and the day warm. It being autumn, the gardeners were busy attending to garden repairs and restoration, planting bulbs and digging up flowerbeds containing summer bedding plants and replanting them with forget-me-nots and polyanthus. The industrious nature of the work drew both women's attention so that their eyes drifted towards the flower borders as they conversed, the clatter and ring of their china and teaspoons adding to the peaceful scene.

Lavinia glanced over at her hostess. It was true that outside the house Millicent seemed to relax, appearing to benefit from the warmth of the sun on her skin and the fresh air in her lungs. Despite this, Lavinia still thought how pale and drawn she looked. There were dark shadows beneath her eyes as if she had smudged her face with coal dust and her skin was so transparent that Lavinia could see the little blue threads of veins beneath the surface. Millicent's hair did nothing to help matters for it was so light as to appear almost colourless, and her lips so bloodless as to be hardly distinguishable.

Lavinia sighed. She was firmly of the opinion that the majority of women benefited from the application of a little rouge and lipstick. Millicent's face was innocent of all make-up. She thought even her dress was the wrong shade, such an insipid pale blue as to be almost white. It was like looking at a ghost. Really, why did Millicent not have on a bright, flower-patterned tea dress or a multi-pigmented tweed suit? She should be wearing something that would bring colour to her face, that would highlight the bright blue of her eyes. She should not be adorned in so anaemic and drab a garment that did nothing more for her than to help her blend into the background and become invisible. Nondescript, that was the word she would use to describe her hostess both in appearance and character, for she just sat there picking listlessly at the material of her dress looking for all the world as if she wished to disappear.

Lavinia was rather regretting her decision to come to Crossing Manor. It was clear that her companion was neither a conversationalist nor an attentive listener. Were she not to give voice to her own idle observations in a light and witty way, there would be an awkward silence, broken only by the labours of the gardeners or the sipping of tea. The news that they would be dining alone had not been welcome. She had visions that the evening would stretch out before them, long and endless. It was therefore a relief when Millicent finally spoke, and a reminder to Lavinia of why she was there, undergoing this unpleasant ordeal.

'Do you know when Miss Simpson will be coming?' enquired Millicent. 'Mrs Field, she's our housekeeper, gets frightfully annoyed if we don't give her much notice of that sort of thing. I suppose she needs to ensure that the bedroom has been properly aired and that there's fresh bedding. She doesn't say anything of course. That she's put out, I mean. But one can just tell. Servants are like that, aren't they?'

'The servants at Sedgwick Court aren't', said Lavinia firmly. 'If they behaved like that, they'd be dismissed. Look here, Millicent. I need to ask you a few questions. That's why I suggested we have tea outside. I should like to gather as much information as I can for Rose in advance of her arrival.'

'You mean, a bit like when the police interview people and one of them takes down notes of what is said?'

'Yes, that's exactly what I mean. Now, tell me, Millicent, who holds the key to your jewel box? Is it you or your lady's maid?'

'Cooper does. She was most insistent.'

'Well, it is usual for the lady's maid to hold the key,' said Lavinia, rather dismissively. A thought struck her. 'Eliza always puts my jewellery back in my jewel box when I retire for the night. She locks the box as well and returns it to the strong room.'

'Cooper usually does.'

'But she didn't the night before the necklace was stolen?'

'No.'

Lavinia stared at her hostess.

Millicent averted her gaze and looked down at the lawn. It looked very green and inviting. How wonderful it would be to tear off her shoes and stockings and walk barefoot through the grass … It was with some reluctance that she returned her attention to Lavinia.

'It was very late when I retired to bed that night. The vicar and his wife had come to dinner. You would never think it to look at them, but they keep very late hours. I was tired as anything, but Mrs Kitchen never showed any signs of fatigue. They've never stayed that late before. She's sixty if a day, but she's as sprightly as a lamb.' Two red spots lit up Millicent's cheeks. It took Lavinia a while to realise that her companion was in fact blushing. 'I was dreadfully tired when at last I retired to my room. I have trouble sleeping in this house, you see. Cooper wasn't a bit pleased at having had to stay up. It's not as if it had been a grand dinner party or anything like that. She was quite sulky helping me to undress. I suppose she was quite tired herself. She managed to catch my hair in my dress clip.'

'She sounds frightful,' said Lavinia, thinking fondly of her own lady's maid, Eliza.

'Yes, she is. I wondered if she had done it on purpose; caught my hair, I mean. I said she could leave and I would finish undressing and undoing my hair myself.'

'And the necklace?'

'I didn't realise the jewel box was unlocked. I took off the necklace and laid it out on the top of the box.'

'I see,' said Lavinia.

It occurred to her that both Millicent and her maid were very careless and lackadaisical in their approach to fine jewellery and it was therefore hardly surprising that a precious piece had gone missing. If an extensive search had not already been undertaken of the house, she would not have been surprised to have discovered that the necklace had fallen off the jewellery box of its own accord and become buried in the carpet.

Rose returned the pressed skirt and satin slippers to Lavinia's room. Finding the room empty, she had restored the garment and shoes to a wardrobe faced with mirror-glass and lined with cedar wood. She had then proceeded to the servants' hall, where she was informed that Mrs Grayson-Smith and her guest were taking a turn in the gardens and were not expected to return for a while. This provided her with a few precious minutes to do with as she liked before the servants' supper was served at six o'clock. As yet she was unaware of the arrangements for the meal. It was possible that the upper servants dined alone in the housekeeper's sitting room and were waited upon by the footman. It was equally likely that all the servants ate together, with the butler presiding over the proceedings. Whatever the custom, Rose was resolved to make best use of her time while the hall buzzed with activity as servants returned from their allotted tasks and immersed themselves in their leisure activities.

She had expected the servants to busy themselves sitting in little clusters exchanging gossip, but the room was unexpectedly absent of any chatter. Instead, one or two sat in easy chairs around the room reading newspapers or books and a young maid of lowly status was sitting drawn up to the huge scrubbed table engrossed in doing what appeared to be sums. At the other end of the table a maid was sewing furiously with a Singer machine. On closer inspection, it was revealed she was making herself an outfit for her Sunday best.

Rose hovered on the threshold of the room. It was evident that everyone was making best use of their few snatched minutes. While one or two of the staff had looked up and eyed her with curiosity, a new face among the old, she considered it unlikely that they would welcome any interruption. Even if her company had been sought out by one or two of the more inquisitive maids, the lack of conversation meant that any words uttered, or conversation entered into, would be overhead by everyone in the room. She had envisaged taking one or two of the servants aside and making discreet enquiries into the theft. In practice, however, such an approach did not appear possible.

As if reading her thoughts regarding the industrious pursuits of the staff and the subsequent lack of conversation, Mrs Field appeared at her shoulder eager to inform.

'Mr Mason encourages the staff to use their idle time wisely,' the housekeeper explained. 'He is an advocate of everyone trying to better themselves.' She gave an admiring smile, as if the man were there before her and could note her approval. 'He considers the pursuit of knowledge to be above all else,' she continued. Bending slightly, the housekeeper whispered in Rose's ear in a conspiratorial manner. 'He is quite a forward-thinking man, is our Mr Mason. He realises times are changing and he encourages learning as much for the girls as for the boys. He still wants things to be done proper, mind. Look at Hettie there, poring over her sums. The girl could hardly read or write when she first came to us. Mr Mason set himself the task of teaching her. Taught her the alphabet, he has, and sets her sums himself, he does, and marks them too.'

'Does he indeed?' said Rose with approval, trying to reconcile this image of Mr Mason's enlightened character with that of the rather stern and intimidating man who had greeted her on her arrival. 'How very modern of him.'

'Oh, don't let him hear you say that, Miss Denning,' said the housekeeper, clasping her hand to her mouth in horror. 'He wouldn't like to be considered modern, not one little bit. He associates it with a fall in values. He says, and of course he's right, that we must keep up standards. He doesn't like the way things have slipped since the war.'

Mrs Field was proving surprisingly talkative. Rose doubted whether the housekeeper would have spoken so candidly to a servant in the house for whom she had responsibility. She had seized the chance to talk openly to a stranger, presumably being of the view that there was little harm in confiding in an upper servant who would be staying only very briefly in the house. It was obvious that the woman was in awe of the butler. Rose hoped that the man in question held Mrs Field in similar high esteem.

Rose looked up and saw that the other servants, intent on their leisure occupations, were seemingly oblivious to their conversation. She was aware, however, that should Mrs Field become excited or agitated, her voice would carry in this vast, quiet room. She could not, however, waste the opportunity given to her of the housekeeper being in a verbose mood. Now was her chance to broach the subject of the thefts, if she could only think of an excuse why they might retire to the housekeeper's sitting room to ensure privacy …

She had taken too long. The housekeeper had gone as quickly as she had appeared and Rose was left hovering, awkward and undecided, at the door. She knew she could not stay there indefinitely in the position of casual observer of a life which was foreign to her. Nor could she squander her time which was all too precious. She turned tail and retreated down the passage, not towards the wooden staircase or the green baize door, but in the opposite direction, retracing her steps along the passage that led to the outside. The door at the end was ajar. With one swift movement she opened it and emerged into the courtyard. The sunlight and fresh air hit her immediately and lifted her spirits. She felt a sense of liberation, certainly of warmth and light. She had been trapped in passages and rooms that were dark and drab in colour, dull greens and greys, but predominantly browns. In comparison with the gardens, the courtyard might be considered dull and uninviting, leading off from the basement as it was, but judged against the servants' quarters, it was a pleasant environment indeed.

A couple of clothes lines had been strung up in the courtyard and on these were pegged a number of bedsheets and table linens that billowed in the wind like sails. The effect of this was to separate off odd stretches of the yard, the washing becoming fragile walls obscuring the small areas from sight. It gave the misleading illusion of privacy for, while those standing behind the sheets and linens were for the most part hidden, their words still carried, particularly as was the case now when she suddenly heard voices, risen above whispers.

Rose edged forward. Under normal circumstances, she would never have considered trying to eavesdrop on what was very obviously a private conversation. However, reminding herself of her purpose for masquerading as a servant, the sleuth in her took precedence and she approached cautiously. Two people, a man and a woman by the sound of them, were having what appeared to be an agitated conversation behind the veil of laundry. Unless she was mistaken there was also the muffled sound of sobbing as if the woman was attempting to stem her tears.

'Martha, why won't you listen to me?' said the voice of a young man. It did not sound particularly educated and the words were delivered in a brusque manner. 'I haven't got it,' the voice continued. 'Listen to me, I'm telling you the truth.'

There was a murmur from his companion. Rose could not distinguish the words themselves, if indeed such were uttered. It might have been that the girl merely sighed or there was a fresh outpouring of tears.

'Why won't you believe me?' There was a pleading note in the man's voice now, coupled with something of an irritating whine. Rose imagined that the young man was clutching the housemaid's hands in his own, staring at her imploringly, or else holding her by her shoulders at arm's length, begging with every gesture of his being for her to see reason.

'Of course you have it,' sobbed the maid. 'Why must you keep on lying to me, Albert? If you would only tell me the truth –'

'I am telling you the truth.' The words were almost spat out. There was a dangerous edge to the voice now, as if the speaker verged on anger, all his pleading having been to no avail. 'But if you won't believe me –'

'How can I believe you?' cried Martha. 'Oh, don't you think I want to?'

'I don't know, do you? If you loved me, you'd believe me.' The voice was clearly annoyed now. 'And what's with all this crying? Do you want everyone to suspect me? Do you want me to be hauled up before the magistrate?' The man gave a laugh that was far from pleasant. 'Perhaps you'd like me to be kept under lock and key where you can keep an eye on me.'

'Albert, no. Of course not …'

Rose quickly made her way back to the door. Any moment now, she imagined the man would lose patience and storm back to the servants' hall, the maid following miserably in his wake. To be caught in the act of listening to such a damning conversation when the man's mood already appeared so agitated and volatile, did not bear contemplating.

She hurried back down the passage and into the servants' hall. The sewing machine and books and newspapers had been cleared away; the table freshly washed and laid. All the chairs had been drawn up neatly to the table and a considerable number of servants had congregated, among them Mrs Field and Velda Cooper. Rose breathed a sigh of relief. It appeared that they were all to dine together in the hour before the gong was sounded for Mrs Grayson-Smith and her guest to go up to dress for dinner.

The servants began to take their seats, leaving the chair at the head of the table vacant for the butler. The housekeeper went and sat right of the empty chair and the lady's maid looked as if she were about to sit opposite her, on the other side of the butler, until she was arrested by a glare from Mrs Field. Whether there would have been an exchange of words between the two women, Rose was never to discover, for Mason chose to arrive at that very moment. On his entrance, the servants rose from their seats in one collective show of deference. He nodded and went to his seat.

'No, no,' he said, glancing down the left hand side of the table. 'You will all need to move down one seat to accommodate Miss Denning. You too, Miss Cooper. In this house visiting servants are seated according to the rank of their masters and mistresses. Miss Denning, if you please.' The butler indicated the chair to his left and Rose found herself seated between Mason and the lady's maid, acutely aware that Miss Cooper was scowling at her in a most unfriendly fashion. If she thought for a moment that the situation could not become more awkward, she was wrong. The kitchen staff were bringing in the dishes and when she lifted her head she found herself looking into a familiar face. The kitchen maid staring back at her, with a look of amazement, was none other than little Edna, former scullery maid at Ashgrove House.

Chapter Eight

For a moment, Rose did not know what to do. It was quite possible that she was mistaken and the girl was not Edna at all. However, she certainly looked like her. She appeared to be about fifteen years of age and had filled out a bit since Rose had last seen her. Strands of black hair had escaped untidily from her mop cap, reminding Rose of when she had first encountered Edna, sobbing bitterly in the kitchen garden at Ashgrove House. If she was in two minds as to the girl's identity, then the girl's reaction was enough to confirm that her suspicions were correct. For the kitchen maid's attention was arrested and then transfixed by the sight of Rose, sitting there so unexpectedly between the butler and the lady's maid. She stood poised beside the table, a dish of potatoes in her hands, and a look of confusion on her face.

'Edna, are you going to serve those potatoes or just stand there letting them get cold?' Mrs Field admonished. 'What's wrong with you, girl? We've had visiting servants here before.'

'Hello. I'm Miss Denning,' said Rose quickly. 'I'm lady's maid to Lady Lavinia.'

'Oh,' said Edna, recovering a little. 'Are you really? If you don't mind my saying, you look awfully like –'

'Yes, I am,' said Rose rather sharply, holding her breath and all the while praying that the girl would not persist.

Their eyes met and she gave the girl an imploring look. Whether by luck or by design, it happened that when Edna stood beside her to serve her potatoes, a few moments later, the other servants were sufficiently engaged in conversation to provide Rose with an opportunity to whisper: 'Please don't give me away.'

She had spoken so softly that for a moment she was afraid the girl had not heard what she had said. Edna progressed around the table, serving the potatoes as was her custom. Was it Rose's imagination or did her hand seem to tremble as she deposited the vegetables on each plate? Rose sat there feeling wretched and on edge. If she was discovered to be Rose Simpson instead of Daisy Denning, how would the servants react? She would have to leave, her investigation barely started, her reputation in ruins. It did not bear thinking about.

The kitchen maid made her way to the door, presumably to return to the kitchen to have her own supper with the rest of the kitchen staff. Rose willed the girl to turn around, catch her eye, give some sort of sign that she was going to comply with her wishes. On the threshold, the kitchen maid hesitated. She turned around and looked up and down the table, as if to make sure she was not being observed. Only then did she focus her gaze on Rose. She gave her the briefest of nods, turned tail and disappeared.

Mason picked up his knife and fork and on his signal the other servants followed suit, Rose among them. The conversation faltered and all attention was focused on eating the food laid before them as soon as possible. Rose was very aware that it would not be long before the gong was sounded for Mrs Grayson-Smith and her guest to dress for dinner. She would be required to leave the servants' hall and help Lavinia dress, whether or not she had finished her own supper. Eliza had warned her that in some households, when the butler laid down his knife and fork, the other servants had to do the same. She glanced nervously at Mason out of the corner of her eye. To her relief, she noticed that he was eating slowly. She ate her own food hungrily.

'Well, Miss Denning, how are you finding Crossing?' enquired the butler. 'You see we have our food before the family eat theirs and not last thing at night when all the work is done. The staff prefer it that way and I agree with them. Going to bed on a heavy stomach does nothing for the digestion. It discourages sleep.'

'We follow the same practice at Sedgwick Court, Mr Mason,' said Rose.

'Do you indeed? Well, well.' He smiled and bent towards her, so only she could hear what he was saying. 'I do not know why the practice is not adopted by all households. Asking servants to serve a five course meal when their own stomachs are empty will only ever lead to trouble.' He straightened and spoke a little louder. 'The pilfering of food is something I will not abide.'

'Perhaps, Mr Mason, you should tell that to the kitchen staff,' said a voice Rose recognised at once. 'They keep the best cuts of meat for themselves, so I've been told, and heap their plates. Eat better than the family, they do. Mrs Field, you should keep a better eye on the cook and on the household accounts.'

'Albert, that will do.'

The butler's face was quite red. The other servants had been arrested in the act of eating by Albert's outburst, their forks frozen halfway to their lips, their mouths open in astonishment. One or two had even put down their cutlery to give their full attention to the spectacle. Rose glanced down the table at Martha, whom she recognised by her parlour maid's dress. The girl looked as pale as anything save for her red swollen eyes, evidence of her recent sobbing.

'You will not speak in that insolent way.' The butler spoke quietly, but there was a dangerous edge to his voice. 'You will apologise to Mrs Field immediately.'

'I'm sorry, Uncle,' Albert said in a sulky manner. 'I apologise unreservedly to you too, Mrs Field.'

There was so little sincerity behind the young man's words that the room was silent, a few of the servants blinking in disbelief at Albert's rudeness. Mrs Field snorted and looked fit to burst, bristling with indignation. Rose shot a quick glance at Martha. The girl was staring fixedly at her plate and looked to be on the verge of shedding fresh tears. She had discarded her knife and fork and her hands were clutched together trembling visibly.

'Albert, you will see me in my pantry as soon as supper's over,' said the butler. His face had a grey hue to it, which was almost sickly in appearance. 'In the meantime, you will not utter another word.'

'If there is a pilferer among us, I doubt it's the cook,' said Velda Cooper quietly.

The lady's maid alone seemed to find the spectacle amusing. Her lips had curled up into that unpleasant smile of hers. That the woman was intent on exacerbating the situation, and took great delight in doing so, was obvious. What surprised Rose the most, having already received an indication of the woman's character, was that she should be so blatant about her purpose. The other servants looked equally taken aback by her antics. If they expected Mason to admonish her, then they were disappointed, for it was the housekeeper who leapt into the affray.

'That will do, Miss Cooper.'

'Albert has the cheek to suggest there is a thief among us, when we all know that if there is a thief, it's him.'

'Miss Cooper –' began the butler, his face now quite flushed.

'It's no good, Mr Mason. We all know as how he took the snuff box and you made him put it back –'

'That's a lie!' cried Albert, jumping up from his chair and knocking it over in the process.

'Sit down, Albert,' Mason demanded, his voice raised.

After a little hesitation, the young man complied with some reluctance. Martha had stared at him imploringly, willing him to be quiet. The fact that he had risen briefly had provided Rose with an opportunity to study him more closely. If Albert were to be judged merely on his appearance, he would be considered an outstandingly handsome young man. He was tall and well-proportioned in physique and his footman's livery set off his figure to perfection. He was dark in complexion, with hair that was almost black and which fell in untidy curls around his face giving him an exotic if unkempt air, strangely at odds with the neat splendour of his uniform. Had he smiled or merely looked attentive then his face with its even features would have been almost beautiful. Now, however, with fury blazing in his eyes and anger distorting his countenance, his face was only striking. Standing, looming above the table, he had looked almost menacing, sitting he still looked hostile and ill-humoured, his character marring his good looks.

'That will do, Miss Cooper,' the butler said quietly, reiterating the housekeeper's words.

Mason had regained something of his usual composure, sufficiently to imply aloofness. His tone was such that few in the room would have dared to challenge his authority. Velda Cooper did not appear to share such scruples. Having at last given voice to her grievances, the lady's maid showed no sign of being silenced. If anything, she seemed more determined than before to make her point.

'He took the snuff box and he took madam's necklace. You may shake your head, Mr Mason, but there can be little doubt in anyone here's mind that he is the thief.' The lady's maid turned to glare at the footman. 'It's not right, so it's not, that he should be walking around as bold as brass while we, with not a blemish on our characters, are all under suspicion.'

There were faint murmurs of assent from the other servants.

'Nonsense,' said the butler. 'The situation with the snuff box was a misunderstanding, nothing more. It had been removed to be cleaned, that is all. And there is no reason to suppose the necklace has been stolen. It has simply been mislaid.'

'That's not what the mistress thinks,' retorted Miss Cooper. 'She warned Lady Lavinia not to bring her jewels with her. Told her there was a thief among her servants, she did. If you don't believe me, ask Miss Denning here.'

Rose blanched as all eyes turned to her. How she wished she had not been so outspoken. She had intended to be all but invisible, melting into the background, a casual observer. To have drawn attention to her presence in the house, to have alluded to her purpose … She cursed her own impetuous nature. If only she had kept quiet. If nothing else, she was responsible for this outburst in the hall. The lady's maid's contribution to it, anyway. And now the servants were looking at her suspiciously or, understandably, at least with some reservations. She was not one of them and yet she knew their business. The theft that had haunted them all the last few days was known to her. Why, her mistress was very likely discussing it this very minute with their mistress as the two women roamed the grounds together.

'Is this true, Miss Denning?' demanded Mrs Field.

'Yes. No,' began Rose. 'That's to say it is true that Mrs Grayson-Smith recommended that Lady Lavinia did not bring her jewels with her. On account of a theft having occurred in the house, she said. I don't think she said the thief was one of the servants.'

'Well, there we have it,' said Mason bestowing the assembled servants with something akin to a smile. 'A precaution. Let us not read any more into it than that.'

The effect of the butler's words, and the tone in which they were delivered, was to bring calm to the servants. They resumed their chatter and Rose was left feeling that she had negotiated a difficult situation with some skill and efficiency. What had threatened to become a disaster had proved the opposite. She had gained a deal of information regarding the thefts without having had to raise the matter herself, and she had also managed to deflect suspicion in connection with her presence in the house. It was only the lady's maid that worried her. Without meaning to, she had made the woman look a fool among her peers, not something that

Velda Cooper was likely to take lightly or forget. The insolent words of Albert had been forgotten, but the humiliation of the lady's maid still showed clearly on the woman's face.

'Come in and shut the door,' said Mason.

He was seated behind the large, wooden desk in his pantry. It was a room he considered very much his own domain, a place where he reigned supreme, even more so than in the servants' hall, where idle servants' chatter could run away with itself as it had done this evening. In some households of which he knew, the butlers that presided over them demanded that the servants' meals be eaten in silence. Privately, he abhorred such practise, considering it close to tyranny. He admitted, however, that such a strict approach to discipline had certain advantages. For example, the conversation that had taken place that evening would never have occurred.

He sighed inwardly and puffed out his pigeon chest, trying to muster his strength. Over the years, and in this very room, he had disciplined and, where deemed necessary, even dismissed a number of male servants. The current situation was nothing out of the ordinary. A spirited young man attempting to challenge the authority that bound the servants' hall and make a name for himself among the servants. A cocky lad trying to impress the women folk, nothing more. He had dealt with such cases a dozen times before. This time should be no different, though of course it was.

'Albert,' he said almost wearily, 'I will not have you speak like that to Mrs Field. And to accuse the cook of pilfering food …' He shuddered.

'I said I was sorry,' said Albert scowling, standing before him like a naughty schoolboy. He did not quite stand with his hands in his pockets, but it was clear that was his inclination.

To the butler, he did not look a bit apologetic. How many times, Mason wondered, have I told him to smarten up his appearance and stand up straight? His manner is sullen and there is always the most unpleasant sneer upon his face. His hair is unkempt with those curls of his falling about his collar in such a bohemian fashion.

The boy was a bad apple, but how to deal with him? That was the question. The butler put a hand to his forehead to conceal his despair. The young man was a disgrace to his profession.

'But you didn't mean it, Albert, just as you do not mean it now. I cannot be seen to tolerate such behaviour.'

'I'm your own sister's son –'

'Don't you think that I know it?' said Mason, banging the desk with his fist. He had not meant to let his anger show, but really the boy would try the patience of a saint. 'Do you think that if you had been anyone else I'd have put up with such behaviour? As God is my witness, I have tried to do my best by you for my own poor sister's sake. But enough is enough, Albert. A life in service is not the life for you.'

'But I like it here,' said Albert. There was a stubborn look upon his face.

'I cannot think why. You do not understand the role of footman or discharge your duties efficiently. At every opportunity you challenge my authority and upset the other servants.' The butler bent forward and leaned over the desk towards him. 'And what have you done to Martha, I'd like to know? The poor girl has done nothing but sob bitterly for these past few days.'

'She's all right,' said Albert quickly.

'Is she? I don't think so and neither does Mrs Field. She rightly considers herself responsible for the girl's welfare and I can tell you she's very worried about Martha. The girl's in pieces, anyone can see that. If you've got her into trouble –'

'I haven't.'

'I'm glad to hear it. Now, Albert, I'm only thinking of what's best for you. You'll be paid up to the end of the month –'

'I said I like it here, Uncle. I'm not going anywhere.'

'Mr Mason. In this house I am referred to as Mr Mason and you know it.' The butler looked exasperated. Why did his nephew insist on being so difficult? 'Now look here, Albert. This really won't do. You know as well as I do that you are not cut out for this life.'

'I'm staying, Uncle.'

'No you are not. I am sorry, Albert, but your conduct is such that you have forced my hand.'

'There are things that I could tell if I wanted to,' said the footman, an unpleasant smirk distorting his handsome face.

'What things?' There was a note of apprehension in the butler's voice.

'Bad things. Things you wouldn't like me to tell. There's not much that goes on in this house that I don't know about.' The young man began to walk about the room, pausing to pick up and look at objects, before proceeding on his way. He stopped for a long time before the safe, staring at it and tracing the key hole with his finger.

'I wouldn't even need to say anything definite as such, Uncle. I could just hint at things, here and there as the mood takes me. Of course, I wouldn't want to get anyone into any trouble, but if my hand was forced, as you might say ...'

Chapter Nine

'I shall have to keep an eye out for that footman of yours,' said Lavinia, applying some rouge expertly to her cheeks. 'He sounds rather interesting. Dangerously handsome, did you say?'

'I did not,' said Rose, laying out a burnt gold-coloured dress, the satin material of which gave it the appearance of liquid metal. 'I said that he was rather good-looking, but a thoroughly ill-bred young man. He was objectionably rude at supper time and awfully unkind to the housemaid who unpacked your clothes, the one that you remarked upon as having been crying. I say, Lavinia, don't you think that this gown is a little too much?' Velda Cooper's condescending words about the slippers still rang in Rose's ears. 'You're dining in tonight and there will just be the two of you. No other guests.'

'More's the pity,' sighed Lavinia. 'I have to admit that I am finding Millie's company rather tedious. It's not her fault, poor girl, but she really isn't able to talk about anything of interest. That's when she opens her mouth at all, I should say. Most of the time she is silent as the grave and just sits there quietly agitated, wringing her hands, mopping her brow, that sort of thing.' Lavinia looked down at her splendid dress. 'And she has no eye for clothes at all.'

'Hardly any point in dressing up, then,' said Rose.

'You know me, I always like to make an impression. Now, be a dear and fasten my necklace for me before you go, will you?' Lavinia stared at her reflection in the mirror. 'It's not quite right, but I suppose it will have to do. I do wish I'd brought my diamonds with me. They offset the gold dress beautifully.'

'For goodness sake, Lavinia,' said Rose. 'Do let us get down to business. Remember why we are here. It is not for you to show off your wardrobe. I have to get back to the servants' hall in a minute, or I'll be missed. I have to sit there and pretend to sew or something equally mundane. Do think of me while you are enjoying your five course dinner, won't you?'

'Oh, I shall,' said Lavinia sweetly.

'Now, the conversation I was telling you about that I overheard between Albert and Martha was certainly suggestive, don't you think? And they were at pains to keep it secret.'

'I should say it was! From what you've said, the housemaid as good as accused the footman of taking Millicent's necklace.'

'Well, she didn't actually mention the necklace by name, but I can't think what else they could have been talking about. It couldn't have been the snuff box because that had been taken some time ago and put back. Anyway, Albert denied taking whatever it was and got frightfully upset when Martha refused to believe him.' Rose began to pace the room. 'He also denied stealing both the snuff box and the necklace when Cooper accused him outright of doing so in the servants' hall.'

'Well, he would say that, wouldn't he? It's not the sort of thing he'd admit to unless he wanted to get into trouble. It just means he's a liar,' said Lavinia dismissively. 'And from what little you've told me about his character, it's hardly surprising if he is. If he hadn't been old Mason's nephew, I daresay he'd have been out on his ear before now.'

'Yes, I think that's safe to assume. Under normal circumstances, if there was any suspicion that a servant was a thief, he would not still be employed. Now, what I found particularly interesting was that all the other servants appeared to be of the same view as Cooper. That Albert was definitely the thief. That he had taken the necklace, I mean. And yet if it had been proved beyond all doubt, being the butler's nephew wouldn't have counted for much. Don't you think it strange that nothing has been done about it? Albert has not been made to put the necklace back as he was with the snuff box.'

'You think someone made him put the snuff box back?'

'Yes, I think his uncle did. I say, I feel a little sorry for poor old Mason. I think he's torn between wanting to maintain the highest of standards and wanting to do the right thing by his sister's son. You should have seen him in the servants' hall. He tried to pretend that no theft had occurred.' Rose sighed. 'I suppose he does not want to be seen as being unduly lenient towards his nephew.'

'Well, he has been,' said Lavinia. 'It may well be that we won't be able to locate the necklace, but at least we will be able to tell Milly whom the thief is.'

'We don't have any proof yet,' warned Rose. 'We've just been speculating. Oh, I almost forgot to tell you –'

'What?' demanded Lavinia, her hand paused in the act of patting a curl.

'One of the servants is Edna.'

'Edna?'

'Yes. She used to be a scullery maid at Ashgrove House.'

'Oh.' Lavinia spoke the one word with a forced indifference. Only her hands gave her away. She drummed her fingers on the dressing table top, a tuneless, unmelodic sound. 'Oh, I see.'

Rose was not surprised by her reaction. Inwardly she cursed herself for having been so thoughtless and insensitive. Mention of Ashgrove House brought back sad memories, ones that her friend would doubtless prefer to forget. She remembered the pain and anguish and Lavinia's subsequent flight to the Continent, leaving her brother to deal with the aftermath as best he could.

'Did she recognise you?' asked Lavinia. A vein throbbed in her neck, betraying the tremendous effort she was making to regain her equanimity.

'Yes,' said Rose quickly, keen to distance herself from the mention of Ashgrove. 'She wasn't certain at first. My disguise confused her, you see. I think it was the spectacles. She almost gave me away. She didn't mean to. I managed to stop her before she did, and she promised not to say anything to the other servants.'

'Do you think she will keep to her word?'

'Yes, I do. Just as I was coming up to see you, she stopped me and said she would be bringing me my cup of tea in the morning. It will be an opportunity to talk to her privately and explain why I am here and in disguise.'

'And you really think she can be trusted?'

'Yes,' said Rose. She might have added that Edna had helped her with the business at Ashgrove, but thought better of it. Instead she said: 'She'll be able to help answer a few questions that I have. Her presence in this house might well prove very useful. She'll be able to tell us about the household's routine. We should be able to establish from that who had an opportunity to steal the necklace.'

'I can tell you that,' said Lavinia. 'I've been thinking about that since we last talked about it.' She had returned her attention to repairing her face. 'The housemaids, the housekeeper and the lady's maid. The weather has been so fine that I doubt whether the scullery maid's been bringing up coal and laying fires in the bedrooms. Not in the morning at least.'

'What about the footman?' asked Rose. 'Albert's the footman. Would he have had any occasion to come upstairs in the morning and go into Mrs Grayson-Smith's bedroom?'

'No, I don't think so. His presence at this end of the corridor at that time of day would certainly have been commented on. I suppose it's possible he might have arranged a clandestine meeting with Martha while she made the bed or changed the bedding. You got the impression they were sweethearts, didn't you?'

'But if the housekeeper caught him, there would be hell to pay,' said Rose. 'I'm sure she'd have sent him away with a flea in his ear, I can tell you, Mason, or no Mason, which means that –'

'Something like that happened to poor Eliza once, though it wasn't her fault,' giggled Lavinia. 'Not at Sedgwick, I hasten to add. It was at another house when she was a young housemaid. There was a new footman, you see. He'd never been in service before and he found working in a grand house rather daunting. It was his first day and he got terribly lost. He went into the daughter of the house's bedroom instead of the mistress' sitting room. Eliza was in there plumping up the pillows and it gave her an awful fright. She screamed and the housekeeper came running. The poor footman got a clip round his ear by the butler and –'

'But don't you see what this means?' interrupted Rose. 'It's highly unlikely that Albert's the thief. He may well have stolen the snuff box but I can't see how he could possibly have stolen the necklace.'

'Miss Cooper, I'm surprised at you. Making a scene at supper like that. Quite disgraceful. And in front of a visiting servant, too.'

Mrs Field bristled with indignation. While the lady's maid was not directly answerable to her, she considered it her place to berate the woman for her unseemly conduct. To this end, she had been waiting for a suitable opportunity to give the woman a piece of her mind ever since the servants' supper had been cleared away. The chance had presented itself soon enough when the lady's maid returned from dressing Millicent Grayson-Smith for dinner. Fortuitously, the servants' hall happened to be empty at that moment. The butler and the footman were busy in the dining room, the kitchen staff were in the kitchen making final preparations for the dishes and Miss Denning was still with Lady Lavinia. Mrs Field could not have asked for more favourable conditions in which to unleash her anger. Even so, she took the precaution of persuading the lady's maid to accompany her to her sitting room on the pretext of indulging in a glass of sherry.

'Someone had to say it, Mrs Field.'

There was a touch of contempt in Velda Cooper's voice as she uttered the word "Mrs". It was only a courtesy title after all. Mrs Field was as much a spinster as she was herself. Not that the housekeeper didn't harbour secret thoughts of being married one day. Anyone could see that. They'd all seen the look in her eyes when she addressed old Mason, the way she fawned over him and tried to ingratiate herself with him. It was pitiful, that's what it was. Velda Cooper smiled her nasty little smile. She'd caught all the servants gossiping and sniggering about it at one time or another, even the scullery maid who hardly ever left the scullery. And pompous old Mason, who thought himself so very proper, had no idea of the fluttering that he caused in the housekeeper's withered breast. Quite blind to it all he was. At least that's the impression he gave. It was possible that he was more astute than she supposed. Either way, he wouldn't want to encourage the old bat. It was clear to even the errand boy who delivered the groceries once a week that the butler had not a morsel of interest in her …

'No they did not.' Mrs Field could feel her cheeks burning a deep crimson shade. The lady's maid's thoughts were so transparent. They appeared on her face in that awful sneering grin of hers as clearly as if she had written them in pen and ink on her forehead. 'And if you wanted to speak as you did, why you couldn't have waited until this evening when you might have spoken to Mr Mason and me in private, I don't know.'

'I was not going to just sit there and let Albert talk to us in that manner. It was disrespectful saying what he said, calling the cook a thief and saying how you could not do your sums.' Miss Cooper smiled. She had seen the housekeeper wince at mention of her deficiency with figures. 'It's a cheek, it is, when we know as eggs are eggs as how he's the thief. Why Mr Mason lets him get away with it, I don't know. He may be his kin, but even so.'

She paused and looked around the room. Her position was an odd one, she always thought. She straddled both worlds. Her existence was lived out in the gloomy servants' quarters, but she also had sight and experience of her employers' bright and splendid world. It was true she was more an observer of the latter world than an inhabitant. She watched her mistress enjoying it rather than being permitted to partake of its advantages herself. But she could take in the wonderful furnishings, the very opulence of it all. How poorly this little sitting room compared with the lavish comfort of her mistress' equivalent room. It grated on her the disparity of it all. It made her grit her teeth. When she looked about her as she did now, the general impression was of a room having fallen on poor times. There was a genteel shabbiness to it, with passed down furniture, which in its heyday had graced the drawing room, but was now worn and faded, a bit like their lives, she thought. They were supposed to feel grateful, being given things their betters no longer wanted or required.

'You know as well as I do that if anyone else had spoken like that, Mr Mason would have been down on them like a ton of bricks, so he would,' the lady's maid said with bitterness in her voice, reflecting her recent thoughts.

She usually took a delight in talking disparagingly of the butler's conduct in front of the housekeeper. She liked to see the little woman bristle, her expression pained at having the object of her adoration mocked. Today, however, it did not seem enough. It could not make her feel any better about her situation or her station in life. Whatever she said could not transform Mrs Field's sitting room to a grandeur it had never known; it would always look like a servant's room.

'That's as may be,' said the housekeeper, regaining her composure a little. 'But it wasn't your place to do it, Miss Cooper, in front of all the servants and all. Disrespectful, that's what I call it. And what Miss Denning would have thought, I don't know. I don't doubt she went running off to her mistress to tell her what sort of a house we run here. We can only hope that Lady Lavinia doesn't say anything to madam.'

'I can't see how it matters what Miss Denning thought. It's not as if she's a proper lady's maid.'

'Oh?'

'It's her cousin whose lady's maid to Lady Lavinia. Gone and got herself ill, she has. Miss Denning's filling in for her, as you might say.

Told me herself she did, when we were doing some ironing.' Miss Cooper sighed. 'It doesn't seem right, does it, me having to move down a seat at the table to accommodate her. We don't know what she is. She could be a scullery maid for all we know. She doesn't know a thing about ironing, I can tell you that.'

'Doesn't she?' The housekeeper looked preoccupied. 'I do hope she's not here to cause trouble. We have enough of that with young Albert. We don't need no more.'

'She seems a timid girl to me, Mrs Field. Easy enough to keep in her place. Wants to do right while she's here. I just wish we could say the same about Albert. That's a young man who will come to a sticky end, you mark my words if he doesn't.'

Chapter Ten

When Rose awoke the next morning she forgot for a moment where she was. The miserable and barren little attic room, with its lack of furniture and dull walls, seemed foreign to her and brought no recollections of the day before. In those few moments of bewilderment, she lay tense and rigid in her bed, the bedclothes pulled up to her chin. It was only when she set eyes on Edna walking timidly towards her, carrying a cup of tea, that she remembered she was at Crossing Manor. She realised that she must have been awakened by the sound of Edna knocking quietly on her door. The reason for her visit to the house returned to her so forcefully that she sat up, alert and fully conscious.

'Oh lor, I spilt a bit,' cried the kitchen maid. 'I'm ever so sorry about that, miss. Those stairs are treacherous, so they are, when you're carrying something you don't want to drop or spill. The tea's still steaming, I'll say that for it. It's come straight from the teapot.'

'Thank you, Edna,' said Rose, taking the proffered cup and saucer and taking a sip of tea. 'I say, this tea's very good. I think it's the best cup I've had in a long while.'

'I made it myself,' said Edna, with something akin to pride. 'Pearl, she's the scullery maid here, takes Cook her cup of tea in the morning. Likes it so strong, she does, it looks like treacle. You could stand a spoon up in it, as my father would say.'

'Well, this tea's just right,' said Rose, taking another sip. 'Neither too weak nor too strong. It's just the way I like it.'

She looked up at the maid who was hovering awkwardly beside her bed, her hands clutched behind her as if she did not know quite what to do with them now that she had dispensed with the tea. Under Rose's scrutiny, the girl began to fidget, shifting her weight from one foot to the other in a childish fashion.

'Won't you close the door and pull up a seat?' Rose indicated the solitary chair in the room. 'It's very good to see you again, Edna. You do look well. I'm sure you've grown a bit since I last saw you. How old are you now?'

'Sixteen, miss, though I know I don't look it. Mother says as how I've filled out a bit since I came here.' Edna had initially perched herself gingerly on the edge of the chair. Now she leaned forward with enthusiasm. 'I wasn't sure it was you, Miss Simpson, not at first. Not with you dressed so strange. I think it was the spectacles. They made you look different. And your hair of course.'

'Yet despite my elaborate disguise you recognised me,' said Rose smiling.

'I'd have recognised you anywhere, miss,' said Edna, with feeling.

Unbeknown to Rose, she had made quite an impression on the maid at Ashgrove. Ever so kind, Edna had thought her, when Rose had found her crying her eyes out in the kitchen garden. Edna remembered her surprise when Bessie, the kitchen maid there, had told her that Rose worked in a dress shop. 'But she's got ever such nice manners and she talks quite posh, you'd never know.' That's what she had said at the time, and she blushed at the recollection. 'I don't care that she's just a shop girl. I think she's a real lady.' The words came floating back to her as if she had uttered them only yesterday. It was, however, with a certain degree of smugness that she recalled now that she had been quite right. Despite Rose's humble origins, Edna had predicted a marriage between Rose and Cedric. Perhaps one day Miss Simpson would be a countess; that's what she had told her friend.

Rose saw the admiration now in the younger girl's eyes and smiled. She remembered how Edna had confided in her with regard to her own career aspirations and had sought her advice concerning information that she had overhead which she thought might have some relevance to the murder investigation, in which they were embroiled. She had been correct on that score. She had also been able to provide Rose with some additional vital details that had helped her solve the case.

'Are you still hoping to be a cook one day, Edna? I suppose that's why you changed jobs and came to work here. How do you find Crossing Manor?'

'It's all right,' said Edna, making a face. 'Mr Mason is a bit like Mr Stafford, though, he's ever so strict, which Cook says is no bad thing knowing what girls can be like these days. But he's kind. His heart's in the right place as my mother would say. And it's nice not having to scrub the vegetables or clean the pans no more now that I'm a kitchen maid. I cook all the servants' meals myself and help Cook with the sauces for the family's meals.'

'For Mr and Mrs Grayson-Smith? Well, it sounds to me that you are well on the path to becoming a cook.'

'That's what my mother says. She says I've done well for myself and shouldn't complain, but –'

'But you'd rather be doing something else?'

'That's just it, Miss Rose, I would,' said Edna excitedly. 'It's not that I mind a life in service, because I don't. But being kitchen staff is quite lonely. It is here, anyway. We're always the first up in the morning and we never get to eat with the other servants. We see the same four walls every day. The kitchen windows are that high up that we never get to see what the weather's really like. And that's not all.' She paused a moment to catch her breath and muster her indignation. 'Cook works her fingers to the bone preparing the dishes, and I do my bit standing over a hot stove making the sauces, and we never really know if the family enjoys our food.' She smiled. 'To give him his due, Mr Mason does report back the odd favourable comment, but I never know whether to believe him or not. He's kind, he is. Sometimes I think he only says what he does because he knows how much it means to Cook and me.'

'Isn't there anyone else you could ask?'

'Only Albert,' said Edna, with obvious distaste, 'and I wouldn't ask him. You can't believe a word that comes out of his mouth. He's the sort of fellow who takes a delight in upsetting people. He once told Cook that her soup was so foul tasting that the master had been forced to spit it out. Had her in tears, he did. And it was a lie and all, of course. Mr Mason was ever so cross with him, called him wicked, so he did.'

'Well, from what little I've seen of Albert, I tend to agree with the butler. He seems a thoroughly unpleasant young man,' said Rose with feeling. 'I'm rather surprised that he's employed here.'

'That's only because he's Mr Mason's nephew. His younger sister's son, Albert is. Mr Mason's devoted to his sister, so he is. Poor woman's had a hard life. Not very strong and she was widowed ever so young and left with four mouths to feed. Albert's the eldest. Mr Mason felt sorry for her and so he gave Albert a job. I bet he regrets it now. All Albert does is cause him misery and embarrassment.'

'And the servants think he's a thief, don't they?'

'Oh, you mean the snuff box? Well, yes they do. We all do. He was in trouble with the law, you see. Before Mr Mason gave him a job, I mean. Poaching, I think it was. It might even have been taking the church collection. But that's the same as stealing, isn't it? Poaching I mean?'

'Taking the church collection certainly is,' said Rose, who secretly had some sympathy with families forced to poach during the current hard times. 'Look here, Edna. You haven't asked me why I'm here pretending to be a servant. Surely you were surprised?'

'Well, I was and I wasn't, miss. Once I knew it was you, it occurred to me you were investigating the theft of madam's necklace. You've been involved in ever so many murder cases if the newspapers are to be believed, and I know you have a knack for it, solving crimes, I mean. They don't say as much in the papers, but you solved the case at Ashgrove, didn't you?'

'Well, I have helped the police in a number of murder investigations,' admitted Rose. 'Though trying to solve a theft is a bit different.' She leaned forward and clasped the girl's hand. 'Listen, Edna. Nobody knows I'm here apart from you and Lady Lavinia. You mustn't say anything to anyone. Not even Mrs Grayson-Smith knows. She thinks I'm coming to stay in a few days' time.'

'But you thought you would come as a lady's maid because you'd get more information from the servants?' Edna lowered her voice until it was scarcely above a whisper. 'You think it's a servant who done it, took the necklace, I mean?'

'Yes. It all sounds rather ludicrous doesn't it, me coming in disguise? I can't tell you how ridiculous I feel wearing those silly spectacles all day.'

'I think it's an awfully good idea.' Edna, her face bright and shining, clapped her hands together in glee. 'And it's the most exciting thing that's happened to me since I've been here.'

Rose made her way from the basement up the bare servants' stairs, which were uneven from both age and neglect. The state of the staircase or the fact that their condition might prove hazardous to any servant struggling with a heavy load did not, however, at that moment occupy her mind. Her thoughts were focused on other matters. Rose reasoned that whoever had stolen Millicent Grayson-Smith's necklace had been faced with the problem of how to get the jewellery out of the room unobserved.

Initially, she had assumed that the thief had hidden the diamonds on their person. However, following a brief scrutiny of the servants' uniforms and being in possession of a more detailed description of the missing necklace, courtesy of Lavinia's own investigations, it became apparent that such a scenario was unlikely.

The housemaids' aprons had boasted no convenient pockets in which items might be hidden and the black dresses of the lady's maid and housekeeper, with their high necks and tight cuffs, had likewise provided no scope for jewellery to be concealed within their folds. Furthermore, the necklace had not consisted of a delicate gold chain with a diamond cluster pendant, as Rose had first thought. It had been something altogether more exquisite and valuable, comprising instead of one hundred graduated sections, half of which were mine-cut diamonds. These in turn had swung freely from fifty moulded gold leaves like sparkling glass flowers. The overall effect was not dissimilar to that of a heavy diamond and gold collar.

A thorough search had been undertaken of Millicent Grayson-Smith's bedroom as soon as it had been realised the necklace was missing. It had not been found, yet reason dictated that the necklace must surely have been hidden somewhere in that room, but so cleverly as not to have been uncovered in the search. Rose racked her brains as she tried to identify a possible place that might have been overlooked by the searchers. She soon realised it was useless to attempt such a feat without first setting eyes on the room itself. With renewed vigour, she set out to accomplish this without further ado. Of course it was too much to hope that the necklace was still there in its original hiding place. The thief would, in all probability, have removed it to a place of safety as soon as the opportunity arose. However, if she could only ascertain where it had been concealed, the place itself might offer up a clue.

Rose opened the door to the landing and, as always, was struck by the stark contrast of the family's domain in comparison with that of the servants'. There were no bare stairs and passages here, no floors broken into different levels by the occasional, oddly positioned step. Everything was smooth and graceful and, above else, exquisitely adorned. It was hard to reconcile the two very different parts of the house reserved exclusively for the use of their particular occupants. For a moment, it occurred to her that the opulence and richness of the family's rooms was ostentatious and almost obscene.

It was in this frame of mind that she made her way to Millicent Grayson-Smith's room, safe in the knowledge that the mistress of the house and her solitary guest had embarked on a walk to the village. By Rose's reckoning, the housemaids had now finished tidying the bedrooms and been set more mundane and laborious tasks downstairs. The lady's maid's whereabouts was unknown, though Rose had a sneaking suspicion that she had retired to her room. Mrs Field, she had seen with her own eyes, was currently engrossed in a heated discussion with the cook concerning the provision of supplies. There was no reason for any other servant to be in this part of the house and so it was with little caution that Rose opened the door to the bedroom of the mistress of the house.

A second or two later she wished that she had been more reticent in her actions, had paused for a moment or two to listen for sounds within the room before she opened the door. For the room was occupied by a lady of obvious consequence. The woman in question, her dark hair elaborately styled, her face expertly made up, was dressed in an evening gown of royal blue silk satin, cut on the bias with a slight cowl neckline and sleeveless except for ruffled panels of silk satin, which descended from the shoulders in an uneven fashion, giving almost a feathery effect. The woman's attention had been given exclusively to staring at her reflection in a full-length looking glass. So preoccupied was she in this pursuit that she was for a moment unaware that she was being observed. This provided Rose with an opportunity to study the woman more closely. Of one thing she was certain. It was not Millicent Grayson-Smith that stood before her. If she believed in ghosts, she might have thought the woman to be the first Mrs Grayson-Smith, so closely did her appearance match Lavinia's description of the great portrait that hung downstairs in the drawing room.

The noise of the door opening, accompanied as it was by the sound of Rose's sharply drawn intake of breath appeared to have struck the woman belatedly. Or perhaps she had become aware of Rose's eyes focused on her, staring at her quite mesmerised. Whatever it was, it had the effect of making the woman abandon her perusal of the looking glass. In one sudden, frightened movement she turned to confront the newcomer. With a jolt of surprise, Rose discovered that the woman's identity was known to her. For she found herself looking into the face of Velda Cooper.

Nothing was going right, thought Millicent. Worse than that, it was all going wrong. A dark miasma hung about her like a shroud, suffocating her so that she found it an effort even to breathe. It was not just the loss of the diamond necklace. She had now become resigned to never seeing it again. It was not even the thought of breaking the news to Edwin so that he might acknowledge her own carelessness and unpopularity with his servants. There had been a time when to see disappointment in his eyes had been the thing that she dreaded most. Now it seemed no more than the inevitable conclusion to an unwise marriage.

She stole a glance at her companion. Lady Lavinia Sedgwick was looking decidedly bored. She had given up all pretence of finding her hostess' company amusing and it was this situation above all else that Millicent was finding an unbearable strain. It had been a mistake to invite her to Crossing Manor, and then she remembered that of course, she hadn't. Her invitation had been intended for Rose Simpson, whose background was not so very different from her own. It had been at her guest's insistence that she come in advance of her friend's arrival and now it seemed that Miss Simpson would not come. What other explanation could there be for why Lavinia was being so elusive as to the date of her arrival?

Millicent could not bear another night of being alone with Lavinia, surreptitiously stealing glances at the clock on the mantelpiece, trying to rack her brain for something interesting to say. She had long exhausted what little conversation they had. If only she did not care what her guest thought of her. Now all she could do was smile and pretend to be gay when all the time she nursed an inner dread of failure. The situation was too frightful to contemplate and so she had surrendered. Tonight their numbers would be swelled. They would be joined at dinner by the vicar and his wife, despite the unfortunate association of them in her mind with her poor necklace. Millicent was not fool enough, or sufficiently deluded, to pretend that Lavinia would find their company amusing. But Mrs Kitchen could be relied upon to keep the discourse flowing with little, if any, contribution from her listeners. The old woman was quite happy to monopolise the conversation if circumstances so demanded.

Having exhausted all that the village of Crossing had to offer, the two women set off back towards Crossing Manor. If it had been up to Millicent, that is to say, if she had undertaken the journey alone, she would certainly have dawdled, keen to prolong her return. Lavinia, she noticed, had other ideas and was walking earnestly, with a spring in her step.

All too quickly for Millicent, the strange half-timbered, red-brick building that was her home came into view and they were walking down the drive. Before they had a chance to pause for a moment on the great pillared porch, the front door was opened to them by the ever attentive butler and they were ushered inside like two wayward children. Their coats were taken from them in a similar fashion by the footman. How Millicent wished she had Lavinia's spirit and confidence and could hand them her hat and gloves with complete indifference. Why must she, Millicent, catch their eye and wonder what they were thinking of her.

It was easy enough to read the thoughts of the tall, dark footman they called Albert. He always stared at her with such an insolent look upon his face. His eyes seemed to penetrate her soul so that she was forced to look away lest he read her thoughts. She shivered. She knew his type. He was dangerously good-looking. That was to say, he knew himself to be handsome and would use it for his own ends. She did not doubt that he left a trail of hearts broken and stamped on in his wake. He caught her eye and involuntarily she blushed. She was rewarded with a sneering grin that made her cringe inwardly.

In that moment, she felt the danger in the house as if it were a real, tangible thing. Afterwards, she wondered if she had had some sort of premonition that something awful was about to happen. Had she but known, it was about to put the loss of the necklace totally in the shade.

Chapter Eleven

Rose went quickly into Millicent Grayson-Smith's bedroom and shut the door behind her. She turned and faced the lady's maid, whose expression was a mixture of emotions, foremost of which appeared to be outrage. Gone was the façade of elegance and breeding. Instead a strange combination of feelings fought to show themselves on the woman's face. The effect was to dull and distort her natural beauty. The layers of refinement had been peeled away, and Rose found standing before her an anxious, angry servant, full of bluster, in fear of losing her job.

'What do you want? Why didn't you knock?'

Velda Cooper almost spat the words out. She was trembling and a vein throbbed in her neck. Now that the lady's maid had turned to face her, Rose saw that the woman was holding in one hand, rather awkwardly, the corner of a cape of silver fox fur, which she had no doubt intended to drape over her shoulders to complete the ensemble. Now, however, she threw it aside in one swift movement to land on her mistress' bed and stared at it with something akin to distaste. It was almost as if the fur had burnt her fingers. The next moment, she had gathered it in her arms and was stuffing it haphazardly back in the wardrobe. It occurred to Rose that it was an expensive fur and really warranted better treatment. She said nothing, but puzzled over the maid's sudden aversion to the cape.

Rose was roused from her musings by the slamming shut of the wardrobe door. This was followed by Velda Cooper leaning back against it, as if she feared it would fly open of its own accord.

'I didn't think there would be anyone here,' Rose said quietly. 'Lady Lavinia was curious to know whether this room was decorated in the same gold tones as her own. I promised her I'd take a look.'

'I see.' The lady's maid took a deep breath. She appeared to relax a little, but still did not release her grip on the wardrobe door. 'Well, you've had your look. You can go now.'

'Do you always dress up in your mistress' gowns when she's not here?' asked Rose. She paused a moment before continuing to allow the words to linger in the air. 'Doesn't she mind? Lady Lavinia would mind awfully. She'd have a fit if I tried on one of her dresses.'

'I suppose you're off to tell Mr Mason?' There was a note of bitterness in the woman's voice. 'You'd like to see me lose my job, I don't doubt.' Despite being frightened, a defiant look had crept upon her face.

'No.'

It was as if a spring had suddenly snapped. As Rose looked on, the woman half slumped against the wardrobe door. It looked now as if she were leaning against it for support. There was something rather pitiful about Velda Cooper. The fine gown, which now drooped and creased, looked strangely at odds with the pale, anxious face of the wearer.

'You don't know what it's like dressing someone like madam. You're not a real lady's maid. You wouldn't understand.' A pained expression showed itself on the woman's face. 'I trained, I did. Hairdressing and sewing. I scrimped and saved and paid to put myself through courses and have lessons. Good at them too, I was. Thought it would put me in good stead for a proper position. I fancied I would travel and see something of the world.'

'You still might.'

'Not with Mrs Grayson-Smith, I won't.' Velda Cooper made a face. 'She's a poor specimen to dress. No eye or interest in fashion and travel; she hardly leaves this house. I thought she'd be like Mr Grayson-Smith's first wife. She was a one for having her picture in the society pages. A proper socialite she was and a real beauty. Elegant too. She liked her clothes, you could just tell. A bit like your Lady Lavinia. Madam's not a bit like that. If I'd known I'd never have taken this job. Never.'

'Why don't you get another position if you're not happy here?'

'It's not as easy as all that.' The woman turned away slightly and caught sight of her reflection in the mirror. She looked down at the gown and played idly with the fabric, running it between her fingers.

'Tell me, Miss Denning, what did you think when you first opened the door? You didn't recognise me, did you?'

'Not at first,' admitted Rose.

'I looked like a proper lady, didn't I? One that would have her own house and servants to wait on her. All it took was the right clothes. And I'd make a much better go of it than madam. She's no better than the rest of us. Worked in a shop, that's what we reckon downstairs. If Mr Grayson-Smith had chanced to meet me on his holiday, happen I'd be the second Mrs Grayson-Smith now.'

'But he didn't,' said Rose quietly.

'No, more's the pity. And there aren't that many gentlemen with his means and so heartbroken about the death of his wife as to marry the first woman who shows him a bit of sympathy.' She sighed. 'If only I could set myself up in some lodgings. With clothes like this, I could pass for a distressed gentlewoman, a widow perhaps. I'd secure a wealthy husband, I can tell you. Just see if I couldn't.'

'You caught her doing what?' exclaimed Lavinia, later that day. 'Oh, how frightful! It's always been a fear of mine that a servant would try on my clothes while I was out visiting. It's one of the reasons I chose Eliza to be my lady's maid. I knew she wouldn't be able to fit into any of my dresses without bursting a seam.' She giggled. 'Are you going to tell Mason?'

'I promised her I wouldn't. And I can't say I wholly blame her. It must be an awful temptation. But you do see what this means, don't you?'

'That she doesn't like or respect Millicent?' Lavinia yawned in an uninterested fashion. 'We knew that already, didn't we? Millicent told us as much herself.'

'It means that Cooper had a very good motive for stealing the necklace. Don't you see? She would like to secure a wealthy husband and believes all she requires to do so is a little money. With the proceeds from the necklace, she could set herself up in a modest house and employ a servant. Why, I wouldn't put it past her to take some of Millicent's gowns with her.'

'How dreadful. Do you think I should warn Millicent?'

'No. It's only a theory,' said Rose, slumping down on to her friend's bed. She took off her spectacles, gave them a look of disdain, and flung them across the eiderdown. 'I need to see Mrs Grayson-Smith's bedroom in daylight. Do you think you could think up an excuse for me to go there? I don't fancy running into Cooper again. I think she may already be a little suspicious of me.'

'Oh, I'm sure I can think of something.'

'I say, it feels awfully strange just sitting here with nothing to do.'

'Is that what you are doing? Sitting, I mean. I would have said you were lying down. Definitely lounging.'

'What I meant,' continued Rose, ignoring her, 'is that if I were on the other side of the green baize door now, I would be running about with no time to call my own. I really don't think you have any idea, Lavinia, of what it's like to be a servant. I wish I could take you with me to the servants' hall so you could see for yourself.'

'Perish the thought,' exclaimed Lavinia, looking horrified. 'Now, do you think you could press that chiffon dress for me? I want to wear it tonight. You will be careful with it, won't you? The fabric's very delicate.'

'If you are that worried,' said Rose, scooping up the dress in her arms, 'I suggest you do it yourself. I can show you to the ironing room if you like.'

Millicent gave a furtive glance at Lavinia's lady's maid. The girl seemed all right, agreeable even. Certainly her face was pleasant enough and the eyes behind the spectacles looked kind, if half hidden. Really, the girl was not at all what she had been expecting. She realised now that she had been half afraid that she would resemble Cooper, only worse. But this maid had nothing of her arrogance. She seemed an ordinary sort of a girl. Millicent certainly did not feel judged or intimidated by her, as she had thought she would.

'It's awfully kind of Lady Lavinia.' Millicent paused to pick up and fiddle with the hairbrush on her dressing table, running her fingers over the bristles. 'Oh dear, I'm sure you must be awfully busy. It's a frightful imposition, I ...' Her words faltered into nothing.

'Not at all, ma'am,' said Rose Simpson, gently but firmly, removing the hairbrush from Millicent's grasp.

Secretly, Rose wondered what Lavinia could have been thinking of, suggesting that she do this woman's hair. Her hairdressing skills were minimal at best and Lavinia, an expert in the field herself, had seen fit to do her own hair while at Crossing Manor. For Lavinia to think that she could in some way replicate her own elaborate hairstyle ... Still, it gave her the chance to see Millicent Grayson-Smith's bedroom in the daylight. It also provided her with an occasion to see the woman in the flesh. For her first sight of the hostess on their arrival had been fleeting to say the least. Rose had been too preoccupied with locating the servants' entrance to give the woman more than a cursory glance. Now that she had the opportunity to study the mistress of the house more closely, she found that Lavinia's description of her was born out. The woman was nervous and self-effacing. She was not at ease in this house, even here, in her own room. Her friend had described the woman as insipid and certainly she was very pale. Her skin was almost translucent, but not in the luminous way that Lavinia's was. Instead it had a sickly pallor to it and there were dark smudges under her eyes. In build she looked insubstantial, as if the smallest gust of wind would blow her over.

Hurriedly, Rose brushed Millicent's thin, dry hair and arranged it in an approximation of Lavinia's hairstyle. She stole a glance around the room. She could see no obvious place that might possibly have been overlooked during the intensive search for the necklace.

'Thank you. Very nice. Yes, very nice indeed,' said Millicent, putting a hand to her hair when Rose had finished, a shy smile of gratitude upon her face.

It was a relief that the woman did not ask her to hold up a hand mirror so that she might see the back which, even to Rose's inexperienced eyes, looked far from neat. Fortunately, she seemed content just patting the back of her head with her fingers. Rose walked over to the window and looked out. The view was marvellous. The room overlooked a gravel terrace, decorated with great stone flowerpots, standing on plinths, leading down to neat, formal gardens, reached from the terrace by stone steps sunk into the lawn. There was, however, no convenient ivy or creeper growing up the side of the house, where a thief might lean out of the window and stow a piece of illicit jewellery.

Millicent gave a delicate little cough and Rose returned her attention to the room. Her eye was drawn immediately to the dress hanging on the wardrobe door. The woman appeared to follow her gaze, for she said immediately:

'Cooper put that dress out for me to wear tonight. She says it suits my colouring.'

Rose disagreed. There was nothing very wrong about the dress itself; it was beautifully made and of a fine material. But it was all wrong for Millicent. The colour was far too pale, too indifferent. If the woman were to wear that dress tonight, she would fade into the background, a shadowy, ghostlike figure, half hidden from her guests. Rose thought of the rich scarlet-coloured gown that Lavinia intended to wear that evening and shuddered. In that moment she remembered the evening dress of royal blue silk satin. She had not worked in a dress shop without knowing which shades and styles suited a woman's figure and colouring. The rich blue, the bias cut, the slight cowl neckline and ruffled panels of silk satin would do more for Mrs Grayson-Smith than the gown hooked on the door of the wardrobe ever would.

'I think a stronger colour would suit you better, ma'am. If I may ...'

Before Millicent could say anything to the contrary, Rose had pulled open the wardrobe door and begun searching through the clothes until she came upon the blue dress. She held it up for the woman to inspect. Millicent looked flustered and a little taken aback. She opened her mouth as if to speak, but no words came out.

'I think you should wear this dress tonight,' said Rose firmly.

'Oh, do you think so?' Millicent said at last. 'Of course, it is a lovely dress. But Cooper did look out that other dress for me. Oh dear, I think she might be a little offended if I –'

'Perhaps if you could say Lady Lavinia picked this dress out for you to wear?'

'Well, I –'

It seemed to Millicent that before she had a chance to protest, Lavinia's lady's maid had somehow managed to leave the room and return with her mistress by her side.

'Oh yes, Denning is quite right. This dress will suit you much better than the other one,' exclaimed Lavinia. 'That shade of blue will bring out the colour of your eyes beautifully. And perhaps a little rouge to give a faint blush to your cheeks?' She clapped her hands together in an excited fashion. 'I say, do try the dress on now. I'm dying to see what you look like in it. I'll make up your face as well, shall I? Oh, no!' Lavinia had just caught sight of the back of Millicent's head. 'Denning, this really will not do. You haven't done that at all well. Here, let me do your hair again for you, Millicent.' She caught Rose's eye. 'Denning, you really must practise more.'

Rose made a face at Lavinia, which fortunately Millicent did not see, the woman in question being preoccupied at that moment with changing into the blue gown.

'There, that's better,' said Lavinia, a little while later after she had finished her ministrations.

Millicent permitted herself to be steered towards the full-length looking glass. She heard a sharp intake of breath and realised that it was her own. For a moment, she could hardly believe that she was looking at her own reflection. For the woman who stared back at her was someone she did not recognise. Her hair had been brushed and teased into the most becoming of styles. The vivid blueness of her gown seemed to complement, rather than accentuate, the paleness of her skin. And perhaps most surprising of all, her eyes shone and her face looked animated.

Later, when the house was filled with policemen and there was death in the air, she was to remember those precious moments, standing there before the mirror, flanked by Lavinia on one side and the girl she took to be her lady's maid on the other, seeing in the glass the woman she aspired to be.

Chapter Twelve

In the early hours of the following morning, Pearl Jones crept across the floor of the tiny attic room she shared with Edna. Barely fifteen years of age, she was employed at Crossing Manor as scullery maid.

Before continuing her journey, she paused for a moment in the doorway to make sure that the kitchen maid was sleeping soundly. It was still dark outside and she found it difficult to make out the form in the other bed. At best, it was a dark mass, an inert mound of bedclothes. However, when she listened carefully, she could just distinguish the faint noise of breathing, which sounded quiet and regular to her keen ear. Reassured, she quietly let herself out of the bedroom, softly pulling the door to behind her.

Pearl made her way gingerly down the corridor, careful not to tread on that one, treacherous, squeaky floorboard, trailing her hand along one wall as she felt her way in the dark. Eventually she found what she was seeking, the old oak door which enclosed the servants' staircase. As she descended the stairs, she did not find them to be as intimidating as the corridor. Even on the brightest and sunniest of days they were only ever half-lit, benefiting from no natural light. Negotiating her way down them now, when it was all but pitch black, was nothing new. Neither was the silence that engulfed her like a cloak. For she was always the first person to rise at Crossing Manor, entrusted as she was to light the stove before the rest of the house stirred.

It was true that Edna was often not far behind her, sometimes only a few minutes. This morning, however, she did not expect the company of her friend. For Pearl had decided to rise a full hour earlier than usual. It was a decision she had made last night when she had spotted Miss Cooper's *Mabs* magazine tucked into the seat of her chair, half hidden. If she had not been so very tired from cleaning and scrubbing the pans in the scullery until all hours, Pearl would have sat down there and then to read the magazine. Instead, she had resolved to snatch a few hours' sleep before tomorrow's long and tedious day stretched out before her.

Pearl really preferred *Women's Weekly* to *Mabs* magazine, but beggars could not be choosers, as her mother was inclined to say if Pearl saw fit to grumble. In particular, Pearl liked the simple and straightforward advice provided in that periodical by Mrs Marryat in response to readers' troubles. Really, it was astonishing the sorts of questions people asked, when anyone with anything about them could see the answer as clear as day … Still, *Mabs* was better than nothing, particularly for someone like herself who could not afford to buy a copy of her own. And Pearl was not a girl to waste an opportunity. Miss Cooper so seldom left her magazines in the servants' hall for the other servants to glance through. If she had not been called away unexpectedly to attend to her mistress, she would not have forgotten her *Mabs* magazine. There was no doubt about that in Pearl's mind. It would be lying now discarded somewhere in her room, probably only half read, not left tucked into her chair for all to read. Tight, that's what she was. Pearl had said as much to Edna as they huddled under their respective bedclothes in their tiny attic room. Mean and spiteful, that Miss Cooper. Thought she was so much better than everyone else, the way she looked at you as if you weren't there. And to say what she had said the evening before last at supper. It wasn't right. How poor Mr Mason didn't lose his temper, she'd never know.

With these thoughts uppermost in her mind, Pearl set off down the passage towards the servants' hall. She didn't like this bit. It was now that she almost lost her nerve. It didn't feel right for this passage, and the rooms that led off it, to be so quiet and deserted. She was used to them being populated with servants by day, going about their business, accompanied by the comforting sound of chatter and bustle. Craning her neck, she peered into the empty depths of each room as she passed, nervous glances as if she feared what she might see lurking in the shadows, under the tables, behind cupboards. She always felt the same when she went to light the stove, conscious that she was the only breathing person awake in the great, old house. She knew she was being a fool, but at such times she felt the history of the house bearing down upon her. Out of the corner of her eye she could almost fancy that she saw a flicker of the ghosts of servants who had gone before. She quickened her pace before her mind ran away with her. She had thought to read the magazine in the servants' hall, curled up in one of the chairs. But now she found that such a prospect had lost its appeal. However, she told herself, there was nothing to stop her from grabbing the magazine and taking it back up to her little attic room to read. She could light a candle and sit up in bed. She envisaged in her mind the welcome warmth of the bedclothes, the sound of Edna breathing peacefully in the next bed. Miss Cooper would be none the wiser for she could return the magazine when she came down to light the stove. No one would know …

Peering into the gloom of the servants' hall, she could just make out the great scrubbed table. She tiptoed inside. Now, could she recollect which chair Miss Cooper had been sitting in? The magazine had been stuffed hurriedly down one side of the seat, she knew that, which meant that it must have been one of the old armchairs … Yes, she remembered now. It was the chair upholstered in shabby red velvet. The material had faded to an unflattering shade of dusky pink long before it had been consigned to the servants' hall. A relic of the drawing room that had served its purpose and was no longer required upstairs.

All of a sudden she felt the hairs on the back of her neck stand on end. There was no reason for it that she could see. True, the room was eerily silent, but no more so than the passage or the other rooms she had passed along the way. There was something though, she felt sure of it. Something that was gnawing away at the edges of her consciousness. It was a feeling she had that everything was not as it should be, that things were definitely not quite right. As her heart thumped loudly in her chest, she felt an icy coldness steal upon her as realisation dawned. She was not alone. There was someone else in the room with her, residing in the dark. It must be someone ghostly, for she could not hear the sound of breathing.

Her eyes, now more accustomed to the dark, alighted on a figure crouched and huddled in one of the chairs drawn up to the hearth. She wondered why the person chose to sit in the dark. Perhaps, she thought, they had fallen asleep. Pearl fought the temptation to turn tail and flee. Her quest to purloin the magazine had been scuppered, but she could no more return to her room now than call out. Before she lost her nerve, she retreated to the door, but only so she could fumble for the Bakelite ceramic light switch. The room was immediately swathed in light, a brightness that hurt her eyes and for a moment hindered her vision. Pearl turned and faced the occupied chair. The figure was sitting facing away from her. She could see nothing but the back of its head. The only thing that registered in her consciousness was that the hair was very thick and black, good hair, her mother would have said. And something was smeared on it, something sticky that caught the light and glistened.

Transfixed, she moved forward. The figure appeared deaf to her presence, for it had not moved a muscle at her approach. A moment later and she knew instinctively that the person was dead. Almost without thinking, she stretched out her arm to touch the gummy substance. She withdrew her hand as quickly as if she had burnt her skin. Her fingers were stained with something. Looking down, she realised that it was blood.

Chapter Thirteen

Martha couldn't sleep. It was possible that she had dozed a little, but she did not think so. From the moment her head had touched the pillow until now, it seemed slumber had eluded her. Tossing and turning restlessly in her bed, she felt that she had not slept properly for days. Certainly, she knew from bitter experience that, when she got up, there would be a heaviness behind her eyes, which would ache and throb relentlessly. Of course, weeping didn't help matters. But what else could she do when she carried such a dark secret within her? She couldn't breathe a word about it to anyone but Albert, and he was no use at all. She stifled a sob, careful as always not to disturb the sleeping Agnes, snoring softly in the next bed, seemingly oblivious to all the cares in the world. How she envied her fellow housemaid.

Not for the first time, Martha wished heartily that she had never laid eyes on Albert Bettering. It was from that moment that everything had started to go wrong. She had loved him, probably still did if truth be told, but now there was something else. She hardly dared admit it, even to herself, but she was afraid of him. He had never hit her as such, not struck a blow, not yet. However, he had raised his voice to her and spoken sharply and she had heard the anger behind his words. Now, it was when he spoke to her softly that she was frightened of him most. There was no tenderness in his voice. When he spoke quietly, there was a coldness that ebbed out of him and chilled her to the bone. She did not think it would take much to make him snap and lash out. She cursed herself for her own foolishness in ever having anything to do with him. How easily he had been able to manipulate her to do his bidding. She had offered no resistance, at least not much. And now look at them. They had done a dreadful thing and, worst of all, Albert didn't seem to care. No, she corrected herself, *she* had done it, not Albert. Admittedly on Albert's instructions, but he was unlikely to admit that if asked. He would not hesitate to lie to protect himself. She knew that. He would let her take the blame and, in the eyes of the law, she alone would be guilty.

She knew things always appeared more awful than they really were in the early, indeterminate hours between night and day. It was easy to exaggerate the importance of things, to imagine the worst. Only of course she had no need to use her imagination. Matters would seem no better in the daylight than they did now. Martha allowed herself to sob quietly, finding solace in the bitter saltiness of her tears as they touched her lips. She could not continue like this, blinking and starting like a frightened rabbit. She knew she resembled a wretched shadow of her former self, close to falling apart at the least provocation. If that was not bad enough, everyone had noticed something was wrong, even Pearl who spent her days ensconced in the scullery, her arms up to the elbows in potato peel. And Martha had seen all too clearly the worried looks exchanged between the butler and the housekeeper. It was obvious what they feared. The housekeeper had asked her outright if anything was the matter and did not appear at all convinced when she had said there wasn't. She was not surprised. She had only to look in the mirror to see the physical effect of her worries upon her face. Her complexion was sallow, her cheeks pinched and sunken, and fine lines had etched themselves around her eyes, which were red and swollen from crying.

She took a deep breath. There was nothing for it but to speak to Albert tomorrow. Not for a moment did she think it would be pleasant. She would need to stand firm and not allow herself to be intimidated or swayed. She would insist on them having a proper conversation. Not a hurried talk, snatched between tasks, standing in the yard between the washing. A proper conversation where they could sit and talk and decide what to do. And if he refuses, or won't listen to reason, what then, said a little voice at the back of her mind. Martha sighed, a distressed, heartfelt little sigh, which almost had her in tears again. Then she'd tell him that she would tell Mr Mason everything. It might well cost her her position, and Albert's too, but anything was better than this. She had had enough.

Rose awoke with a start. She was unsure whether this was due to a knock on her bedroom door or the noise in the outside corridor which seemed, even in her half-conscious state, sufficient to wake the house. She fancied she had heard, a few moments before, the sound of running feet and loud whispers, which suggested that a number of people were about. This seemed odd in itself, stranger yet when she realised that it was still dark outside. But what was most alarming of all was the vision of Edna, now staggering into her room, still dressed in her nightgown, her hair tangled and uncombed, falling down unchecked on to her shoulders. She was holding no welcoming cup of hot tea. Instead, her hands were clenched and there was a bewildered look upon her face.

'Oh, Miss Rose, Miss Rose –'

'What is it, Edna? Whatever is the matter?' Rose enquired, hurriedly sitting up in bed.

'Oh, it's awful, it is. Awful.'

Edna's eyes were wide and Rose had an impression the girl was trembling. Instinctively she put out a hand to her. The girl's skin was icy cold. Rose immediately sprang up from her bed and motioned for the girl to sit down upon it.

'Here, get under the covers, Edna. You'll freeze to death.'

Edna did as she was bid and Rose proceeded to arrange the bedclothes around her.

'You look as if you've had an awful shock. What's wrong, Edna? What's happened?'

'There's been a death, miss.' Edna spoke in a dull voice, scarcely above a whisper, so that Rose was obliged to lean forward to catch her words. 'It's awful, it is. There's been a murder in the servants' hall.'

'A murder?' Rose felt her heart quicken. 'Did you say a murder?'

Edna nodded and Rose felt the colour drain from her own face. She sat down on the bed beside the girl and put an arm around her thin little shoulders. Edna was shivering now.

'Pearl found the body. Poor little thing. She's just turned fifteen, so she has. It's not right.' Edna pulled the bedcovers more tightly around her and stifled a sob. 'Mrs Field was ever so upset. Said how it should have been her that found the body, not Edna.'

'I expect she feels responsible for you both, what with her being housekeeper and you under her charge.'

'I suppose you're right. That's what Mr Mason said. Ever so kind he was. But I don't look at it like that. We answer to Cook, Pearl and me do.' Edna passed a thin hand over her eyes. Rose thought how tired the girl looked. 'He's telephoning the police now, Mr Mason is.'

'Good. Where is Pearl now?'

'Agnes is with her. I didn't like to leave her alone. But I had to see you, miss, it being a murder and all.' Edna sniffed. 'I still think Mrs Field was awful hard on her. Almost gave her a scolding, she did, as if she hadn't been through enough. Asked her what she was doing in the servants' hall, like she had no right to be there.'

'Oh?'

'Well, she don't normally go there. Her job's to go to the kitchen first thing and light the stove. She had no call to go to the servants' hall. And she went ever so early, so she did.' Edna bent forward and whispered: 'Miss Cooper, she'd left her magazine there and Pearl wanted to read it. She had it all planned. She was going to curl up in a chair and read it. But then she saw the body. Sat in one of the chairs, it was. Its head was all bashed in, covered in blood …' Edna covered her face with her hands and wept.

'Did you see the body, Edna?' Rose asked, prompting her gently. 'I expect she went and got you straight away, didn't she?'

Edna nodded. 'Yes, she did. She said she was so scared, she didn't even scream. She couldn't remember running up the stairs and coming to get me neither. You should have seen her, miss. She was in such a state. She could hardly get a word out. She wouldn't go back down again with me, though I begged her. It was awful. I didn't know what to do, whether to wake Mrs Field, I mean, or go down by myself. I'll admit I was that frightened, but a little part of me wondered whether it was real. I mean to say, I didn't want to make a fuss and wake the house over nothing. I thought as she might just have had a bad dream.'

'So you decided to go down alone?' The kitchen maid nodded. 'That was very brave of you, Edna.'

'Yes. Oh, miss, it was horrible. Ever so horrible. It was just like she'd said.'

'I'm sure it was. Now, Edna, you keep mentioning it being a body.'

'That's what it was, miss. A cold, lifeless thing. I couldn't think of it as being a person.'

Rose clasped the girl's hands in her own.

'Listen to me, Edna. I need to know whose body it was. Who's been murdered?'

Millicent Grayson-Smith was also awoken from her sleep at an unaccustomed hour. Instinctively, before she had opened her eyes or a word had been uttered, she knew that something was afoot. It had nothing to do with the earliness of the hour, more with the tread of the person who came to wake her. It was not the loud, impatient tread of Cooper, more a light, hesitant step, which she considered surprising. She opened one eye to discover that it belonged to the rotund little housekeeper.

'Mrs Field, what are you doing here? Where's Cooper?'

'Madam, I regret to inform you that Miss Cooper is currently indisposed.'

'What do you mean indisposed? Has she walked out?' Even as the words left her lips, Millicent felt a lightness of spirit. Of course it was too much to hope for. The woman probably just had a head cold or some minor ailment.

'I am afraid there has been … an accident, ma'am,' said the housekeeper quietly, hesitating slightly over her words.

'An accident? What sort of an accident? Has Cooper been hurt?'

'Yes, madam. I'm afraid … I'm afraid it's worse than that … she's dead.'

'Dead?' Millicent said stupidly, as if the word were foreign to her. She had sat up in bed and was rubbing her eyes. 'What do you mean … dead?'

Before Mrs Field had a chance to explain, the door to the room was flung open and Lavinia bound in like a gust of wind, dressed in a negligée thrown carelessly over her silk pyjamas.

'Oh, Millicent, you poor thing,' exclaimed Lavinia, running over to her and draping herself on the edge of the bed. She patted her hostess' hand in what she considered to be a comforting gesture.

'Lavinia, Cooper's dead,' Millicent said weakly.

'Yes, I know. Murdered. Dreadful, isn't it … Denning's just told me all about it.'

'If you don't mind my saying so, m'lady, she had no right to gossip. No right at all,' Mrs Field said rather stuffily. 'Mr Mason won't be best pleased. He doesn't want to upset the servants, the younger ones, that is. He is saying how Miss Cooper has had an accident.'

'Nonsense,' replied Lavinia, glaring at the housekeeper. 'My maid had every right to tell me. And if your Mr Mason thinks he can keep all this quiet, well, he had better think again.'

Mrs Field went a deep shade of crimson and looked at the floor. Perhaps the woman's distress touched a nerve, or Lavinia just wished to display her superior knowledge of how such an occasion should be dealt with, for when she spoke next, it was in a kinder tone.

'Believe me, Mrs Field, I know what I am talking about. One might say I have been rather unfortunate. I have, what one might call, some experience of murder.' Lavinia gave the woman what she intended to be a sad little smile. 'You see, I have been involved in two previous murder investigations.'

'Murder?'

Millicent spoke the word so quietly that the two other women had an effort to hear her. However, it drew to their attention that they had all but forgotten her presence in the room. Mrs Field was quick to remedy the situation, going to stand at the woman's bedside, momentarily obscuring Lavinia from Millicent's view. This slight was not lost on Lavinia. She drew herself up from her lounging position and went around the bed to sit on the other side so that she might remain visible to her hostess.

'Murdered?' repeated Millicent, apparently oblivious to the shenanigans going on about her. 'Why would anyone want to murder Cooper?'

'Well, that of course is what we shall need to find out,' said Lavinia. She gave the housekeeper a haughty glance. 'Thank you, Mrs Field. You can go now. I'll look after Mrs Grayson-Smith. I've asked my maid to bring us some hot tea with plenty of sugar in it.' She turned her attention to her hostess. 'That's what you need, Millicent. Hot, sweet, tea. It does wonders for the shock.'

Mrs Field pointedly looked at her mistress for acquiescence before moving from her position, making it abundantly clear that she had no intention of taking her orders from Lavinia, even if she was the daughter of an earl. Millicent gave a faint nod and closed her eyes. Even then, the housekeeper showed a reluctance to leave, hovering for a moment in the doorway, before closing the door softly behind her.

'Ah, that's better,' said Lavinia. 'What an annoying woman. She really doesn't know when she's not wanted, does she?'

'She was just being kind,' said Millicent. She passed a hand across her brow. Her head throbbed and she felt both hot and cold, if that were possible. 'I can't believe it. Cooper murdered! It all seems so ridiculous, like a bad dream. I keep thinking that I am going to wake up in a moment and find that none of this is real.'

'Well, I'm afraid it is,' Lavinia said, more firmly than she had intended. She found the woman's overt weakness in the face of adversity frustrating. Millicent could be rather pathetic when she chose to be. She really did put women in a poor light. It was no wonder that her servants took advantage of her placid nature. What the woman needed was a little backbone.

'Edwin!' All of a sudden Millicent became animated. She grasped Lavinia's arm, her fingers pinching the flesh so that the girl winced. 'Edwin must be told.'

'I'm sure your butler is doing that now,' said Lavinia, retrieving her arm. 'He seems a capable sort of a fellow. He's already telephoned the police. Rose told me. They will be here shortly.'

'Rose? Do you mean Rose Simpson? How does she know what has happened? Have you telephoned her? Is she coming down?' Millicent sounded eager, as if a weight were being lifted from her shoulders, or else she saw a light at the end of a very long tunnel.

'Er … no,' began Lavinia, desperately trying to decide how best to reply. 'No, she –'

'She's already here.'

Both women looked up in surprise. They had not heard the door open.

It's Lavinia's lady's maid, thought Millicent dully. She's bringing in the cups of tea. But how does she know about Rose Simpson?

'Oh, thank goodness we don't have to pretend any more,' exclaimed Lavinia, jumping up and taking the tray from Rose. 'It has been very trying. Now, I'll be mother and pour, shall I?'

Millicent looked from one to the other of them in something akin to bewilderment.

'I'm Rose Simpson, Mrs Grayson-Smith,' explained Rose, coming forward and extending her hand. 'You must forgive me. I'm not really Lavinia's lady's maid. I've been playing a part. I've been in disguise, you see. I thought it was the best way to find out which of your servants had stolen your necklace.'

'You're Rose Simpson?'

'Yes, I am Rose Simpson. And I am very pleased to meet you properly, Mrs Grayson-Smith.'

'But you did my hair …'

'Yes, and what an awful job of it she did too,' said Lavinia, making a face as she poured out the tea, spilling some in one of the saucers. 'It was just as well I was on hand to sort it out. Now, let me see. Plenty of milk I think, that would be best, and lots of sugar. That's good for shock, isn't it?'

'I can't take it all in, said Millicent, rather weakly. 'It's all too much …'

'Well, I daresay it is,' said Lavinia. 'But you have got to try, Millicent. You must pull yourself together. I mean to say, it's not as if you liked the woman very much, is it? Cooper, I mean?'

'Lavinia!' Rose said appalled. She had removed her spectacles and her resemblance to a lady's maid was diminishing before Millicent's eyes. 'May I call you, Millicent?' she said kindly. Millicent nodded vaguely. 'What Lavinia is trying to say,' she paused to glare at her friend, 'is that this will all be very unpleasant, perfectly horrid in fact, but we shall be here to give you support.' Rose smiled. 'You really mustn't worry. It won't do any good.'

'But how can I not worry?' asked Millicent rather feebly. 'It's all so awful. I suppose they will think I did it, won't they?'

'Who will think what?' asked Lavinia sharply, looking up, her hand paused in the act of putting sugar into one of the teacups.

'The police, of course. They'll think I murdered Cooper, won't they? They'll think I'm the murderer.'

Chapter Fourteen

'Why should they think that?' asked Rose sharply.

She stared at Millicent curiously. From what Lavinia had said, and from what little she had seen of the woman herself, Millicent Grayson-Smith appeared to have a natural tendency for nervousness. Rose wondered if this was her usual condition, for it was perfectly possible that this propensity towards anxiety had only developed following the theft of the necklace. Particularly as it had occurred hot on the heels, as it were, of a rather hasty marriage and a significant change in Millicent's social position. With this in mind, it was tempting to dismiss Millicent's words as the normal apprehension experienced by anyone of a nervous disposition on finding themselves embroiled in a murder investigation. Rose reasoned that it was unlikely to be an admission of guilt as such, more a genuine fear at the prospect of being considered a suspect. Even so, there had been a note of genuine distress in Millicent's voice. Her eyes had been large and the words had appeared to slip from her lips instinctively, before she had had the sense to check them. Now the woman looked close to tears. Rose could feel the desperation in the room.

It was perhaps fortunate that at that very moment Lavinia, never one to keep her thoughts to herself, intervened before Rose could probe further or Millicent could say anything more self-incriminating.

'Millicent, do stop talking such nonsense.' Lavinia spoke with some scorn in her voice. She rose from her seat and began to pace the room as if to emphasise that she found such melodramatic statements to be irritating. 'Why ever should the police suspect you of killing your lady's maid? I have never heard of anything so ridiculous.' An unpleasant thought suddenly occurred to her. 'I say, I do hope you won't make a similarly foolish comment to the police when you are interviewed?'

'No … Of course not.'

Millicent clawed miserably at her bedsheet, pulling it this way and that. The spectacle appeared to further annoy Lavinia, for she marched over to the bed and tore the sheet from Millicent's hand.

'For goodness sake, do stop that, Milly, and listen to me. Really, you must pull yourself together. She must, mustn't she, Rose?'

Lavinia turned to look at her friend for affirmation. However, if she had hoped that Rose would offer support, then she was to be bitterly disappointed. Rose was in a reflective mood and said nothing. It was even possible that she had not heard what Lavinia had just been saying.

'Rose? Rose, did you hear what I said? Tell Millicent how ridiculous she is being.' There was an impatient note to Lavinia's voice now. She had ceased to look imploringly at Rose. Instead, her eyes flashed with annoyance.

'It is not ridiculous to suppose that the police might consider you a possible suspect,' Rose said after a while, addressing Millicent. She chose her words carefully. 'They are unlikely to rule out anyone at first. However, I think, particularly given where Cooper's body was found, they will be focusing their efforts primarily on your servants.'

'Well, of course they will. There you are, Millicent,' said Lavinia, having decided to make the best of it. 'You are no more a suspect than Rose is. Or I am myself, come to that.' She sighed wearily, thoroughly bored of the conversation.

'I suppose it does stand to reason that it must be one of them. I wasn't thinking properly … Really, I don't know what I was thinking. You must think me very silly,' stuttered Millicent apologetically. No one said anything. The silence appeared to unnerve her. 'I can't bear to think about it,' she said hurriedly. 'In this very house … but who could have done such a thing? Surely it can't have been Mason or Mrs Field or … or one of the housemaids? They are so very young. Oh, I don't think I can bear it … really I don't.'

'You see what I have had to put up with?' said Lavinia a little while later, when she and Rose were alone. 'Millicent really is impossible. It's a pity that the police will have to interview her at all. She's frightened of everything. Who knows what she will say?' She paused a moment to give her friend something of a hard stare. 'I say, Rose, you weren't much of a help just now. Couldn't you see that the woman needed reassuring? Really, if I'd known I was going to have to play nursemaid, I don't think I would have come here at all.'

Rose did not reply at once. It occurred to Lavinia that her friend had been unusually quiet since they had left Millicent's room and entered her own. She shut the door behind them and turned on her friend.

'Look here, Rose, this really won't do.'

'Do remember, Lavinia, I'm not really your lady's maid,' said Rose, with a spark of her usual spirit.

'I realise that. But I say, Rose, why did you behave as you did just now? It wasn't like you at all.'

Rose answered Lavinia with a question of her own.

'Didn't it strike you as very odd what Mrs Grayson-Smith said?'

'Of course it did. I said as much at the time.'

'No. I mean … I don't think she said what she did just because she was nervous –'

'Really, Rose, must you insist on talking in riddles? I have absolutely no idea what you are talking about.'

'I think she said what she did because she has something to hide,' said Rose. The words came out of her mouth before she could stop them. 'Didn't you see the look on her face? She looked horrified at her own stupidity.'

'Well, I did think she looked rather upset,' conceded Lavinia.

'It made me wonder.'

'Wonder what?' asked Lavinia, though the look on her face suggested that she knew the answer already.

'It made me wonder whether Mrs Grayson-Smith did do it. Murdered her own lady's maid, I mean.'

'Oh, Mr Mason!' Mrs Field exclaimed, bustling into the butler's parlour.

The housekeeper's complexion was deprived of its natural high colour. Instead, her face looked strained and was tinged an unhealthy shade of grey. Her hands, always busy at the best of times, played with the fabric of her black dress, clenching it between her hands repeatedly and then releasing it, leaving the material scrunched and creased. Had the butler been more himself, he would have noticed and thought how it set a bad example to the lower servants.

'What is it, Mrs Field?'

Mason passed a weary hand across his brow. In appearance, he was similarly pale to the housekeeper, though this was not vastly at odds with his usual complexion. However, Mrs Field thought there was a tiredness about him and, when he looked up at her, she was aghast. It was as if he had aged ten years in the space of a few hours, so dull and lifeless was his face. In her surprise, she clutched a hand to her chest. On his part, the housekeeper's intrusion on his solitude was most unwelcome. Had he been a different man, he might well have asked her to leave.

'Why, Mr Mason, you do look awful, if you don't mind my saying,' said Mrs Field. Immediately her own worries were forgotten. She saw a rare opportunity to put a caring arm around his shoulders. 'You come with me and sit in my sitting room for a while. You can rest your feet and we'll have a nice cup of tea just like madam and that Lady Lavinia. It must have been something of an ordeal, talking to the police on the telephone. Did you manage to get hold of the master?'

The butler said nothing, but allowed himself to be steered to the room in question. He did not throw off the housekeeper's arm or insist that he was quite all right. A part of Mrs Field rejoiced, another part of her worried at his wretched condition. It was not like him at all, this melancholy. She had seen him discipline errant servants and see off unwelcome guests. True, murder was a particularly nasty business, but even so she had expected him to take it in his stride, and deal with it in his usual efficient and professional manner.

It was while the housekeeper was dwelling on this point and finding the butler sadly wanting, that to her relief she remembered that only a short time before he had performed his role admirably, keeping his inner turmoil well hidden. No one could have asked for more. The way he had gathered the servants together and informed them in the quietest and most gentle tones of Miss Cooper's unfortunate accident. There had been no hint that the death had been intentional. The word "murder" had not escaped his lips. Mrs Field made a face, instinctively shying away from the word herself. They had had to use the kitchen, the body still residing untouched in the servants' hall. Cook had complained that the presence of so many in her domain was a hindrance to her work, until Mr Mason had rather sharply pointed out in something of an icy voice that it was unlikely that anyone would require much breakfast. He had spoken kindly but firmly to the servants, some of whom were in tears, with the authority that became his position. He had made it quite clear that questions were neither invited nor would they be welcomed. The servants would be told only what they needed to know. Meanwhile, he had instructed them to go about their business as best they could. Mrs Field had been proud of him.

Only in her presence had he seen fit to let down his defences and show his real emotions. It was another side of him that she had not known, and she found that it rather appealed to her. He was still the same upright and respectable man whom she looked up to, but now she saw a sensitive, vulnerable side to him, that brought out her maternal instincts. It was this side of the butler that had compelled him to take in his sister's wayward son and give the boy a job against his better judgement.

She steered him into one of the old armchairs and he fell heavily on to its seat as if his frame had been large and ungainly, not tall and thin. The housekeeper glanced at him a moment to satisfy herself that he would not leave as soon as her back was turned. She had decided to make the tea herself rather than call for one of the maids. Much better that no one else should see him in this state. He'd feel awkward about it later when he came to his senses.

A few minutes later they were sipping their tea. The housekeeper was relieved to see that a little colour had returned to the butler's cheeks. He was still distant, brooding in his own world, but in a short while she felt certain she would be able to coax him into speech. For the moment, however, she was content just to watch him surreptitiously out of the corner of her eye. She was sorely tempted to lean back in her own armchair, close her eyes and imagine what things might have been. With a considerable effort, she did not give way to her inclination, but brought herself back to the present. It did not do any good to wish for what could never be. And this was not the time to daydream. It was enough that they were sitting here together either side of the hearth enjoying a quiet companionship.

There had been a time, years ago, when she had hoped for more. Housekeepers and butlers married all the time, she'd told herself, so why shouldn't she and Mr Mason? It had seemed the logical extension of their professional partnership. Only Mr Mason didn't appear to think so. He had given her no sign, uttered no warm or tender words. For a while, she had been content to admire him from afar. As the years progressed, she had made her own tentative and hesitant advances. They had been gently, but effectively, declined. It became obvious, even to her own lovelorn heart, that he did not feel the same way about her as she did about him. Initially, the realisation had left her distraught. In time, she had come to accept the situation, had made do with the platonic companionship that he did offer her. But unrequited though her love might be, her heart still ached and burned only for him. There had never been anyone else. In her own way, she had grudgingly made do with loving him in a quiet, unobtrusive manner.

'They're not much more than children, Pearl and Edna,' the butler said at last. 'It is a pity it was them that found her. It near breaks my heart to know they saw what they did.'

'They had no reason to be in the servants' hall that time of day,' replied the housekeeper, herself close to tears. 'It should have been me that found her, Mr Mason.'

'Far better if it had been me, Mrs Field.' He leaned back heavily in his armchair. 'I don't mind telling you that I never thought something like this would happen in a place where I was butler. I feel I've let them all down, the family and the servants.'

'No more did I, Mr Mason,' said Mrs Field, deciding not to comment on his feelings of responsibility. It would only prolong his despondent mood, and the police would be here soon. She didn't want them to see him like this. She leaned towards him in a conspiratorial fashion. 'I know one shouldn't speak ill of the dead, but I never liked Miss Cooper, no I never. Thought rather a lot of herself, she did. A bit of a looker, as you might say, and didn't she know it. There'll be a man involved in this, you mark my words. I've been giving it a bit of thought, so I have. How it could have happened, I mean. I reckon she let him in, don't you? Waited for us all to retire to bed. She must have been one of the last up, what with the mistress entertaining. She waits for the coast to be clear and then lets him in as bold as brass. They must have had an argument and he done her in. I say, Mr Mason,' she tried to get his attention, for he was staring into the distance, 'don't you think I'm right?'

'No, I'm afraid I don't,' replied the butler gravely. The air of desolation hung about him like a cloak. 'I cannot tell you how much I should like to believe that the murderer came from outside. A mythical young man as you describe, Mrs Field, or a tramp perhaps … what a relief it would be to believe that such a man existed and that he gave Miss Cooper the fatal blow.'

'But that's how it must have happened, Mr Mason,' the housekeeper said, a note of urgency in her voice. Her bottom lip was trembling. She had stopped what she was doing so that her cup was paused halfway to her mouth. Next her hand shook, and for a moment it looked as if she might spill her tea. 'Surely you're not suggesting that the murderer was someone in this house? How could you think such a thing?'

'Because I know it to be true.'

The harshness of the words hung in the air. The housekeeper, for her part, felt as if she had been hit squarely in the face.

'How?' she demanded. 'How could you possibly know such a thing?' She felt the anger rise up within her. Why must he pour cold water on the version of events she had created in her mind, the only scenario that was bearable? She took a deep breath in an attempt to quell her resentment. She hoped vehemently that he would not say as much to the police.

'Because Miss Cooper would not have been in a position to let a stranger into the house, even if she had had a mind to. No,' the butler raised a hand as the housekeeper made to protest, 'hear me out, if you please, Mrs Field. It really is quite simple. She did not have a key.'

'Nonsense,' said Mrs Field. 'The key to the servants' entrance is always kept on the hook beside the door.'

'It certainly used to be,' agreed Mason. 'But, since the disappearance of madam's diamond necklace, I have been in the habit of removing it each night lest the thief should seek an opportunity to escape with his spoils.'

'Very well, then,' said the housekeeper, thinking rapidly. 'Perhaps she chose instead to go through the main house and to let him in through one of the French windows. I admit it would take some nerve, but I don't think you would have found Miss Cooper wanting there.'

'I'm afraid that would not have been possible, either. You see, Mrs Field, I also took the precaution of locking the doors into the main parts of the house. I did not want to risk another theft.' The butler bowed his head. 'I am sure you understand what that means. No one could get in to the servants' quarters and –'

'No one could get out.' The housekeeper stifled a sob. 'You are saying it was one of us?'

'Exactly, Mrs Field. Miss Cooper's murderer must have been one of the servants.'

Chapter Fifteen

Somewhere in the depths of her lethargy and despair, Millicent was reminded of her duties as hostess. In truth, it was the minute Rose had re-entered the room in that hideous maid's dress of hers. No, Millicent reflected, she was being a little uncharitable. There was nothing wrong with the outfit itself save that it was a little old-fashioned, even by Millicent's standards. But to know, as she did now, that the girl was about to marry into the British aristocracy … well, it seemed a little ridiculous that she should still be wearing that unflattering ensemble. Rather to her surprise, she noticed Rose had returned the spectacles to sit on her nose, which had the effect of altering her appearance considerably. For a moment, a little part of Millicent wondered whether she had been dreaming. Perhaps this girl really was Lavinia's lady's maid and Rose Simpson was still at Sedgwick Court, making the final arrangements for her forthcoming marriage. So much of the events of this morning had seemed unreal. Therefore, would it be so very surprising if she had conjured up Rose Simpson's presence in her house, a figment of an over active or exhausted imagination?

'I must ask Mrs Field to prepare you a room,' she said, addressing Rose. 'There's no reason for you to stay in the servants' quarters now. The theft of my necklace is the last thing on anyone's mind after … after what's happened. Lavinia said she would join me for breakfast in my room. You will too, won't you? I'll just ring for another plate. And do please call me Millicent.'

'No,' said Rose rather abruptly.

'Oh?' Millicent was taken aback. Perhaps the events of the morning had all been a dream after all.

'No,' repeated Rose hurriedly. 'Please don't do that, Mrs Grayson-Smith.' She rushed over to Millicent and clasped her hand in an effort to secure the woman's full attention. 'That's why I'm here, why I came back. I've come to ask you to keep my identity a secret, please. From the other servants, I mean.'

'Is that really necessary?' Millicent withdrew her hand from Rose's and looked at it rather as if it had been contaminated. 'Surely I should at least tell Mason and Mrs Field?'

'No, I don't want you to do that. The situation has changed. Don't you see? We are no longer discussing a missing necklace. We are now talking of murder.' Rose paused to look in the mirror and adjust her spectacles. 'It will give me an advantage to remain as a servant.'

'An advantage?'

'Yes, in trying to solve the case,' explained Rose. 'Of course, I shall be obliged to tell the police who I am.' She sighed. 'It's unfortunate, but hopefully I can persuade them to be discreet.'

'You are going to try and find the murderer?' said Millicent slowly, her face pale. 'Do you think that wise? Won't it be dangerous? Hadn't you much better leave it to the police?'

'Oh, she couldn't possibly do that,' exclaimed Lavinia. Unobserved by either woman, she had entered the room quietly and had evidently overheard the latter part of Millicent's speech. 'Rose has rather a thing for murders, as you know, and she's frightfully good at solving them.'

'I … I don't know,' Millicent said rather hesitantly. 'That's to say, I might forget. I will probably call you Rose or Miss Simpson or even your ladyship, in front of the servants by mistake. I'm afraid it's the sort of thing I might do. I have a tendency to get rather nervous, you see.'

Lavinia made a face and opened her mouth to speak, no doubt a disparaging remark forming itself on her lips. Rose intervened hurriedly.

'You needn't worry about that. I'm going back to the servants' hall now. I've been gone too long as it is. There is no reason why you need see me again until … until this business is all over. In fact, I shall go out of my way to ensure that you don't. One of the housemaids can attend to you.'

'I … I don't know,' repeated Millicent. 'It makes everything so complicated, more complicated than it is already, I mean. And what should I say to Edwin? When is he coming home, do you know?'

'I don't, I'm afraid,' said Rose. 'You will need to ask Mason. It was he who telephoned Mr Grayson-Smith.' She gave Lavinia an imploring stare.

'I will see what I can do,' Lavinia's answering look seemed to say. She patted Millicent's arm absentmindedly in what she considered to be a reassuring gesture. Millicent appeared not to be of the same view, for she withdrew from her into the bedcovers.

'Now, I need to telephone Cedric,' Rose said, smiling at the spectacle. 'He will need to know what's happened. If nothing else, we will probably be prolonging our stay.'

She made to go to the door.

'Oh no you don't.' Lavinia said, half rising. 'Not if you want the servants to think you're my lady's maid, that is. I know what you will be like, whispering sweet nothings and giving the game away. No,' she held up her hand as Rose made to protest. '*I'll* telephone Ceddie and tell him what's happened. It will be all I can do to stop him coming down here. If he hears your voice, there will be no hope. And he'd be absolutely hopeless at pretending that you're just my lady's maid. He could never act, poor lamb, even when we were children. You should have seen him when he pretended to be St George attacking the dragon –'

'Oh, very well,' said Rose, rather dejectedly. 'I suppose you are right. It wouldn't be very sensible.'

It had been the one bright spark in the whole of this affair, she thought, an excuse to speak to Cedric. Yet Lavinia's reasoning was sound. Much as she may try, Rose could not fault it. How could she possibly talk to Cedric without casting off her trappings as a maid and being herself? Oh, to have him here now, helping her to solve the case as he had done on previous occasions. He had considered himself Watson to her Holmes, but in doing so he had done himself down. His very presence inspired her and fuelled her imagination. And how much more bearable everything would be to have him here. Instead, she must contend with a difficult Millicent on one hand and the hierarchy of the servants' hall on the other. Suddenly the whole ludicrousness of the situation occurred to her. Here she was, on the eve of her wedding, embroiled in a murder investigation that had very little to do with her. Really, there was nothing to prevent her from leaving and returning to Sedgwick …

But, even as these very thoughts played out in her mind, she knew that there was something that kept her here. It had nothing to do with upholding her reputation as an amateur sleuth. That meant very little to anyone but Lavinia, and only to her as a means of explaining why her brother, one of the most eligible men in England, had seen fit to choose a shop girl for his bride. The real reason she could not contemplate leaving had to do with the diamond necklace or, more precisely, her investigation into its disappearance. For at the back of her mind lurked a little, but persistent, voice, nagging at her, whispering in her ear that had she not been there raking up the dust in the servants' hall, encouraging gossip and prying into secrets that were none of her concern, the lady's maid might still be alive today.

'So, what's the local inspector like? Do you know him, Millicent? Is he any good?'

Lavinia's words roused Rose from her musings with a jolt.

'The local inspector?' Rose queried, before Millicent had a chance to answer Lavinia's question. 'Won't they be calling in Scotland Yard?'

'Over the death of a lady's maid? Well, of course not,' Lavinia said, openly derisive. 'Really, Rose, what were you thinking? It is hardly likely to be the most complicated of cases. The woman looked the sort to have a sweetheart. I think we'll find that the murderer was a jealous or rejected lover.' She beamed. 'You'll probably have it all solved by teatime, Rose.' Lavinia turned her attention to focus on Millicent. 'Rose probably hoped it would be one of her friends from Scotland Yard. The rude Inspector Bramwell, perhaps, or the young and rather dashing Inspector Deacon …'

Rose blushed. Mention of Inspector Deacon brought back with it recollections of the last time she had seen the man in question. It had been at the conclusion of the last murder inquiry in which she had found herself, an investigation into the murder that had occurred at Renard's dress shop. Inspector Deacon, who was already known to her from previous cases, had been the officer in charge of the investigation. He had not welcomed her help due to fears for her safety, being of the view that the murderer was very likely to be someone she considered a friend or acquaintance. Her cheeks flushed crimson. Goodness knows what he would think now, she thought, if he could see her dressed up like this and pretending to be a servant. It was almost a relief to know that she would not be required to explain to him the reasoning behind her disguise.

Her thoughts drifted to memories of Madame Renard's little flat. She remembered her very last conversation with the inspector. The scene itself flooded back into her mind. They had been standing in the makeshift kitchen-cum-bathroom, an area partitioned off from the main room by a curtain. They had been washing up and drying the tea things. A cup and a saucer, that had been all that had been left to do. Inspector Deacon had been waiting for an excuse to talk to her. He had had something to say to her, something important. And she had panicked because she had known that once it was said, it could not be unsaid. There had been a brief moment ... and then Cedric had arrived and told Inspector Deacon about their engagement ...

Rose made her way quickly back to the servants' quarters. She flew down the steep flights of stairs, her feet tapping loudly on the wooden boards so that the noise echoed within the confined space. Yet, she had seen and heard Agnes run up and down these very steps so quietly as to make hardly a sound. Looking down at her feet, she realised that the girl must have trodden on what remained of the old, dull linoleum, which was so worn in places as to be almost non-existent. The same linoleum, though in better condition, continued down into the passage, leading to the servants' hall. Rose took a moment to pause and study its dull brown and cream design. She saw that the small pattern evident on the stairs had given way to a more elaborate design of leaves and flowers, bordered by a bold design of thick plaited rope. The overall illusion was that the floor was covered by a long linoleum rug.

It was while engaged in this activity that Mrs Field came upon her, her stiff skirts bustling as she walked.

'Oh, there you are, Miss Denning. We were wondering where you'd got to. Mr Mason and I are requiring a word, if you please.'

Similar to the butler before her, Rose found herself expertly manoeuvred into the housekeeper's sitting room. Mr Mason, it appeared, was already in occupation, clutching a lukewarm cup of tea in one hand and a saucer in the other.

'Ah, Miss Denning.' He rose from the old armchair and discarded the china on a convenient occasional table. 'I understand from Mrs Field that you are appraised of the ... eh ... exact nature of Miss Cooper's death?'

'Yes. Edna told me. Poor girl, she was very frightened.'

'That girl needs to learn when to hold her tongue!' said Mrs Field crossly. 'Gossiping to visiting servants like that –'

'She was in shock,' said Rose rather abruptly. 'She needed someone to talk to.'

'That's as may be –' began the housekeeper before she was quickly interrupted by the butler.

'I am sure Miss Denning can appreciate that this is a particularly nasty business,' said Mr Mason, 'and that, as such, it requires delicate handling.' He began to pace the room, considerably hindered in his progress by both the lack of space and the abundance of worn furniture. 'It's an awful business, but we, as senior servants, have a responsibility to the staff. We must ensure that they are not unduly upset and that the house continues to operate as smoothly and efficiently as possible.'

'That is all very well,' said Rose, finding herself annoyed by what she took to be the butler's rather pompous attitude, 'but a murder has been committed and the police are likely to want to interview all the servants. The staff will need to be told the truth.'

She cast a glance around the sitting room with its shabby but genteel furniture. It looked worn, very like the butler and housekeeper themselves, all trying desperately to keep up appearances. It seemed to her a losing battle, the sagging seats, the faded velvet, the old rug, threadbare in places, Mr Mason and Mrs Field, their faces lined and a ghastly shade of grey …

'I agree we must do our best,' she said more gently. 'However, I am afraid that the orderly running of this house will not be their first priority.'

'Not for the police, perhaps, but it will be for us,' Mrs Field said firmly. 'If this business is not handled properly we'll be having staff handing in their notice willy-nilly. And good servants are hard to come by. Girls these days want to work in shops and offices. They don't want the long hours and poor pay. They want the evenings to themselves, they do, so they can go out dancing –'

'Thank you, Mrs Field,' said the butler quickly, before the housekeeper could stray any further on to what was evidently one of her favourite hobby-horses. 'Quite so.'

'Is that why you didn't tell them Miss Cooper had been murdered?' inquired Rose. 'You said she had met with an unfortunate accident –'

'I did not wish to alarm them unduly,' began Mason.

'But they will have to know,' protested Rose. 'The police will be here in a moment. You will need to tell them before then. That's a point,' she said looking around, 'where *are* the police? Shouldn't they be here by now? The body was found quite a while ago, wasn't it?'

'That's Constable Smith for you,' said the housekeeper, with something akin to contempt. 'The man can't deal with no more than a couple of drunkards staggering home at closing time. Petty theft and damage, that's what he's used to and all he's good for. He took fright, so he did, when Mr Mason telephoned him about Miss Cooper's death. Told us to lock the servants' hall and wait for the inspector. He's over Bichester way.'

'I see,' said Rose. Privately she thought Constable Smith guilty of a dereliction of duty.

'I wanted them to get used to the idea of Miss Cooper's death,' said the butler in so dull and quiet a voice that his words were very nearly inaudible. Indeed, both women were obliged to move a step or two forward to catch what he said. Rose thought that it was almost as if he had not heard the discussion concerning Constable Smith's various professional failings, for his mind dwelt still on her original question. 'To tell them it was murder … something so wicked as that ... it doesn't bear thinking about …'

'I'm sure she had it coming to her,' said Mrs Field brusquely, though there was a tear in her eyes, which suggested that she was not unaffected by the butler's words. 'I know her sort. The servants, they'll be pretty shaken up, and that's a fact.' She glared at Rose. 'Mr Mason, he's doing right by them, surely even you can see that?'

Mrs Field's hostility filled the room. She had moved to stand beside the butler to illustrate her support for his way of thinking. They might have been an old married couple sharing an impossible burden. All at once, Rose felt that her presence in the room was no longer desired. Indeed, Mrs Field had all but turned her back on her as she patted the butler's arm. It was tempting to take the unsubtle hint and leave. After a moment, she made to do just that. However, she was arrested by the housekeeper's voice, loud in the prevailing silence and somewhat dismissive.

'I take it, Miss Denning, that you will be attending to madam?'

'No … no, I won't. I'm afraid I have more than enough to do with her ladyship,' Rose lied. 'Perhaps one of the housemaid's –'

'No. If you can't be minded to, I shall see to madam myself.' The housekeeper looked at her coldly. 'But why you can't look after madam when she's no trouble at all, I don't know.'

Before Rose could make to protest or attempt to justify her position, the housekeeper had gathered up her skirts and disappeared from the room in a cloud of black. Her antagonism lingered in the air like a whiff of perfume. Rose, feeling she had made a bad job of things, made to follow her into the passage.

'Don't mind Mrs Field.'

She had all but forgotten the butler, who had lowered himself into one of the armchairs, his expression half hidden by a hand, which he held to his forehead as if to shield his face from her gaze. 'She's upset, she is. We both are. Mrs Field … she doesn't mean to take it out on you, Miss Denning. That's just her way.' He hesitated for a moment before continuing. 'It's one of us, you know.'

'What do you mean?' cried Rose. She was aware of her own sharp intake of breath. If that was not enough, she could feel her heart beating in her chest. 'What do you mean, it's one of us?'

'It's one of the servants,' explained Mason. 'No one else could have got into the servants' hall. Kept it locked at night, I did, more's the pity.'

He tapped the breast pocket of his waistcoat, which presumably held the key, with his free hand, the other still partially obscuring his face. This time Rose wondered whether its purpose was to prop up his head to prevent him from slumping back into the chair.

'One of the servants murdered Miss Cooper? I suppose that's to be expected, what with it happening in the servants' hall.'

'Yes. But that's not all, Miss Denning. Mrs Field and I, we have an inkling we know who did it.'

Chapter Sixteen

Rose did not press Mason to divulge the name of the person who had killed Miss Cooper. The drooped shoulders, the air of utter despondency and the recollection of the housekeeper fussing around and ministering to him were sufficient clues as to whom the two of them believed to be the murderer. It might well be, she thought, that they had had sight of, or were in possession of, some incriminating piece of evidence. She would not have put it past Mrs Field to remove a bloodied knife. Or it could just be no more than a suspicion, honed and perfected so that in their minds it was now almost fact. However, she could not help but think that there was a great deal of difference between theft and murder, a great number of steps to climb to ascend from the lesser crime to the greater. It would mean crossing a line after which there would be no going back.

She had walked out into the passage, somewhat dazed, not sure what to do next or where to go. The ordinary routine of service was in disarray, despite the butler's fine words to the contrary. In normal circumstances, Rose would no doubt have drifted aimlessly towards the servants' hall where the staff had a tendency to congregate when they had an odd moment to spare or sought company. Today, of course, the room was closed to them all, hiding as it did the hideous crime that had befallen Crossing Manor. Instead, the servants stood around in little groups, some in the stillroom, others in the pantry and a few in the passage causing something of an obstruction. They spoke in hurried whispers, glancing up at her guiltily, caught gossiping about Velda Cooper's death by a visiting servant, the words frozen on their lips. Some had tried the patience of the cook by veering off into the kitchen, the warmth of the stove and the aroma of cooking providing comfort and solace from the situation in hand.

Rose knew she had a duty to mingle, to glean from the servants what little she could before the arrival of the police. Sudden death had unnerved them, particularly the demise of a woman still in her prime. The realisation that it was murder would frighten them further. And it was not at all certain, she reminded herself, that the police would acquiesce with her wish to keep her identity a secret. The servants were unlikely to talk to her freely once they knew who she was. Indeed, her presence in the servants' quarters was unlikely to be tolerated, certainly not accepted. At best, they would think she had played a mean trick on them and, on reflection, perhaps she had.

A noise at her shoulder brought her to her senses. The butler, it appeared, had followed her example, for he had shuffled out into the passage in her wake. Immediately he came upon the staff, his posture changed. Gone was the hunched, dejected figure. Mason had drawn himself up to his not inconsiderable height and puffed out his weak pigeon chest. In different circumstances, the effect might have been considered comical. To Rose, it seemed almost pitiful, but she admired the man's dogged determination to fulfil his part. The servants looked up to him and he in turn felt the responsibility that such a position bestowed. He viewed them with something of a paternal air. Together, with Mrs Field, he was responsible for their moral welfare, there to provide guidance and offer protection. Never more had this latter duty come into play than this day. For in a few moments' time he would inform them that Miss Cooper's death had not been the result of natural causes.

Rose held back a little as the butler summoned the servants to congregate once again in the great kitchen. She followed slowly in his trail and was one of the last staff to enter the room. The kitchen was crammed full to bursting and Mason had already commenced his speech when she entered. She took up her position at the butler's side, a lone attendant in Mrs Field's absence. Such a vantage point afforded her a good view of the servants; she would be able to observe their individual reactions to the distressing news. She began by searching out Albert and Martha, who were standing as far away from each other as possible.

The butler's words brought an immediate effect. Edna and Pearl, to whom the details of Velda Cooper's death were not a surprise, clung to one another, tears pouring down the scullery maid's little face. Agnes's lip quivered and she looked very pale. Gone was the talkative maid that Rose had met on her arrival. In her place was a silent and reflective girl, pulling at her apron with hands that did not know what to do with themselves. While all the colour had drained from Martha's face, even from her eyes, which had been red and swollen from excessive crying. Now they looked strangely dull and colourless. She was standing on the spot, her feet seemingly rooted to the ground, but her body swaying. Any moment now,

Rose thought, she is going to faint. Agnes was obviously of the same opinion because she put out a hand and clutched at the girl's arm before propelling her into an old wooden chair.

It was, however, Albert's reaction to the news that interested Rose most. She had half expected him to sneer, even to look a little amused, so despicable a fellow did she find him. But he did none of these things. Where the others sobbed and grew pale, twisted their hands and toyed with their aprons, the young footman stood motionless, frozen to the spot. He might have been one of the stone statues that graced the gardens, he was so still. Even the expression on his face did not change. It was only his eyes that betrayed his emotions. Black as coal, like his hair, they flashed brilliantly in the dim light of the kitchen, the only sign that he was a living, breathing person, and that his uncle's words had not fallen on deaf ears. He's frightened, thought Rose. Mason has not even told them that the murderer must be a servant and already he's afraid.

It was while these thoughts filled her head and she stared at the young man more keenly, that the housekeeper appeared, bustling into the kitchen as was her wont. She alone looked flushed, presumably from her exertions at helping Millicent to dress and rushing down the servants' back stairs, for her hair had come slightly undone from its bun as if a strand or two had got caught on something. She went and stood beside the butler, her manner flustered. It was clear she was trying to catch her breath. There was a look of anxiety on her face. From the way she turned her eyes to look first at the butler and then at the servants, it was obvious that she was curious to know what she had missed. After a minute, the housekeeper's gaze lingered only on the staff. Her eyes combed the audience, as Rose's had done only moments before her. She was looking for someone. She gave an involuntary start. She appeared to have found the person she was looking for, for her gaze settled at last. Rose turned to follow her line of vision. She had expected to find Mrs Field staring at Albert. Much to her surprise, she found that the person who commanded her attention was the little scullery maid, Pearl.

'This is a rum go and no mistake,' muttered Inspector Connor, as soon as he had hung up the telephone receiver.

'Oh?' enquired his nephew politely, though in point of fact he was more interested in tucking into the plate of eggs and bacon that his aunt had thoughtfully seen fit to set before him.

'Yes, indeed,' replied his uncle. 'Seems there's been a murder up at the big house in Crossing village. You know the one, that great patchwork of a place? Ugly, I call it, made up of bits and pieces. Tudor here, Victorian there. Why he didn't just pull it down and put up another in its stead, I'm sure I don't know, given the amount of money he has and all.'

'Who has?'

'Edwin Grayson-Smith, of course. You may well think we're out in the sticks here, and so we are, and what with you being a fine London gentleman now with your fancy ways, but we have our characters just the same. You must have heard of him, Charlie? He's a businessman of sorts, what you might call an entrepreneur or a financier or some such. Rich as kings, some say.'

'Yes, I've heard of him,' admitted Charlie, looking decidedly more interested in what the inspector had to say. He took a swig of tea and cleared his throat. 'I say, Uncle, you're not telling me someone did him in?'

'Not him, Charlie my boy. One of his servants. A lady's maid would you believe? Down in the servants' hall and all. Her head bashed in good and proper!'

'Murder in the servants' hall, that's a new one on me. Was Mr Grayson-Smith home at the time?'

'No, not he. He was away on business making his money. There was only his wife at home and a young lady she had staying. Fancy sounding name … yes, here we are,' said the inspector glancing at the notes he'd hurriedly written down. 'Lady Lavinia Sedgwick.'

'The Earl of Belvedere's sister?' said his nephew, his fork, with a piece of bacon on it, arrested in mid-air.

'Met her have you?'

'No, I haven't. But I've heard of her. Quite a character if my superior's to be believed.'

'Well, I've got to hurry over to Crossing Manor now. That's the name of Grayson-Smith's house. The local chap's only a young constable and not used to dealing with suspicious deaths. Sounds as if he took fright. Hasn't even gone over to the place to take preliminary statements. Just told the butler to keep the room locked and we'd be over directly. The cheek of the man!' Inspector Connor looked distinctly put out. 'I've a good mind to give him what for, I have. Incompetent, that's what the fellow is. Only a constable, he may be, but he should know what's to be done in a case like this.' He sighed. 'I've asked the fingerprint chaps to meet me there and the police surgeon. Hopefully not too much time's been wasted.' He looked gloomily at his plate. 'I suppose I can say goodbye to my breakfast. Make sure you leave me a morsel.'

'I will,' said his nephew, through a mouthful of egg. 'Have a good day, Uncle. I expect to hear all about it this evening.'

The inspector made to go and then hesitated a moment to regard the young man with affection. He had no children of his own and regarded his nephew very much like a son, particularly as the young man was in the habit of taking his summer holidays at Bichester. He was a smart lad, as the inspector often said to his wife. Was making something of himself in London, so he was. A pleasant and cheerful young man who'd go far, even if he was a bit too well groomed for his own good and would insist on wearing his hat at that ridiculous jaunty angle whenever he went out. Still, they probably did things differently in London ...

'Look here, Charlie. It doesn't feel right my asking you, and I know it'll be something of a busman's holiday for you, but how say you give me a bit of a hand?' He paused a moment to give his nephew an opportunity to protest. Charlie, however, merely looked up expectantly, a cheeky grin on his face. Encouraged, his uncle continued. 'Constable Jones is not the only one all at sea here. We're not used to many murders in these parts, not murders in the houses of the rich, that's for certain. I'm not saying it's beyond me, because it isn't. I know my duty as well as the next man and I reckon I'll make a decent enough stab at it but –'

'But you'd like to use my expertise?'

'Well ... you may put it like that if you like. I was thinking more in the way of experience. You have more murders in London than we do, and what with you being a Scotland Yard detective, it stands to reason you could be a help. Nothing official, mind.' The inspector looked at his nephew gravely. 'We're not calling in Scotland Yard on this one, but if you want to liven up your holiday a bit, well, it would be something to tell your superiors about, wouldn't it?'

'It certainly would,' agreed Charlie, 'and I have to say that I am rather intrigued to meet Lady Lavinia.'

'Well, I don't think we'll be seeing much of that lady, what with the murder happening in the servants' hall, but I daresay you'll get to meet her.'

'Very well, Uncle, I'm in.' Charlie grinned at him. 'Now, just let me gobble down this last bit of toast and have a slurp of tea and we'll go. Aunt won't know herself, it'll be so quiet.'

'It certainly will be without you around to liven up the place.' The inspector's face became grave. 'Now, when we get to Crossing Manor, I'll be referring to you by your rank in the police force, none of this "uncle" and "nephew" business, do you hear, lad? We'll need to do things properly.'

'Certainly, Inspector,' said Charlie adopting a mock serious manner and saluting. 'Sergeant Perkins at your service and reporting for duty, Inspector Connor.'

'You didn't tell them about the locked doors,' said Rose, catching up with the butler as he returned to the sanctuary of his pantry. 'Shouldn't you have told them that the murderer must be one of them? Hadn't you a duty to put them on their guard?'

'So many questions …' mumbled Mason unhappily.

'And have them crying and fainting and screaming?' demanded the housekeeper whom, unbeknown to Rose and much to her annoyance, had followed them into the pantry. 'I think not! We'd never get a stroke of work done.'

What was it with this woman, Rose thought, that she will never leave the poor chap alone? Why does she insist on playing chaperone?

'They will have to know sooner or later,' Rose said, rather more brusquely than she had intended. 'They'll guess as much when the police start questioning them. I can understand, Mr Mason, why you withheld that a murder had been committed until after they had got used to the idea that Miss Cooper was dead, but this … this is far too serious. They might be in danger.'

'Nonsense,' said Mrs Field. 'It stands to reason that the murderer wanted to kill Miss Cooper, and Miss Cooper alone. Why should anyone else be in peril? And why can't the killer be someone we don't know, someone from outside? Who says –?'

'I've told her,' Mason said. He had adopted the familiar stance of putting his hand to his forehead. 'I've told her about the keys.'

'Now, why did you want to go and do a thing like that, Mr Mason?' cried the housekeeper. She put a handkerchief to her eyes and sniffed. 'We could have kept it to ourselves, you and me. I'd never have breathed a word, you know I wouldn't, not without your say so. Oh lor', Mr Mason, what have you done?'

'It's no good, Mrs Field, the police have got to be told the truth, and there's an end to it. Goodness knows, I wanted to say something just now. I wanted to warn him, really I did, give him a chance to escape.' The butler himself seemed close to tears, certainly his face was ashen and he had given way to a stoop. 'But my duty is to the master and it's to justice. Lord knows I've tried to do my best by the boy, but there's no helping some folk. You've said as much yourself, Mrs Field, he's a bad 'un, that's what you said.'

'He's that,' agreed the housekeeper. She appeared to Rose to have regained a little of her composure. Her eyes were still moist and the hand that held the handkerchief shook, but the voice that spoke was steady, if resigned. In a tone that was dull and emotionless, and scarcely above a whisper, she said: 'I suppose if anyone deserves to hang, it's him.'

Chapter Seventeen

Inspector Connor realised as soon as he introduced his nephew to his own sergeant, that the two of them wouldn't get on. Or, perhaps to be more precise, that Sergeant Harris would take an instant, and quite irrational, dislike to Sergeant Perkins. For Charlie was a pleasant and affable enough young chap, though his uncle said so himself and probably shouldn't. Sergeant Harris, in comparison, was considerably senior in terms of age, somewhat set in his ways and had an inbred distrust of what he called foreigners, which to all intents and purposes included Londoners. Of course, Inspector Connor sighed to himself, it did not help matters that his nephew did not look the part of a Scotland Yard detective. True, it was a relief that he was not putting on airs and graces which the solid and reliable Sergeant Harris would have despised and taken umbrage at, but nor did he exactly look like what he purported to be. They had been so quick to abandon their breakfast and make for the scene of the crime that Charlie had not delayed in stopping a moment to change his clothes. He had come as he was, dressed for a day in the country. And Sergeant Harris was staring at him now, openly derisive at his choice of outfit, consisting as it did of pullover, tweed jacket and flannels. All Inspector Connor could say to himself was thank goodness he was wearing a tie, even if it was a horrid little knitted affair.

'A Scotland Yard detective, you say?' Sergeant Harris pointedly looked Charlie up and down. 'Well I never? And is this what passes for professional dress in London?'

'Of course not,' laughed Sergeant Perkins. 'My presence here is strictly unofficial, Sergeant, I can assure you. To the best of my knowledge Scotland Yard's not been called in. I'm here on holiday and have merely decided to tag along as you might say. Hope you don't object? I don't want to step on anyone's toes.'

Sergeant Harris grunted but said nothing, a somewhat sour look on his rather ugly face. His jowl was heavy and fleshy and his eyes had a tendency to look downcast and runny even when he was in a jovial mood. His appearance reminded Sergeant Perkins rather aptly of a bloodhound, and the young man was obliged to turn away slightly to hide his grin.

They were standing in the drive of Crossing Manor. Sergeant Harris, efficient and dedicated to his job in his own way, had arrived at the house a little earlier than the others and had set to carrying out the preliminary inquiries that the errant Constable Jones had so neglected. On hearing the car, he had appeared at the door and come hurrying down the drive to greet his superior. Sergeant Perkin's emergence from the car had taken him aback, as had Inspector Connor's introduction of the young man as his nephew.

The poor chap's jealous, chuckled Sergeant Perkins. It's bad enough to find out I'm his inspector's kin, but to discover I'm a Scotland Yard detective as well. That just about takes the biscuit as far as he's concerned.

Sergeant Harris led them into the house, very purposefully walking beside the inspector and leaving Sergeant Perkins to dawdle behind. This provided the young man with an opportunity to look around him and take in the grandeur of the house, made all the more surprising and impressive by its uninspiring exterior, which had fully prepared him to expect the worst. But it was soon apparent that whatever the outside of the house might be lacking, it was more than made up for by the interior. For this included rich and ornate furnishings of Venetian brocade and heavy velvets, and a great oak staircase which reared up from the entrance hall. At the top of the stairs was a balcony encasing the landing, on the walls of which an impressive collection of old portraits hung and seemed, from their size and elevated position, to bear down on the visitors like sentinels. For a moment he thought one of the old faces had actually moved. It was of course just his imagination, or a trick of the light. Yet, he fancied he'd caught a quick glimpse of something retreating back into the shadows. As he progressed further into the house, he caught exciting peeks into the rooms that led off the entrance hall. Some had walls of highly polished wood panelling, others housed grand fireplaces of veined marble. Sergeant Perkins soaked up the atmosphere which wealth had made possible, something new and fine and opulent drawing his attention with every tilt of his head, so that he found himself mesmerised by the experience and a little over-awed. He therefore listened with only half an ear to what Sergeant Harris was saying, particularly as the conversation was directed very obviously to his uncle rather than to himself.

'I've had a look at the corpse and had a word with the butler. He's of the old school type, knows his duty and wants to protect the family's reputation, as you might expect in a place like this. He's had a nasty scare all right, but he's not about to lose his head.'

'Good,' said the inspector. 'Let's hope the rest of the staff follow suit.'

'Oh, I doubt that, sir,' replied Sergeant Harris rather smugly. 'T'was a young girl who found the deceased. Not much more than a child, the scullery maid. She's in an awful state. I haven't had a chance to talk to her yet. But I've heard her sobbing fit to burst. There's talk of sending for the doctor to give her a sedative, though I've said we'd like to have a quick word with her first. If all else fails, it seems she's talked to the kitchen maid.'

'All right,' said Inspector Connor. 'Now, have they given us the use of a room? The library? Very good. Come with me both of you. Harris, you can give us the particulars of this case as you see them. And then I'd like to view the body. I suppose we'd also better have a word with the lady of the house.'

'I believe she's still dressing, sir,' said Sergeant Harris.

'Good. It was really only out of courtesy. I'd rather interview the servants first. We'll start with that respectable butler of yours.' The inspector made his way towards the library. 'But before we do anything, you'll need to tell us what you know about this business, Harris.' He hovered for a moment at the entrance to the room. 'I say, any chance of a cup of tea? My breakfast was rather rushed this morning, to say the least.'

As soon as the library door shut behind the policemen, Rose emerged from her hiding place. She had been loitering on the landing, on the pretext of holding a bit of lace up to the light to see if it required mending, standing a little way from the balcony, keen to catch a glimpse of the inspector as soon as he arrived. For she had been unable to get the thought out of her head that she would know as soon as she laid eyes upon him, by his general demeanour and build, whether he was the sort of man who'd be agreeable to the proposal that her true identity remain a secret from the servants. It was illogical, she knew, and, to make matters worse, her first glimpse of the man had not been promising, for he bore a striking resemblance to Inspector Bramwell, a policeman who had harboured an aversion to any type of amateur detective.

Rose had recognised the young man in country dress as someone she knew, though at first she could not place him. It was only when he lifted his head to stare up at the old portraits that she had known him to be Sergeant Perkins. The realisation had taken her quite by surprise, for hadn't Lavinia laughed at the idea that Scotland Yard would be brought in to investigate the death of a domestic? Her astonishment had the effect of dulling her senses and preventing her from reacting immediately. For while she could hope for no better advocate of her detective abilities than Sergeant Perkins, to have him acknowledge her and call out her name in the open environment of the entrance hall was the last thing that she desired. It was true that Mason appeared to be elsewhere and there was no sign of the footman or a maid lingering covertly in the shadows to overhear any exclamation of recognition, but who knew who might be situated out of sight behind a half closed door or concealed on the servants' staircase?

After what seemed like quite a few moments, her wits had returned, and she had taken a step or two backwards into the shadows until she was all but hidden from view. Though Sergeant Perkins had visibly started, which might indicate he was aware of a presence above, she was tolerably confident that he had not recognised her. Certainly he had not called out to her, nor drawn her presence to the attention of the other policemen.

Rose stole down the great staircase as quickly and quietly as she could. The rich pile of the carpet under her feet contrasted sharply with the old wooden boards covered in deteriorated linoleum that she had become accustomed to in this house. It was also the first opportunity she had had to study the grand hall, her duties since her arrival at Crossing Manor having been confined to the servants' quarters and Lavinia's bedroom. She did not, however, pause for a moment to take in her fine surroundings. For there was an urgency about her task. Curiosity could not be allowed to hinder her steps. While she had been hovering in the darkness with bated breath lest her identity be revealed, she had made up her mind what to do. She would go straight to the library and make herself known to the policemen.

Resolute and determined in her purpose, she had just reached the penultimate stair, when the library door opened and someone came out. It was Mason. He wore an agitated look, which turned to surprise when he saw her perched guiltily on the stair. He took a step back, drew himself up to his full height and gave her a hard, penetrating stare. Rose shrank from such a look. She did not doubt for a minute that she looked mortified. She had been caught in the act and her cheeks flushed crimson.

'Miss Denning, what are you doing using the main staircase?'

'I … I was getting a book from the library, Mr Mason. Her ladyship thought she had left her book on the table.'

'I am afraid that is quite out of the question. The police are now in possession of the library and are not to be disturbed under any circumstances.' He permitted a frown to crease his brow and a tut-tutting sound to emit from his throat. 'Servants are required to use the back stairs at all times, Miss Denning. I know you are relatively new to service, but really!' He proceeded to adopt something of a schoolmaster manner, as if he were addressing a wayward child. 'The main staircase is for the sole use of the family and their guests. Except of course when it is being cleaned by the housemaids. But they are careful not to be seen by the family and to spend as little time upon it as possible.'

'Yes, Mr Mason.' Rose lowered her eyes and hoped she appeared suitably contrite.

'Have you seen Albert?' asked the butler, changing the subject and looking about him. 'I thought he'd be here in the hall. The policemen require refreshments –'

'I'll go and tell the kitchen,' said Rose, eager to redeem herself in the butler's eyes and divert any suspicion that he might have concerning her purpose for being on the stairs.

She made her way to the servants' quarters by way of the back stairs, and waited while Edna boiled the kettle. The kitchen maid was regarding her with a mixture of curiosity and apprehension, but the kitchen appeared to be the new haven of the displaced servants and Rose had no opportunity to speak to her in private. All the time she stood there waiting, Rose's mind was racing. It had not occurred to her before how stifling and confining the rules of staff etiquette would be. While remaining in the guise of a servant, she must be seen to adhere to them. Had she been Rose Simpson and not Daisy Denning, then she would have been quite at liberty to venture into the library without being challenged. Certainly she would not have been rebuked by Mason and scolded for using the wrong stairs. Now, however, it appeared that accomplishing her mission was going to prove quite a feat.

She must have daydreamed for she was brought to by the chink of china as the cups and saucers were arranged on the tray. The teapot, with its boiling water, was added, as was a milk jug and sugar bowl. Edna, she noticed, was looking about her for a convenient footman or parlour maid to take in the tray. Before the girl had a chance to hail anyone, Rose grabbed the tray from her.

'Ssh! I'll take it in.'

'Mr Mason won't like that,' whispered the kitchen maid, a worried look on her face. 'It's a footman's duty or a parlour maid's. He'll be ever so cross. He likes things to be done proper, does our Mr Mason.'

'Well, that is just too bad,' muttered Rose. 'If questioned, I'll say I couldn't find Albert. He's always sneaking outside to smoke. You see, I need an excuse to get into the library. I must speak to the policemen, Edna, tell them who I am.'

Rose had spoken so softly that her voice was barely audible, even to her listener. Even so, she looked around quickly, anxious in case their exchange had been overheard. To her relief, everyone seemed too engrossed in their own tasks or conversations to pay her much heed.

Rose staggered up the servants' stairs with the laden tray. Negotiating the steps was more difficult than she had imagined, so confined and dark was the space. At one point she almost slipped. Certainly she could not help some of the tea slopping on to the saucers and the tray. By the time she had emerged in the hall, she was thinking how deft the maids and footman must be. To her relief the hall appeared to be deserted. Quickly she put the tray down on one of the occasional tables that littered the entrance hall and mopped at the spilt tea with her handkerchief as best she could. The result was rather slipshod, but she could not afford to waste any more time. Any moment now, a servant could appear and take the tray from her and the opportunity to appraise Sergeant Perkins of the charade she was participating in would be lost.

She tapped on the library door and stood impatiently before it, holding the tray in front of her. To her dismay, the door was opened by the ever present Mason, who stared at her aghast.

'Albert couldn't be found and I wanted to make myself useful,' she mumbled hurriedly.

She had intended to hold her head up high and catch Sergeant Perkins' eye as soon as she entered the room. Now, however, this was the furthest thing from her mind. With the butler still in the room and eyeing her suspiciously, she must conceal her identity at all costs. She bowed her head and prayed that the old-fashioned spectacles were sufficient to disguise her appearance. Because her head was bent over the tray, her view was obscured, and she could only imagine the reaction to her arrival in the room. In her mind's eye she saw Sergeant Perkins staring at her, mouth open. Any moment now he would surely call out her name.

She scurried over to a table conveniently placed at the other side of the room, as far removed from the policemen as possible. With her back to them, and with trembling hands, she proceeded to pour out the tea, all the time straining her ears to hear the welcome sound of the door opening and closing behind the butler. It was quite possible of course that he might choose to remain until she had finished her task so that they could go out of the room together. It would provide him with another opportunity to scold her. She only hoped that he had better, and more pressing, things to do with his time.

As if in answer to her prayers, she heard the door open and close softly. She stole a glance around the room. The butler had gone. The only inhabitants now were herself and the three policemen.

'Ah, tea, just what we need,' Inspector Connor was saying. 'Just leave it there please, and we will help ourselves. No need for you to wait on us –'

The inspector broke off from what he was saying. For a most astonishing spectacle was playing out before him. The maid, having abandoned the tea things, had leapt across the room in the least decorous of fashions, drawn a chair up to the desk and dropped herself into it with a heartfelt sigh. Before any of them could utter a word, she had discarded her spectacles, which she had then thrown carelessly on to the desk. The bowed head had looked up, but he found that it was not at him she was staring or addressing her attention. For some reason, his nephew had caught her interest and, by the look of him, she his.

'Oh, Sergeant Perkins,' said the maid. 'Thank goodness. You don't know how difficult it has been to get here. But I've managed it at last.' She smiled sweetly at his vague, bewildered face. 'You do recognise me, don't you?'

Chapter Eighteen

For a moment, no one said a word. It was so quiet in the library that the ticking of the clock on the mantelpiece was the only sound in the room, loud and intrusive. Rose sat there impatiently, and for the first time a little nervously, waiting for the spell to be broken and for Sergeant Perkins to acknowledge her in his usual amicable way. She imagined that it would be a matter of only a few seconds before his face erupted into its characteristic grin, or an excited exclamation of recognition leapt from his lips. However, the young man remained oddly silent, as he peered at her closely and the time ticked by. She felt awkward and self-conscious, and disinclined to make an announcement of her own, though the prolonged silence seemed to necessitate it. The other two policemen showed various degrees of confusion and astonishment at her initial outburst, which was hardly surprising, a young woman in maid's uniform tumbling into the room and assuming a degree of intimacy with one of its inhabitants. After a minute, this display of emotions was joined by something akin to a sneer on Sergeant Harris's jowly face, as if he found the whole situation highly amusing. Particularly so, because it appeared to be to the detriment of Sergeant Perkins. Conversely, Inspector Connor's complexion became red and angry, his manner indignant, as if he himself were embarrassed by a faux pas. His jaw had dropped as he had witnessed Rose's rather unorthodox behaviour. Now, having recovered a little from his initial surprise, it was obvious, even to the most casual observer, that he wished to get matters back on to an even keel. The interruption had been highly irregular and he had found it displeasing. He would not permit it to cast a lasting shadow over his investigation.

'Charlie, do you know this young woman?' he demanded sharply.

For all his talk about referring to each other by police rank, the surprise seemed to have taken the wind out of his sails. Sergeant Perkins was once again his young nephew, the very same boy whom had so often in his childhood been up to mischief.

'Er … yes, Uncle, I think I do.' Even so, Sergeant Perkins sounded rather uncertain, as if it was only an impression he had, rather than a certainty he felt.

'Got something of a record, have you, miss?' enquired Sergeant Harris. 'Enjoyed some time in prison, I daresay?'

'Certainly not!' retorted Rose.

It was not lost on her that the older sergeant was apparently rather enjoying the discomfort of the other two policemen. Rose found that this, coupled with his assumption that she must have a criminal record, adversely coloured her view of him. She did not delude herself that he would regard her more favourably once she made known her true identity. If anything, she rather thought he might think worse of her.

'Look here, Miss ... em ...' began the inspector, pausing to look down at the list of names on the table in front of him.

'Denning,' volunteered Rose. 'Though, of course, that's not my real name.'

'It's like that, is it, miss?' This was from Sergeant Harris, who stared at her smugly.

'No,' said Rose firmly. She might have been tempted to say more, certainly to give the sergeant a withering stare, if the other sergeant had not chosen that very moment to awaken from his stupor and become animated.

'Oh, I say!' Enlightenment finally dawned on Sergeant Perkins. 'Is that really you, Miss Simpson? Surely not?' All the while he had been looking at her keenly, as if he feared his eyes were playing tricks on him. Now he thumped the table with the palm of his hand and laughed. 'I must say, you had me fooled.'

'I don't blame you at all for not knowing me when I first came into the room.' Rose smiled at him. 'I can hardly recognise myself when I look in the mirror.'

'Sergeant Perkins, will you kindly explain how you know this young lady,' said Inspector Connor. His humour had not improved during the pleasant exchange between his nephew and the maid. If anything, he had become more irritated.

'Perhaps she's your young lady?' began Sergeant Harris, clearly enjoying the situation.

'No,' said Sergeant Perkins blushing furiously. 'I know Miss Simpson in an official capacity. She is by way of being a private detective and –'

'Huh!' snorted Sergeant Harris loudly.

The noise, a vocal emission of disgust, seemed to rumble around the room and linger there. That he held that particular occupation in very low esteem was beyond doubt. Indeed, he was regarding Rose even now in a most objectionable way, much in the manner as if she were something unpleasant that had got stuck to the bottom of his shoe, and which he was trying desperately to scrape off. Her dislike of the man intensified, not least because she felt he was trying to do Sergeant Perkins down in the inspector's eyes.

'A private detective?' began Inspector Connor, gulping hard and looking considerably displeased by the revelation.

'No,' said Rose firmly. 'Really, I am no such thing. At best something of an amateur sleuth. You see, it's not my occupation. I don't get paid a penny for it.'

'I see,' said the inspector, though the expression on his face suggested otherwise. Rather than try to fathom out what the girl meant, it was apparent that he had decided instead to clutch at the facts. 'Answer me this, young lady, if you please. Are you, or are you not, lady's maid to Lady Lavinia Sedgwick?'

'Yes … no. That's to say that I am pretending to be Lavinia's lady's maid –'

'That's no way to refer to your mistress,' said Inspector Connor curtly.

He spoke more brusquely than he had intended. It was an opportunity for him to assert his authority on a situation that all the while he felt was running away from him. Lost in a mire of confusion, he grasped at anything that he could take a hold of.

'I don't see why,' replied Rose rather primly. 'Lavinia is by way of being a friend of mine. Why, in a few days' time she will become my sister-in-law.'

'Oh?'

This involuntary interjection was from Sergeant Harris. His unpleasant face glowed as the others turned to look at him. His colour heightened. It was obvious he was annoyed that he had been unable to stop himself from voicing his interest in developments.

'Yes. Miss Simpson is about to marry the Earl of Belvedere,' answered Sergeant Perkins rather smugly. Now that he had mastered his surprise, he found that he was rather enjoying developments and, in particular, Sergeant Harris' obvious discomfort. 'He's Lady Lavinia's brother, don't you know? I say,' he continued, addressing Rose, 'perhaps I should start practising and refer to you as your ladyship.'

'Yes, doesn't it sound grand?' Rose laughed.

She looked about her, very aware that the other two policemen did not share their amusement. Now that she had established her identity, it was time to conclude matters as quickly as possible. She had spent too long sitting in the library. Any moment now, the butler might return and there were things she needed to say before she was banished to the servants' quarters.

'I didn't know Scotland Yard had been called in,' she began tentatively. She regarded Sergeant Perkins' attire rather dubiously. It seemed to her that his dress was as much at odds as her own.

'Oh, I'm not here officially,' Sergeant Perkins said hurriedly. 'The inspector here is my uncle. I thought I'd just tag along.'

'Well, I'm very glad you did. It's nice to see a friendly face.'

'Miss Simpson has made quite a name for herself at Scotland Yard, Uncle,' Sergeant Perkins said, addressing the inspector, keen to put things right. 'We hold her in very high esteem there, we do. That's to say, I, myself, Inspector Deacon and even old Inspector Bramwell who has quite a thing against amateur detectives as a rule. Quite a favourite of ours, she is. Why, one or two of the murder cases we've investigated might never have been solved if it had not been for Miss Simpson, least not so quickly anyhow.'

'Is that so?' said Sergeant Harris, sounding very sceptical.

'What's brought you here, Miss Simpson?' asked the inspector wearily. It was obvious that he had had enough of the games and intrigue and had decided to cut to the chase. This young woman was delaying his investigation and he wanted to put a stop to it. 'I assume you didn't know that a murder was going to be committed?'

'No, of course not, Inspector. I was investigating the disappearance of a diamond necklace belonging to Mrs Grayson-Smith.

'Oh, is that so?' The inspector looked faintly interested.

'Any reason, miss, why you had to do that dressed up as a servant?' asked Sergeant Harris. 'I mean to say, what with you becoming a countess any day now, so we're told.'

The look which he gave Rose suggested that he was far from convinced of the truth of Sergeant Perkins' claim regarding her forthcoming elevation in society. Sorely tempted to be outspoken and put him in his place, Rose, after a moment's reflection, considered it more prudent to pretend to be oblivious to his scepticism. She reminded herself that she would require the cooperation of all the policemen, not just Sergeant Perkins, if she wished to keep her identity a secret from the servants. How easy it would be for Sergeant Harris to let her name slip from his lips as if in error.

'Mrs Grayson-Smith was of the opinion that her necklace had been stolen by one of her servants. Having obtained the facts, I am also of that view.'

Rose got up from her seat and began to pace the room. It might well have been assumed by the others that her legs had become stiff due to her sedentary position. The reality, however, was that she was very much afraid that Mason would return to the library at any moment. To find her still there when she had clearly finished pouring the tea was one thing, but to discover her seated and in animated discourse with the policemen was quite another.

'I didn't think the servants would be very forthcoming with their answers if I were to interview them as Rose Simpson,' she continued. 'Mrs Grayson-Smith had already tried and failed, you see, as had the butler and the housekeeper. To disguise myself as a servant seemed the best way to ascertain the truth.'

'Well, you certainly had me fooled.' This was from Sergeant Perkins, who was grinning at her warmly.

'Any luck?' This, a sharp interjection from Sergeant Harris.

'I've made some progress,' said Rose carefully. 'I've narrowed down the possible suspects, one of whom was the deceased.'

'Ah! Now we are getting somewhere,' said the inspector.

Inspector Connor sounded relieved. To the senior policeman, the conversation thus far had seemed to veer off on a strange tangent. Now it was winding its way back to the matter in hand. It was just possible that this young woman before him, decked out as a maid but purporting to be someone rather more grand, might be in possession of some information that would help with his murder investigation, rather than divert his attention away to lesser, trivial matters.

'There has been no mention of a theft of a diamond necklace that I can tell,' said Sergeant Harris rather brusquely, stubbornly holding on to his initial view that Rose was nothing more than a nuisance. 'When did this happen? I am assuming Mrs Grayson-Smith reported the matter to the police?'

'A few days ago. And … no … well, no … she didn't report the theft. She wanted to make the minimum of fuss, you see. I think she thought the necklace might just reappear of its own accord.'

Sergeant Harris raised his eyebrows and gave Rose the most cynical of looks. She knew that she was making the most awful mess of things. It was a simple case of explaining why she was there. But she could not help fluster and falter. Really, the man was most disconcerting. It was as if he were willing her to fail and look ridiculous.

'She wished for discreet enquiries to be made,' Rose said, pulling herself together. 'Before she went to the police, I mean. Why, she hadn't even told her husband of the disappearance of the necklace. She wanted to tread carefully before she went about accusing his servants of theft.'

'Worth a lot, was it, this necklace?' asked Sergeant Harris. He sniffed disparagingly.

'Yes, a small fortune, I believe. Look here,' said Rose, turning her attention to the inspector, 'I may be wrong, but it seems to me that there is a strong possibility that the theft and the murder are connected. Oh, I know,' she put her hand up, as the inspector made to protest, 'that they are two very different crimes. But it does seem rather a coincidence, don't you think, that they should occur within days of each other?'

'Possibly. Possibly not,' said Sergeant Harris.

The large bulk of the man seemed to tower above her, forcing his opinions on the room so strongly that even if the inspector were tempted to believe her, or even give her the benefit of the doubt, then Sergeant Harris' very presence in the room would squash such an inclination. Rose appealed to Sergeant Perkins, standing in the shadows in his inappropriate dress, careful not to overstep the mark, yet eager also to make an impression. Whether or not the two sergeants were aware of it, they were both vying for the inspector's attention, she thought; the nephew in an amiable, pleasant way, Sergeant Harris in an aggressive and offensive manner. She had thought herself to be in luck when she had recognised Sergeant Perkins in the hall. Now she wondered whether her association with him would diminish her standing in the other policemen's eyes. It was clear that the inspector did not wish to appear to his subordinate to be giving his nephew unfair favour and Sergeant Harris on principle was inclined to dislike anyone associated with Sergeant Perkins.

Sergeant Perkins stepped forward in response to her silent appeal.

'We will certainly bear it in mind, Miss Simpson. I say, are you suggesting that we may find the necklace hidden among the deceased's possessions?'

'It is possible, though I think it highly unlikely. It's more probable that the murderer has it. It may well be the reason Cooper was murdered, to procure the necklace, I mean.'

'We will instigate a thorough search of all the rooms, beginning with the servants' quarters,' said the inspector. 'Sergeant Perkins, perhaps you could oversee that? Good. Now, Miss Simpson, what are you intending to do?' He eyed her suspiciously. 'Once you have given us a statement, I think it advisable for you to leave Crossing Manor.' He coughed decisively as Rose made to protest. Even the two sergeants looked surprised. 'It is not something I would recommend under normal circumstances. But you cannot remain here in disguise. And once your true identity becomes known … well … I do not think it will be feasible for you to stay here as a guest. I would rather you leave and the servants not know that they have been spied upon. It will make them resentful and uncooperative when we come to interview them.'

No,' said Rose. 'I wish to stay. And I should like to keep up my disguise. Only Lavinia and Mrs Grayson-Smith know who I really am … oh, and Edna of course, but she won't breathe a word.'

'That is quite out of the question,' began Inspector Connor.

'It needn't be,' said Rose. 'Don't you see? I feel responsible. If I hadn't been here investigating the theft of the necklace, this murder may never have happened.'

'Nonsense,' said Sergeant Harris.

'Miss Simpson, I hardly think you should consider yourself to blame – ' began Sergeant Perkins gallantly.

'I cannot possibly leave now,' Rose continued doggedly. 'If nothing else, don't you see what an advantage it could be for you to have me remain here in disguise? I could find things out that you couldn't possibly. Gossip among servants and all that.'

'It would be highly irregular and far too dangerous,' replied the inspector.

'Only if my true identity becomes known. They all believe I'm Lavinia's lady's maid. No one suspects me of being anyone else. Really, I'm quite safe.'

'Miss Simpson is a one for danger, Uncle,' said Sergeant Perkins. 'She won't be told. You should have heard Inspector Deacon on the subject. He talked to her until he was quite blue in the face, he did.' He grinned at Rose. 'You showed him, though, didn't you, miss? I reckon you can look after yourself.'

'Thank you, Sergeant. I think I can.'

'I don't like it,' said Inspector Connor with certain misgivings.

'I will be very careful, Inspector, I promise.'

The inspector had been thinking as much about the unwelcome presence of an amateur detective in their midst as to her safety if she were to persist with her subterfuge. It was enough that he had his nephew there in an unofficial capacity. And look how well Sergeant Harris had taken that! He stole a glance at his subordinate, who was not bothering to hide the glare upon his face. Even so, the inspector's mind started working, an independence and strength of character coming to the fore that until that moment had seemed lacking. He was not a man to be dictated to by an underling, not even one as belligerent as Sergeant Harris.

He reminded himself also that his nephew was there at his invitation. It was also true that it was unlikely that he could deter the girl from following her chosen course of action now that she had put her mind to it. She was a stubborn one, he could see that. Of course, he could denounce her in front of the staff, though caution forbade him to do so. If what Charlie said was correct, and he had no reason to suspect otherwise, indeed the girl had corroborated his claim, she was on the verge of marrying into the British aristocracy. In which case his own superiors would wish him to tread carefully. There was no use being heavy-handed for the sake of it. Besides, there might be certain advantages in having an accomplice in the servants' hall. He had a strange feeling about this case. He had only been in the house a little time, but the servants would close ranks, he felt sure of it. They would prefer that some things stay hidden …

'Righto, that settles it,' said Rose cheerfully.

Even to her own ears, it was a rather ludicrous statement to make. Matters had very clearly not been concluded, yet she tore from the room before the inspector, deep in thought, could say anything to the contrary.

As she hurried to the safety of the kitchen through the green baize door and down the servants' staircase, the sound of her footsteps echoing loudly on the wood, she was very aware that the situation was not as she had envisaged. In her mind's eye, as soon as she had spotted Sergeant Perkins in the hall, she had imagined her presence would be welcomed, if not with outstretched arms, at least tolerated. She had fully intended to sit down and tell the policemen all she knew. In particular, Mason's theory about the keys. It would add support to her argument to remain in disguise. Now, however, she realised that to do so would jeopardise her position. Two of the policemen were not particularly agreeable to her involvement in the case, indeed, one of them was openly hostile. She must give them no cause to dismiss her proposal. It was far better to leave the library before the inspector had the opportunity to voice his opposition. She thought it unlikely that he had been swayed by her argument. Indeed, had he not said as much? He was uneasy about her subterfuge. But until Inspector Connor forbade her outright she would remain here in her servant disguise. She would stay in the shadows, watchful and alert, waiting for the murderer to make an error or reveal himself in the mistaken belief that she was of little threat or consequence.

Chapter Nineteen

The library door closed behind the retreating figure of Rose Simpson, and a moment or two of silence followed as the three policemen took a minute to collect their thoughts. Sergeant Harris, the least affected of the three by the unexpected turn of events, was the first to recover his faculties and articulate his feelings.

'Well, I'll be blowed! An amateur detective. Just what we need in a case like this to unsettle things and make everything more complicated than it need be. And a good friend of yours, too, Sergeant Perkins, so it seems.' The older sergeant gave the younger one a far from pleasant look. 'And you'd have us believe you didn't know the young lady would be here?'

'Of course I didn't,' retorted Sergeant Perkins, though he could feel his cheeks growing crimson in spite of himself. The situation was not helped by the way his uncle was also regarding him somewhat suspiciously, as if he thought there was some truth in his sergeant's accusation. Ignoring Sergeant Harris' contemptuous stare, he addressed the conversation to his kin.

'I tell you, Uncle, I had no idea that Miss Simpson would be here. It's true I knew she was an acquaintance of Lady Lavinia Sedgwick, but it never occurred to me she would be here in this house, and certainly not in disguise.' He paused a moment before continuing, as if he were thinking over his words carefully before uttering them. 'I will admit I was rather keen to lay eyes on Lady Lavinia. You see, I've heard one or two things about her from Inspector Deacon and Sergeant Lane which made me rather interested to meet her in the flesh, so to speak.'

'What things?' demanded Inspector Connor rather brusquely.

In reply, Sergeant Perkins might have said that neither gentleman had given her a particularly glowing reference, which had only made her appear a more fascinating and intriguing character in the young man's eyes. To further whet his curiosity, it could be argued, particularly by those who did not like her, that Lady Lavinia had been indirectly responsible for a death that had occurred at Renard's dress shop. This had been due to her last minute decision not to model at a fashion exhibition held there. Sergeant Perkins decided, on reflection, to say none of this, even though it had greatly influenced his decision to accompany his uncle on the case in hand.

Perhaps his uncle did not expect him to elaborate, for he did not press his nephew when it became apparent that he was disinclined to go into details. An awkward silence returned to the room. Partly to escape it, Sergeant Perkins turned his thoughts instead to Rose Simpson, a woman for whom he had the greatest of respect. He had an unsettling feeling in the pit of his stomach that he had somehow let her down. She had been relieved to see him, there was no doubt about it for it had shown in her expression. Her face had lit up at the not unreasonable thought that he would fight her cause, as he had once done with Inspector Deacon. Yet in this present situation, where he was little more than an observer, he had felt unsure of his position. Matters had been made worse by Sergeant Harris' open hostility. He did not wish to be accused of encroaching on matters that were not his concern. Much as he wished the situation were to the contrary, it was painfully obvious that his uncle was now rather regretting his rash decision to invite his nephew to participate in the case.

Certainly it placed the inspector in something of a personal dilemma, for the man was torn between his feelings of loyalty towards both his subordinate and his nephew. Sergeant Perkins sighed inwardly. He wondered if Rose would have fared better if he had not been there to influence Sergeant Harris' first impressions of her. Certainly both policemen were likely to have heard her out rather than turning against her as Sergeant Harris had done immediately he had become aware of their association. Sergeant Perkins did not know whether matters had been made worse or better by Rose bolting from the room the way she had. For one thing, she had not waited for the matter to be satisfactorily resolved. Instead it hung languishing and inconclusive in the air. For, while the inspector had not actually condoned or endorsed her behaviour of subterfuge, nor her expressed intention to conduct her own investigation, neither had he forbidden her outright to proceed along such lines.

In the end, if only to clear the air and move the investigation forward, Sergeant Perkins had decided to follow Rose's example and seek a temporary stay of execution by appealing to his uncle's good nature. He had no wish to reopen the argument, nor to be perceived by his uncle as rattling swords with Sergeant Harris. That said, he had no intention of giving way, or providing his adversary with the belief that he had won the argument. Instead, he sought a middle ground.

'A decision doesn't need to be made this very minute, Uncle,' Sergeant Perkins said quickly, before the other sergeant had an opportunity to expand further on why Rose should not be permitted to continue on her chosen path. 'We will be speaking to Miss Simpson again during the course of our interviews with the staff. Why not wait until then to decide what to do? Miss Simpson will have the opportunity to tell us what she has discovered –'

'If anything,' interjected Sergeant Harris with a sneer.

'Yes, if anything,' agreed Sergeant Perkins, quietly confident that Rose would have found out quite a bit by then and thus proved her worth. But would she divulge everything she had uncovered? A nagging little voice at the back of his mind suggested she might not, particularly if the ears that listened were not particularly receptive.

Inspector Connor looked from his nephew to his sergeant, mulling over the proposition put before him. He felt himself to be in an uncomfortable position, which was particularly vexing as some of it, at least, was of his own making. There was no getting around the fact that he did not like his nephew's suggestion. To have this stray girl conducting her own investigation and putting herself into goodness knew what danger was something he was inclined to put a stop to immediately. If truth be told, his views on the matter echoed his own sergeant's. He was sorely tempted to demand that the girl leave Crossing Manor at once for her own safety. But there was something holding him back from that course of action. Quite simply, he resented the smug look on his subordinate's face. The way the man regarded Charlie riled him. Quite justifiably, the inspector took some pride in the young man's achievements; he had followed in his uncle's footsteps in terms of profession and was working for Scotland Yard, no less. The inspector could not just sit there and watch his nephew be mocked and ridiculed. Besides, Charlie had provided him with a temporary way out of the immediate dilemma, a way of placating his sergeant while also supporting his nephew. With some reservations, he chose to seize it.

'Very good,' said Inspector Connor, resuming charge with a thump on the desk. 'We'll see what Miss Simpson has to say for herself when we interview her later. I'm not promising anything, mind, Charlie. Now,' he pushed back his chair and rose to his feet, 'I think we've wasted enough time on all this, don't you? We've a body to see. Lead the way, Sergeant Harris, there's a good man.'

'You haven't been pouring tea out all this time?' demanded Mrs Field, her small currant eyes bright with righteous indignation, her whole body bristling. From the way the housekeeper had pounced on the girl as soon as Rose had entered the kitchen, it was clear she had been awaiting her arrival with a degree of impatience. 'Whatever can Edna have been thinking giving you the tea tray to take up to the policemen?'

She turned to glare at the kitchen maid, who shrank back from her and hastily immersed herself in some kitchen task or other, her face flushed.

'It's not Edna's fault. I offered to take up the tray,' replied Rose rather coolly. She had no wish for the kitchen maid to be reprimanded for her own actions. 'Albert was nowhere to be found and the maids were in a state of shock. If you remember, Mr Mason had only just informed them that Miss Cooper had not died of natural causes.'

'Even so, it wasn't your job to do. Mr Mason was ever so put out when he opened the library door and saw you standing there with the tray. It's not how things are done here at Crossing.'

'Surely allowances must be made at a time like this, Mrs Field?' cried Rose, the effects of the pent up frustration she had felt following her conversation with the policemen suddenly welling up inside her, seeking a suitable outlet. 'Miss Cooper has been murdered after all!'

'Ssh!' The housekeeper looked about her apprehensively, as if she were afraid that their conversation was being overheard. Though as it happened they had generated little interest among the other servants, who were too occupied with their duties or own conversations to give much heed to what they said.

'There's no need for caution now, Mrs Field. Everyone knows,' said Rose rather brusquely. 'Miss Cooper has been murdered and there's no use pretending she hasn't been.'

In her annoyance, she had raised her voice rather unnecessarily, the effect of which to make Mrs Field wince. Rose found the housekeeper's rigid determination that the general routine of the house be maintained at all costs, and her manner of pretending nothing had happened, strangely irritating, though it occurred to her that the other maids might find such an approach comforting in a time of confusion and distress. On reflection, she found herself softening slightly in spite of herself, for it occurred to her that perhaps it was only for the sake of the staff that the housekeeper was so insistent on adopting such a stance.

'You don't need to go on so,' said the housekeeper in a thin voice. 'Things are quite bad enough without you making a song and dance. It's times like these, Miss Denning, that things need to be done properly. I daresay you're too young to remember much about the war. Things were allowed to slip, and now look at us. We are nothing without standards. They need to be upheld.'

'Blow your standards and rules,' Rose said dismissively.

The words, foremost in her thoughts, had sprung from her mouth before she could stop them. She had felt a certain sympathy for the woman's feelings, the longing to preserve what had been before. Yet it would not do for her to consider the housekeeper's sensitivities unduly. She could not let herself become too sentimental. They could not pretend that the murder had not happened, that a lifeless body did not at this very moment languish in the servants' hall ...

'It's not for you to say that,' retorted the housekeeper quietly. Her face was ashen and she looked quite taken aback at such impertinence.

Rose felt a well of desperation and helplessness engulf her. Her head throbbed and she wanted, more than anything, to escape the confines of the servants' quarters; to go outside into the gardens and feel the fresh air on her face.

'I don't answer to you or to Mr Mason,' she said rather weakly. 'You are not my mistress.'

'That's true enough, Miss Denning. But while you are a servant staying in this house ...' began Mrs Field.

The housekeeper, however, faltered, as if she did not know what else to say or as if she found it too much of an effort to keep up the pretence. Certainly she seemed to flag, groping around for a chair and lowering her ample bottom on to its battered seat. Rose's melancholy mood appeared to have affected her. For the moment at least, she was speechless. It was this, coupled with the crestfallen expression on her face, that brought Rose sharply to her senses. She had no wish to make an enemy of the housekeeper, and besides, the woman was a sight of abject misery; shock mingled with fear coloured her movements and brought dark shadows to reside under her eyes. For the first time, Rose saw the world as Mrs Field perceived it. The ordered realm that the older woman had so carefully built up about her, and to which she had devoted much of her life, was showing significant cracks. Worse than that, it was threatening to come tumbling down about her ears.

'I'm sorry,' Rose said gently, stretching out her hand instinctively towards the older woman. 'I didn't mean to be unkind. I'm afraid I can be rather thoughtless. You've every right to feel the way you do. It must have been an awful shock. Edna fetched you to see the body, didn't she? When the murder was first discovered, I mean?'

'Yes, she did.' Mrs Field's voice was a dull whisper. 'And such a sight I never wish to see again. I didn't want to believe it. These young girls have such strange fancies. I kept hoping that she was mistaken, that we'd find Miss Cooper snoring gently in the chair.' She wrung her hands together. 'Oh, I wanted so much for it to be just a bad dream that the silly girl had had. Pearl is a one for them, you see.'

'I suppose you knew her well? Miss Cooper, I mean.'

'No, not really. She has … had only been here a few months,' sighed the housekeeper. 'She was engaged not long after the master married the mistress. The first Mrs Grayson-Smith's maid had found another position, you see.' She bent forward to whisper in Rose's ear. 'It sounds awful to say it, but I can't say I took to her. Kept herself to herself for the most part, she did. She didn't like it here, Miss Cooper didn't. Didn't think her mistress was grand enough. She kept telling Mr Mason and me how she was used to waiting on socialites and wives of ambassadors, not women who shut themselves away at home and had no visitors. A waste of her talents, so Miss Cooper was wont to say. I've an idea she was looking for another position.'

'Oh?'

'Just from the little things she said. That she wouldn't be here long. That sort of thing.' She paused a moment as she reflected. 'Well, she got her wish, didn't she? Only she will be leaving this house in a box, not to attend some great lady.' Mrs Field turned anxious eyes on Rose. Unshed tears threatened to spill. She put out a small plump arm and snatched in a desperate fashion at the girl's fingers in an attempt to draw her closer so that she might whisper in her ear. 'I'm frightened, Miss Denning. You see, I'm desperately afraid that things won't go back to the way they were.'

Rose was prevented from the necessity of responding by the sharp ringing of one of the servant bells. Mrs Field, roused from her contemplations, looked up and consulted the bell board.

'The Sovereign Room. That will be for you, Miss Denning. You'd better go. Don't keep that mistress of yours waiting.'

It was with some relief that Rose left the kitchen. Inwardly, however, she cursed Lavinia for summoning her. It was true that she had desired an excuse to escape Mrs Field's despondent brooding which, coupled with the recent unexpected hostility she had received from the policemen, did little to inspire her to instigate her own investigation into the death. A sense of duty, however, made her determined to embark on her enquiries. To this end, she had in mind to speak to Pearl or Edna to establish the facts concerning the discovery of the body. To return to Lavinia, therefore, felt like taking a backwards step.

It was consequently with little enthusiasm that she once again mounted the servants' staircase, scarcely hurrying up the flights of stairs. To emerge into the splendour of the main house, however, was as always something of a shock. Gone were the dismal and depressing greys and browns, the old and chipped wooden stairs, the faded and broken linoleum. All this was left behind and with it there came about a lightening of her mood so that her pace quickened and she almost ran down the landing, eager to enter the golden room with its plush surroundings. Lavinia would be there to greet her and for those few precious moments she would be able to discard her disguise and the pretence of being someone else, much as she would claw off those awful spectacles and throw them on to the bed.

Before she could feel herself fully assimilated with her surroundings, however, the door to Lavinia's bedroom opened. She had scarcely had a chance to knock on it before she found herself pulled inside by the room's occupant, the door closed firmly behind her.

'Is this really necessary, Lavinia?' said Rose indignantly, detaching herself from her friend's grip. 'I know you like ringing for me and all, but I've only just finished talking to the policemen. I wanted to speak to Pearl before –'

'Oh, do shush!' said Lavinia.

Her eyes were bright and there was a radiance about her complexion, which seemed wholly inappropriate given the gravity of the occasion. She appeared to Rose like an excited child, keen to impart some illicit information.

'You're not the only one who has been investigating, Rose. I have something awfully exciting to tell you.'

'Blackmail?' exclaimed Rose. 'Are you quite sure?'

'Well, it was you who put the idea into my mind,' retorted Lavinia. 'You thought Millicent might have something to hide because of the odd thing she said. You know, about the police assuming she'd killed her lady's maid.'

'Well, it seemed such a very strange thing for her to say. It was as if the words escaped from her mouth before she could think what she was saying. And certainly she appeared to regret what she had said. It did make me wonder …'

'As it did me,' said Lavinia, clapping her hands together in an excited fashion. 'As soon as you'd gone, I told her she should tell me everything, that it would be much better if we knew the very worst.'

'I'd say! And so she told you?' said Rose, finding it hard not to sound surprised.

'Yes, as a matter of fact she did,' said Lavinia. 'After all, she regards me as a friend. It was only natural that she should want to tell me all about it. She's been keeping it bottled up inside her all this time. I'm surprised she didn't burst.'

'So Cooper was blackmailing her,' said Rose to herself. 'And what a strange thing to blackmail her over. I suppose Cooper saw an opportunity and took it. I say, it does reek a bit of clutching at straws, doesn't it? I mean, trying to find something, however far-fetched, to blackmail her over?''

'If Millicent had anything about her, she would have stood her ground and weathered the storm,' said Lavinia, making a face. 'But you know what she's like, timid as anything and frightened to death of putting a foot wrong. I'd say she was pretty easy prey.'

'And this all started last night?'

'Yes, I've told you. Cooper didn't actually use the word blackmail or threaten Millcent as such. I daresay she was too clever for that. She just hinted and implied, if that makes any sense? Anyway she left poor old Millicent in very little doubt that it would be in her best interests to comply with her wishes.'

'And it provided Mrs Grayson-Smith with a very good motive for wishing her dead.'

'Oh, you can't possibly think Millicent had anything to do with this Cooper woman's murder?' exclaimed Lavinia. 'Really, Rose I think the woman would have difficulty swatting a fly, don't you? Hardly murderess material, I would have said.'

'I daresay you are right,' conceded Rose, sitting on the bed. 'Though who knows what a desperate person might do?' She stared at her friend suspiciously. 'I do hope you advised her to tell the police about the blackmail. They will have to be told and it will be much better if it comes from her own lips.'

'Well, of course I did no such thing. What a very stupid idea, Rose.' Lavinia gave her an incredulous look. 'I'm surprised at you, I am really. As you yourself have just said it gives Millicent a perfectly good motive for the murder. I told the poor girl to say nothing at all about it to the police.'

'You didn't!'

'Well, of course I did. Do you want to see her arrested?'

'Lavinia, she must tell them.' Rose leapt up from the bed and took her friend by the shoulders, and shook her gently. 'Lavinia, listen to me. She must tell them before someone else does. It will come out in the end, it always does. Don't you see? It will look bad for her if it's thought she tried to conceal it.'

'I don't see why it should come out,' replied Lavinia rather sulkily. 'I jolly well won't tell them and I hope you shan't either. You're just making things worse for poor Milly. Can't you see that? She feels bad enough thinking ill of the woman and wishing her gone, without having to endure the embarrassment of telling the police about the blackmail. Think of it from her point of view. Can you imagine anything more awful?'

'Yes, I can. Being arrested for murder, for one thing. No,' said Rose hurriedly, as Lavinia made to protest, 'hear me out. Even if we all decide to say nothing, it is bound to come out.'

'I don't see why –' reiterated Lavinia.

'Because there was another party to it. That's to say, someone else who knew what had happened and might be tempted to use that knowledge for their own means. I'm not saying that they knew about the blackmail, but they would know Cooper had in her possession information that could be used for such a purpose.'

'You mean –'

'Yes,' said Rose firmly. 'Millicent is in a dangerous position. You must encourage her to tell the police about the blackmail before anyone else does.'

Chapter Twenty

The three policemen made their way through the green baize door and down the staff staircase, towards the servants' hall. As they walked, they passed servants in various degrees of occupation, and heard snatches of conversations, undertaken in hushed tones. The effect of their sudden appearance in a territory that was not their own, and to which they were very obvious strangers and interlopers, was not lost on the policemen. It quelled speech and dispersed the staff so completely as to give the impression of fleeing shadows. Without its decoration of staff, the passage became dull and dowdy, only accentuating the changed environment from that of the splendid library to the sombre colours and sparse furniture of the servants' quarters. The change of setting had a corresponding effect on the mood of each policeman. They had commenced their journey by mulling over one or two particulars of the case and giving voice to such contemplations. Now, however, they were rendered silent as almost unconsciously they took in the drab surroundings, a foretaste to what was awaiting them in the servants' hall. For it seemed to all of them fitting, somehow, that a person should be murdered in such a climate, far from the ornate backdrop of the main house.

There was a young, uniformed constable stationed at the door to the murder scene. Until he had spotted the policemen, he had looked rather lost in his own thoughts. Now he saluted them perfunctorily on their arrival. With a sense of occasion, he slowly unlocked the door and the inspector and sergeants entered the room to commence their examination.

'The fingerprint fellows have done their stuff,' began Sergeant Harris. 'The police surgeon's seen the body. Wants it moved to the mortuary, only he knew you'd want to see it first, in situ, so to speak.'

'Quite right,' muttered the inspector, though he was only half listening, being more interested in looking about him.

He glanced quickly around the hall, taking in the large, scrubbed wooden table, which appeared the dominant feature of the room. Drawn up to it was rather an ill-assortment of hard backed chairs, in various stages of repair, which looked oddly abandoned, as if each were awaiting its respective occupant. A handful of battered and faded armchairs, far inferior to those that graced the housekeeper's sitting room, offering only shabby comfort and sagging seats, were clustered around the fireplace. The windows, recessed, and located high up in the walls, gave the room the feeling of something akin to a large, communal prison cell. The men shivered, coming as they did from the light of the library with its large French windows, which commanded an impressive view of the gardens beyond.

'Can't say I'd enjoy working in this sort of a place myself,' commented Sergeant Harris, his expression grim. 'You'd feel like you were buried alive. The wife's niece is a scullery maid in a grand house like this one. Hardly sees daylight, poor girl.'

The inspector coughed in an irritated fashion, keen to get down to the business in hand. With this in mind, he strolled purposefully over to the assembly of armchairs, the majority of which had their backs to the door, so that it took him a moment or two to establish which was occupied by the corpse.

The deceased was propped up in a high-backed armchair, her head slumped a little to one side on the head rest, giving the illusion of someone sleeping. It was only the deathly stillness of the body, the lack of a gentle breathing rhythm or the soft sound of snoring that showed this to be a lie. A step or two closer and the matter was left in no doubt. A great, gaping wound revealed itself on the drooped head. The sight was not a pretty one and the inspector had to steel himself not to take a step or two back in disgust. Sergeant Harris did not appear to share his superior's feelings of repulsion, for he leapt forward to point out the various particulars of the injury.

Sergeant Perkins, though wishing to have sight of the deceased to satisfy his natural policeman's curiosity, held back a little, keen not to be perceived as overstepping the mark in a case in which he was not officially involved. He did not know whether it was out of respect for the deceased, or a desire that the details of the death be kept from him, but whatever the reason Sergeant Harris appeared to keep his voice purposefully low. The consequence of which was that only the odd word floated into the young sergeant's hearing. It was only by concentrating hard that he obtained the general gist of what was being said. He gathered that Miss Cooper was unlikely to have known anything of the blow that killed her, having her back to the murderer as she had done, and that death would have been instantaneous. He supposed it was a blessing. If one were destined to be murdered, it was best to die quickly and in ignorance of the fact. However, it did mean that Miss Cooper had been provided with no opportunity to defend herself, no chance to see off her assailant and save her life.

'Do we know the murder weapon?' inquired Inspector Connor, withdrawing from the body with a sense of relief. 'One might suppose a poker. It would be convenient, being only a few feet away.'

'But it would be hard to get the right angle,' said Sergeant Harris. 'Hard to get a good swing too with the deceased sitting as she was in the chair.'

He paused a moment to give a practical demonstration and then uttered a noise which sounded surprisingly like a chuckle. Given the situation, the inspector looked appalled.

'Oh, I don't mean to offend you, sir,' said his sergeant quickly. 'But it's a rum go. The murder weapon, we've found it, so we have. It was left on that great table over there, as bold as brass. And you'll never guess what it was, sir, not in a month of Sundays.'

'Get on with it, man,' grumbled the inspector. 'There's no need to make a meal of it. What is this weapon that you are making such a song and dance over?'

'A copper saucepan, sir, of the ordinary sort.'

'A copper saucepan?' exclaimed Sergeant Perkins before he could stop himself. Sergeant Harris gave him a look of satisfaction.

'Indeed, Sergeant. Bet you didn't think of that? A copper saucepan that was left for all to see out on that table there. It had blood on it and hair from the deceased.'

'What about fingerprints? Did our chaps find any?' asked the inspector with a degree of both urgency and optimism.

'They did not, sir.' For the first time Sergeant Harris lowered his eyes in regret. 'The handle had been wiped clean. The murderer had enough presence of mind to do that, even if they did leave the saucepan on the table in full view.'

'What was it doing here in the first place?' demanded the inspector. 'Shouldn't it have been in the kitchen or the scullery? Are we saying that our murderer went out into another room to get the saucepan? Certainly sounds like a premeditated crime to me.'

'No, sir,' said Sergeant Harris. 'It was here on the table all the time. It was probably the closest weapon to hand. The servants had a custom, you see, a routine you might say. A saucepan of soup was brought into this room at the end of the evening. They all used to help themselves to a cup, them that had to stay up late, that is. The lady's maid would probably have had a cup after she had helped undress her mistress for the night, the butler after he'd done his final rounds, the –'

'Thank you, Sergeant, I think I get the idea. What you are saying is that they all knew it was here and that the murder might have been a spur of the moment thing. Our murderer wants to do our young lady in, sees the saucepan lying on the table and picks it up. I take it, it was empty?' he added as an afterthought looking at Sergeant Harris, who nodded.

'Yes, sir, they only had a dribble of soup each, so the butler told us. Just enough to keep them going. Tide them over to breakfast like. A long day some of them had.'

'Yes,' muttered Inspector Connor, as if to himself. 'Else there would have been soup slopped all over the place. And a copper saucepan would have been an easy enough weapon to wield. If you got a good grip on the handle, that is. You could have come straight up to the chair like this and … hello, what's this? One of those women's magazines, if I'm not mistaken. Our lady here was probably reading it, proper engrossed in it, she probably was. Least my wife is when she's reading one of these things. Have to shout to get her attention, so I do. So, our Miss Cooper here is reading her magazine. Our murderer creeps up behind her –'

'Or perhaps she knows the murderer is in the room but is not afraid of him,' suggested Sergeant Perkins, thinking it was about time he made a contribution. 'We're thinking that the murderer was one of the servants, after all. It would be quite natural for him to be here in this room.'

'Well, there would have been that of course,' conceded Inspector Connor rather gruffly. He resented the interruption when he was in full flow, as he called it. 'Either way, there would have been nothing to stop our murderer pausing while he took careful aim. The first blow would have stunned the deceased, the second or third would have killed her. All a matter of a few seconds' work, I'd have said, certainly less than a minute.'

'And that's not all,' said Sergeant Perkins, suddenly finding himself keen to exert his expertise as a Scotland Yard detective. 'It wouldn't have taken much force. The murderer would have had the opportunity to take careful aim as you've said and the saucepan would have been an easy enough thing to wield, particularly as our murderer would have been able to come right up behind the victim without being observed.'

'Yes, yes, we've said all that, Sergeant,' said Sergeant Harris, looking at the young man with a degree of irritation. 'Unless of course you've something else to add? I'm sure we'd love to hear your pearls of wisdom.'

'Yes, we would,' said Inspector Connor firmly, resenting his sergeant's tone when addressing his nephew. 'Out with it, Charlie.'

'It is only that it occurred to me that it would have been just as easy for a woman to have done the deed as a man, that's all,' said Sergeant Perkins. 'Why, there's no saying that the little scullery maid that found her couldn't have done her in.'

'Well, I suppose that's possible,' admitted the inspector rather grudgingly. He exchanged a look with his sergeant, who nodded reluctantly. 'It seems a very vicious act for a woman to do. The attack, it looks almost frenzied, doesn't it? I suppose a girl might have done it, if she were angry enough, whipped up into a fury and all.'

'It doesn't seem very likely, sir,' said Sergeant Harris. 'Tiny little mite the scullery maid is, and the kitchen maid not much better. Hardly anything to them, all skin and bones.'

'You will admit, however, that it is possible a woman might have done this crime?' said Sergeant Perkins somewhat impatiently, moving out of the shadows to stand next to the corpse.

As always, he saw in the inert body indications and suggestions of what the person might have been like in life. She had been young and pretty, he could tell that even with only one side of her head fully intact. The fact made the deed seem more awful somehow, as if destroying beauty rather than plainness was a horrendous act in itself. Of course it was irrational, all life being sacred. But he felt himself moved as he contemplated the waste of a bright, young life. He thought there were indications about the face that she had been an intelligent woman; the high, smooth brow, the clear dark eyes, blank and glazed now, but which in life would have been bright and animated. He thought he detected also a haughtiness about her. It was difficult to tell with her head slumped over on one side as it was, but he imagined that she had carried herself well. In different clothes she might well have been mistaken for a lady, rather than a servant. Now, however, the black dress was strangely appropriate and fitting for the occasion. It reminded him of widow's weeds. Inwardly, he uttered a sigh of relief. They had Rose, he must remember that. She would tell them what this woman had been like in life, whether she had been despised or well-liked, whether anyone would miss her now that she was gone.

The three policemen traipsed out of the room quietly and thoughtfully. They barely acknowledged the constable on the door, a clear vision of the deceased still occupying the better part of their minds, obliterating all else, so that they were hardly aware of his presence. Each felt that he would retain the image of the dead woman, that it would linger in his head as they interviewed each witness and suspect, a woman with a gaping wound, cut down in her prime. Even as they made their way back to the library, they wondered who could have done such a thing. More than likely, it had been a fellow servant, someone who had sat beside her at meal times, had laughed and cried with her, had shared a joke and endured the same miserable existence below stairs. It didn't seem possible, but they would find out in the end who was responsible; they would see that justice was done.

Rose hurried down the hateful, mean little staircases and associated passages back to the servants' territory. Once again she reflected how easy it would be to miss one's footing on the steps and come tumbling down. The atmosphere appeared to her to have become more oppressive, as if the staircases and passages were bearing down on her like evergreens in a forest, dark and brooding, shutting out the light. Certainly it was as if the very house appeared to begrudge the space the servants' quarters occupied, as if the area behind the green baize door had been torn unwillingly from the main house by force. As a consequence, the servants' living conditions had been made as cramped as possible, forcing a large number of staff into a relatively small space. Rose thought back to the spacious dimensions of the library, a room which she imagined was often left empty and unoccupied for days on end.

She sighed and tried to rid herself of her indignation, forcing herself to consider the matter in hand. She supposed that it was just possible that the policemen were still viewing the body. While she experienced a natural revulsion at the idea of undertaking such a task herself, she admitted it was not without merit. She had gleaned very little from Edna as to the cause of death or the weapon used. Understandably, the girl had still been in shock and consequently Rose had not pressed her on the matter. Now, however, it was imperative that she find out as much as she could. At any moment, she felt, the policemen were likely to decide to banish her from the house or, at the very least, reveal her identity to all, making any attempt to carry out her own investigation nigh on impossible.

Rose allowed her mind to drift back to her recent conversation with Lavinia. She wondered if she had impressed upon the girl sufficiently the importance of Millicent Grayson-Smith advising the police herself that she was being blackmailed by the deceased. Knowing her friend as she did, it was the sort of thing Lavinia might dismiss as soon as Rose had walked out of the door, certain that she knew best. Rose had been sorely tempted to go and knock on Millicent's door and speak to the woman herself. Only her desire to speak to Edna and Pearl as soon as possible had prevented her from doing just that. She could not be in two places at once. She must leave Millicent to act as she thought best and as her own conscience dictated. It was difficult to tell if there was wisdom or intelligence behind those frightened eyes. What little she had seen of the woman did not inspire confidence. Perhaps, though, Millicent suffered only from nerves and an inferiority complex, and faced with officialdom would do her duty and disclose all.

Rose sighed and quickened her pace. It did not do to dwell on the matter any further. She must focus on what was important. Without a doubt, that was to commence her own investigation before the way forward was barred to her and she was all but turned out on her ear. She was a woman of considerable substance but with little hope of obtaining the cooperation of the servants in the event her identity became common knowledge. They would consider themselves to be of a different class. On the surface they might treat her with deference, while underneath they would simmer with resentment and anger, quite rightly considering themselves having been cruelly tricked and deceived.

The constable stood in front of the closed door to the servants' hall, looking bored and preoccupied with his own thoughts. His presence brought Rose up sharp so that she found herself lingering idly in the passage unsure whether or not to continue on her journey. However, the matter was resolved for her before she was forced to make a decision, for the door suddenly opened from the inside bringing both herself and the young constable to attention. Quickly she retreated to stand further down the passage, where she was partially hidden in the shadows, a nondescript servant who would incur little interest.

'I suppose we should speak to the girl who found her,' Inspector Connor was saying to his sergeant as he emerged into the passage.

Sergeant Perkins, Rose noticed, was following a little behind in their wake, much as if he were their collective shadow. She was inclined to try and get his attention, but thought better of it.

'Poor little mite, frightened half to death, she is,' muttered Sergeant Harris. 'Scarce more than a child. Reminds me of the wife's niece.'

'Awful thing to happen to the girl,' agreed the inspector, with sympathy. 'But we'll have to talk to her sooner or later all the same. Though perhaps we'll give her a little longer to compose herself.'

'I wouldn't mind speaking to the butler first,' said Sergeant Harris. 'Get the lie of the land and all that. He seems a sensible sort of a fellow from what little I have seen of him, honest too.'

'Not forgetting Mrs Grayson-Smith,' said Inspector Connor. 'We'd better see her for form's sake as soon as we've interviewed the butler. Not that I expect she can tell us much. Still, I expect she was one of the last to see the deceased alive. She'll be able to tell us what time she dismissed the woman for the night, if nothing else.'

Rose, lurking in the passage, could not believe her luck. She waited until the policemen had disappeared up the staircase before she made her way to the scullery. Pearl was not there. Neither was she in the kitchen where the cook huffed and puffed over the stove.

'Where's Pearl?' Rose whispered urgently to Edna.

It appeared that she had not spoken quietly enough, or perhaps the cook possessed particularly good hearing, for it was that woman who answered. She had turned away from the stove and was standing heavy and squat, facing Rose. She wiped her hands on her apron in a brisk fashion before resting them on her hips so that she resembled something of a teapot with two handles.

'I've sent her to her room, not that it's any business of yours, I might add. Agnes is with her now. The poor girl couldn't be left alone, could she? Not after what she's been through. And I couldn't spare Edna here, much as I'd have liked to. As I said to Mrs Field, when she was all for making a fuss, there's still meals to be made whether or not anyone feels like eating. And likely as not them upstairs won't notice if a room's not been swept, or a desk polished. But they'll need food to keep up their strength at a time like this, even the mistress, who eats scarce more than a bird at the best of times. It's a pity the master isn't here. He has a healthy appetite, he has, and he's always encouraging the mistress to eat a little more.'

Having had her say, the cook returned her attention to the stove and barked one or two orders to Edna, who threw Rose a furtive glance. An apology of sorts was written in the expression on her face. Rose, feeling herself to have been suitably dismissed by the cook, turned tail and returned to the staircase, where she made her way slowly up the endless stairs to the attics above. It was something of an unseen blow that Edna had remained in the kitchen while Agnes had been sent in her stead to nursemaid Pearl. She wondered how the two girls would take her sudden and rather unexpected appearance in the little attic room. Her presence was unlikely to be welcomed and certainly would be considered a little strange, particularly as she was only a visiting servant. That she would be intruding on some private grief, she felt sure, and it left rather a nasty taste in her mouth. But it could not be helped, she told herself. The best thing that she could do for them all was to find out who had killed Velda Cooper. Until they knew that, the servants' hall would forever be in the possession of a troubled soul, and behind the twists and turns of the darkened staircases, enclosed and shut off from the passages as they were, a threatening menace might lurk still in the shadows ready to strike. Fear would linger in the air, much like stale tobacco, until it seeped its way into the very wood itself so that it became as much a part of the fixtures and fittings as the battered stairs and the cracked and broken linoleum.

Chapter Twenty-one

Rose had not been precisely sure which was Pearl and Edna's room. She had envisaged being obliged to look in at the open door of each room that she passed, or to open the doors that were closed until she found the right one. In practice, however, this proved unnecessary, for she heard the soft murmur of voices as soon as she had reached the attics and had proceeded down the passage.

Each sound that her feet made on the bare wooden floor seemed to echo and vibrate about the place in an alarming fashion. There was an eerie silence about the rooms as she passed them. Due to the sparseness of furniture and lack of decoration they appeared unoccupied and abandoned; only one or two had personal touches which made them appear a little lived in. Pearl and Edna's room, she discovered, was one of the latter, for rudimentary attempts had been made to make the room appear homely. In dimensions it was only a little larger than the one which had been allocated to Rose, and shared the same dull sage green painted walls. However, the drab colour had been relieved somewhat by the addition of one or two illustrations torn from the pages of magazines, which had been affixed to the walls by the means of soap. A small bunch of flowers, now rather wilted, resided in a crude earthenware vase on the top of the chest-of-drawers and a bright crocheted blanket was folded neatly at the end of one of the small, single beds, which added a splash of much needed colour.

On the other bed a quilt of the patchwork variety was draped around the shoulders of a girl she took to be Pearl. The girl herself sat crouched on the bed, her knees drawn up to her chin, and her arms hugging them to her for all she was worth. Beside her, in the only chair that the room possessed, sat Agnes, looking on in a disconcerted fashion, a cup of warm milk clutched in her hands. It was apparent from her actions that Agnes was trying to persuade Pearl to drink the milk and equally obvious that the girl was oblivious to her efforts, despite Agnes's soft words of encouragement.

Rose hovered awkwardly in the corridor, a few feet from the open door. She felt she was intruding, trespassing on a scene that was not meant for her eyes. The two girls had been too preoccupied to be aware of her approach, so now she looked on helplessly, unsure how to proceed. She wondered whether she should cough or clear her throat, or give any other unobtrusive sign that would announce her presence. But, as it happened, she was obliged to do neither. Perhaps Rose cast a shadow on the wall, or perhaps Agnes heard her breathing, for suddenly, as if on a whim, she looked around, her face showing signs of panic.

Agnes leapt to her feet, almost spilling the cup of milk in her haste. Even little Pearl was persuaded to look up from her pursuit of staring at her bed, her arms still clasped about her knees.

'Miss Denning,' began Agnes, 'I … oh, you did frighten me –'

'Forgive me, I didn't mean to startle you,' Rose said quickly. 'Please, do sit down. Cook told me you were here. I thought I might be of some help. I have a little experience in this sort of thing. Dealing with shock, I mean. And Lady Lavinia doesn't require me at present. So you see, I'm rather at a loose end …'

'Very kind of you, I'm sure,' muttered Agnes, though her voice sounded anything but grateful and she glanced nervously back at Pearl as if she feared that the girl might make some sort of protest. Certainly Pearl, her eyes large and puffy from crying, looked a little scared. She bit her lip anxiously.

'Here, you'd better have my seat,' said Agnes, looking at Rose with barely concealed hostility, and beckoning rather reluctantly to her recently vacated chair.

'Not at all,' said Rose, 'you have it. I'll perch myself here on the end of the bed.'

She edged herself down on to the little wrought iron bed, slightly nervous lest Pearl should recoil from her, viewing the move as an imposition. When she looked up, however, much to her surprise, she found that Pearl was looking at her keenly, all traces of fear having disappeared from her face. Instead the girl appeared to be eyeing her curiously. Agnes, it seemed, still harboured some reservations. Gone was the careless chatter associated with their first meeting, when the girl had only to concern herself with showing Rose to her room and changing her uniform from the blue cotton twill dress of the housemaid to the black alpaca dress of the parlour maid. In its place was a quiet, sullen girl, who gave her the odd suspicious stare.

'I'm glad you're here,' said Pearl, smiling shyly. 'Edna said you were ever so nice.'

Agnes looked from one to the other of them, shrugged her shoulders and got up from the chair.

'Will you be all right if I go to the lavatory? Pearl doesn't want to be left alone, but seeing as you're here and she's happy to see you …' Agnes allowed her words to drift off, her eyes still showing some signs of wariness.

'We'll be quite all right, won't we Pearl?' said Rose firmly, taking Agnes's seat before the girl had a chance to change her mind. Inwardly she cheered; she could not believe her luck. 'I'm only glad to be of assistance, do my bit and all that.'

Pearl waited for Agnes to disappear down the corridor before she leaned forward and spoke to Rose in a confiding manner.

'Gone to the lavatory, my eye! She's sneaked out to have a fag. I just hope Mrs Field don't catch her. She's ever so old-fashioned about women smoking. Don't hold with it, she don't.'

Rose ardently hoped that Pearl was correct. If Agnes had crept out into the kitchen courtyard to smoke an illicit cigarette, then she might be afforded a little more time to question Pearl in private than she had initially thought. Certainly every additional second counted; she would do well to make best use of her time.

It was while she was trying to make up her mind how best to proceed without Pearl becoming suspicious as to her uncommon interest in the murder, that the girl in question cut through her thoughts with something of an exploding rocket.

'I'm ever so glad to see you,' she said. 'Edna's told me all about you, you being an amateur sleuth, I mean.'

Rose looked up appalled. For a moment she was lost for words. It had not occurred to her that Edna would not keep her word. That the girl had revealed her true identity so casually and quickly was a cause for concern. Rose wondered who else she had told.

'Oh, you needn't worry,' said Pearl, as if she could read the other's thoughts. 'She's only told me, no one else, and I won't say nothing to no one. And she only told me this morning, in case you're wondering, after I'd found the … Miss Cooper. She wouldn't have said nothing otherwise.

Only, she could see how scared and upset I was, and she said as how she knew someone who could help.'

'I see,' said Rose. While it would certainly make questioning Pearl a great deal easier, it was worrying to know that the number of people aware of her real purpose for being at Crossing Manor was steadily increasing. It was surely only a matter of time before the murderer got wind of the truth. 'Look here, Pearl,' she said urgently, gripping the girl by the arm in such a manner as to make her wince, 'it's very important that you don't tell anyone else why I'm here.' She took a deep breath before continuing, to emphasise the point. 'It could put my life in danger. Do you understand?'

Pearl stared at her with eyes like saucers. Rose felt the girl's arm tremble beneath her fingers and immediately she felt guilty.

'I won't tell a soul,' Pearl whispered. 'Strike me down if I do.'

'Good,' said Rose, releasing her hold on Pearl's arm. 'Now, I should like you to tell me everything. About finding the body, I mean.'

Pearl obligingly proceeded to give an account of the discovery. She was not one for embellishing her narratives, adhering to the facts as far as was possible, though she perhaps gave slightly more emphasis to her feelings of foreboding than she had experienced at the time. Certainly she gave voice to her fears of the shadows and her impression of the presence of ghosts of long dead servants who prevailed over the passages and kitchen in the early hours, when the rest of the house was still.

'At first I thought she was just asleep. Miss Cooper, I mean.'

'Oh?'

'Of course, miss,' said Pearl, 'I didn't know it was her at first.' She paused a moment, as if conjuring up again the awful image before her. 'You see I could only see the back of her head.'

'So it could have been anyone?'

'I suppose it could have been. Though I realised it was her as soon as I went up to the body. The black hair, it was ever so thick, good hair. But … oh, it was awful,' Pearl covered her face with her hand. 'I could tell it was smeared with something, something that was sticky. I don't know why I did it, but I put out my hand to touch it, the sticky patch, that is. I knew she was dead and I still did it, stretched out my hand and touched the … the blood.' She held out the offending hand in front of her, almost as if she thought it had a will of its own and might still be stained red.

'What did you do then?'

'She came and got me,' said Edna who, unobserved by either of them, had appeared at the door. Rose resolved to listen out more carefully for Agnes's return. 'Mrs Field is giving Agnes ever such a talking to,' continued the kitchen maid. 'She caught her smoking in the yard. She was crouched behind one of the bedsheets. Mrs Field says it will have to be washed again 'cause it smells of smoke.'

'What nonsense. The fresh air will get rid of that,' said Pearl, making a face. Her posture had relaxed, however, and a smile had lit up her face. The effect was to make her pretty in a waif-like fashion. It was abundantly clear to Rose that Pearl was keen to return her thoughts to the more innocuous and routine matters of the house.

'Anyway, I thought I'd take my chance and see how you were doing. Cook got caught up in the argument, you see. She as good as told Mrs Field to leave Agnes alone and let her smoke, so she won't miss me for a while.'

'I know this is hard, Pearl,' said Rose, keen to return the girl's thoughts to the murder and to continue with her interview. 'But you're doing ever so well. Tell me, you didn't stop to look at the body or search for the weapon?'

'No. I just ran up here as fast as I could and woke Edna.' She gave a small, frightened smile. 'I'm surprised that I didn't wake the whole house, I made that much noise.'

'She could hardly speak, poor thing,' said the kitchen maid, sitting down beside her friend and putting an arm around her shoulders. 'Shaking and crying, she was. It took an age to find out what was wrong, and then I thought she'd only had a bad dream.'

'Yes, you told me this morning,' said Rose rather brusquely, keen to progress the interview lest the admonished housemaid return. 'Edna, you went down and viewed the body, didn't you? Before you went and got Mrs Field, that is? Is there anything you didn't tell me about this morning? Anything additional that you can remember, no matter how small? It may be important, you see.'

'No … I don't think so. Oh, miss, I can't quite remember what I told you.' Edna put a hand to her head and screwed up her eyes in concentration. 'I was in such a state, so I was. I could hardly think straight. I really thought Pearl had had a bad dream, I did really. She has them every so often, you see. I never thought there had been a murder and in the servants' hall of all places. It was ever such a shock seeing the body there. It gave me an awful fright, it did.'

'If you can remember anything –'

'I don't know … oh, wait, I think I can.' Edna's eyes became large and expressive, her mouth forming the shape of an orange. Her brow was no longer furrowed and a light had lit up her eyes so that her whole being appeared animated. 'There is something. I didn't tell you about what was used to kill her, did I, miss?'

'Ah!' exclaimed Pearl, who looked on the verge of fresh tears. Certainly she shivered and her bottom lip trembled. With half fumbling fingers she pulled the quilt tighter around herself.

'Sorry, Pearl, I didn't mean to upset you,' said Edna, touching the girl's arm affectionately, 'but that's the sort of thing you want to know, isn't it, miss?'

'It is indeed, Edna,' said Rose. 'It's just the sort of thing I want to know.'

'Well, you'd never guess, miss.' Edna bent forward, her face lowered. 'It was the copper saucepan.'

'Not the one that held the soup?' Rose made a face.

'None other,' said Edna triumphantly, a gleam in her eye.

'Are you quite sure?' asked Rose.

She had availed herself of some of the soup from that very receptacle the previous evening. She felt a tightening in her throat and an inclination to retch which she fought stoutly. It would not do to succumb to a feeling of nausea. In front of the two young girls before her she must appear strong and above such things.

'Yes. It was the saucepan all right,' said Edna, grinning in spite of herself. 'It was on the table. The shine from the copper caught the light and drew my attention to it. And then I saw the smear of blood.' She shivered. 'It was horrible.'

'I'm sure it was,' said Rose rallying. 'Do you remember anything else? Something unexpected or which struck you as odd, for instance?'

'Well, now that you mention it, there was something,' said Edna. 'It didn't strike me at the time, but now that I think about it, it was a little strange.'

'Oh? And what was that?'

162

'Miss Cooper had on her black dress, as you'd expect. The one with the lace at the neck. Honiton lace, she always said it was, but Pearl and me, we never believed her.'

'But you said there was something odd?' pressed Rose.

All the while she had been listening for footsteps, and now her ears had detected them dim and faint at the other end of the corridor. Perhaps Edna had heard them too because she turned towards the open door and looked into the passage furtively.

'She was wearing her coat,' said Edna, scarcely above a whisper. 'It wasn't done up, which was how I could still see the dress, but she was wearing it all right.'

Before Rose had a chance to react to such news, the footsteps had quickened and become louder. In a moment, Agnes was in the doorway, holding on to the doorframe. She was in something of a dishevelled state. Some of her hair had come down from her bun so that it poked out untidily beneath her maid's cap. It was her eyes, however, that drew their attention. They were red and puffy and her lip trembled. To some extent she resembled Pearl. But she had not been the one to find the murdered woman, Rose reminded herself. And Agnes had merely been admonished by the housekeeper for smoking and spoiling the washing. It was something which was probably a regular occurrence. Hadn't Pearl said as much? Why then had it produced such a dramatic response from the girl? As she looked on, it occurred to Rose that the girl had been crying about something else entirely.

Chapter Twenty-two

'Well now, it's Mason, isn't it?' Inspector Connor, his voice somewhat gruff, appraised the man standing before him.

The old type of servant, he would have said, the sort that was hard to get these days. They weren't made the same way they were before, not since the war. For a moment he was almost tempted to chuckle, for his brief, instinctive summing up had little to do with his own thoughts. Instead, it had been based on the observations of his old maiden aunt. The very words she would have uttered had come to his mind almost as if she had been there to utter them herself. So instilled in him was her assessment and views of servants that he found it difficult to view them objectively. With a concerted effort, he tried to rid his thoughts of all but his own perceptions.

That Mason was the same man who had attended on them following their arrival at Crossing Manor hardly registered with the inspector, for then the butler had been no more to him than a servant in a house that was evidently full of them. It had nothing to do with Mason's station in life, or the class from which he came. Had he been a member of the landed gentry, he would have been of little more interest to the policeman. It was only now that the butler was both a witness and a potential suspect in his investigation that he was worthy of note in the inspector's eye. He had been elevated to a level of importance in the policeman's mind that he had not held before. Putting his maiden aunt and her distinctive views firmly from his mind, Inspector Connor set to evaluating the man thoroughly, making no pretence at doing otherwise.

It was difficult to determine whether Mason, his face impressively impassive under such scrutiny, would have been relieved to know that he had made a favourable impression. In the inspector's own words, he had 'passed muster,' based purely on the man's ability to stand upright and adopt a manner that was at once deferential without being annoyingly subservient. Of course, the inspector thought, it was a pity about the man's chest. Pigeon chested, they called it, if he wasn't mistaken, the breastbone protruding forward as it did in an almost comic fashion. He resisted the temptation to smile, even as the thought came to him suddenly that the butler looked as if he were wearing a corset, so severe was his deformity. Such an uncharitable observation was swiftly followed on its heels by one of pity, for the inspector was of a sympathetic disposition by nature.

'Yes, sir.' Straight backed, despite the offending chest, Mason stood with his head held firmly aloft, his figure tall and lean, his expression attentive, without being inquisitive.

'Been butler here long?' enquired the inspector. It seemed fitting to him to adopt a chatty manner, to tempt the man to deviate from his natural propensity for being reserved.

'Twenty-nine years, sir, almost to the day.'

'Indeed? Well, I never. I daresay there's not much you don't know about this place?'

'No sir.'

'I suppose a house this size requires a great deal of management?' There was the faintest inclination of the butler's head. 'To make sure everything runs properly and efficiently and all that?' persisted the inspector.

'Yes, sir.' The two words were said blandly and without sentiment. It occurred to the inspector that the man must spend his days uttering them.

'Have to ensure there are no bad eggs and all that to spoil the broth?'

This was met with silence and a fixed, glazed expression appeared on the butler's face. The inspector tried again, deciding that the best course of action was to be more direct.

'A man in your position needs to keep an eye on things. Needs to make sure everyone is pulling their weight, no one sneaking out for a cigarette when their services are required, that sort of thing.'

The inspector spoke in such a tone of voice as to imply that what he was saying was a given fact rather than a question.

'I pride myself in thinking that not much occurs at Crossing Manor without my knowledge.' Mason permitted himself to incline his head very slightly, and for a smile to hover for the briefest moment across his distinguished face.

'Would that include murder?' Sergeant Harris interjected sharply before the inspector could follow the same line of questioning at a more leisurely pace. His superior inwardly cursed the man for his impatience. The butler had showed signs of thawing. Now he would close up again, with the shutters put back in place. As if in adherence to the inspector's prediction, the butler paled slightly, but he did not falter. No word of horror escaped his lips. Instead, he said politely, but firmly: 'No, sir.'

'You pride yourself on knowing your staff well though?' persisted Sergeant Harris, not to be outdone. 'I wager you know which one would be more likely than another to do a young woman to death?'

He was met with an icy silence. A moment or two elapsed before Mason deigned to give a reply. Pointedly looking the sergeant in the eye, he said: 'I cannot believe that anyone here at Crossing Manor is capable of such an act, certainly no one among the staff.'

'Oh? Are you suggesting that we should look further afield? Among the family, perhaps, or the guests?' Sergeant Harris' manner was impertinent. Inspector Connor looked away, somewhat embarrassed by what he perceived to be his subordinate's unnecessarily aggressive stance. The butler, however, remained silent, looking fixedly ahead of him as if he were focused on something in the middle distance.

'You see our problem though, Mason, don't you?' said Sergeant Perkins gently, entering the conversation for the first time. 'The murder occurred in the servants' hall and by your own admission the outside doors and the doors from the servants' quarters to the main house were locked. I understand you told Sergeant Harris that when he arrived?' The butler nodded. 'Well then, it stands to reason that the deceased must have been killed by a servant. You do see that, don't you? There is no other explanation.'

He looked at the man kindly. Unlike Sergeant Harris, he was of a sufficiently sensitive disposition that he could sense the servant's distress. What they were telling him, the man knew already.

'I say, I suppose there's no chance you could have overlooked fastening one of the doors or windows?' Sergeant Perkins felt compelled to ask. 'One of the shutters to the window in the scullery, perhaps?'

'No, sir, all were locked and barred. I'm very particular, I am, when doing my rounds. I try every door and window in turn after I've closed and locked them, just to make sure that they're fast.'

'Is it usual to lock the doors into the main house?' asked the inspector, a little sharply. 'What would happen if there were to be a fire?'

The butler swallowed hard, but said nothing. It was obvious, even to the most casual observer that he was trying to concoct a suitable reply.

'Ah, if I were a betting man I'd say you only started doing that since the theft of the necklace,' said Sergeant Harris. He was watching the butler closely and smiled when he perceived his remark had had an impact.

'The theft of the –?' Mason did not finish his sentence and a note of something akin to both surprise and fear revealed itself in the butler's voice. That he had been taken greatly unawares by the suggestion was obvious.

Sergeant Perkins, watching on, fumed inwardly at the callous disregard shown by his fellow sergeant. By revealing their hand so early on in the investigation, they were risking Rose's exposure. The matter of the theft should not have been raised, at least not until after they had interviewed Millicent Grayson-Smith. It would have appeared quite natural to all for the mistress of the house to refer to the disappearance of her diamond necklace during the course of her interview. However, for Sergeant Harris to have mentioned it now before anyone had been interviewed and no report of the theft had been made to the police …

Looking across at his uncle, it was clear that Inspector Connor was of the same opinion. He was glancing at the butler nervously, as if he wondered what was going through the man's mind. Even Sergeant Harris looked as if he had realised his mistake. His face had reddened and he appeared unusually interested in studying a particular spot on the floor, as if it provided a very significant clue. At length, he raised his head as if about to speak. However, before he could say anything further, the inspector, arguably not before time, seized the reins and took command of the situation by thumping his fist on the table. For a moment it looked as if his cup and saucer might go flying; certainly the china made a disquieting, rattling sound.

'Look here, Mason. From what you have just told us, it must be as clear to you as it is to us that we are looking for a murderer from within the servants. You're a wise sort of a chap, I can see that, and you have a sense of duty both to the family and to the law. Now,' he paused and raised a hand as the butler made to protest, 'I know this is a rum old business. It's never nice to be forced to accept something which is highly unpalatable. But there it is, I'm afraid. And who other is better placed than yourself to suggest a culprit?'

'I can suggest no one, sir,' said Mason stubbornly. His face was white and, for the first time, his gaze was averted, so that he stared at a spot on the wall a little above the inspector's left shoulder.

He won't look us in the eye, thought Sergeant Perkins. He has some one in mind, all right, but he won't let on.

'Your loyalty to your staff does you credit,' began Inspector Connor. 'But it'll do no good. Trying to protect the guilty party, I mean. It'll all come out in the end; it always does. Now, let's take this fellow Albert Bettering. The chap's got something of a criminal record, I believe, as I'm sure you're aware. I wouldn't have thought it usual myself for a chap like him to be employed in a place like this. Too many temptations for one thing, and I can't see Grayson-Smith accepting it. He's just the sort of man who'd be most particular about his staff, I'd have thought.'

'Just youthful high spirits,' the butler said rather weakly. 'He's a good fellow, Albert is. He has the makings of a fine footman.'

'Is that so?' Sergeant Harris sounded his usual sceptical self.

'Yes,' said Mason firmly, though his face flushed crimson.

'Not a relative of yours by any chance?' suggested Sergeant Harris.

It was a lucky shot, but all three policemen saw at once that it had hit home. Gone was the professional façade. Instead Mason's face seemed to crumble. Certainly there was a marked twitching of the eye, and one hand was clenched, the knuckle showing white.

'He's my sister's son.' He said slowly. His voice was quiet and dull. If they had not seen the outward signs, they would have been forgiven for believing the voice lacked emotion.

'Ah, I thought as much,' said Sergeant Harris, a smug look on his face. 'Grayson-Smith doesn't know about your nephew's criminal past. Vouched for him, did you?'

'He's a good boy,' Mason mumbled, his voice scarce above a whisper, almost as if he were talking to himself. Sergeant Perkins was of the opinion that the man lacked conviction, as if the words that sprang from his lips were not of his own choosing.

There was a strong possibility that the interview would falter and come to an end almost of its own accord, before the routine questions had been quite dealt with. Inspector Connor, keen to resume his original line of questioning which had focused on more mundane matters, cleared his throat and rustled the papers before him to signify a shift in the form of questions to be asked.

'Well, there you have it, sir,' said Sergeant Harris as the door closed behind the retreating form of Mason. 'Clear as day, it is. The butler's nephew did it. The uncle as good as said as much.'

'The butler has his suspicions certainly,' said the inspector more cautiously. 'At the very least he knows it looks bad for the boy. And even if the lad didn't kill the lady's maid, he more than likely stole the necklace.'

'No doubt about that,' agreed his sergeant, 'not when you take into account his record. Been in trouble with the law ever since he was in long trousers.'

'I wonder if Miss Simpson is right,' pondered Sergeant Perkins aloud. 'That there is a connection between the two crimes, I mean.'

'Maybe,' Sergeant Harris grunted somewhat reluctantly. 'Though our Miss Simpson's just using it as an excuse to keep on snooping.'

'Right,' said Inspector Connor quickly. The topic of Rose's rather contentious role in the investigation was not one he wished to pursue. He did not want the discussion to disintegrate into an argument. 'Look back through your notes, Harris, there's a good chap, and remind us what the butler had to say for himself. If you remember, I missed some of the interview because I had to take that telephone call from the Chief Constable. I'm not saying I missed anything of importance, but I can't be too sure. No need to go through all of it, mind. I know the bare bones of it. Mason did his rounds as usual. Left everything locked and barred and shipshape, according to his account, and we've no reason as yet to doubt it.'

'If anything, quite the reverse,' said Sergeant Perkins, keen not to be excluded from the conversation. 'It would have been in his interests to be vague. To protect his nephew, I mean.'

Sergeant Harris raised his eyebrows, as if to suggest that the interruption was unwelcome, or even that he was a little bored by it.

'What I'm trying to say,' continued Sergeant Perkins, aware that his uncle's eyes were upon him, 'is that he could just as easily have said that he was not certain. He could have left a margin of doubt, said his attention had been diverted, that type of thing.'

'The man's an honest sort, doesn't like to tell a lie,' said the inspector, 'not if he can help it. You can see that as soon as you set eyes on the man. It doesn't come natural to him, not like it does to some.'

'That nephew of his, for instance?' This contribution was from Sergeant Harris.

'Quite. Now, let's get back to this butler fellow,' said the inspector, keen not to be diverted from his purpose. 'He must have been one of the last persons to have seen Miss Cooper alive.' He began to pace the room in a thoughtful fashion. 'Now, whichever way you look at it, he couldn't retire to bed until the last servant had returned to the servants' quarters, on account of his having to lock the doors to the main house behind them. Five doors in all, there are, one opening out on to the entrance hall and two on either end of each landing, opening out from the servants' staircases.'

'According to his statement, sir,' said Sergeant Harris, flicking through the pages of his notebook until he had found the relevant note, 'the deceased was the last to return last night from doing her duties in the main part of the house. Yes … here we are. The footman, our friend Albert, had brought down the coffee tray from the drawing room and gone outside into the kitchen courtyard for a smoke. The housekeeper didn't hold with smoking in the servants' hall. Thought it encouraged the maids to take up the habit. Averse to it, she was. Sounds like a bit of a martinet, if you ask me. So the fellow had to go out into the cold. Mason waited from him to return and locked the door behind him directly he had come back inside. The butler says his nephew then went straight to bed, though that's not to say he didn't come downstairs again.'

'There would have been nothing to prevent him from doing so?' asked the inspector.

'I don't think I quite understand–'

'The butler didn't lock the doors on the attic landing leading from the servants' bedrooms to the back staircases?' clarified Sergeant Perkins.

'Ah, I see what you mean, sir,' said Sergeant Harris, addressing his reply to his superior, and very pointedly ignoring the young sergeant. 'No, those doors weren't kept locked. The servants could come and go from their bedrooms to the servants' hall and kitchen as they saw fit. It was only the main house they couldn't visit at night.'

'Right, I think that's clear,' said the inspector, pausing in his pacing to make a note of his own. 'What we are saying is that any one of the servants could have come down in the middle of the night and killed the deceased. That reminds me, does the police surgeon have any opinion on the time of death? I know old Collins doesn't like to commit himself until after he's done the post-mortem but even so, he must have some idea.'

'Any time between about midnight and three o'clock in the morning he told me, sir, unofficial like,' said Sergeant Harris. He chuckled. 'He said it ever so grudgingly. He was all for not saying anything and us having to wait for his report.'

The inspector groaned. 'None of the servants are likely to have alibis for that time that can be proved or disproved. All asleep in their beds they would have been. Only our murderer up and about.'

'One or two of them share a room, sir,' said Sergeant Harris.

'Yes, but given the hours they work and the strenuous nature of their employment, I'd bet that each and every one of them is asleep as soon as their heads touch their pillows.'

'I am sure what you say is right, sir,' concurred his sergeant, 'but we might discover one or two of the servants decided to sit up late in the servants' hall reading the day's newspaper, or the scullery maid was kept busy in the scullery scrubbing the pots and pans until all hours.'

'Well, we'll find out soon enough during the course of the interviews. Right, now that we have dealt with young Albert, who, according to the butler, was left to return from the main house?'

'Just Miss Denning … or Miss Simpson, should I say?'

'Stick with Miss Denning. We'd better not refer to her as Miss Simpson, even in private. Walls have ears, particularly in a place like this.' Inspector Connor looked around furtively, as if he expected a servant to be crouching in the shadows.

'Very well' said Sergeant Harris, though the look on his face showed that he clearly thought this an unnecessary precaution. 'Well, Miss Denning, she came down next, after seeing to Lady Lavinia. She poured herself a mug of the soup, though it was only lukewarm, and went straight to bed. I daresay she was tired, her not being used to hard labour.'

'Until recently she worked in a dress shop,' cried Sergeant Perkins, leaping to Rose's defence. 'She is quite used to hard work and working long hours.'

'That's as may be, but it's not the same as a life in service. You ask the wife's niece. Now, where was I? You made me lose my place … ah, here we are. I've got written down here that a few moments later Miss Cooper came down. Ah, now, this is interesting, I'd forgotten about that. The butler said she was in something of an agitated state, whatever that means. 'Couldn't settle', those were the very words he used. She told him she would stop downstairs and have some soup. But when she went to have a look in the saucepan there wasn't any soup left, on account of Miss Simpson having taken the last bit. So she said she'd boil the kettle and make herself a cup of tea instead.'

'Miss Denning, not Miss Simpson,' corrected Sergeant Perkins through gritted teeth.

'Ay, her,' said his fellow sergeant.

'Go on,' said the inspector beginning to become irritated by the sergeants' constant bickering, though he admitted to himself that his own man was mostly to blame.

'The butler was still there in the servants' hall when she returned with her tea. He had half a thought that she'd go straight to her room. Liked to keep herself to herself as a rule, she did. Didn't tend to sit down with the others when she'd finished for the day, though occasionally she drank her coffee in the housekeeper's sitting room. But more often than not she preferred her own company.'

'But last night she decided to stay in the servants' hall? I say, that's interesting,' said Sergeant Perkins. 'Do you think it possible that she had arranged to meet one of the servants there? Now, who else was about? If I remember, the butler did say.'

'Just the housekeeper, Mrs Field. She was in her sitting room doing the household accounts.'

'I suppose it is just possible that someone else might have been lurking unobserved in the passage outside or in one of the other rooms, waiting until the coast was clear? The butler might have been none the wiser, not if they had pretended to go up to bed and then slipped down again when Mason's back was turned,' suggested Sergeant Perkins.

'Well, it is a rabbit warren of rooms down there,' conceded Sergeant Harris. 'Plenty of places to hide if you had a mind to. But according to Mason, there was only him and the housekeeper about, and as soon as Miss Cooper had come into the servants' hall with her cup of tea, he went and bid Mrs Field goodnight, telling her not to stay up too late. Then he retired for the night. His bedroom's off his pantry.'

'Is it indeed?' exclaimed the inspector. 'Well, there's a thing. Rather surprising, don't you think, if that's the case, that he didn't hear anything? No sound of a cry in the night or of the saucepan being wielded?'

'Well, his pantry's at the other end of the passage,' said Sergeant Harris. 'And he says he sleeps very deep. He plugs his ears with bits of cotton wool, you see. It helps him sleep like anything. As soon as his eyes are closed, nothing wakes him until he is brought in his morning cup of tea. Of course this morning he was wakened early by the housekeeper.'

'How very inconsiderate of him, the cotton wool, I mean,' grumbled the inspector, returning to his seat behind the desk. 'Well, I daresay we'll find out soon enough from the housekeeper if any of the servants came down to read their newspapers or whatnot, before she took her leave and retired for the night.' He gathered up his papers. 'Well, there's no use putting it off any longer. We'd better see the mistress of the house next. Likely as not it will be a waste of time and she'll have nothing to tell us. But we'd better get it over with.'

The inspector was not to know, as he sat there shuffling his papers, that before many minutes had elapsed, he would be forced to eat his words.

Chapter Twenty-three

Still pondering Agnes's tear-stained face, Rose made her way back down the corridor, absentmindedly staring through the open doorways to catch glimpses of the attic rooms beyond. Idly she compared the rooms where the occupants had made efforts to personalise them with pictures and their own possessions, as Pearl and Edna had done, with those where the inhabitants had been content to leave them as they were, plain and unadorned; the dull sage green paint dominant on the walls, the uninviting bare floorboards on the floor. Rose was just thinking how different and warm the rooms could be made to look with a little care and attention, and a few homely touches, when a sudden thought occurred to her. This caused her to halt abruptly and for Edna, who was accompanying her and walking a little behind her due to the narrowness of the corridor, to walk straight into her.

'Oh, miss, I'm ever so sorry. I didn't see –'

'It was my fault entirely, Edna. I shouldn't have stopped like that. A thought had just occurred to me, that's all.' She bent her head a little and leaned towards the girl so that she might speak in a low tone. 'Tell me, Edna, do you know which room was Miss Cooper's?'

'That one there, miss. The one with the door closed.' The kitchen maid pointed to a door a little further down the corridor. 'I've never peeked inside, myself. Miss Cooper was one for keeping her door firmly shut, she was. Insisted on doing her own cleaning and dusting too, she did, and making her own bed. Wouldn't let Agnes or Martha do it for her, though it was their job to do it. Not that they minded of course. It meant less work for them.'

'I'm curious as to what the police are doing now,' muttered Rose. 'I wonder if they've searched Miss Cooper's room yet.'

'I don't think they have, miss. They've been too busy talking with Mr Mason. He's in with them now, least he was a few minutes ago. Martha told me when I was trying to make up my mind whether to pop up here. Cook was busy having a go at Mrs Field. And Mr Mason, he was in with the policemen. It made me decide to seize my chance, you see. I didn't think I'd be missed.'

'Well, I think I'll take a leaf out of your book, Edna, and seize my chance now,' said Rose, walking purposefully towards the door of Miss Cooper's attic room. 'Hurry up. You had better come inside with me. I don't want to arouse Agnes's suspicions by you waiting outside for me in the corridor.'

'Oh, miss, do you think we ought to? The police will be ever so cross if they find us there and Miss Cooper ... well, she wouldn't have liked it, us rummaging through her things, I mean.'

'I'm afraid it can't be helped, Edna. And if the police find me ... well, they won't be surprised. But you needn't worry, you won't get in any trouble. I'll take the blame.'

Despite these words of reassurance, the kitchen maid still looked worried.

'Oh, Edna, how very silly of me and selfish too. There's no reason why you need to come in Miss Cooper's room with me at all. Go back downstairs. As a matter of fact, it would be much better if you did, in case you're missed and someone comes looking for you.'

Still the kitchen maid hesitated, biting her lip and moving her weight from one foot to the other. She was a picture of indecision, but Rose could not afford any more time to wait for the girl to make up her mind what to do. With one last passing comment over her shoulder to the effect that if she wished to be of help the girl might keep an eye on the library door and come and warn her should the policemen emerge from that room and begin to prowl, Rose hurried into Miss Cooper's room, shutting the door firmly behind her.

Leaning back against the door, Rose took a moment or two to survey her surroundings. To all intents and purposes, the room was very similar to her own in both dimensions and décor. Like some of the other servants, Miss Cooper had taken steps to make the room her own. In her case, the attempt had been successful, showing both a tasteful eye and an appreciation of fine things. The pictures that adorned the walls were pleasing reproductions of flower paintings, which had been mounted and framed and hung properly; cord and nails had been used in place of wet soap. The cushion, plumped up on the obligatory lone chair, was covered in Italian flame-stitched needlework and, such was its quality, would not have looked out of place in the Grayson-Smiths' drawing room. A figured mohair rug on the floor beside the bed, which Rose was to discover was exceptionally soft to the tread, relieved the bareness of the wooden floorboards. Instead of the usual chest-of-drawers, an old wooden wardrobe of modest dimensions stood in one corner of the room, its door tight shut.

For the first time, Rose was thankful that the servants' rooms were so sparsely furnished. It made the process of undertaking a thorough search a relatively quick affair. With no time to waste, she commenced a methodical examination of the room, starting with the obvious hiding places. The rug was turned back and inspected, the bed stripped of its sheets and blankets, the underside of the mattress examined and the bedframe itself scrutinised. Rose took the pictures from the walls, just falling short of removing the backs to ascertain if anything had been slipped behind the pictures. Though sorely tempted, she felt it would not be possible to do so without leaving evidence of her activities. The pictures returned to the walls, the bed made and the rug put back in position, she turned her attention next to the wardrobe. She felt a shiver of excitement pass through her. Of all the places where something substantial might be hidden, she thought it would be here.

The wardrobe was what could best be described as a gentleman's wardrobe, being small in stature. It was made of polished walnut, scratched in places, and consisted only of a series of open shelves on one side and a pull out central hanging rail. Before she made an investigation of the inside, however, her eyes were drawn to a small, leather suitcase, scuffed and shabby, perched at an untidy angle on top of the wardrobe, as if it had been thrust there hastily. With the aid of the chair, she got it down and put it on the bed. Rose wrestled with the clasp, which appeared faulty, for certainly it was hard to open. It was only when she had succeeded in doing so that she realised the difficulty had arisen due to the presence of an obstruction, a small bit of blue fabric which had got snagged in the fastening. To her disappointment, particularly after all her efforts, Rose found the suitcase to be empty save for some badly folded brown paper, the corner of which was torn, and a length of string. She tossed the offending article aside in disgust.

Next she concentrated on the inside of the wardrobe. It took no more than a few minutes for Rose to examine the shelves, taking out the neatly pressed clothes, shaking them out lest anything be hidden within their folds or seams. Once she had restored them neatly folded to the shelves, she removed the two pairs of shoes from the shoe rack positioned at the bottom of the wardrobe and felt inside the toes. Next she inspected the wardrobe floor itself. Finally, her attention turned to the clothes that hung from the rail. She discovered that as a consequence of the rail being central rather than horizontal, she could see only the nearest garment, the others being stacked behind it out of sight. To make a thorough examination, she would be obliged to take out each garment in turn. She paused a moment before she began this task. It seemed to her that she had been in the attic room a considerable length of time. It could be only the matter of a few minutes before she was disturbed. She threw a quick glance at the door. She could hear no sounds beyond it, no footsteps marching down the corridor, no voices raised. She hoped fervently that Agnes was still busy attending to the scullery maid, the policemen employed elsewhere in other rooms. Despite her earlier show of bravado to Edna, she did not relish being caught in the act of rummaging through the murdered woman's possessions.

The first garment she examined was evidently Miss Cooper's second best lady's maid's uniform. Plain and austere, it hung in the wardrobe like a dark shroud, the blackness relieved only by a small amount of white lace at the neck. She threw the dress on to the bed and proceeded to inspect the other clothes in turn. There was a sombre grey wool tweed suit, a day dress in a brightly coloured print, a tea dress in rayon chiffon. These she scrutinised and discarded, throwing them haphazardly on the bed, caring not that in her haste one or two came off their hangers and slipped on to the floor. She came to what she considered was the last garment, a black wool coat, practical but not stylish. It was sufficiently bulky to fill the space entirely. Eagerly she examined the pockets, but they revealed nothing of interest.

Rose was just about to return the other clothes to the closet, when it occurred to her that the wardrobe went further back than she had first supposed, its depth surprisingly spacious. The coat, therefore, was not at the back of the wardrobe as she had assumed. Considerable space lay beyond it. With trembling fingers, she tore the coat from its hanger and threw it carelessly on to the floor.

The sound of a sharply drawn breath surprised her. She was almost tempted to look behind her; it took a moment to realise that the noise was her own intake of breath. For the sight that greeted her eyes was an evening gown of royal blue silk satin, cut on the bias with a slight cowl neckline and sleeveless except for its ruffled panels of silk satin. It was Millicent's gown, the one she had worn the previous evening, the very same that the lady's maid had furtively put on so that she might stare at her own reflection in the mirror. Rose pulled out the gown to assure herself that it was the same. There was no mistake. And behind it hung other dresses, other evening gowns in taffeta and silk satin and beyond those chiffon day dresses ...

Rose sat down heavily on the bed beside the discarded clothes. She knew that she must gather her thoughts and make sense of them. But for the moment, all she could think was that Millicent must have lied to them. First she had omitted to tell them about the blackmail business and now it appeared she had deliberately misled them, or perhaps she only wished to portray herself in a better light. Whatever the reason, it was apparent that she had not told them the full truth.

It was then that she heard footsteps coming down the corridor. It was a heavy tread; a man's tread. She stood up. There was no time to restore order to the wardrobe. Surrounded by the strewn clothes as she was, she braced herself to face the unpleasant consequences of her actions. She turned to face the door in time to see it open slowly and rather hesitantly. She wondered idly if she had betrayed her presence in the room by making too much noise. Yet, for the last few minutes she had done nothing more than sit quietly on the bed. In those last few seconds, as the door was opened wide, an unpleasant realisation came upon her. The man who entered was not one of the policemen, as she had expected. It was true that he shared Sergeant Perkins' youth. His face, however, was impossibly handsome and there was a nervousness about him that Rose did not associate with any of the policemen.

The man started, as if he'd seen a ghost.

'Miss Denning! What are you doing here?'

'I might well ask you the same question,' said Rose with bluster, though she felt herself inwardly tremble, 'creeping furtively into this room. I've a good mind to tell the policemen. As to why I'm here, I was asked to go through Miss Cooper's possessions,' she lied, 'to see if anything was missing.'

'I don't know how you'd know that,' retorted the young man, relaxing a little. 'You hardly knew the woman. Mrs Field would have been better placed to do that.'

'She's far too busy,' said Rose quickly, eager to change the subject. 'Now, I wonder why you are here?' Her enquiry was met with an ominous silence. She hurried on. 'Shall I make a wild guess?'

The young man stared at her, fear and surprise showing on his face in equal measure. With a deep breath, Rose decided to take the bull by the horns.

'I think you are looking for the diamond necklace, Albert. The one that's missing. Am I right?'

It was not a promising start. Inspector Connor realised that as soon as the door opened and admitted the woman he took to be Mrs Grayson-Smith. He saw at once that she was of the fragile-looking, nervy type that he knew well, having encountered that sort often enough in his career. He groaned inwardly and, catching his sergeant's eye, saw Sergeant Harris do the same. Her kind usually made the worst interviewee. They had to be handled right or else they went to pieces. One awkward question, or a sharp tone of voice, and they dissolved in tears and there was nothing you could do about it, save provide a clean handkerchief, which would be returned to you crumpled, complete with smudges of make-up on it that would never wash out. And you might as well give up there and then with the questioning, because it was no use hoping that after the crying subsided you'd be able to get any sense out of them. Frightened of their own shadows, they were. They gave hesitant answers, doubting their own memory of events so you did too. Others would not utter a word unless it was torn grudgingly from their lips and then it would only be feeble nonsense, or information of the useless kind. Nothing of any substance.

Inspector Connor cleared his throat and tried to empty his head of such disconsolate thoughts. It did not do to start an interview with such negative expectations. If he treated the woman like a hothouse flower, then likely as not she would act like one. And people could surprise you. She might look as if she lacked a backbone, would scream as soon as look at you, but it was just possible she contained an inner strength hidden behind that delicate shell. If she was treated with care, she might bloom under questioning rather than wilt. With these thoughts uppermost in his mind, the inspector attempted to put the woman at her ease. He arranged his face into a kindly expression and adopted a genial tone of voice as if he were playing the part of a favourite uncle. Patience, that was the key thing; he must be patient. He only hoped that Sergeant Harris, not a man renowned for his forbearance, would follow his lead and not intimidate her with that face of his, which looked gloomy at the best of times.

'Mrs Grayson-Smith, I'm Inspector Connor. Won't you please take a seat?'

The inspector beckoned to the chair in front of his desk, so positioned as to obscure from view, and hopefully also from mind, the two sergeants. The older of the two had drawn up a chair in which to sit and take notes unobtrusively, the younger lounged in a nonchalant fashion against a bookcase beside the door. Both were notable only by their silence and the way they seemed to disappear into the very fabric of the room. Certainly Millicent did not appear to see them, her focus being solely on the inspector, whom she viewed warily and with not a little apprehension. Before she had seemingly given it any thought, or intentionally acquiesced, she found herself seated in the allocated chair. She did not remember walking over to the seat, nor sitting down upon it. She bit her bottom lip and clasped and unclasped her hands in her lap. She was restive, and she did not wish to be. She wanted to compose herself, portray herself in a good light, and give the inspector her full attention. Instead she averted her gaze and stared unseeing at the carpet, much as Sergeant Harris had done earlier when he had realised he had made an error in mentioning the disappearance of the diamond necklace to Mason before they had interviewed the lady of the house.

'I appreciate this must be difficult for you, Mrs Grayson-Smith,' began the inspector, 'what with the deceased being your lady's maid.'

'Oh? No. I didn't know her very well, you see.' Millicent, obviously flustered, put a hand to her mouth. 'She had only been with me a few months at most ...' She allowed her voice to dwindle to nothing, not quite sure herself what she was intending to say next.

'Even so, it must have been –'

He got no further, for the door burst open and a woman, who was patently everything Millicent Grayson-Smith was not, rushed into the room. It was true that she shared Millicent's sense of fragility and delicate features, but there the similarity ended. Where Millicent's face appeared strained and wan, hers was bright and animated. It took a moment for Inspector Connor to realise that it was this vitality, compared with Millicent's lethargy, that made the greatest impression. Her tall, willowy figure and cool, aristocratic beauty might draw Sergeant Perkins' attention, and Sergeant Harris would have much to say about the platinum dyed hair, but it was the girl's obvious energy that attracted the inspector. The woman standing here before him was not a creature who would answer questions with monosyllabic answers. She would show no self-restraint in the expression of emotion, the words would flow from her lips before she gave a thought to stop them, regardless of the consequences.

'Oh Millicent, there you are. Why didn't you wait for me?' Millicent made a half-hearted attempt to answer and then stopped, staring up at Lavinia with something of a bewildered look upon her face, her eyes large and doleful. To the policemen, who watched her closely, she seemed to shrink back a little in her seat.

'Hello, our frightened little goose never intended that her confident young friend should accompany her,' said Inspector Connor to himself. 'Now, that is interesting. She's just the sort who needs someone to hold her hand. So why doesn't she want her ladyship here?'

'Never mind, I'm here now,' Lavinia was saying. Whether or not she realised an answer would not be forthcoming, she did not bother to wait for Millicent to speak. 'No harm done. Mrs Grayson-Smith is a little nervous, Inspector. She's never encountered this sort of thing before, whereas of course, I have.'

'Indeed?' said the inspector.

'Oh, yes,' said Lavinia, seating herself comfortably into a chair that Sergeant Perkins had kindly drawn up for her.

The inspector decided not to pry. This type of woman required no encouragement. If he were to show any interest in what she was saying, he was afraid she would not stop talking. That sort never did; too fond of their own voices, they were. Momentarily, he felt a little at a loss. With Lady Lavinia Sedgwick present he did not doubt that he would receive detailed answers to his questions. The problem was that they would not come from Mrs Grayson-Smith's lips. For this reason, his preference was for witnesses and suspects to be interviewed alone, particularly if they were impressionable and apt to be swayed by others. He looked at Millicent's pale and drawn face. He noted the way her lip trembled and her hands fidgeted. He remembered the way she had already barely comprehended his first few questions and stumbled over her answers. Somewhat against his better judgment, he decided rather grudgingly to permit her friend to stay.

'You are welcome to remain, Lady Lavinia,' he said. 'To give moral support, that is. But I should like Mrs Grayson-Smith to answer my questions herself. Do you understand what I am saying Miss ... em ... m'lady?' The inspector coughed awkwardly over the oral address. He felt it placed him at a disadvantage by emphasising their very different stations in society.

'But of course, Inspector.' Lavinia smiled sweetly apparently oblivious to any discomfort on the inspector's part.

'Very well. Now, Mrs Grayson-Smith,' began the inspector adopting a firmer tone than he had originally intended, to cover the feelings of inferiority he was experiencing, 'I'll be asking you the routine questions about how long Miss Cooper had been employed here as your maid and her references and such like in a minute. But what I am interested in at the moment is getting a picture of the events of last night. Your butler's given us a bit of an account from the servants' perspective. Now I'd like one from yours.'

'I ... I'm not sure I understand,' began Millicent, something of a frightened look creeping back upon her face.

'Well, of course you do, Milly,' said Lavinia, squeezing the woman's hand. She might have been speaking to a child or to a person with marred intellect. 'The inspector wants to know what time Cooper left you last night and the type of mood she was in. Isn't that right, Inspector, you want to know that sort of thing?'

'Yes, indeed, m'lady,' muttered Inspector Connor almost under his breath.

Sergeant Perkins turned his head away to hide a smile. If truth be told, he was enjoying himself immensely. There was much to be said for being on the fringes of an investigation. Lady Lavinia Sedgwick was proving herself to be a most lively and interesting woman, everything he had hoped for in the form of entertainment. He could see why such a woman had riled Inspector Deacon. He wondered how his uncle was going to fare.

'Well,' began Millicent rather hesitantly, 'she appeared to me in much the same state of mind as usual. Of course we were not by way of being friends.'

'I appreciate that, Mrs Grayson-Smith. But did she, for example, appear excited at all or perhaps a little agitated?'

'No ... I don't think so.'

'And yet, if you don't mind my saying, you sound rather hesitant. Are you quite sure she wasn't upset about something?'

'Yes, I'm perfectly certain ... at least I think I am. It's difficult to remember.' Millicent hung her head a little as if ashamed at the apparent inadequacy of her memory. 'We weren't on familiar terms.'

'Well, of course they weren't,' said Lavinia rather indignantly. 'After all, Cooper was only a servant, Inspector.'

'I am quite well aware of that,' said the inspector coldly.

'I can't quite remember what time she left me,' continued Millicent quickly. 'Let me see. She helped me undress at the end of the evening. Oh, yes. I remember now. She took my gown. That's to say, the one I had been wearing. She said it needed repairing.'

'And what time did she leave you for the night?'

'Oh. I have just told you I'm not certain.' She turned to her friend. 'Lavinia, do you know?'

'About a quarter to eleven, I should think. I wasn't looking at the clock. But Mrs Grayson-Smith doesn't keep late hours, Inspector. Even when she entertains.'

'Did you actually see her go? The deceased, I mean?' Inspector Connor asked her sharply.

'Well, as it happens, I did. She was in the corridor when Rose ... Miss Simpson, opened my door to leave,' said Lavinia. 'She must have just come out of your room, Millicent. I remember she was carrying your dress. The one you had been wearing. I think I recall it because of the colour; it was such a vivid blue.'

'I see. Now, Mrs Grayson-Smith,' Inspector Connor said in a tone which suggested that the interview was drawing to a close. 'I'm obliged to ask you this question. It's a mere matter of routine. I doubt very much whether you'll be able to help me, not being one of the deceased's fellow servants or a particular friend.'

'Oh?'

He heard the apprehension in her voice. Her hands, which a moment before had been neatly folded in her lap, now jerked alive of their own accord and clung to the sides of her seat. His interest aroused, he said quickly, before the momentum was lost: 'Do you know if the deceased had any enemies?'

'No,' said Lavinia quickly, 'of course Mrs Grayson-Smith doesn't know.'

'Yes,' said Millicent. 'She did.'

'Oh?' Inspector Connor stared at Millicent, his eyes glued to her as if he found her fascinating. Even Sergeant Harris had paused in his note taking, his pencil hovering impatiently above the page.

'Me.'

'You?' exclaimed the inspector. He stared at her with incredulous horror.

'Shush, Millicent, don't be silly,' began Lavinia. For the first time during the interview she looked worried.

'Be quiet, Lady Lavinia, if you please,' commanded Inspector Connor. 'You were saying, Mrs Grayson-Smith?'

'It's no good. Don't you see?' Millicent said, looking imploringly at Lavinia. 'It'll come out in the end.'

'Yes it will,' said Sergeant Harris ominously from the depths of the room.

The two women had forgotten that he was there and both started visibly.

'Oh do shut up,' cried Lavinia with feeling. She was ostensibly addressing the sergeant, but few in the room would have doubted that she was also speaking to Millicent, begging the woman to hold her tongue.

'I suppose you would say Cooper was blackmailing me, Inspector,' Millicent said quietly. Now that she had released her burden, she seemed strangely at peace. 'She caught me in a … a compromising position. But it wasn't my fault. That's to say, it wasn't how it looked.'

'Of course it wasn't,' said Lavinia, rallying a little. 'Mrs Grayson-Smith happened to be upset one day and the footman … well, he is an impertinent fellow. He took advantage of the situation and put his arm around her shoulders.'

'Would that be Albert Bettering?' enquired the inspector.

'Yes. I think he was just trying to be kind, Lavinia,' said Millicent, her cheeks going crimson. 'I don't think he meant anything by it.'

Sergeant Harris snorted and the inspector frowned.

'Of course I pushed him away,' said Millicent, 'but not before Cooper caught us. It was all rather embarrassing. I didn't know where to look. I thought she would pretend she hadn't seen anything. But later that evening when I was dressing for dinner and she was brushing my hair, she said men were funny creatures and apt to think the worst. Of course I asked her what she meant. She said that in her experience husbands were prone to think that their wives were up to no good when there was a perfectly innocent explanation, and wouldn't it be awful if my husband happened to find out that the footman had held me in his arms.'

'I see. She hinted that she intended to blackmail you?'

'Yes. I was frightened, Inspector. My husband is a jealous man. I … I didn't know what to do. In the end I asked her what she wanted. I said I didn't have much money of my own. She said that she didn't want money.'

'Oh? She did, did she?' The inspector sounded surprised. 'What did she want?'

'She said it was usual for mistresses to give their lady's maids dresses they no longer wanted, and that she would like to take one or two of the gowns I didn't wear.'

'And you agreed to this?'

'I didn't see the harm. I was relieved. She seemed to be asking for so little.'

'I know what you are thinking, Inspector,' said Lavinia, 'that this gives Mrs Grayson-Smith some sort of a motive for wishing Cooper dead.'

'Lavinia!' Millicent shrank back in her seat, as if she had been stung.

'There is no need to look so alarmed, Millicent. I was just going to explain that this only happened last night. Hardly enough time to take it on yourself to kill the woman. Why, she probably hadn't even decided which dresses of yours to take.'

'But she had,' said Millicent. Having recovered from her initial shock, her voice was now quiet, and her tone dull. She sounded resigned, a heavy weight slipping from her shoulders, to come tumbling down to deliver the final blow. 'She took my best ones.'

'But –' began Lavinia.

'I'm sorry, Lavinia. I'm afraid I lied to you. Do forgive me.' Millicent stared at her hands while she spoke and worked the fabric of her skirt between her fingers. 'It all happened last week, not last night. When she blackmailed me, I mean. I wanted to tell you the truth, really I did. But I was so embarrassed. She took my best clothes. I knew if I refused to let her she'd tell Edwin. I didn't know what to do. I was awfully afraid of what she would ask for next.'

Chapter Twenty-four

Albert took a couple of steps forward. As he advanced on her, Rose wondered whether he intended to strike her. Certainly he appeared sufficiently angry. His good looks were momentarily marred with rage, and his dark eyes blazed dangerously like two lumps of coal. She also fancied she saw his hand twitch, as if in preparation for being raised.

She had been a fool. In those few seconds of uncertainty, while she waited to see how Albert would react, she cursed herself for her own stupidity. To goad a man such as him had been an act of madness. She had already seen him display a violent temper in the servants' hall. There had been others present then to restrain and placate him. Now she was very aware that she was entirely alone and vulnerable.

There were no witnesses, should he decide to hit her. There would only be her word against his and he might well decide that the odds were sufficiently in his favour to take the chance. In that instant, her nerve almost broke and she was sorely tempted to tell him who she really was, believing it would be sufficient to stay his hand. On a second's reflection, however, she considered it might place her in worse peril. For she would be forced to give the reason for her deceit. To admit that she was an amateur sleuth, when Albert might at best be a thief and at worst a murderer, would be placing herself in even greater danger.

Looking wildly around the room, she saw there was no obvious means of escape. To get to the door she would need to brush past Albert and he would surely grab her. Of course she could always scream, but she doubted anyone would hear her, hidden away as she was high up in the attics. It was true that Pearl and Agnes might hear her muffled cries, but in their highly distressed and agitated states, might they not flee below in fright rather than take a moment to investigate from whence the noise had come?

What had threatened to become a deadly situation, in the end strangely resolved itself peaceably enough. So much so that Rose almost felt cheated by the outcome, being as it was something of an anti-climax. For the footman to all intents and purposes backed down and withdrew. Perhaps she had not, after all, provoked him sufficiently, or possibly he had thought better of it than to strike a visiting servant amidst a murder investigation while the police still lingered in the house. Whatever the reason, Albert straightened and lowered his hand to his side. The expression on his face returned to its usual one of insolence, which had the odd effect of accentuating his good looks. With an air of assumed indifference, he shrugged and retraced his steps to the door.

'Whatever made you think that?' Albert laughed over his shoulder. It was not a pleasant sound. 'If you must know, I was going to my room to get a … a handkerchief. I heard noises coming from this room and thought it my duty to investigate.' He turned and stared at her, as if challenging her to question his version of events. 'But I must say, Miss Denning, I find your being here highly suspicious.'

'Well then, I suggest you speak to the inspector,' retorted Rose, having recovered a little from her fright. 'He will confirm my story.' She felt it imperative that she appear undaunted, and she knew full well Albert was unlikely to approach the police of his own volition.

It was a relief when Albert finally left the room, banging the door closed behind him. She heard him whistling as he proceeded down the corridor. She had not realised how very frightened she had been until she noticed she was trembling. Slowly, Rose lowered herself on to the bed and shivered. More than anything she wished to flee from Cooper's room, to leave it far behind her and pretend that the confrontation with Albert had not occurred. But she was frightened of running into the footman, to whom she was determined to give a wide berth, at least for a while. She put a hand to her throbbing head. For the first time she acknowledged her precarious position. By continuing with her disguise and undertaking her own investigation she would be rubbing shoulders with both the thief and the murderer, treading on eggshells lest she give herself away. As she looked around her, the room took on a sinister air. The attics were so very far removed from the rest of the house, both from the main part of the manor and from the servants' hall and associated workrooms. Here anything might happen, and it almost had. Confined to the servants' quarters as she was, she felt herself to be an anonymous, faceless individual, unlikely to be missed.

She proceeded to give herself a severe talking to. It did not do to let her thoughts run wild and lose her head. She had suffered a fright, that was all. It would pass. It might well be very tempting to retreat to

Lavinia's room and hide, but it would not progress the investigation. She must find the murderer and the thief, who might well be one and the same person.

With a renewed sense of purpose, Rose quickly let herself out of the murdered woman's room and peered cautiously along the corridor which, to her relief, was empty. She thought of the enclosed servants' stairs and shivered as a vision appeared before her of Albert lurking in the dark, waiting for her. She heard the muffled voices of Pearl and Agnes a little way off. In her present feeling of loneliness, they were a welcome sound indeed. Even before she had given any thought to what she was doing, she found herself making her way towards them, as if her feet had a mind of their own. She reminded herself that she had a perfectly good reason for seeking them out. For she needed to talk to Agnes. She had wanted to speak to the girl ever since she had first heard about her crying and seen her tear-stained face.

It was only when she appeared at the girls' door, and saw their upturned faces staring up at her apprehensively, that she realised, with all the excitement of recent events, she had entirely overlooked the significance of what she had found during her search of the dead woman's room. Then her focus had been on completing the task as quickly as possible before she was disturbed. Only now, walking down the corridor and collecting her thoughts had she had an opportunity to evaluate her findings. With a sudden burst of comprehension, she realised that she had unknowingly unearthed two clues.

'I'm not being rude, Miss Denning, but I don't see what it has to do with you,' said Agnes indignantly.

The girl had not gone to any pains to conceal the fact that Rose's unexpected return to the sickroom was, at least from her point of view, most unwelcome. This was in sharp contrast to the reception Rose had received from Pearl. The girl had given her a warm smile and motioned for her to enter and to sit down on one corner of the bed.

'Edna told me that Mrs Field had scolded you for smoking in the courtyard,' Rose said, attempting to adopt a sympathetic tone in spite of Agnes's surly manner.

'What if she had? It was my own fault. I know old Fieldy doesn't like me smoking.' Agnes stared miserably at one of the dusty floorboards. 'I should have come up to my room and opened the window. That's what I usually do. Smoke out the window, I mean.' She gave a bitter laugh. 'Then I steal into the kitchen and eat some mint. Works a treat, it does.'

'Why, what a lot of effort you have to go to just to have a smoke,' said Rose. 'It doesn't seem very fair. Why shouldn't you smoke a cigarette if you want to?'

Agnes eyed her suspiciously, as if she doubted the sincerity of Rose's words.

'Well, as I said it's my own fault,' the housemaid muttered. 'I know what the old dragon's like.'

'You must have been particularly upset this time.'

'What do you mean?' Agnes asked her warily. 'I was no more upset than usual. She's just a silly old woman with old-fashioned ideas. Martha and me, we don't take any notice of her.'

'Edna said you cried like anything. Terribly upset she said you were,' Rose said, not altogether truthfully.

'Did she indeed? Well, she should learn to keep her mouth shut.'

'Agnes!' The scullery maid looked aghast.

'I'm sorry, Pearl. I didn't mean to upset you, but Edna's no business gossiping about me to all and sundry.' She gave Rose an insolent glance. 'Begging your pardon, Miss Denning, I'm sure. But it's not right, it isn't. I've a good mind to –'

'Agnes, it's obvious you were crying about something else,' said Rose quickly. The interview had started inauspiciously and continued in that vein. She had neither the time nor the patience to try and coax the truth out of the girl by gentle means. A more direct approach would be necessary. 'I think something else upset you, something that has been worrying you for a little while. Am I right? You lit a cigarette as an excuse to go out into the kitchen courtyard to be alone, so you could decide what to do.'

Agnes gaped at her, her mouth wide open, her eyes large and frightened. She began to tremble in obvious distress, whether as a result of astonishment at Rose's mind-reading skills, or due to the knowledge she held so guiltily within her, it was hard to tell. An ominous silence had fallen upon the attic room like a heavy rain cloud; the other two had caught some of the girl's nervousness. Pearl, her eyes bright, looked as shocked as Agnes. But she betrayed no furtive gestures, no trembling lip.

Instead, she was brimming with excitement, as if some thrilling drama was about to be played out before her to enliven an otherwise drab existence. Even Rose was affected. She had thought it possible, because of the changed manner of the girl, that Agnes was hiding some piece of information that was causing her distress. But she had in ignorance assumed it was something relatively trivial. Only now she felt less certain. With bated breath she waited for the girl to speak, but the silence seemed to drag. There was no clock ticking to relieve the quiet, no sounds associated with the servants going about their business; only the noise of three women breathing, two in anticipation and one in dread.

In the end the prolonged silence was broken by Agnes, not with a vehement denial as Rose had feared, but with a droop of the shoulders, followed by a sigh of resignation. The housemaid stared down at her lap and worried the fabric of her uniform with fingers that clenched and unclenched.

'I don't know how you know what you do. I thought I'd been ever so careful.' Her voice had sunk to a whisper. Gone was the bluster and the sullen temper. Instead, here was a frightened girl staring at the world through unshed tears, wondering what to do for the best.

'It would be much better to tell us what is worrying you,' Rose said gently.

'Why should I?' A defiant spark still existed in the girl's breast. 'You're just a visiting servant. It's nothing to do with you. If I tell anyone, it will be old Fieldy or one of them policemen.'

'Very wise,' said Rose. 'Only I don't think you will.'

'If I know something, why shouldn't I tell them?'

'Because you are afraid.'

Agnes looked up startled and then looked down again at her crumpled skirt. There threatened to be another prolonged silence. Rose bit her lip with impatience. Perhaps Pearl felt the same, for it was she who broke the silence this time.

'Tell Miss Denning, Agnes, do,' said Pearl, learning forward and squeezing the girl's arm. 'She's ever so kind. Edna says so and you know how good she is at reading people. Miss Denning will know what to do.' She stared at Rose, as if for reassurance. 'You will won't you, miss?'

'Yes,' said Rose quickly. She had a sudden dread that Pearl might be tempted to reveal her identity.

'I don't want to get anyone in trouble,' sobbed Agnes. 'I wish I hadn't seen them, really I do. It was just my bad luck, it was.

'What did you see?' asked Rose, slightly more sharply than she had intended.

'I can't,' sobbed Agnes. 'I can't tell you. Martha's my friend, you see.'

'Martha?' The word of surprise had sprung from the scullery maid's lips. Looking at Pearl, Rose saw that the girl had turned pale. The look of excitement had gone from her eyes, to be replaced by one of trepidation. 'Perhaps you shouldn't say anything, Agnes. We don't want to get Martha in trouble.'

'Listen, both of you,' said Rose. She spoke firmly and clasped the hand of each. 'You must say what you saw, Agnes, if not to me, then to the police. It'll all come out in the end, it always does. If Martha's in trouble, and I very much hope she is not, I shall do my best to help her.' She stared at their scared faces and said quietly: 'I daresay she was provoked.'

'It isn't Martha who's in trouble, miss,' said Agnes. 'Though it'll hurt her something terrible, it will.'

'Are you saying that you know something that will get Albert in trouble?' asked Rose.

Inwardly she uttered a sigh of relief. Martha was not implicated in the murder. Rose knew it to be a weakness of hers, an inability to detach herself and keep her personal feelings from influencing her investigations. On at least one previous occasion she had tried to shield someone she had feared might be guilty of a crime. But, try as she might, she had not been able to rid her mind of the image of Martha, a desolate creature, eyes puffy and red from frequent crying, sobbing bitterly as she pleaded with Albert to tell her the truth about the missing necklace. She remembered the way the footman had spoken to the girl so roughly, with hardly a care. Rose recollected that her sight at the time had been hindered by the existence of the bedsheet hanging between them like some great screen. She had been forced, therefore, to rely solely on her hearing. With her sight obscured, her other senses had been heightened so that she could recall not only the very words that had been spoken, but the tone in which they had been uttered.

There was a sharp intake of breath. It was her own. She realised now something that had not struck her at the time. Something that she had disregarded, much as she had overlooked the clues in Velda Cooper's room.

'Yes,' Agnes was saying. 'Poor Martha. It'll break her heart, it will. He'll never do right by her. I've told her and told her 'till I'm blue in the face, but she won't listen. Headstrong she is when she wants to be. He's a wrong' un and a wastrel. Even Mr Mason thinks so, and Albert's his nephew. If it weren't for his good looks ...' Agnes blushed, suddenly aware that her voice had run away with her. 'I shouldn't have gone on like that, not to you Miss Denning. But when I get started on something, I can't stop. My mother says it's a failing. I just –'

'What did you see, Agnes?' Rose said, trying to keep the impatience from her voice. A few minutes ago she had been prepared to hang on the girl's every word. Now her thoughts were elsewhere. With the sudden realisation of what the scene played out before her with the bedsheet represented, she was eager to be gone. Agnes's next words, however, brought her up sharp.

'I saw him kiss her. I saw Albert kiss Miss Cooper.' Agnes smiled in spite of herself as she saw Pearl's eyes grow large in disbelief.

'You never!'

'I did. Ever so passionate it was, the kiss. I thought, hello, what's going on here?' Her face became serious again. 'I've been that worried. Yesterday, it was, I caught them. In the library they were, as bold as brass. 'Course that room don't get used much when the master's not here. They thought they'd not be disturbed. But I'd left my duster in there by mistake and I went to get it before Mrs Field noticed.' She bent forward and spoke in a conspiratorial fashion: 'She follows Martha and me around the house. Wants to make sure we've dusted proper. Runs her finger over the furniture, she does, tops of bookcases and the like. Ever so particular, she is.'

'Did they see you?' asked Rose, her mind racing.

She had fully expected Agnes to tell them about her being witness to a further altercation between the pair, a continuation of the row that had erupted in the servants' hall the day before. It had never occurred to her that Albert and Velda Cooper might be lovers. Idly she recalled to mind Lavinia's observation, which she had dismissed so readily, that in all likelihood the murderer was a jealous or rejected lover.

'I don't know. I saw them as soon as I opened the door. I closed it again awful quick, but it must have made a noise. I ran all the way back to the servants' hall.' All mirth had gone from Agnes's voice now. 'I've been so worried. I didn't want to get Albert in trouble, and I was scared he'd know it was me that had seen them. He's been giving me ever such strange looks.' She lowered her voice to a whisper. 'Do you think Miss Cooper threatened to tell Martha about them? Is that why he done her in?'

'We don't know that Albert did kill Miss Cooper,' Rose reminded her. 'But it certainly gives him a possible motive. I suppose he might have killed her to keep her quiet.'

'She'd have been the sort to tell Martha, all right,' said Agnes with feeling. 'Full of spite she was. She would have taken a delight in telling her. And Martha, she'd not have stood for it. Albert carrying on with another woman, I mean. Albert would have known that. He'd have lost her and, though he doesn't treat her right, he loves her in his own way and she him.'

Pearl nodded in agreement. To Rose, she looked a little scared. Rose remembered her own fear when Albert had come upon her unexpectedly in the deceased's room. She had not doubted for a moment that he would not flinch at using force to still her tongue. It was, therefore, perfectly feasible that, if provoked, he might have stuck the lady's maid with the first suitable instrument that had come to hand.

Rose reassured the maids that they had done the right thing in disclosing what they knew and told them that the innocent had nothing to fear from the truth being known.

As Rose left the maids to ponder on the footman's guilt, it struck her as rather odd that neither of them had given voice to the other possibility. If Martha had become aware of Albert's deception, which might well have happened if Velda Cooper had spoken to her as they thought likely, might it not have been she who had struck the fatal blow to rid herself of a rival for her lover's affections?

Chapter Twenty-five

'Lavinia,' said Rose, closing the door behind her and sinking gratefully down on the bed, kicking off her shoes, 'it really is absurd you ringing for me all the time.' She removed the hated spectacles and flung them across the bed; so careless was her gesture that they landed on the floor. 'You do know I am trying to investigate a murder? Had you forgotten? I'm not really here to be your lady's maid.'

'Don't I know it!' retorted Lavinia rather haughtily. 'I just thought you might appreciate a nice hot cup of tea, that's all. I don't suppose you have anywhere to drink one downstairs. I take it you aren't allowed back in the servants' hall yet?' She patted her nose with a powder puff. 'And it would look awfully suspicious if I stopped summoning you. Still, I wish I hadn't bothered if you are going to be in this mood.'

'I'm sorry,' said Rose, suitably chastised.

She decided to make amends and helped herself to a cup of tea, pouring one out for Lavinia for good measure, which she took over to her and placed on the dressing table. Lavinia, gazing despondently in the mirror, gave her a brief wave by way of thanks.

'You can't stare at your face all day,' said Rose. 'Surely even you get bored of looking at it?'

'Yes, I jolly well can. And, anyway, there's not much else to do here.'

'You could keep Mrs Grayson-Smith company.'

'Oh, don't talk to me about that woman.' Lavinia made a face in the mirror and swivelled around in her seat to face her friend. 'I swear she wants to be arrested for that wretched maid's murder. You should have heard her, Rose. The things she told the police! It was absolutely ghastly. And worse than that, she made me look a complete fool.'

'That can't have been too difficult,' Rose said, grinning in spite of herself.

Lavinia retaliated by sticking out her tongue. But the mood was lifted and the artificial roles of mistress and servant, accentuated by their very different clothes, had evaporated and been replaced by the easy camaraderie and familiarity that usually existed between the two women.

The mood, however, turned swiftly from frivolity to one of responsibility. There was a serious note to Rose's voice when next she spoke.

'So Mrs Grayson-Smith told the police about being blackmailed?'

'She did,' groaned Lavinia. 'Even though I told her not to. She really is a very silly woman. Honestly, you should have heard her, Rose. When the inspector asked her if she knew if that Cooper woman had any enemies, she said "Yes, me"'. Lavinia chuckled in spite of herself. 'You could have knocked the inspector down with a feather, he was so surprised. Because of course he was expecting her to say she didn't know, which made it even more ridiculous that she had to go and open her mouth and say something so damning.'

'Good for her!' said Rose. 'No,' she raised her hand as her friend made to protest, 'but seriously, Lavinia. I think she did the right thing. Telling the inspector, I mean. It was bound to come out in the end, and think how bad it would have looked for her if she had kept quiet.'

'I suppose you're right,' admitted Lavinia rather grudgingly. 'But she made me look a fool and I won't forgive her that lightly, I can tell you.' She turned to face the mirror again and patted her hair. 'There was something else I wanted to tell you. Now, what was it?' She paused in the act of pinning a stray curl. 'Oh, I remember. All this blackmail business didn't start last night like she told us. It had been going on a week or so.'

If Lavinia had hoped such news would produce a reaction from her friend, then she was to be disappointed, for Rose showed little, if any, surprise.

'I thought as much. I searched Cooper's room and her wardrobe was stuffed with Millicent's dresses. I didn't think she could have taken them all last night.'

'Millicent said she was too embarrassed and a little afraid to tell us the truth this morning. That her lady's maid had been blackmailing her for some time, I mean. I say, Rose,' said Lavinia, lowering her voice slightly, which seemed an unnecessary precaution given that they were alone, 'you'll think I'm being frightfully mean, but I did wonder if there was any truth in –'

'If there was any substance to the blackmail allegation?' asked Rose. 'Yes, I wondered that myself and then dismissed the idea. I suppose it is possible that Millicent might have been seduced by Albert in a moment of weakness, but I think it highly unlikely. For one thing, I don't think she would have chosen a man like him. She'd find his looks too intimidating and his manner too familiar. Anyway, she doesn't strike me as the type of woman to have affairs. And remember, she's only been married a few months.'

'Yes, it's hardly very likely, is it?' agreed Lavinia. 'It was just a thought, that's all.'

'One thing I have found out is that Albert appears to have been carrying on an affair with Cooper.'

'No! I thought he and the other girl, Martha, were sweethearts. No wonder the girl always looks so upset.'

'I'm not sure she knew anything about it. But it does make you wonder, doesn't it? It would give her a very good motive for wishing Cooper dead. I don't know how long it had been going on. The discovery was only made yesterday. Agnes happened to open the door to the library and caught them in a passionate embrace. I say, if Cooper and Albert were lovers, they may well have concocted the blackmail business between them. Cooper catching Albert and Millicent together like that, I mean. It could all have been part of an elaborate plan.'

'Poor Millicent. First she is blackmailed and then her diamond necklace is stolen.'

'Yes, she hasn't had much luck since her marriage, has she?'

'Rose,' said Lavinia excitedly, a sudden thought having just occurred to her. 'You don't think she gave Cooper the diamond necklace to keep her quiet, do you? Perhaps it was never stolen at all.'

'No, I don't' said Rose, 'She could have reasoned with herself that it was usual for a mistress to pass on clothes to her lady's maid, convinced herself that she wasn't really being blackmailed. But think about it, Lavinia. A diamond necklace is a very different kettle of fish. Firstly, it is valuable and, in the case of the necklace in question, it had belonged to her husband's first wife. Knowing Millicent as we do, she wouldn't have thought it hers to give. And, even if she had, why would she then ask us to investigate its disappearance? It wouldn't make any sense. She wouldn't want us to find out the truth. And why draw everyone's attention to the fact that the necklace was missing in the first place? There was nothing to prevent her from giving Mason an empty jewellery box to put back in the safe cabinet. Surely that is what she would have done if she intended on disposing of the necklace to Cooper. No one would have been any the wiser. It might have been months before it was discovered that the necklace was missing, if at all. And remember it was also she who decided to retrieve the necklace from the safe only a few minutes after she had deposited it there. Why would she do that if she knew for a fact it wasn't there?' Rose stared at Lavinia's disappointed face. 'Of course, that doesn't mean that Albert or Cooper, or both of them together, didn't steal the necklace.'

'Of course you are quite right, you always are,' said Lavinia, taking a sip of her tea. 'So she didn't fake the disappearance of her necklace. I say, Rose, you don't think she could be the murderer do you? She may have thought Cooper might become greedy and demand something more valuable than a couple of old dresses.'

'Cooper didn't take Millicent's old dresses,' said Rose. 'Remember, I had a look in Cooper's wardrobe. She'd chosen her best dresses, including the blue silk satin gown Millicent wore last night.'

'The darned cheek of the woman!' exclaimed Lavinia with feeling. 'Why, I think Milly is well rid of her.' Her face turned pale as she realised what she had said. 'I didn't really mean –'

'It certainly would give Millicent a good motive for killing her lady's maid,' Rose said. 'A woman like Cooper wouldn't have been satisfied with dresses for long, even if they were good ones. Remember what her aspirations were, Lavinia. She needed money for that. More than she'd get for a few splendid gowns. It was only a matter of time before she asked for money. Millicent would have known that.'

'Look here, Rose. You can't really think that Millicent would kill her maid? Why, the woman's frightened of her own shadow; she wouldn't say boo to a goose. Of course I haven't killed anyone myself, but I'd have said it would take some nerve. Not Millicent's sort of thing at all. The woman would go completely to pieces. She'd confess to the crime immediately.'

'According to you, that's what she did do. At least one could argue that she as good as confessed by admitting that she and Cooper were enemies, and that she had good cause for wishing the woman dead.'

'I don't believe a word of it,' said Lavinia. 'I've never heard such rot. Really, Rose, if that's the best you –'

'All I'm saying at this stage is that Millicent had a decent motive. But she certainly wasn't the only one. Martha might have discovered that

198

Cooper was carrying on with her sweetheart and killed her in a fit of jealousy, and likewise Albert may have wanted to stop Cooper from telling Martha about their affair. I daresay I'll find that some of the others had motives for wishing her dead too. She wasn't very well liked.'

'Well, it serves her jolly well right, if you ask me. Cooper, I mean. If anyone deserved to be murdered –'

'Anyway, you needn't worry about Millicent,' said Rose, quickly interrupting what she feared would be another rant. 'There is a very good reason why she could not have killed her lady's maid even if she had wanted to do so.'

'Oh?'

'If you remember, the servants were unable to go into the main house at night. Mason saw to it that all the doors were locked. Which means, of course, that Millicent would not have been able to get into the servants' quarters to kill Cooper.'

'The key!' exclaimed Lavinia. Her hand had sprung to her mouth and there was a look of horror on her face. 'I forgot to tell you about the key. The inspector asked Millicent whether she knew if Edwin had a key to the servants' quarters. Apparently, he thought it strange that there should only be one key; in case of a fire and all that.'

'Oh? What was her reply?' asked Rose, with some misgivings. She had an inkling what Lavinia was going to say even before she opened her mouth.

'That her husband kept a spare key in a drawer in his dressing room. Millicent even offered to show the inspector which compartment.'

'I see.'

'Oh, what exactly do you see?' cried Lavinia with frustration. 'That Millicent Grayson-Smith is a very silly woman who is determined to get herself hanged?'

'Or a very clever woman pretending to be stupid.'

'Huh!' said Lavinia dismissively. 'You haven't had to sit with her for hours on end. Believe me, if you had, you would be left in very little doubt about the extent of that woman's mental abilities.'

'You're probably right. But it does mean that she had the same opportunity as the servants to carry out the crime, and of course she did have a motive. So we can't rule her out quite yet, I'm afraid.'

There followed rather an uncomfortable silence, relieved only by Lavinia's occasional banging down of a hairbrush or comb on the dressing table surface.

'Oh, please don't sulk,' said Rose finally, helping herself to another cup of tea. 'It's bad enough downstairs. Apart from Edna and Pearl, I don't think anyone else wants me there. I feel like I am intruding on other people's grief.'

'Well, they most probably think you did it,' sniffed Lavinia, 'Murdered the lady's maid.' But she brightened considerably, and there was a twinkle in her eye.

'I bet they do wish I was the murderer,' said Rose. 'It would make it much easier for them if they thought it wasn't one of them. It's not knowing whom to trust that's so awful. Mrs Field is insisting that the younger maids do their jobs in pairs. They even have to accompany each other to the lavatory.'

'Doesn't anyone have any suspicions?'

'Well, both Mason and Mrs Field think that Albert did it, though they won't say as much. At least not to me. Agnes also thinks Albert did it on account of him and Cooper being lovers. I think even Martha fears he may be implicated.'

'Poor Albert. I almost feel sorry for him,' said Lavinia. 'I say, it would be a bit hard on him if we find he's innocent.' She gave Rose a hard look. 'Do you think he did it?'

'Well, I certainly think he's quite capable of doing it. He is completely unscrupulous and he has a wicked temper, as I know to my cost.'

'Were you very frightened when you were alone with him in Cooper's room?'

'Yes, I was. He wanted to hit me, I could see it in his eyes. But then fortunately he thought better of it. If he had been sufficiently provoked by Cooper, I don't think he would have hesitated to kill her. Not if he felt threatened.'

'You haven't really told me what you found out,' said Lavinia. 'I've told you all about the key and Cooper having blackmailed Millicent for longer than she said. You've only told me about Albert disturbing your search of Cooper's room and that he and Cooper were secret sweethearts. Haven't you found out anything else?'

'Well, yes I have,' said Rose. She put her shoes on and started to pace the room. 'If you remember, it was Pearl, the scullery maid, who found the body. She shares a room with Edna, the girl I told you about who was a maid at Ashgrove House. Edna thought at first that Pearl might have been dreaming when she told her about finding the corpse. So Edna went down to make sure there really was a body in the servants' hall before she woke up Mrs Field.'

'What of it?' said Lavinia, sounding a little bored.

'Well, I asked her if she remembered anything unexpected, or which struck her as a little odd. And she said that now she came to think of it, Cooper had been wearing a coat.'

'Is it chilly in the servants' hall? Perhaps she was cold.'

'I wouldn't have said it was, not especially. And she wouldn't have put it on to go outside to smoke a cigarette because she didn't smoke. Anyway, the butler had already locked the doors by the time I returned to the servants' hall. He told me so. He'd just locked up after Albert. Mason told me that he was just waiting for Cooper to return and then he intended to retire for the night.'

'Didn't Cooper walk down with you?' Lavinia asked, surprised. 'She came out of Millicent's room at about the same time that you left mine. I saw her in the corridor.'

'No. She said she wanted to go to her room first.'

'Well, there you are. She was getting her coat.'

'No. I think she went to her room to do something else. She went back later to get her coat. But the point is, why was she found in the servants' hall wearing it?'

Lavinia shrugged. 'I've already told you. She was feeling the cold.'

'I think she was planning to leave Crossing Manor that night.'

'What? Well, what about the locked doors?' objected Lavinia. 'How did she intend to get out?'

'She could have taken the spare key from Mr Grayson-Smith's dressing room. If Millicent knew about the key, it's possible that Cooper did too. All she had to do was take it at some point during the day. She would have had plenty of opportunities to do so.'

'But the key was still there. One of the sergeants went to have a look for it as soon as Millicent mentioned its existence.'

'The murderer could have put it back.' Rose leaned forward. 'Do you know what else I think, Lavinia?'

'No, but I'm sure you're going to tell me.'

'I think Cooper had arranged to meet someone in the servants' hall after all the staff had retired for the night. Someone who was intent on leaving the house with her.'

'You surely don't mean Albert?' Lavinia's eyes were wide in disbelief.

'Yes, I do. Agnes had caught Albert and Cooper embracing in the library yesterday. She says that she closed the door as soon as she saw them and that they didn't see her. But that does not mean they didn't know they had been spotted. Agnes had just had a severe shock as you might imagine. I doubt she closed the door very quietly behind her. I think, in all probability, that Albert and Cooper heard the door close and realised they had been found out.'

'So they decided to leave Crossing Manor last night?'

'Yes. They knew there would be all hell to pay if they didn't.'

'You mean they would have been dismissed?' asked Lavinia. 'I say, that does sound rather harsh. I realise there would have been some unpleasantness. I daresay that poor girl Martha would have been frightfully upset but –'

'I think there was another reason why they wanted to leave Crossing Manor.'

'Oh?'

'I believe at least one of them was responsible for the theft of Millicent's diamond necklace. I think they wanted to get it out of the house before anyone could stop them.'

Chapter Twenty-six

Not wishing to encounter Albert on the servants' stairs, Rose took a chance and hurried down the main staircase. Despite Lavinia's protests to the contrary, she felt she had been gone from the servants' quarters for far too long. She was likely to be missed, particularly by Mrs Field and Mason as they tried desperately to maintain order and decorum in what was a horrendous situation, striking as it did at the very core of their world. For a moment, she considerably aged them in her mind and thought of them as two old retainers desperately trying to cling on to the traditions and morals of the past in an ever changing world. She reasoned it would not be long before the life they had known and worked towards had ceased to exist or, at the very least, dwindled into a mere shadow of its former self. The days of a house full of servants were coming to an end. She wondered whether the murder in the servants' hall would accelerate the rate of change in this particular house. Would Mrs Field and Mason have trouble recruiting staff, or conversely would new servants be drawn to Crossing Manor solely because of its macabre association with death?

Reaching the bottom step, she sighed. She must free her head of such thoughts and distractions, and focus her attention instead on catching the murderer and the thief, who might, or might not, be one and the same person. Try as she might, she could not rid herself of the feeling that there was a connection between the two crimes, that the theft had precipitated the murder or, at the very least, had in some way contributed to the lady's maid's death.

She glanced furtively at the library door, which was steadfastly closed, and wondered idly whom the police were interviewing at that very moment. Who was sitting nervously in the seat that she had not so very long ago vacated, twisting their hands in their lap or looking resolutely forward? Suddenly she gave a start. For, unless her eyes were deceiving her, the door was opening, as if of its own accord. Momentarily she was mesmerised, frozen where she was on that last step, wondering if the concentration of her thoughts had in some way depressed the door handle and caused it to open.

In light of her previous experience, she did not much relish the prospect of another encounter with the policemen. It was unfortunate then that, by the time she had recovered her wits sufficiently, it was too late to make a dash for the green baize door. She felt much like an animal caught in a trap. They would see her as soon as they came out of the library. They would catch her loitering on the stairs and be reminded of her purpose for being in the house. In her mind's eye she saw Sergeant Harris' contemptuous sneer and the inspector's worried frown. Worst of all, however, she knew it would provide them with an opportunity to renew their calls that she should leave.

It was, therefore, something of a relief when only Sergeant Perkins emerged from the library. He saw her at once, and quickly closed the door behind him, lest she be spotted by the others. Instinctively she ran to him.

'Quickly, I must talk to you. I need to ask you something,' said Rose. 'But not here.'

She looked wildly about her. The entrance hall appeared empty, but it was just possible that someone might be on the landing above or lurking in one of the rooms that led off the hall, with the door ajar. Her thoughts flew rapidly until they settled on Edwin Grayson-Smith's study, which was certain to be empty for the man himself had yet to return. Grabbing Sergeant Perkins rather unceremoniously by the arm, she marched him across the hall and led him into the study, closing the door firmly behind them.

'I say, Miss Denning, this is most intriguing,' said Sergeant Perkins with a deal of humour. 'You are the only person who has been pleased to see me since I entered this establishment. I'll have you know I have spent the morning trying to avoid stepping on Sergeant Harris' toes or ruffling the old boy's feathers. I rather think my uncle regrets asking me to tag along.'

'Who are you interviewing at the moment?' asked Rose, ignoring his jovial manner.

'The housekeeper, Mrs Field. I'm afraid she is not being very forthcoming. She's indignant that a murder has occurred in this house, but that's all she'll say on the matter. Keeps looking at the clock. Says she must find a room for the servants to have their meal. It will be time for the mistress' lunch soon and they can't keep her waiting and she won't have the servants working on empty stomachs.' He made a face. 'She doesn't want standards slipping. Apparently, even a murder occurring in the house under her very nose does not warrant an upset to routine.' He looked at Rose quizzically. 'Though I rather gathered she was none too fond of young Albert. Am I right?''

'Yes. She doesn't like him much; very few do. She and Mason, and a number of the other servants, think he did it; murdered the lady's maid.'

'Do they indeed? Well, I shall let you in on a little secret,' he paused for effect, 'so do we!' He gave her a sudden, penetrating stare. 'But I suppose the question is, do you think he did it, miss?'

'I really don't know,' Rose answered truthfully. 'Everything seems to point to him being the murderer. He and the deceased appear to have been lovers. Did you know about that?'

'No, I didn't. Well, I'll be blowed! I thought he was fond of the other maid, the pretty one.'

'Martha? Yes, he is. I'm afraid Albert doesn't appear to have any scruples about anything,' Rose paused a moment before continuing. 'Mrs Grayson-Smith's told you about the blackmail business?'

'She did indeed, much to Lady Lavinia's annoyance. She's quite a character isn't she, that friend of yours?' He chuckled. 'I think she could give old Sergeant Harris a run for his money. Now, what's with all this cloak and dagger stuff, miss? You said you needed to ask me a question.'

'Yes. Tell me, did you go with the other policemen to view the body?'

'I did,' said Sergeant Perkins, his manner at once becoming serious. 'It was not a pretty sight.'

'I'm sure it wasn't. Will you tell me please, what … what was she wearing?'

Sergeant Perkins raised his eyebrows in surprise. The question was not one he had been expecting.

'Do you mean in the way of clothes?' Rose nodded. 'Well, she had on a dress a bit like yours. Rather a sombre affair, if I remember. Black, save for a bit of white lace at the cuffs and neck.'

'Was she wearing anything else?'

Sergeant Perkins gave her a puzzled look.

'No. I don't think so. What sort of thing did you have in mind?'

'A coat. Was she wearing a coat?'

'A coat?' He looked surprised. 'No. She wasn't wearing a coat. And before you ask, I am quite sure. I studied the body quite closely. I would have remembered if she had been wearing a coat. She wasn't. She was just wearing the black dress.'

'Would it surprise you to learn that she was wearing a coat when her body was first discovered? Edna told me. If you remember, she went down to make sure there really was a body before she roused the housekeeper.'

'The kitchen maid? The friend of the scullery maid who found her?'

Rose nodded.

'She must have been mistaken.'

'I don't think she was,' said Rose. 'I think Cooper was wearing a coat when the body was found.'

'If that's the case, what's happened to it? We must make a search of the house. It can't have gone far.'

'There's no need, Sergeant. You see, I know where it is.'

'Where?'

'It's hanging at the back of Cooper's wardrobe.'

'I ... I don't understand,' said the young man, clearly puzzled.

'It's really very simple, Sergeant. At some time between Edna viewing the body and your viewing the corpse, someone removed the coat and hung it up in the deceased's wardrobe.'

'Why would anyone go to all that trouble?' asked the sergeant, looking bemused.

'To hide the fact that the deceased was intending to leave Crossing Manor.'

'What? In the middle of the night? Are you quite sure? Why wouldn't she wait until morning?'

'I think she had her reasons. But at the moment, it's pure conjecture on my part, so I don't really want to say any more at present until I have some proof. Now,' Rose said, holding up her hand as the sergeant made to protest, 'will you tell me something else? Have you interviewed Albert Bettering yet?'

'No.'

'Good.'

'My uncle's all for leaving him to last. He thinks his nerves will do for him if we make him wait. He fancies he'll go to pieces and make a full confession.'

'Does he?'

206

'Of course we didn't know then that Albert had been carrying on with the deceased. That will be another nail in his coffin.' The sergeant smiled. 'I reckon you've earned yourself a pat on the back, miss.'

'Well, I do hope the inspector will think so,' said Rose, 'because I should like to be present when you interview Albert Bettering.'

Rose emerged from the study. She hurried across the entrance hall and slipped through the green baize door, eager to reach the servants' quarters before Mrs Field came out of the library. When she arrived in the passage, the orderly air that had prevailed seemed to have dissolved into chaos in the housekeeper's absence. For servants were running this way and that and she could hear the raised voice of the cook, scolding one of the unfortunate maids.

'Everyone's behind with their duties,' explained Agnes, who had appeared at her shoulder. 'And Pearl has just upset a saucepan of soup much to the chagrin of Cook. Not got time to make any more so she says, not with no help all morning. We're to make do with a bit of bread and dripping and cheese if we're lucky. I don't know what old Fieldy will say. And there's nowhere to sit and eat, only the scullery and we can't all fit in there. We'll have to eat in shifts, so we will.'

'Where is Mr Mason?'

'He's in his pantry, He's been in there ever since he came back from seeing the policemen. Deathly pale he was, so Martha says. She happened to pass him in the passage.'

'Where is Martha now?'

'I don't rightly know. She said something about going to her room. If you're wanting some lunch, I'd go to the scullery now, before there's nowhere to sit.'

Rose thanked her, though she had no intention of taking her advice. Following her discussion with Sergeant Perkins, she had only one object in mind. She must talk to Martha. For she felt that the girl held the key to the mystery. Something had upset Martha long before the murder, something that had made her so miserable and dejected that it had been readily commented upon by the rest of the staff. It could not be explained by the girl having a vague suspicion that the man she loved was a thief. There must be some substance behind her belief. Of course, it appeared to be common knowledge among the staff that Albert had pilfered one of

Edwin Grayson-Smith's snuff boxes. However, the item had been returned undamaged and really it was quite another thing to steal a valuable diamond necklace, which was still missing.

Rose found herself going against the tide, for it seemed that all the other servants were now making their way towards the scullery, keen to secure a seat before all the chairs were taken and they were obliged to prop themselves against tables or eat standing up, as they partook of their very humble meal. Consequently, she found herself being pushed and pulled as they filed passed her in the narrow corridor. It was, therefore, something of a relief to find herself at the bottom of the servants' staircase, a solitary figure, her eyes stretching to look up to the floors above as she considered the number of steps she had to climb to reach the attics.

It was not until she had started on the second flight of steps that she realised she was not alone. She had caught a faint glimpse of movement out of the corner of her eye, fleeting, but long enough to have registered in her brain. She paused for a moment on the stairs and strained her ears. No, she had not imagined it. She could just make out the faint sound of someone breathing. Her own heart beat painfully and noisily in her chest. Someone was hiding in the dark at the top of the flight of stairs waiting for her. She fought desperately for an innocent reason to explain why anybody might wait for her in the shadows. Perhaps they thought there was not enough room for them to pass on the stairs and out of courtesy had held back to let her come up first so that they might pass on the landing where there was more space.

She stood stock still, not sure what to do. The temptation was to turn tail and run down the stairs two at a time. However, the idea of turning her back on a possible assailant was unbearable and besides, deep down she did not think she would make it to the bottom of the stairs before she was overpowered by a being much stronger than herself. Instead, she remained where she was and waited for the next move. It appeared, however, that her unseen adversary had made a similar decision. Save for the faint sound of breathing and her own beating heart, silence engulfed the staircase. Undeterred, she waited. It was only when the seconds became minutes, which seemed to her, in her highly agitated state, more like hours, that Rose could endure the endless waiting no longer. She felt at that moment that it was better to know the worst, than to be stuck in an unfathomable limbo.

'Who's there?'

She heard the waver in her voice, and her words themselves seemed to reverberate queerly in the confined space, producing an eerie echo.

A bitter laugh, which confirmed her worst fears, was the only reply she received. She heard the figure walk out of the shadows before she saw it standing perched at the top of the stairs looming over her. She did not need her eyes to tell her that it was Albert towering above her, a menacing expression distorting his handsome face.

She fought the impulse to scream aloud for help, for she did not want him to know how terrified she was. Besides, it was unlikely that anyone would hear her cries being huddled as they all were in the scullery.

The next minute, before she could think what to do, Albert had bounded down the stairs and was upon her, pushing her against the wall with sufficient force to make her stumble. He shoved his face so close to hers that she could feel his breath on her skin. Instinctively Rose recoiled, turning her gaze away from his face, but not before she had noticed the fury and hatred in his eyes. These violent emotions had the effect of disfiguring the young man's good looks to such an extent that she wondered why she had ever considered him handsome.

'Where is it?' Albert snarled. His voice was hardly recognisable.

'Where is what?' Rose asked, trying to keep the fear from her voice.

'I'm not in the mood to play games, Miss Denning. The diamond necklace, of course. Where is it?' He gripped her arm painfully and she winced.

'I don't know what you're talking about, Albert. I haven't got any diamond necklace.'

'Don't give me that! You accused me of going to Cooper's room to look for the necklace and you were right. Only you were there, so I couldn't look for it. Not then. Well, I've just come back from there now. Made a thorough search of the room, I did. And it wasn't there.' He bent towards her so that his face completely filled her vision. 'Still, you knew that already, didn't you? Because you took it.'

'I didn't,' said Rose, 'I promise I didn't.' This time she could not keep the fear from her voice.

Rose closed her eyes. Albert did not believe her and there was nothing she could say to make him. Any moment now, he would fasten his hands around her throat and later they would find her lying crumpled in a heap at the bottom of the stairs. This was the moment for her able mind to find a solution, but she felt as if all her inner strength had been drained from her. Even as these thoughts raced through her brain, she felt Albert's hands upon her neck. She imagined the inspector and Sergeant Harris exchanging knowing looks, satisfied that their misgivings and predictions had proved correct. With a sob, she saw Cedric's face as he waited in vain for his bride to appear. She would never now walk down the church aisle to greet him. Never would he see her in the wedding dress that had been so lovingly made by her mother ...

'Albert! What are you doing?'

The voice, unexpected as it was, jolted her brain and she was brought back to reality. It appeared to have had a similar effect on Albert, for he immediately released his grip on her throat. He then lurched forward, stumbling down the steps in his haste, pushing past the man who had so mercifully interrupted them, before disappearing through the door at the bottom.

'Miss Denning. Are you hurt?' The man moved a step or two forward. 'What happened?'

'I'm all right, thank you, Mr Mason,' said Rose, collecting her scattered thoughts. Apart from her arm, which ached a bit, she was somewhat surprised to find that she was indeed physically unharmed. 'I will come and see you in your pantry in a minute and tell you all about it. But first ... first I must speak to Martha.'

'But Miss Denning –'

Rose looked down at the butler. His face was pale and drawn, and he was trembling a little. It was patently obvious that the scene he had just witnessed had given him a considerable shock. 'If you wish to help me,' she said more gently, 'please keep an eye on Albert.'

Before the butler could respond, Rose was racing up the stairs, leaving him further and further behind. She did not stop to take a breath until she had reached the attics, and then she only paused for a moment. Then she was running almost blindly down the corridor, banging with her fist on any door that happened to be closed and flinging it open. Her feet stomped on the bare floorboards, making sufficient noise to wake the dead. But she was oblivious to all this, aware only that she couldn't find Martha. Each door she opened revealed a room that was empty. Panic threatened to overpower her, and she began to fear the worst.

It was only as she neared the end of the corridor that a door was flung open and the figure of Martha appeared. Her eyes were large with fright, her face pale and white. She might have been a ghost had it not been for the red rimmed eyes. Her lips trembled and she clung to the door, as if she intended to use it as a weapon.

It was only then that it occurred to Rose what a sight she must look and how bizarre her behaviour must seem, running down the corridor, opening and shutting the doors like a creature possessed. Martha had been in an agitated state for days, on the verge of going to pieces. Rose had no wish to alarm her and add to her suffering.

'Martha.' Rose put out a hand to touch her arm, but the girl shrank from her, and looked for a moment as if she might retreat back into her room and lock the door behind her. 'Martha. Please, listen to me. I know you're frightened, but I want to help you.'

'No one can help me,' said Martha. Tears filled her eyes at the unexpected kindness in the other girl's voice. She made no further attempts to retreat. Instead she leaned against the doorframe, as if she did not have the strength to stand without support. 'I'm going to prison.'

'No you're not,' said Rose firmly, though even as she uttered the words, she knew she had no right to give such an assurance.

'It's very kind of you, I'm sure, but I don't see how you can possibly help me, Miss Denning,' mumbled Martha.

There was a look of hostility on Martha's face. She had regained some of her composure and was eyeing Rose suspiciously, as if she did not trust her. Certainly she must think her unduly interfering and inquisitive. Rose realised then that Martha was not the type of person who would answer questions simply to satisfy someone else's idle curiosity, particularly as to do so was likely to place her in a more precarious position. It seemed to Rose then that there was only one course of action.

'I'm not Miss Denning,' she said, removing her spectacles. 'I'm not even a lady's maid. My name is Rose Simpson, and I am a sort of amateur sleuth. Mrs Grayson-Smith engaged my services to recover her diamond necklace. I am also now investigating the murder of Velda Cooper. The police know who I am and why I am here in this house masquerading as a servant. Now, Martha, if you please, I should like to ask you one or two questions.'

Chapter Twenty-seven

For a moment it did not look as if Martha would relinquish her position by the door. The colour had drained from her face following Rose's disclosure and with trembling hands she clutched the door to her, as if warding off a dangerous spirit. However, following a few persuasive words of encouragement, the housemaid reluctantly released her hold and fell back against the wall sobbing bitterly. She made her hand into a ball and used it to mop ineffectually at her eyes. Rose passed Martha her own handkerchief and waited for the crying to subside, before steering Martha back into the room she shared with Agnes. It was almost an exact replica of Pearl and Edna's. Heartily sick of looking at the same sage green walls, Rose encouraged Martha to sit on the one solitary chair, while she herself perched on the end of a bed.

'Am I in trouble?' sniffed Martha through her sobs. 'Will I lose my job?'

'I don't know,' said Rose truthfully. 'I rather think that might depend on what you have done.'

'Albert made me do it. I didn't want to. I knew it was wrong.'

'I don't doubt it.'

'He can be awful persuasive, can Albert. When he wants to be, he'll be as kind as anything. I've never known a man be so tender.' This description of the young man's character was accompanied by a sad little smile from Martha.

Rose, whose thoughts drifted back to her recent encounter with the said Albert on the stairs, when the man had been anything but gentle, felt not a little riled by Martha's misplaced sentimentality. She had a very good mind to get up and shake the girl by her shoulders, or splash her face with cold water. Resisting the temptation to do either, she said: 'I'm sure he can be.'

'And he has matinee idol looks, don't you think so? He could have had any girl, but he chose me.'

Rose thought of Velda Cooper and the mistress of the house. She wondered if Martha knew about Albert's affair with the lady's maid, or his attempt to seduce poor Millicent. She was inclined to enlighten the girl for her own good, but on reflection decided that to do so would be unwise, particularly given the girl's present fragile state. It might also hinder her investigations, and she must speak to Martha before Albert intervened. But neither did she wish to have to sit there and hear about the admirable qualities that poor, deluded Martha thought her young man possessed.

'Look here, Martha,' she said, 'We might not have much time. The police will want to speak to you in a minute and I should like to ask you a few questions first.'

'Oh?' The haunted look returned to Martha's eyes and she seemed to withdraw within herself.

'I overheard your conversation with Albert in the kitchen courtyard the day before yesterday,' said Rose, deciding that a direct approach might be best. 'I didn't mean to eavesdrop,' she lied, 'but I couldn't help noticing that you sounded upset. I was rather anxious about you, you see.'

Martha stared at her apprehensively, but chose to say nothing. The colour had drained from her face except for two bright spots of pink that had appeared on her cheeks.

'You were discussing the diamond necklace, the one that is missing,' said Rose, though in fact neither had referred to it by name. 'You told Albert you knew he had it.'

'I was upset,' replied Martha, rallying a little, 'I was thinking about that stupid little snuff box, the one that caused so much fuss. I thought just because he'd taken that, he must have taken the necklace as well. It was silly of me to think such a thing because you see he put the snuff box back. It was just a silly prank. He didn't mean any harm by it.'

'I'm sorry, Martha, but I'm afraid that really won't do,' said Rose firmly. 'I couldn't see your face because of the bedsheet. It made me listen all the more carefully to what you were saying and the way that you said it.' She paused a moment. 'You see, I realised that it wasn't so much that you suspected Albert had stolen the necklace. You *knew* he had taken it.'

Martha mopped her eyes with the handkerchief and looked at the floor. After a short while, she lifted her gaze so that her eyes met Rose's.

'Albert didn't take the necklace.'

'Of course he —'

'I know Albert didn't take the necklace because I did,' said Martha quietly.

'You did?'

'Yes. That morning, Miss Cooper came down into the servants' hall in ever such a foul mood. She'd just taken the mistress up her morning cup of tea and she'd spotted the necklace on top of the jewel box, ever so careless like. She said if people couldn't be bothered to look after such valuable jewellery properly, well then they didn't ought to have it.'

'And that is when you decided to steal it?'

'It was Albert who decided we should. To teach the mistress a lesson, so he said. I was to take it and then, when she discovered it was lost, he'd produce it from under the carpet or some such place and say he'd found it there. He said she'd be ever so grateful that she might even give him a reward.'

'But she might not have realised it was missing for months,' protested Rose. 'It was only by chance that she discovered it was gone when she did.'

'Well, it wouldn't have mattered. I was to keep it safe for her,' said the housemaid adopting a defensive tone. 'I'm not saying I might not have taken it out and looked at it every so often when I was alone, because I might have done. I might even have put it on, just to see how it looked. But I would have kept it safe for her, and as soon as she knew it was missing, we'd have pretended we'd found it. So there would have been no harm in it.'

'Is that what Albert told you would happen?' asked Rose incredulous. She could not refrain from adding: 'And you believed him?' She wondered at that moment whether the girl was incredibly stupid or remarkably naïve.

'I did then,' admitted Martha blushing. 'Of course, I don't believe him now.'

'You must have slipped in to Mrs Grayson-Smith's room while she was in the bathroom having her bath?'

'Yes. Albert said it wouldn't look odd if anyone were to catch me. I could say something like I was checking to see what would need dusting later.'

'I suppose you were afraid that the necklace would be locked away in the jewel box if you waited until you came up to tidy the room?'

'Yes. And you see, it wasn't my turn to do her room. Agnes and me, we take it in turns. It makes the job more interesting.'

'What I don't understand is how you managed to get the necklace out of the room. Your apron doesn't have any pockets, and the necklace was too large and bulky for you to hide it about your person.'

'I threw it out of the window, miss. I'm a good shot on account of having four brothers.' For a moment Martha looked rather proud. 'We was always playing cricket when we were children, or our version of it, anyway. I threw the necklace into one of those stone flowerpots on the terrace. I knew it wouldn't spoil or break because the gardeners had only just forked over the soil in them the day before, so I knew it would be nice and soft.'

'I see. Most ingenious. I take it you had arranged with Albert that he should take the necklace out of the flowerpot?'

'Yes. He was to remove it when the coast was clear, and give it to me to hide in my drawer of the chest-of-drawers where Agnes wouldn't see it.' She got up from her chair and pulled out one of the drawers to illustrate. 'I was going to wrap it up in a handkerchief and put it here under my stockings. It would have been quite safe. Only, of course, that's not what happened.'

'And thank goodness!' exclaimed Rose. 'It would have been discovered when the search was made of all the servants' rooms and then you would have been in no end of trouble, Martha.'

The housemaid bit her lip, and looked as if she were about to cry again.

'Something went wrong with your plan though, didn't it Martha?' said Rose quickly.

'Yes. Albert said he couldn't find the necklace. According to him, it wasn't in the flowerpot. He said I must have thrown it into another one by mistake. Awful cross with me, he was. And I was just as angry with him because I knew I'd thrown it into the right one.' She stared at her hands, which rested in her lap. 'Of course, I knew he was lying about not finding the necklace. He was putting on an act. Even him being furious with me didn't last very long. He pretended we'd have to check all the other flowerpots. 'Course it were all an act. I knew that. He'd stolen it. He wasn't ever going to give the necklace back to the mistress. He was going to sell it and keep the money for himself. He was a thief and he's made me one too.'

'It's possible I may be able to recover the necklace, Martha. I can't promise you I will, but I shall do my very best.'

'Oh, will you, miss? I'd be ever so grateful.'

'Yes. And if we recover it, your mistress might never need to know what happened.'

'You mean I wouldn't lose my job?' Martha brightened considerably. 'And I wouldn't have to go to prison?'

'No.'

Suddenly a cloud passed over Martha's face and her expression again became strained.

'What's the matter?' asked Rose considerably alarmed by Martha's transformation.

'I'd forgotten about Albert.'

'That young man can look after himself,' Rose said with feeling. 'I daresay some time in prison would do him the world of good, though I suppose it'd be too much to expect him to change his ways.' She stretched out her arm and took one of Martha's hands in hers. 'Listen to me, Martha. I know this will be hard, but you must try and forget Albert. He'll never do you any good, and you don't owe him anything.'

'I know that, miss. I know you are right.'

'Well, then –'

'It's not that, miss, that's worrying me. It's … Oh, miss, he did it. Albert did her in.'

'What? Are you saying Albert killed Miss Cooper?'

'Yes,' cried Martha, covering her face with her hands. 'I didn't want to say nothing. I didn't want to see him hang. I know he's wicked but –'

'Martha, how do you know that Albert killed Miss Cooper? Did he tell you he had?' An awful thought suddenly crossed Rose's mind. 'You weren't … you weren't there when it happened?'

'No, miss, of course not,' Martha looked appalled. 'It was just something he said that made me think he didn't like her. Always watching her, he was, as if he didn't trust her. And the things she said about him in the servants' hall. Why, you were there yourself, miss. You must have heard how she went on at him something awful?'

'Yes, I did,' said Rose, trying to hide her disappointment.

For a moment she had thought Martha had something important to tell her, that she was in possession of some evidence that would prove

Albert's guilt. But it appeared the girl knew nothing of substance, her knowledge only confirmed what Rose had already suspected or could ordinarily have assumed. In public, Albert cast only furtive glances at Cooper. To any observer who scrutinised his movements closely, such as the besotted Martha, his manner would naturally appear stealthy and surreptitious. And he had participated in a brilliant charade with the lady's maid, the intention of which had now become apparent. Their aim had been to make everyone think that they violently disliked one another, to divert suspicion from their true relations. She admonished herself severely, for she should have had some inkling that the scene was not as it appeared. The confrontation had been far too staged and dramatic.

'I knew he didn't like her,' cried Martha. 'But still I wouldn't have thought he'd … Last night, when I was in bed, thoughts kept rushing around in my head and I couldn't sleep for worrying. I couldn't get it out of my mind that we'd stolen the mistress' necklace. I knew Albert wasn't going to give it back. It was eating away at me knowing that. And Albert had been avoiding me. He didn't want to talk about it. Well, I'd decided that I had had enough. I couldn't go on like that. It was making me ill, and everyone had noticed and was commenting on it.' She bent forward and whispered: 'I think Mrs Field was afraid I had got myself into trouble, I looked that pale. Anyway, I had made my mind up that I was going to talk to Albert in the morning and let him know I intended to tell Mr Mason everything.'

Inwardly Rose uttered a sigh of relief that Martha had not had the opportunity to do so. But for providence, there might well have been two bodies found that morning instead of one.

'I'd made my decision,' Martha was saying. 'But I still couldn't get to sleep. I got it into my head, you see, that I wouldn't have a chance to speak to Albert in the morning. He'd make sure he was busy or wasn't alone. He didn't want me to go on about the necklace.'

'So what did you do?' asked Rose, her eyes gleaming with renewed interest.

'I couldn't help thinking that there was no time like the present. Albert had a room of his own, you see, so I knew we wouldn't be disturbed. He used to share the room with Archie, who was the first footman, but he went off to London and his position hasn't been filled, nor never will be, if you listen to Agnes.'

'What about your reputation? Weren't you afraid it might be ruined? If anyone had caught you –'

'But they didn't. Oh, miss. I was that upset about the necklace, I couldn't think about anything else. You know, this house isn't like some places I've worked in. There they have a door between the male and female staff's quarters that is kept locked. They don't have one here, which is funny when you think how particular Mrs Field is.'

'Go on,' said Rose. 'Did you go to Albert's room?'

'Yes. I opened his door ever so quiet like and … and he wasn't there. His bed, it hadn't even been slept in. Oh, miss. I was so afraid. I thought he was doing some more thieving while the whole house was asleep. I was that upset, I ran back to my room and cried myself to sleep. It was only this morning when I learned that Miss Cooper had been murdered that I wondered whether –'

'That was what he had been up to?' supplied Rose.

'Yes. But it wasn't just that, miss. Mr Mason, he locks the doors to the main house at night. I never knew that until Agnes told me this morning. So you see, Albert couldn't have been thieving because he wouldn't have been able to leave the servants' quarters. The only place he could have gone was downstairs into the workrooms. And I can't see he'd have had any reason to go into the kitchen or the scullery or the boot room –'

'But he might well have had reason to go into the servants' hall,' said Rose.

The two girls made their way quickly downstairs to eat what was left of the food set out for them in the scullery. Glancing at her companion, Rose was relieved to see that some of the natural colour had returned to Martha's complexion. The girl could not be said to be happy, but there was certainly an improvement in her mental state. She was quiet, but she was not sobbing. She had clearly resigned herself to the situation and decided to make the best of it. The heavy secret she had been carrying, which had been eating her up inside, was gone. The very process of confiding in someone like Rose had been cathartic.

As they came into the passage, Rose caught a brief glimpse of Mason, standing before his pantry. It reminded her that she still had to speak to him, and she wondered whether he had been waiting for her. Telling Martha to go on without her, and that she would catch her up in a minute,

Rose made her way to the butler's pantry. The passage was quiet and almost deserted now, the majority of the servants having had their meals and returned to their duties. Mason himself had already disappeared into the preserve of his pantry, and it was with a strange sense of foreboding that Rose knocked tentatively on the door.

'Oh, do come in, Miss Denning,' said the butler rising from his seat behind the desk. 'Will you not sit down?'

He beckoned to the chair in front of his desk, but Rose chose to remain standing, resting her hand instead on the back of the proffered chair.

'If you don't have any objection, I should prefer to stand,' she said rather primly.

'As you wish,' replied Mason, his manner strangely deferential given his understanding that her position was that of a lady's maid.

For a moment, Rose wondered whether he knew her true identity, but dismissed the idea almost at once. She thought it unlikely that Pearl and Edna would have told him. Martha was the only other person among the servants to know, and she had had no opportunity to do so, for Rose had accompanied her down from the attics and not left her side until she had come in search of the butler. It was only once the conversation progressed that Rose realised that the butler's oddly respectful manner towards her was due to acute embarrassment. He had caught her in an awful situation with his nephew which, by anyone's standards, and certainly by the values of a diligent and upstanding butler, should have led to Albert's immediate dismissal.

There was an awkward silence, with neither knowing quite how to begin. Mason appeared suddenly intrigued by the papers scattered on his desk in front of him, though closer inspection would have revealed his eyes were glazed. Meanwhile, Rose had let her gaze drift to the mahogany safe cabinet, the temporary resting place of the ill-fated necklace.

The butler coughed. 'Albert … Albert –' he began.

'Albert is a very dangerous young man, as well you know, Mr Mason,' said Rose rather abruptly. 'If you hadn't come upon us when you did, I don't even want to think about what might have happened.'

'Albert does have a violent temper that needs to be checked,' admitted the butler, speaking very quietly.

'That is an understatement to say the least!' cried Rose. 'Did you not see that he had his hands about my throat? I feared for my life, Mr

Mason.' She found herself suddenly consumed with an overwhelming anger. It may have been this, or the delayed shock from the incident itself, which had the effect of loosening her tongue so that her words seemed to run away with themselves before she could check them. 'A member of your staff lies dead in your servants' hall, and the police are very much of the opinion that Albert killed her.'

'How ... how can you possibly know that?'

The butler's face was ashen. In a few seconds he seemed to have aged years, the lines on his face had become deeper and more numerous, and the black smudges under his eyes were accentuated by his pale complexion. To even the most casual observer, it was obvious that the news had unsettled him. To Rose, who watched him closely, it was also apparent that her words, uttered so recklessly, also confirmed his very worst fears. Immediately she regretted her outburst. It suggested that she was in the confidence of the police. At a loss as to how she might answer his question, she finally settled on posing one of her own.

'Well, you tell me why you insist on protecting Albert?' She held up a hand as Mason made to protest and her voice rose. 'You suspect him of the murder of Miss Cooper. You are fully aware that he intended to do me harm. And, even before the events of today, you knew him to be a thief. Yet you have not dismissed him.' She gave a sigh of frustration. 'Why, I have never met a man more ill-suited for the position of footman.'

'Miss Denning, please!' cried Mason, looking appalled.

'I know Albert is your nephew and you feel that you have a responsibility towards him and your sister,' Rose said more quietly, 'But you would never accept such disgraceful behaviour and wilful insolence from another servant.'

'I think you had better leave, Miss Denning.' There was a coldness to the butler's voice that Rose found chilling. 'We shall perhaps continue this conversation when you are in a more rational frame of mind.'

'I am in a perfectly rational frame of mind,' cried Rose. 'It is you who are not.'

'Miss Denning!' This time she had sufficiently provoked the butler to induce him to glare at her and raise his own voice. 'Enough. I will not tolerate an outburst of this nature. Really, Miss Denning, I am surprised at your impertinence.' He paused for a moment to achieve maximum effect.

'Please remember that as a lady's maid you are an upper servant, and as such you should set an example by your behaviour.'

'I am sorry if I have offended you, Mr Mason,' Rose said quietly, taking the seat previously proffered, much to the surprise and consternation of the butler. 'But you see, I'm not really a servant so I am not sure how to behave as one. My name is not Miss Denning, it is Rose Simpson. I am what you might call an amateur detective. Mrs Grayson-Smith has engaged me to recover her diamond necklace.' She removed her spectacles. 'Naturally I am now also required to investigate the murder of Velda Cooper. I would, therefore, very much appreciate it if you would answer my questions.'

The butler stared at her dumbfounded. His mouth opened, but no words came out. During what he had called her outburst, he had risen to his full height and stuck out his pigeon chest in an imposing fashion. Now he seemed to falter. His hands clung to the fabric of his waistcoat and he removed an imaginary piece of fluff from his coat. Slowly he lowered himself on to his chair. All the while his lips were working silently, as if of their own accord. It was as if he were trying to formulate sentences before saying them aloud.

''What hold has Albert over you, Mr Mason?' asked Rose gently. A sudden thought struck her. 'Is he … is he by any chance your son?'

'No, he is not, Miss Simpson,' the butler retorted. 'I don't know what made you think such a thing. I am unmarried.'

Rose was relieved to see some colour had been restored to his cheeks. She had an odd desire to laugh at his righteous indignation.

'But he does have a hold over you, does he not? Won't you tell me what it is?'

The butler raised his head and gave a look of resignation. Rose thought he also looked a little relieved at the prospect of relinquishing his secret.

'I suppose it had to come out in the end, Miss Simpson. Albert didn't take the snuff box. I did.'

Chapter Twenty-eight

Inspector Connor did not think that he had ever seen such a disreputable looking young fellow. The footman was dressed in a smart enough livery of striped waistcoat and tails, but the waistcoat had been done up haphazardly, with some of the buttons inserted in the wrong holes, as if the wearer did not give a care about the overall effect. There was a smudge of grease on one of the jacket's lapels, and the man's bow tie was slanted, as if it had been knocked, or had caught on something; it looked almost on the verge of coming undone. To make matters worse, the man's hair did not look brushed, and a lock fell carelessly over one eye.

It was not, however, the man's dishevelled and unkempt appearance that had caused the inspector to arrive at such a negative assessment of him. It had more to do with the way the man had slouched into the room, hands in pockets, whistling softly under his breath. He had fallen further in Inspector Connor's estimations by throwing himself down into a chair before it was proffered, and looking at them impertinently, a grin on his face. Meanwhile, Sergeant Perkins, intrigued by such a blatant show of nonchalance and indifference, said to himself: 'He's our man!' Even Sergeant Harris, not a man given to excessive displays of emotion, could not hide his interest in the man lounging in the chair before them. He moved to take up his usual position, flicking open his notebook and picking up his pencil in eager anticipation.

'Now, young man, we have one or two questions to ask you,' said the inspector, adopting an authoritative tone, 'and you'd do well to answer them truthfully and without any cheek, mind.'

Albert raised his eyebrows lazily and gave the inspector something of a disrespectful look. Inspector Connor glared at him. It was a damn shame that a fellow like that was so handsome, and didn't he know it. He was just the sort of chap girls went mad over and he'd lead them astray all right. Manipulative, that's what he was. You could see it by the look in his eyes, and sly eyes they were too. Why, if he and his wife had been fortunate enough to have daughters, he wouldn't have let them anywhere near the fellow.

The door opened and Rose walked into the library. The insolent look on the man's face disappeared immediately and was replaced by one of apprehension.

''Ere, what's she doing 'ere? She's no business being 'ere. Tell her to leave.'

Sergeant Harris sat up in his chair and gazed at Rose speculatively. It was interesting that the girl's appearance had caused such a reaction in the fellow. He certainly was none too pleased to see her, that was for sure.

'This is Miss Simpson. I think you may know her rather better by the name Miss Denning,' said Inspector Connor, rather enjoying the man's obvious discomfort. 'Miss Simpson is something of a private enquiry agent. She has been engaged by Mrs Grayson-Smith to investigate the disappearance of a diamond necklace. She is also assisting us with our investigation into the murder of Miss Cooper.'

Albert paled visibly and swallowed hard. The inspector thought he could detect beads of perspiration on the young man's brow. There was certainly a look of fear in his eyes. Perhaps suddenly aware that his feelings had betrayed him, Albert made concerted efforts to regain his composure.

'I don't care who she is,' he said sullenly. 'I don't want her here. I don't have to have her here.'

'No, you don't,' agreed the inspector, 'not if you object.'

'Well, I do –' began Albert.

'I am quite sure you don't object to my presence, do you, Albert?' said Rose sweetly. 'If you do, I'm afraid that I might feel it my duty to tell the inspector about our ... our little conversation on the stairs. The one we were having before your uncle interrupted us.'

'You wouldn't dare,' snarled Albert.

'Why ever not?' said Rose coldly. 'I rather think Inspector Connor would accept my version of events over yours, don't you?'

If they had been alone, she thought it likely that Albert would have leapt from his chair and struck her. However, with the policemen present, and with the fear of having some of his more unsavoury behaviour revealed, this course of action was not open to him. It therefore did not surprise her when he did no more than lower his head and make them wait for his reply.

'Oh, all right. Let her stay then. I don't care,' he muttered at last, almost under his breath so that Sergeant Harris was obliged to lean forward in his chair to catch his words.

'Then that settles it,' said Inspector Connor. 'Now young man. I should like to ask you some questions, and as I have already said, I'd advise you to answer them truthfully, if you know what's good for you.' He gave Albert a hard stare. 'If you are innocent, you have nothing to worry about. Thanks to Miss Simpson here, we know a great deal already.'

Albert blanched and threw Rose a dirty look. He had entered the library an arrogant young man. Now the wind had been taken firmly out of his sails and he was an apprehensive one. With one hand he twisted a button on his waistcoat, with the other, he drummed his fingers on the seat of his chair.

'How well did you know the deceased, Albert?' The inspector's stare was sufficient to make the man shift in his chair and avert his gaze.

'Not very well. Just enough to pass the time of day.'

'Is that so? And yet you were spotted embracing in the library yesterday.'

'Who said we were? It ain't true. Martha's my girl. Ask anyone; they'll tell you the same.'

'And yet, as I understand it, you were caught in the act of kissing Miss Cooper passionately. Is that usually how you pass the time of day with mere acquaintances?'

Sergeant Harris gave a chuckle and Sergeant Perkins grinned.

'It's lies, I tell you,' said Albert. 'It's all damned lies.'

'I don't think so. Now,' said the inspector, putting up his hand as Albert made to protest, 'I'd like to clear up this business of the theft before we do anything else. I'd like you to tell me about Mrs Grayson-Smith's diamond necklace.'

'I don't know nothing about it,' Albert replied grumpily, 'it being missing, I mean. I saw the mistress wearing it at dinner when I was serving her. But I didn't steal it. They've all got it in for me in this house, they have. Just because I got into a bit of trouble as a lad. They think I stole that stupid old snuff box and all, and that old Mason made me put it back.' A smug look appeared on the footman's face and he tapped his nose in a secretive manner. 'But I know different.'

'So do I,' said Rose. Without exception, they all turned to look at her in surprise, Sergeant Harris included, his pencil poised in mid-air. 'Your uncle took the snuff box,' she said. 'He told me so himself. You had got yourself into trouble again and you came to him for help. You owed some money to some rather unpleasant characters and you pleaded with your uncle for him to settle your debt.'

'Well, aren't we the clever one?' said Albert rather nastily. 'If you know so much, why don't you tell the policemen here what happened?'

'Very well, if you want me to. Your uncle agreed to help you but, not surprisingly, he did not have the amount of money you required readily to hand. He told you he would need to go to his bank to withdraw some of his savings. He intended to do so the very next day, but you were desperate. You needed the money that evening.'

'He promised he'd help me,' said Albert, his voice a petulant whine. 'He said he'd pawn one of Mr Grayson-Smith's old snuff boxes. He knew the pawnbroker chap, said he was honest and would give him a good price. The stupid box would only have been gone for one night. 'Cause he'd have got it back the next day when he'd got his money from the bank. Nobody would have been any the wiser. The master, he was away and no one else looks at those old boxes.'

'But someone must have done,' pointed out Sergeant Perkins, 'because it was commented upon that the snuff box was missing.'

'It was Mrs Field. Fieldy.' Albert laughed. 'That's what Martha and Agnes call her. She's a right interfering Mrs Grundy,' He made a face. 'She don't approve of me. Always telling Martha she can do much better for herself.'

'I daresay she's right,' piped up Sergeant Harris, not to be outdone by Sergeant Perkins.

'What did you say?' snarled Albert, turning around in his seat to face the older sergeant.

'That will do,' said the inspector, including the sergeant in his glance 'Now, you were saying that Mason took the snuff box to pawn?'

'Only he didn't, did he?' said Albert with a note of disgust in his voice. 'Pawn it, that is. His conscience got the better of him. That's what he told me. Halfway to the pawnbroker's and he changes his mind. He couldn't do it to the master, that's what he said. Made a bit of a sermon of it. A butler must have absolute integrity and be honest. He must be beyond reproach.'

'So he put the snuff box back? But not before it had been missed?' said Inspector Connor.

'That's right, And I didn't get my money until the next day,' said Albert bitterly. 'A broken rib I got because of it and a black eye. I was lucky they didn't break my nose.'

'It wasn't your money,' said Rose coldly. 'It was your uncle's. And I think you were jolly lucky that he gave it to you at all. It was his savings.' She gave him a contemptuous look. 'I doubt you even thanked him, not properly. And ever since, you have been holding that snuff box over him, threatening to tell everyone he is a thief. That's why you are employed here, isn't it, Albert? You would never have got the position of footman otherwise. You are lazy and slovenly and –'

''Ere, are you going to let her talk to me like that?' protested the young man.

'I doubt whether it's any worse than you deserve,' Inspector Connor said. 'Now, Albert, you were telling me about the diamond necklace.'

'I wasn't. I ain't got nothing to tell.'

'Albert, this will not do. I suggest you be cooperative,' said the inspector, finding the young man's attitude tiresome in the extreme. At this rate the interview was likely to last a few hours. 'We have it on good authority that you persuaded Martha to steal the necklace for you. You had discovered that it had been left out on top of the jewel box. I admit it was very careless of Mrs Grayson-Smith and quite a temptation to a fellow like you. Now, tell us what happened. I think we can agree it was a crime of opportunity. We know Martha threw the necklace out of the window into one of the stone flowerpots on the terrace, because she told us so herself, first to Miss Simpson and then she repeated her story to us.'

'I say, you have been busy, Miss Simpson,' said Albert, staring at her with open animosity. 'All right. We decided to borrow the necklace. We weren't going to keep it. We were going to return it as soon as it was missed.'

Sergeant Harris gave a snort.

'Anyway, it was Martha's idea, not mine,' said Albert glumly. 'I didn't want nothing to do with it. I knew I'd get the blame. But Martha, she got it into her head that she wanted to try it on. She wanted to see how it'd look with that dress of hers that she wears to dances, not that she could ever have worn it out.'

'I should think not,' said the inspector with some feeling. 'Now Albert, what we want to know is, where is this necklace now? Did you sell it?'

'No, I didn't! Not on my mother's life,' cried Albert. 'I haven't got it. I never did have it.' He glared at them. 'Why won't you listen to me? Martha told me she'd thrown it out of the window like we'd agreed, but it wasn't there, not in the flowerpot. She swore blind she'd thrown it into the right one, but it wasn't there. We looked in all the flowerpots. It was gone.'

'When did you go on to the terrace to look for it?' the inspector asked sharply.

'Not 'til later that day,' said Albert. 'Course, we'd have gone sooner only the mistress discovered the necklace was missing only a few minutes after Martha had thrown it out of the window. And what a to-do she made over it. You never did see such a fuss; ripping up carpets and emptying drawers. And then when she demanded that all the servants' rooms be searched …' He threw up his hands in a dramatic gesture.

'You were in a panic?' suggested Inspector Connor.

'You're right we were in a panic. We decided it was best to leave the necklace where it was.'

'In the flowerpot?'

'Yes. I told you.'

'So you did,' said the inspector gravely. 'But here's the thing, Albert. I don't say you didn't leave the necklace in the flowerpot until after the search. But I think you retrieved it later. I wager you've still got it. I don't think it was lost, like you said. Now, young man, why don't you give it to us? You know, Mrs Grayson-Smith has never officially reported that it was stolen. She strikes me as a thoroughly decent kind of woman. All she wants is her necklace back. I doubt very much she will press charges.'

'How many more times must I tell you, Inspector? I haven't got that damned necklace. I never had it.' Albert covered his head with his hands. 'Why won't anyone believe me?'

'I believe you,' said Rose.

'Do you?' said the inspector looking interested.

'Yes, I do. For the simple reason, Inspector, that Albert has been spending the whole day looking for the necklace. He came up to Cooper's room to look for it while I was searching the room myself. It gave us both a fright, I can tell you.'

What? You were searching the deceased's room?' cried the inspector, looking appalled. 'Look here, Miss Simpson –'

'And we had a conversation on the stairs, didn't we, Albert?' The man in question steadfastly refused to meet her gaze. 'Albert demanded to know where the necklace was. He was quite insistent that I had it.'

'If this fellow didn't take it, what did happen to the necklace?' asked Inspector Connor gruffly.

'It was picked up from the flowerpot by someone else, someone who witnessed the necklace being thrown from the window.'

'Who?' asked the three policemen in unison. Albert, she noticed, looked only a little curious.

'The deceased,' said Rose. 'I think Cooper was just about to go back into Mrs Grayson-Smith's room when she saw Martha standing by the window. I fancy she watched her from the doorway. She would have been curious to know why the girl was there, particularly as Martha was no doubt acting in a furtive manner. And then, when she witnessed her throwing something out of the window, Cooper was just the type of woman who would want to know what it was.'

'So she found an excuse to go out on to the terrace to investigate?' said Sergeant Perkins. 'I say, miss, she was jolly lucky to find the necklace. I mean, she didn't know that the girl was aiming for one of the stone flowerpots, did she?'

'No, but I think she could have made an educated guess. She was an intelligent woman. She would have realised that if Martha had thrown something straight on to the gravel, it would have been damaged, and when she inspected the terrace she would have seen that the soil in the flowerpots had been turned over and would make a soft landing. Besides, she might have known what she was looking for, which would have made it easier. She might even have spotted one of the diamonds glinting in the sun. And Mrs Grayson-Smith only had Cooper's word for it that she didn't look inside the jewel box to check that the necklace was there after she noticed that it had gone from the top. If she had, she would have realised immediately that the necklace was missing and guessed what she was looking for.'

'And if she didn't go out on to the terrace until later in the day, she would know for certain that the necklace had disappeared, because Mrs Grayson-Smith had found out by then and raised a hue and cry about it?' said Sergeant Perkins.

'Exactly, Sergeant. But the question now of course,' said Rose, 'is where is the necklace now? It wasn't hidden in Cooper's room, as both Albert and I can verify, and you didn't find it on the deceased did you?'

'Well, that's all fine and good,' said the inspector intervening, 'but I think we've wasted quite enough time on this necklace. Likely as not we'll find out what's happened to it during the course of our investigation. Now, I'd like to focus on the murder. Let's see what you have got to say for yourself about that, young man.'

'I think you will find, Inspector,' said Rose, ignoring the inspector's exasperated look at the unwelcome interruption, 'that once we find our murderer, we will discover the necklace.'

'I ain't got nothing to do with the murder,' said Albert, 'and you can't say I 'ave.'

'Is that a fact?' said the inspector coldly. 'And yet Martha has told us that when she decided to go to your room in the middle of the night, to have it out with you about the necklace, you were not there.'

Albert looked taken aback. 'That doesn't prove anything. I … I was most probably in the lavatory.'

'Martha told me that your bed hadn't been slept in,' said Rose.

'Thank you, Miss Simpson,' said the inspector rather brusquely. 'Now, Albert, we know you must have been downstairs in the servants' workrooms. There was nowhere else you could have been unless of course you were in one of the other servants' bedrooms –'

'I wasn't,' scowled Albert.

'I didn't think so,' said the inspector. 'Now let us agree you went downstairs. You couldn't have gone outside because Mason has told us that he locked the doors immediately after you had come back in from smoking your last cigarette for the night. He locked the doors into the main house a little later when the deceased returned. So you see, you could only have gone into the servants' quarters.'

'What if I did?' said Albert warily. 'Who's to say Velda Cooper was there then? For all you know, she was still in her room.'

'That is a possibility,' said the inspector, 'but an unlikely one. You and the deceased were on intimate terms. You had been caught in a passionate embrace that day. I think that we can assume, therefore, that you had arranged to meet with the deceased to discuss how to deal with the situation when it became common knowledge. Now, let us assume for the sake of argument that you had a disagreement. Velda Cooper wants you to end your relationship with Martha. You do not wish to. Instead, you try to end your relationship with the deceased. She in turn threatens to go to your Martha and give her all the sordid details of your affair.'

'No,' cried Albert. 'It never happened like that. I admit that I had arranged to meet her to talk over some matters. She'd teased me in the library about the necklace. Said everyone would think I'd stolen it because of the snuff box. I told her my uncle had taken the box and she'd laughed and said no one would believe me. She'd had a bit of a go at me in the servants' hall in front of everyone a day or so before and so I was none too pleased with her. But she told me that she hadn't meant anything by it and that she'd found the necklace just like you said.' He paused to jerk his head in Rose's direction. 'Said if I could find someone who'd buy it from her and give her a good price, she'd give me some of the money for my trouble.'

'So, what happened, Albert?' enquired Sergeant Harris, leaning forward to appear over the man's shoulder. 'You didn't think it was right that she'd taken the necklace from under your nose? A man like you wouldn't have been satisfied with only a share of the proceeds.'

'I tell you, I didn't kill her,' shouted Albert turning around. 'If you must know, she was dead when I found her.'

'A likely story,' said the inspector sceptically.

'It's true,' cried Albert. 'I found her in that chair with her head all bashed in. Awful it was. I didn't know what to do.'

'You could have called the police,' said Inspector Connor. 'It was your duty to do so.'

'I know,' said Albert, 'but I was in such a panic.'

'Another one? If you don't mind my saying, Albert,' said Sergeant Perkins, 'you seem to spend your life in a perpetual panic.'

'I knew everyone would think I'd done it,' said Albert glowering. 'That we'd had a lovers' quarrel and I done her in. Not that we were sweethearts. We'd only kissed the once in the library on account of her telling me about the necklace and the money she'd give me if I helped her.'

'You had no qualms about not returning the necklace to Mrs Grayson-Smith?' Sergeant Perkins asked with a smile.

'Charlie, please!' protested Inspector Connor. 'Go on, Albert.'

'To make matters worse, she'd packed her suitcase. That was a shock, I can tell you, seeing it sitting there by her chair. I didn't know she'd intended on leaving immediately. I'd have had to go with her to make sure I got my money. We'd probably have had to force one of the locks to get out.'

'A suitcase, you say?' said the inspector, looking up with interest. 'It wasn't there when we viewed the body?'

'No, it wouldn't have been, Inspector,' said Rose. 'Because Albert took it back upstairs and unpacked it, didn't you, Albert?'

'How did you know that?' demanded the footman incredulous.

'When I searched Cooper's room, it was obvious that someone had put the suitcase away rather carelessly on top of the wardrobe. When I opened it, I noticed that a piece of blue material was caught in the catch. It came from the blue silk satin dress that Mrs Grayson-Smith had been wearing that evening, which I found hanging in the back of Cooper's wardrobe.'

'I was in something of a rush,' said Albert, by way of explanation. 'I didn't want to be caught in her room, did I? Not with her lying dead downstairs and me rummaging through her things.'

'So that's why you saw the need to unpack the suitcase,' said Sergeant Perkins with sudden comprehension. 'You wanted to see if the necklace was in it.'

'No,' said Albert rather unconvincingly. 'I didn't want anyone to know she'd been intending on disappearing into the night. Not after that business in the library. They'd all have thought the worst. Said we was planning to elope, had an argument and I killed her, same as you did with your suspicious minds.'

'It is our job to be suspicious,' said the inspector, his tone serious. 'Did you find the necklace in the suitcase?'

'No.' The word was said with an air of defiance.

There followed a somewhat awkward silence.

'Why did you leave her coat?' asked Rose finally. 'She was wearing it, wasn't she?'

232

'That damned coat,' Albert said bitterly. 'With all the fuss and panic taking up the suitcase, it completely slipped my mind she had it on over her dress. And before you ask, 'course the pockets were the first thing I checked. The necklace wasn't in any of them.'

'Go on,' said the inspector, looking at him dubiously.

'Well, as I said, I had forgotten all about the coat and I went to bed. It wasn't going to be me who found the body, that was for sure. Anyway, it felt like I'd just laid my head upon the pillow, though I might have had an hour or two's kip, and blow me if I didn't hear the sound of running feet. It was Pearl, the little scullery maid. She'd found the body.'

'And it was then that you remembered about the coat?' asked Rose. 'You slipped downstairs while Pearl was telling Edna about the body. You intended to remove the coat from the body and hide with it in one of the workrooms until the coast was clear for you to creep back upstairs. You weren't expecting Edna to come down and make sure that there was a body before they woke Mrs Field.'

'No. Luckily I heard the girl before she came out into the passage or else she'd have caught me. I had to run into the boot room and hide.' He threw her a grudging look of admiration. 'I don't know how you do it, I must say.'

'You waited until Edna went back upstairs to wake up the housekeeper,' continued Rose, 'and then you removed the coat.'

'I did and then I went and hid again until I could return to my room without being seen. I kept the coat in my wardrobe, I did, until I knew nobody was about and I could put it back in Velda Cooper's room.'

'Well, Albert, that's quite a story you've told us,' said the inspector. 'I'm not saying parts of it aren't true, but … hello? Who's this?'

For Inspector Connor, on the verge of arresting the footman for murder, was distracted by a knock on the library door. It had been sufficiently loud to make them all start. Without exception, they turned towards it, and stared almost memorised as the door opened.

'Look here, Mason,' began the inspector. 'I know this fellow is your nephew but –'

'Inspector,' said the butler, 'I fear you are about to make a very grave mistake.' He drew himself up to his full height, his face solemn. 'I am here to confess to the murder of Velda Cooper.'

Chapter Twenty-nine

'What's the matter?' asked Lavinia. 'You look terrible. And where are your spectacles? I've become rather used to you flinging them down on the bed every time you come into my room.'

'I don't need to wear them anymore,' said Rose wearily. 'Almost everyone knows who I am, except the housekeeper. I suppose I ought to go and find her in a minute to explain what I am doing here disguised as a lady's maid.' She rubbed her forehead. 'It's funny. She never did consider me a very satisfactory servant. She didn't think me very good at upholding standards. She and Mason are rather alike in that way. He is all for setting a good example to the lower servants.'

'What *is* the matter, Rose?' asked Lavinia, looking at her closely. 'You do seem in rather an odd mood.'

'Mason has just confessed to Cooper's murder.'

'Gosh, has he really?' exclaimed Lavinia excitedly. 'Well I never! I wouldn't have had him down as the murderer.'

'I think it's all my fault, him confessing I mean,' Rose said, collapsing on to the bed. 'I as good as told him that the police were about to arrest Albert.'

'Does it really matter? If he's guilty –'

'But that's just it, Lavinia. I'm not sure he is. Oh, he gave a good enough reason for why he'd done it,' Rose said, getting off the bed and beginning to pace the room. 'I just can't help feeling that something's not quite right. I'm awfully afraid he might have confessed to the crime just to save Albert from the rope.'

'Well, if he did, I expect the police will come to the same conclusion,' Lavinia said, rather dispassionately. 'Now, what you need, Rose, is a nice cup of tea. I suppose we can do away with all the subterfuge now. I'll ring for some. Will it feel strange being waited on?' She made a face. 'Oh. I suppose we should invite Millicent to join us. If we can get her to leave her room, that is. I had no end of trouble trying to get her to come and have lunch. She's kept herself locked in her room all day. She wouldn't even let the maids in to tidy, which explains why my room is in such a mess. I suppose they'd decided that if they were not required to tidy her room, they wouldn't do mine either.'

'Well, they have been kept rather busy. Agnes has spent most of the morning looking after Pearl –'

'Pearl?'

'The scullery maid,' said Rose rather coldly. 'It was Pearl who found the body.'

'Oh, I see. And you needn't look at me like that. You can't expect me to remember everyone's name.'

'Did Millicent say why she was keeping herself locked in her room?' asked Rose curiously.

'She has got it into her head that she will be the murderer's next victim,' said Lavinia, far more casually than the statement deserved. 'I say, she will be pleased to hear about Mason's confession, though good butlers are very hard to come by these days.'

'You needn't be so flippant about it all,' protested Rose.

'I'm sorry,' said Lavinia, 'but you know it's how I'm made. It's the only way I can deal with situations like this.' She gave a high little laugh. 'I say, Milly really is rather a scream. She insisted on locking her bedroom door when we went for our interviews with the police. She even locked her door when we went down for lunch.'

'Did she indeed? I wonder why?'

'She said she was terrified that the murderer was going to creep into her room and hide in the wardrobe.'

It had involved a great deal of persuasion to entice Millicent to leave her room. She had stared at them blankly when they had informed her of Mason's confession, as if the words did not quite register in her brain. Certainly she just sat there listlessly in Lavinia's room, sipping her tea. Rose thought how pale and gaunt she looked. Even Lavinia, who was happily prattling away about nothing in particular, noticed that Millicent was shivering to such an extent that she sent Rose to get her a cardigan.

As she opened the door to Millicent's bedroom, Rose was reminded of a previous occasion when she had opened the door to find Cooper, her dark hair elaborately styled, her face expertly made up, dressed in Millicent's evening gown of royal blue silk satin. For a moment she saw her there, a ghostly image, staring at her reflection in the full-length looking glass. Rose recollected how, on discovering that she had been spotted dressed in her mistress' gown, Cooper had turned with one frightened movement to confront her. It was then that Rose remembered something else which had puzzled her at the time. It had been Velda Cooper's sudden aversion to a cape of silver fox fur that she had held in one hand. With one swift movement the woman had thrown it away from her and stared at it with something akin to distaste.

Alone in the room, Rose ran to the wardrobe and threw open the door. With trembling fingers, she rifled through the clothes in so careless and hasty a fashion that some slipped from their hangers and fell to the floor. She did not pause to pick them up. If anything, she seemed more determined in her quest, her movements becoming more hurried. Eventually she found what she was seeking. It was the silver fox fur cape. She snatched it from the wardrobe and turned it over to inspect its maroon-coloured satin lining. With not a thought to the damage she was causing, she tore a hole in the lining and put her hand inside. Her fingers touched something that was bulky and heavy and felt like pieces of heavy glass. With bated breath she quickly withdrew her hand, bringing out with it the item that had been hidden in the cape's lining. She did not need to look at the object to know that what she held in her palm was Millicent's diamond necklace.

'Mrs Field, may I come in?'

The door to the housekeeper's sitting room was half open, which afforded Rose a glance at Mrs Field before she was conscious of being observed. Unaware she was being watched, the woman was slouched in her seat, her hand playing with the fabric of her dress, her bunch of keys jangling softly, and her eyes staring unseeing into the distance. Rose's voice brought her to her senses and she struggled to her feet.

'Please don't get up on my account,' said Rose hurriedly. 'Would you mind if I sit down?'

'No, miss.'

There followed an uncomfortable silence. The housekeeper's deferential manner seemed strangely at odds with Rose's recollection of the woman. She realised that a gulf had sprung up between them. She no longer belonged in the servants' quarters and she was acutely aware that she was being viewed as trespassing.

All of a sudden words came tumbling out of Mrs Field's mouth as if she had kept them bottled up inside her.

'Albert and the others, they say you are not a servant at all. You're a private enquiry agent, whatever one of those is. They tell me the mistress has engaged you to recover her necklace and find the … the murderer.' She bent her head towards Rose and lowered her voice to barely above a whisper. 'Pearl says you're to be married to the Earl of Belvedere in a few days' time.'

'Yes, it's all true, I'm afraid, Mrs Field. I feel awfully beastly for having deceived you all. I do hope you won't hold it against me?'

'Not at all, miss,' said the housekeeper, though she looked considerably ill-at-ease. 'Do you know what's happening, miss? It's Mr Mason I'm worried about. He and Albert are with the policemen now and he's been gone ever such a long time. Usually he and I, we have our afternoon cup of tea together this time of day, just the two of us. It's not like him to miss it.'

'I am afraid that you must prepare yourself for a shock, Mrs Field,' said Rose gently.

'Why? What has happened? Pray do tell me, miss.'

There was a waver in the housekeeper's voice, and anguish in her eyes. It occurred to Rose that the woman was about to cry.

'Mr Mason has confessed to the murder of Velda Cooper.'

'No!' Mrs Field fell back in her chair and clasped a hand to her chest. 'That isn't right. He didn't do it. I don't believe it. Mr Mason would never do a thing like that. I don't understand. Why should he confess to such a thing?'

'I think he is trying to protect his nephew. You see, the police thought that Albert was the murderer. All the evidence was pointing that way. And he's admitted that he arranged to meet Miss Cooper last night when the rest of the house was asleep.'

'Of course it was Albert,' sniffed Mrs Field. 'Any fool could tell them that. He's a wrong 'un, always was and always will be. Oh, why would a man like Mr Mason risk his neck for that boy?'

'Because he's the boy's uncle.'

'They'll get to the truth, miss. The police, I mean. They'll let him go, just you see.'

'Perhaps, though I must say, Mr Mason gave a very convincing argument for why he had committed the murder.'

'Did he?' The housekeeper looked alarmed.

'Yes. Apparently, it was he who took the snuff box, not Albert as everyone thought. Borrowed might be a better word for it, as he intended to put it back. Of course, he took it for the very best of reasons. It was to help that nephew of his get out of trouble. Unfortunately, Albert told all to Miss Cooper. She, being of a rather spiteful disposition, threatened to tell your master, who I understand is very particular about his servants being honest. It would have meant Mr Mason losing his job.' Rose sat back in her chair. 'To some people, that wouldn't seem much of a motive for murder. But for a person like Mr Mason, for whom the position of butler is everything, it would mean a great deal. He has dedicated his life to serving the Grayson-Smith family. Crossing Manor is his home. I don't suppose he can imagine a different life, do you?'

'No,' said Mrs Field, producing a handkerchief and dabbing at her eyes, 'I don't suppose he can.'

'Oh,' said Rose, sounding more cheerful. 'There is one piece of good news. You'll be pleased to hear that we have recovered Mrs Grayson-Smith's diamond necklace. It's rather a long story, and I don't want to bore you with it, but it was Miss Cooper who had taken it. She'd hidden it in the lining of one of Mrs Grayson-Smith's fur stoles and hung it in your mistress' wardrobe. Rather ingenious, don't you think?'

'Yes.' Mrs Field shifted in her seat. 'Do you think that is why she was murdered? Someone knew she had taken the necklace and wanted it for themselves? Perhaps she wouldn't tell them where it was, or goaded them that she was in possession of it, so they killed her.'

'No.' said Rose. 'You see, Miss Cooper had the necklace with her when she was murdered. She was intending to leave Crossing Manor that night with Albert. In fact, she was all ready to leave. She'd brought down her suitcase into the servants' hall, and was wearing her coat. The necklace was most probably in her coat pocket. She wouldn't have left the necklace upstairs in Mrs Grayson-Smith's room, because she wasn't intending to go back there. And besides, she couldn't, even if she had wanted to, because Mason had locked the doors into the main house.'

'If what you are saying is true, then how is it that you found the necklace in the mistress' wardrobe?' asked the housekeeper. 'How did it get back up there?'

'Oh, that's easy to explain,' said Rose. 'The murderer put it back. During the conversation leading up to her murder, Miss Cooper must have disclosed her hiding place for the necklace. I dare say she bragged a bit about her own cleverness.'

'I see.'

'Do you?' Rose sat forward in her seat. 'There is only one person who had an opportunity to put the necklace back in its hiding place this morning, when the doors from the servants' hall to the main house were unlocked. Mrs Grayson-Smith has kept to her room all day. She has forbidden the maids to tidy her room, and on the few occasions she has left her room, she has locked the door behind her.'

'Surely you're not suggesting that the mistress killed –'

'No, Mrs Field, I am not. I am suggesting that *you* killed Miss Cooper.'

The housekeeper opened her mouth once or twice, but no words came out. She stared at Rose with eyes full of anguish, and then slumped back into her chair.

'You are the only person, other than Lady Lavinia and myself, whom Mrs Grayson-Smith has admitted to her room today. When you realised I would not be attending to your mistress, you were adamant that you attend to her yourself rather than have one of the housemaids do it, which I understand is the usual practice. It provided you with an opportunity to return the necklace to its hiding place while your mistress was having her bath. I daresay you brought it into the room wrapped up in a towel. You would have been desperate to get rid of it. You didn't want it discovered in your room.'

A silence filled the housekeeper's sitting room and the two women looked at each other, one with fear and the other with pity. It was Mrs Field in the end who broke the silence.

'Yes. I did it. I killed her.' She held her head in her hands. 'Even now, I can't believe I did it. I never intended to.' She looked up at Rose through her tears. 'The reasons Mr Mason gave for killing Miss Cooper, you knew they were my reasons too, didn't you?'

'Yes, that's to say, I guessed they were.'

'I'll tell you how it was. I'd like to get it off my chest by telling someone. Something had woken me and I couldn't get back to sleep. Perhaps it was Miss Cooper going down the stairs with her suitcase. I thought I'd make myself a nice cup of tea. How I wish I hadn't! As I was making my way down the passage, I noticed there was a light on in the servants' hall. It struck me as strange. So I went in. And there was Miss Cooper, standing there as bold as brass with her coat on and her suitcase by her feet. She was holding the mistress' diamond necklace in her hand, holding it out to see how it caught the light.'

'It must have given her quite a shock to see you?'

'It did. She knew she'd been caught in the act good and proper. She had nothing to lose but to tell me how it was Mr Mason who'd taken the snuff box, not Albert. She said she was leaving with the necklace and if I tried to stop her she'd tell the master about Mr Mason.' She sobbed. 'He's such a good, upright man, is Mr Mason, he wouldn't have denied it, not if the master had asked him outright. He'd have told the truth. And you're right about the master being very particular about his servants being honest. Mr Mason would have lost his job. It would have destroyed him.' The housekeeper held up her head. 'It would have destroyed me too. Being housekeeper here means as much to me as being butler does to Mr Mason. We've both dedicated our lives to serving the Grayson-Smith family. I can't imagine a life away from Crossing Manor, but it wouldn't have been the same without Mr Mason.' She paused. 'I couldn't imagine a world without Mr Mason in it.'

'Do you love him so very much?' asked Rose softly.

'More than life itself,' declared Mrs Field. 'I've been here at Crossing Manor since I was a young woman, and Mr Mason since he was a young man. We've grown up together as you might say. I loved him from the moment I first set eyes on him. I thought in time he might feel the same way about me. But he never did. Unrequited love, that's what they call it, isn't it? But I cherished what we had, running this house in partnership, taking tea and coffee together in this sitting room. Sometimes, when we sat side by side in front of the fire, I could almost imagine we were a married couple.' She smiled and then her face darkened. 'I wasn't going to let her take it all away from me. I wasn't going to let her hurt him.'

'But to kill her!' said Rose.

'It was her own fault really. She wouldn't let it alone. She had to tease me about Mr Mason. She said he'd never look at someone like me and that it was pathetic for a grown woman to carry on so. Then she picked up her suitcase and went and sat in one of the armchairs and started reading her magazine as if nothing had happened. I was so angry I couldn't help myself. I saw the saucepan lying there. I picked it up and hit her on the head before I knew what I was doing, and then I hit her again and again … I couldn't stop.'

'What did you do next?' asked Rose with a heavy heart.

'After the anger faded, I couldn't believe what I had done. Then I remembered the necklace. It had fallen out of her pocket and was lying on the floor. I wanted to return it to the mistress. I couldn't do anything for poor Miss Cooper, but I could return the necklace. Miss Cooper had told me about her hiding place for it. Very clever she thought she was. I thought I'd put it back there for safekeeping and then in a few days' time I'd produce it and say I'd found it somewhere. Then I went to bed. I didn't know what else to do. I didn't for one moment think I'd fall asleep, not after killing someone. But the odd thing is, I did.' The housekeeper put her hand to her head. 'I meant to be the one to find her. I never meant that it should be little Pearl … Pearl and Edna …. I can hardly bear to think about it.'

There followed another silence, which neither woman seemed particularly minded to break, each lost in their own thoughts.

'You know you must tell the police the truth, don't you?' Rose said at last. 'If you don't, an innocent man may be convicted of Miss Cooper's murder.'

'Yes. I realise that now. I'd never let Mr Mason hang for my crime. I thought it might all go away. Aren't I silly to hope that things would go back to the way they were?' She put a hand to her face, which had unexpectedly turned crimson. 'It will all come out at the trial, won't it? About my feelings for Mr Mason and why I did it? I don't think I will be able to bear it.'

There was another moment of silence. Then the housekeeper patted the arm of her chair in an affectionate manner as if she were saying goodbye to the room.

'Would you mind if I go up to my room first before we go and see the policemen? I'd like to make sure I leave it tidy, and I must get my coat. I daresay it's chilly outside.'

At the door, she paused and looked back.

'Thank you, Miss Simpson, for not going to the police with your suspicions. I appreciate your talking to me first.'

Later, Rose wondered whether she should have stopped her. Instead, she sat in the housekeeper's sitting room, with its faded but genteel furniture, waiting for Mrs Field to return. She realised afterwards that she must have become too engrossed in her own thoughts. With a start, she looked at the clock on the mantelpiece. Too much time had elapsed. She was running to the door and out into the passage when she heard the scream. She heard the sound of running feet, the clatter of shoes on the staircase, and Agnes appeared in the passage, her hair falling down, her eyes wild.

'Oh, miss. Something dreadful has happened. Mrs Field has just thrown herself out of an upstairs' window!'

Chapter Thirty

'Hello Edna,' said Rose, 'I've come to say goodbye.'

It was the following afternoon, and Rose had gone to the kitchen in search of the kitchen maid. She had found Edna busy preparing vegetables for the dinner that evening, under the watchful supervision of the cook, who had looked slightly put out by Rose's sudden appearance in her domain. The woman had taken out her annoyance by making a great show of banging pots and pans and now stood resolutely at the stove with her back to them, vigorously stirring a sauce of some concoction.

'I wish you weren't going, miss. It'll seem awful quiet here without you, what with Pearl gone.' Edna whispered. 'Her father fetched her first thing this morning. He'd heard talk in the village about the murder. I don't think she'll be coming back.'

'I'm afraid I must leave,' said Rose smiling. 'Remember, I'm getting married in a few days' time. I must see Cedric. I've missed him terribly and I have so much to tell him. I'm sure there will be a hundred and one things waiting for me to do when I get back. Final preparations for the wedding and gifts to acknowledge, that sort of thing. Did I tell you that my mother's made my wedding dress? I'm dying to see it all finished.'

'What's your dress like, miss?'

'Well, it's made of pale gold satin and it's cut on the bias so it drapes beautifully. It has a cowl neck and puffed sleeves, which are tapered in at the elbow –'

'Oh, miss. It sounds beautiful, I wish I could see it.'

'Well, perhaps you can.'

Edna raised her eyebrows and looked at her quizzically, the knife she had been holding to slice the carrots slipped from her hand and clattered on to the table. Rose, in response, looked towards the stove and addressed the cook's back.

'Would it be all right, Mrs Mellor, if Edna were to accompany me into the garden? I'll only keep her a few minutes.'

The cook's only response had been to stir a pot with particular vigour, which Rose took to be a sign of reluctant acquiescence.

'Edna,' said Rose as they strolled in the garden, much to the delight of the kitchen maid, who breathed in the fresh air, 'I have something to ask you. Do you remember telling me that you didn't much like working in the kitchens?'

'I do, miss.' Edna sighed. 'And it'll be worse now Pearl's gone. I wish I was doing something else, I do really.'

'Now, don't answer me now, because I should like you to think about it, but I was wondering if you would be interested in becoming my lady's maid. It –'

'Oh, miss, I should love it more than anything,' cried Edna, clapping her hands together. 'Though I should tell you that I haven't any experience of that sort of thing.'

'Neither had I when I came here. You should have seen the mess I made of Lady Lavinia's hair,' laughed Rose. 'She was so cross. But seriously, Edna, Lavinia's lady's maid, Eliza, is the most wonderful teacher and I shall arrange for you to go on courses in hairdressing and fashion.'

'Would you really? Oh, miss, I can't wait,' exclaimed Edna, skipping around the garden in her excitement.

'Close the door behind you, Albert,' said the butler.

In Albert's opinion, his uncle was eyeing him rather too coldly. He shifted uncomfortably from one foot to the other, gazing nervously around the butler's pantry, awaiting the inevitable reprimand for his recent bad behaviour.

'Albert. I'm dismissing you from your position as footman in this house with immediate effect.'

''Ere, uncle, you can't do that,' protested Albert, patently shocked. 'The mistress, she ain't going to press charges about her damned necklace and –'

'I am very well aware of that,' said Mason brusquely. 'You should consider yourself very fortunate. Most employers would not have shown such leniency. Now, I'll pay you up to the end of the month, which I think is more than generous given the circumstances. I'm afraid you can't expect me to give you much of a reference –'

'I don't want to leave,' said Albert sulkily. He looked at his uncle slyly. 'I'm sure the master would be very interested to learn the truth about who took the snuff box –'

'He already knows the truth. I told it to him this morning,' said the butler, raising his voice a little.

'And he's letting you keep your job?' asked Albert, looking taken aback. 'Blimey.'

'He is. The master appreciates all that I have done for the family during my years in service and is prepared to overlook the incident.' Mason paused and stared down at the papers on the desk in front of him. His eyes appeared glazed and it was doubtful that he saw them. 'I should have told him before. Then none of … of this awful business would have happened.'

'It wasn't my fault that it did,' said Albert sulkily. 'If Velda Cooper hadn't –'

'You may be innocent in the eyes of the law, Albert,' said the butler, getting up from his seat and coming to stand rather menacingly in front of his nephew, who flinched visibly. 'But I consider you bear more than some responsibility for the tragic events that have taken place here. Two women are dead, one of whom …'

He could not continue, for his voice broke a little and there were tears in his eyes. He took a deep breath and stood up to his full height, which was not inconsiderable, and puffed out his weak pigeon chest. Mrs Field, had she been there, would have thought him very handsome.

'I wish you well, Albert. Make something of your life and make your poor mother proud of you.' The butler resumed his seat. 'Now, will you be so good as to shut the door when you go out?'

You've done what?' exclaimed Lavinia. 'I have never heard of such a thing!'

'You were the one who told me that I would definitely need a lady's maid when I became the Countess of Belvedere,' said Rose. 'I think Edna will be very suitable. She is a quick learner and very enthusiastic.'

'But she has no experience,' protested Lavinia. 'She'll probably decorate your hair as she would a strawberry charlotte.'

'You do talk a lot of rot, Lavinia. Now, what do you think of Edwin Grayson-Smith?' said Rose, keen to change the subject. 'He wasn't at all what I had expected.'

'I know exactly what you mean,' replied Lavinia enthusiastically. 'I'd imagined someone very loud and gruff and rather intimidating. But he seemed terribly sweet and jolly fond of old Millicent in a quiet and undemonstrative sort of a way. Of course, I think it helped that she wasn't wearing one of those awful insipid dresses of hers, and that I'd done her hair for her.'

'I'm sure that helped enormously,' laughed Rose. 'I thought they appeared rather well suited, Millicent and her husband, I mean. I do hope that their marriage will prove a success. It's a great pity that Mr Grayson-Smith doesn't spend more time here at Crossing Manor with Millicent. She'd get to know him better and she wouldn't be so lonely and bored.'

'Well, it's funny you mention that,' said Lavinia, with something of a mischievous grin. 'I admit that I did take him aside this morning and propose that he take down that portrait of his first wife in the drawing room and commission one to be done of his second. I also suggested that he take Millicent on a nice long holiday to recover from this awful business which, I will say for him, he thought was a terribly good idea.'

'Well done,' said Rose, who could imagine the scene perfectly, and felt a little sorry for Millicent's husband. 'And we shall also make a point of seeing them often. Sedgwick is so very close.'

'I don't think I shall ever want to come back to Crossing Manor,' said Lavinia, with a shiver. 'I say, I wonder if Millicent will make an effort with her appearance when we are gone. I do hope so. She really is quite pretty. I have made it my mission to find her a suitable lady's maid, with Eliza's help, of course.'

'Well, you'll be able to see for yourself in a few days' time,' said Rose. 'I've invited Millicent and Edwin to the wedding.'

'Have you really? I say that … hello? Here's that tame policeman of yours. I expect he has come to congratulate you on a job well done. Hello, Sergeant Perkins. How are you?'

'Very well, thank you, your ladyship,' said the man in question, strolling over to them. 'I've just come to bid you farewell and to hope that the weather stays fine for your wedding, Miss Simpson.'

'Thank you, Sergeant. I do hope Inspector Connor and Sergeant Harris don't think too badly of me for interfering in their investigation?'

'Well, I'll say this,' said the sergeant, rather diplomatically, 'you certainly made quite an impression on them. Even old Harris had to rather grudgingly admit that you made a valuable contribution to the gathering of information.'

'Contribution?' Lavinia gave a snort. 'Rose solved the case. If it hadn't been for her, you would have arrested the wrong person.'

'I'm sure the truth would have come out in the end,' said Rose quickly. 'Are you going back to London, Sergeant? You will give my best wishes to Inspector Deacon, won't you?'

'I am and I will, miss. He'll be very interested to hear all the details of this case, and your involvement in it, I am sure.' He grinned and bid them a fond farewell.

The two women watched the retreating form of the policeman as he made his way down the drive.

'I wonder,' said Rose, 'whether I shall become involved in any more murder investigations. I suppose things will be different after I get married.'

'Nonsense,' retorted Lavinia. 'You will still be an amateur sleuth, Rose, or a private enquiry agent, or whatever you want to call yourself. And your services will still be required whether you are Miss Simpson or the Countess of Belvedere. I shall also have to tell my friends that you are awfully good at recovering stolen items, not just solving murders. You will be in great demand! And besides ...' Lavinia paused.

'Yes?'

'Murder does seem to follow you around wherever you go, doesn't it? Life certainly won't be dull for me having you as a sister-in-law.' She squeezed Rose's hand affectionately. 'Won't it be exciting? Now, we really must get back to Sedgwick. We've a wedding to attend to and I want to talk to you about my bridesmaid's dress. I was wondering whether it wouldn't look better if ...'

WITHDRAWN

WITHDRAWN

Printed in Great Britain
by Amazon